"There is no friend as loyal as a book."
- Ernest Hemingway

*The Constitution is the guide which I
never will abandon.*
- President George Washington

Sexual scandals, political intrigue, and hidden agendas . . . Ms. Burns has captured the very essence of Washington D.C. politics within the pages of this scrumptious political thriller. An attempted assassination of the President of the United States leads to the first woman sworn into office as Commander in Chief. Who will win the race to discover the culprit . . . government agencies, or a political blogger and her ex-fiancé journalist? *Capitol Secrets* is dripping with dirty little secrets and more than enough backbiting drama to satisfy the fussiest readers. From first page to the last—a delicious read!

Lori Leger - 2015 R.O.N.E. award winner
for "One Year to Forever"

Capitol Secrets

Capitol Intrigue Series:
Book One

By

Karen Sue Burns

Copyright

ISBN 978-0-98960-277-8

Credits

Editor — Cajunflair Publishing

Cover — The Killion Group

Washington, D.C. map graphic — Purchased from www.123rf.com, credit for profile: nicolarenna/123RF Stock Photo.

Source for Democracy vs Republic — www.diffen.com

Author Notes

This novel was born from frustration—frustration as one of The People, frustration at Congress, frustration at the White House.

Regardless, this novel is pure fiction and gleamed one hundred percent from the author's imagination. Truly. It's not intended as a "true account" of anything related to the actual workings of the U.S. federal government. Of course, the plot may have received a smidgeon of inspiration from actual current and past events.

The author wishes to thank JP Willis and Carolyn Ross for their support, their friendship, and their twisted brainstorming with the plot.

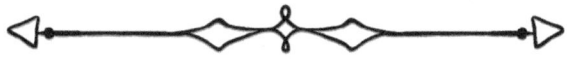

Which form of government do you prefer?

The omnipotent majority rules a **democracy**. In a democracy, an individual, and any group of individuals composing any minority, have no protection against the unlimited power of the majority. It is a case of Majority-over-Man.

A **republic** is a representative democracy with a written constitution of basic rights that protect the minority from being completely unrepresented or overridden by the majority.

Washington, D.C.
(Points of Interest)

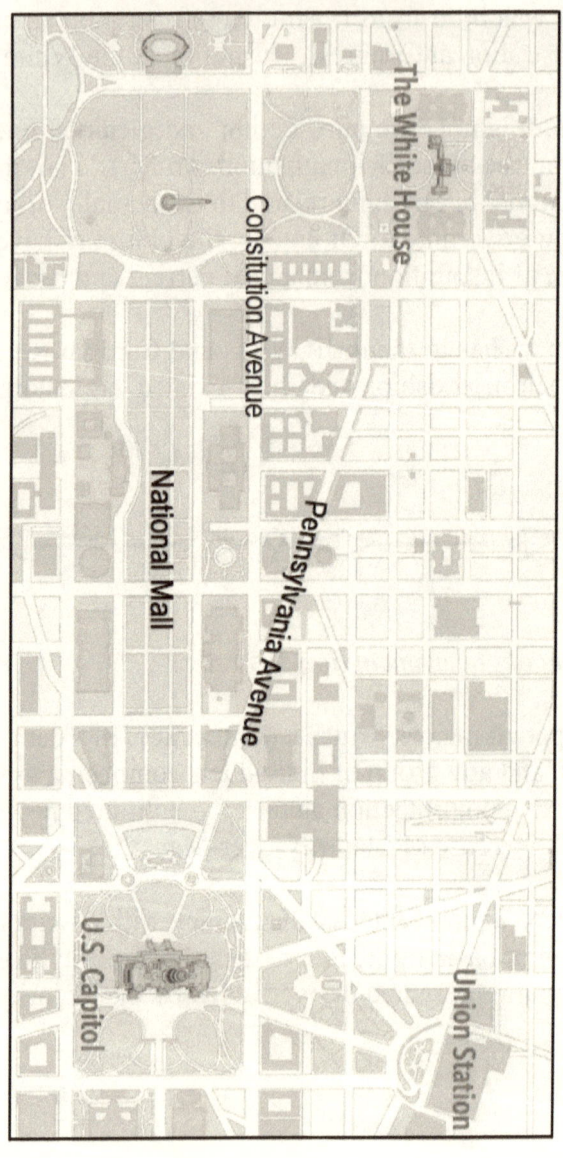

The President's Players
(Primary Cast of Characters)

Adam Martinez – Director of the Federal Bureau of Investigation (FBI)

Betty Flowers – White House Secretary for President Daniel Gardner

Candy Lawson – Retired police detective

Carol White – Personal assistant for Vice President Georgia Ross

Carolyn Helms – Aunt of Nick Romano

Daniel Gardner – 45th President of the United States

Ed Burnett – Director of the National Security Agency (NSA)

Elizabeth Gardner – Mother of President Daniel Gardner

Emmett Garrett – White House Chief of Staff under President Daniel Gardner

Frank Meredith – Head Secret Service Agent guarding Vice President Georgia Ross

Georgia Ross – Vice President of the United States with President Daniel Gardner

Gina O'Brian – Best friend of Nita Andrews

Gracie Evans – White House Chief of Staff for Vice President Georgia Ross

Harry Roberts – Speaker of the United States House of Representatives

Helen Capstone – Secretary of the Department of Homeland Security (DHS)

Jake and Drake Gardner – Twin sons of Daniel and Rosie Gardner

Jeff Cannon – White House Deputy Chief of Staff of Policy under President Daniel Gardner

Jessie Smith – Wife of John Smith, decease

The President's Players

(Continued)

Jim Brooks – Director of the Central Intelligence Agency (CIA)

Jimmy Crystal – Head Chef at Renoir Restaurant

John Smith/Patrick Warren – The Shooter

Julie Jordan – White House Press Secretary under President Daniel Gardner

Justin Jamison – FBI Special Agent

Mary Legend – Mother of sailor killed on the USS Barak Obama

Mike McCain – Majority Leader of the United State Senate

Nick Romano – Former reporter for the *Washington Chronicle*

Nita Andrews – Conservative political blogger for BetterPolitics.com

Peter Ross – Husband of Vice President Georgia Ross

Rosie Gardner – First Lady of the United States

Special Agent Brown – Secret Service agent at the White House

Valerie Jones – White House Senior Advisor under President Daniel Gardner

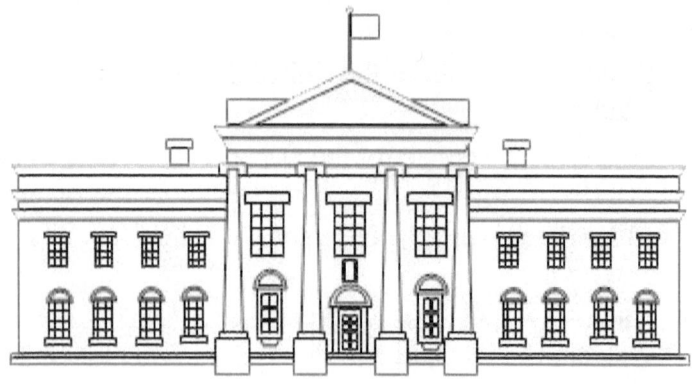

Chapter One

"MR. PRESIDENT . . . you make me so fucking hot. I'm about to explode."

"Go for the gold, sweetheart." Daniel Gardner, forty-fifth President of the United States, glanced at his Rolex. He'd be late if he didn't get this evening meeting wrapped up real quick. He grabbed the ass of his senior advisor with a hand on each cheek and squeezed as she rode him. "Come on, baby girl, bring daddy home."

They rocked and rolled until Danny finished the job in his usual triumphant style. He pushed her away and she jumped off the bed.

"We don't have much time and I don't want to be late," she said, clutching a wrinkled sheet to her chest.

"Get dressed and get out of here." Naked, he swung his legs over the side of the bed. She straddled him and pushed her generous breasts against his chest, wrapping her arms around his neck. He pinched each nipple, hard. She gasped and pulled back.

"Jesus, Danny, you don't have to man-handle me." She slapped at his hands and slid back from his lap, standing upright as a giggle escaped. After grabbing her clothes from the floor, she slipped them on while he watched. She sashayed to the door and looked back at him over her shoulder. "See you at the speech." Blowing him a kiss, she winked and quietly let herself out of the room.

Danny strolled to the small closet and pulled out a white terrycloth robe. He donned it and casually walked out the door. His security detail would take care of the soiled clothing and clean the small bedroom tucked into a third floor corner of the White House. Damn, he loved having good help around.

He walked down the center hall without noticing his surroundings. His wife would no doubt be on his ass for being a few minutes late. He didn't give a shit. His world and the White House revolved according to *his* schedule. He whistled as he trudged down the stairs to the second floor. He slipped into the dressing room adjacent to their bedroom to avoid Rosie and her bitching about his tardiness.

He headed straight to the shower, tossing the robe on the floor. He nodded in approval at the reflection of his rocking fifty-year-old body in the long mirror.

After a quick shit, shower, and shave he exited the presidential bedroom dressed to his usual perfection. He entered the family living room, also known as the West Sitting Hall, and found the full crew huddled around a widescreen television.

"Someone pour me a drink." Five sets of eyes turned their gaze toward Danny.

"Daniel, where have you been?" His eternally nosy mother, Elizabeth Gardner, rose from the sectional sofa and strolled to the bar along the opposite wall.

"I was getting dressed." Rosie hurried to him and kissed his cheek, then fiddled with his tie. He gently brushed her hands away. "It's fine."

"Of course." His wife looked at him with the same gentle understanding she'd had for the last twenty years. She nodded then returned to her place on the sofa.

"What are you guys doing?" Danny accepted a drink from his mother.

"Gee, Dad, this is awesome," Jake said. "Fox News is doing a summary of your first three years in office. It's not very nice."

"Maybe you should drive them out of business. You know, have the feds shut 'em down." Drake grinned like he'd made a joke. He and Jake were sixteen, good-looking, and identical twins, the only children of Danny and Rosie. They loved living in the White House with all the perks and benefits of being kids of the president.

Danny sipped his scotch and glared at the television. "Those people are assholes but I can't shut down a whole network. They don't do anything illegal."

Elizabeth stood next to him. "Maybe they should be found doing something unlawful." She lifted her eyebrows. "If you get my drift."

"Mother, don't be ridiculous." The same thought had crossed his mind a hundred times. Fox was the one news outlet that didn't kowtow to the liberal Democrats and just reported the news. He hated them.

"Mr. President, I think we need to get on the road." Emmett Garrett, Danny's chief of staff and long time friend, stood and walked around the sofa. "There are several people you need to see before the address."

Danny nodded and drained his glass. "Come on, Rosie, let's get a shake on." He turned to his sons lounging on the sofa. "You two watch my speech. You might learn something."

"Sure, Dad," the twins said in unison. He knew they'd be on their smartphones the minute the door closed.

Elizabeth rubbed his back then gave him a one-armed hug. "Knock 'em dead, kiddo. And, don't be nervous. This isn't your first State of the Union."

Danny rolled his eyes. "Thanks for the update, Mother." He pulled away from her and headed for the door. Might as well get this damned thing over with. He had a couple of college basketball games being DVR'd during his address. Giving speeches was so easy for him that he barely had a twinge of nervousness. Of course, the one thing he did enjoy was the adulation and worship from his fellow Democrats. The jackass Republicans could hardly contain their distaste for him. He loved it.

~~*

John Smith wiped his mouth with a napkin then threw it on a paper plate on the table. He looked at his watch, nine o'clock straight up. He gathered his backpack and stood. It was time.

He strolled out of Pizzeria Uno on the mezzanine level of Union Station and turned left. This level of D.C.'s downtown mall was shutting down; few customers remained at the tables and didn't seem inclined to follow him to the parking garage elevator. Just as well.

He punched the up button and the doors opened immediately. Maybe that was an omen. Yes, things would go smoothly for the next hour. The elevator cab headed to the fourth floor. Within seconds, he exited and walked south to his vehicle parked along the outside row. This floor was almost full, which he concluded was due to the goings-on at the Capitol and the garage's superior location for D.C. tourists. He had another reason for selecting it.

John turned his head from left to right and back again, as he walked. Looked like the floor had no unexpected visitors. He reached his Nissan Murano, which he'd backed into the parking space, and clicked the button on his key fob to open the tailgate. He sat on the edge of the cargo area and pulled a cardboard box to his right side. He pulled his laptop out of the backpack and placed it on the box. Next, he retrieved his cell phone from the inner pocket of his bomber jacket and set it to the left of the computer. He'd practiced these steps a dozen times.

He checked his watch again, 9:04. Perfect.

After opening the computer, he entered his password and selected his phone's hotspot as his Internet connection. He clicked on the Internet icon on the desktop for the White House and quickly signed into the server with hacked credentials, assuming control of the desktop computer used by Mrs. Betty Flowers, secretary and long-time confidant of President Daniel Gardner. Asshole was more like it from John's point of view.

That jerk, and his lack of leadership, had cost John almost everything. And now he sat in the back of his SUV less than a mile from the U.S. Capitol with a laptop connected to the White House. Gardner would soon learn that payback was a bitch.

From Betty's desktop, John opened the Internet and logged into a tool to track and operate Jessie. From his own PC, he logged into Fox News and their web feed for the State of the Union address. Gardner was close to the front of the House Chamber, still shaking hands. Perfect. John had enough time to do one last check of Jessie.

~~*

Nita Andrews popped the cap off of a longneck and brought it and a bowl of popcorn to her living room sofa. Although muted, the wide screen television over the fireplace was tuned to President Gardner's third State of the Union address. She settled in with the popcorn to her right side and her tablet and keyboard to her left, resting on the low arm of the couch. The beer sat between her legs along with the TV remote after she hit the Record button.

She sipped the beer as she watched Gardner shake the last hand then quickly trot to the podium. He turned to the crowd, waved with both hands, and slipped behind the lectern. He waved again, smiling broadly and gestured the "sit down" motion with his hands. Nita turned up the TV's volume. Finally, this show would start. Vice President Ross and Speaker Roberts sat directly behind Gardner, both wearing blank faces.

"Mr. Speaker, Mrs. Vice President, Members of Congress, my fellow Americans, tonight we turn the page. Tonight we shut one door and open another. Tonight we walk boldly into the future with our heads held high and our hearts intact. Tonight is the dawn of a new America. This is the time for action and the time for contemplation."

Nita rolled her eyes and entered a note into her tablet—swagger/arrogant. Along with taping the address, she would jot down her emotional reaction to Gardner's demeanor and words. So far, same old Gardner. As a political blogger and owner of the conservative website BetterPolitics.com, she had a duty to track the activities of the president and his administration, as well as Congress. Not only that, she found all the antics in Washington as interesting as hell. They'd be comical if most weren't so damned scary—like the hacking and theft of the personal identity information for millions of taxpayers from the IRS two years ago, at the end of Gardner's first year in office. His reaction? Gee, that sucks, sorry y'all.

At the words "new system of taxation" she stopped her musing and her attention snapped back to the television.

"Yes, you heard me correctly." Gardner paused and smiled at the attendees and the television cameras. "By the end of next month, I'll be sending a bill to the House for a new and much simplified taxation system. This includes a budget proposal to build a brand new twenty-first century java-based computer system. This system will fully implement the new tax law and the processing of simplified tax returns. The bill also includes funding for the training of IRS employees."

"Holy shit," Nita exclaimed. "Is Gardner finally coming through with a campaign promise?" She keyed in another note on her tablet.

Always the politician, Gardner paused to enjoy the thunderous applause. Jesus, you'd think he'd announced the second coming. Nita grabbed her beer, took a long pull, and tucked the bottle back between her legs. As her gaze returned to the television, Gardner's right side shuddered then his head jerked, and he moved backwards, straight into the half wall in front of the Vice President and Speaker Roberts who sat slightly above. It looked like he bounced off the wall then fell out of sight.

"Oh my God. What just happened?" She turned up the volume, straining to hear the commentator over the shouting. Numerous people had descended on the podium where President Gardner must be on the floor. A boom echoed and many people looked up as something drifted down from the ceiling. The clapping stopped and a hush floated over the chamber.

"Viewers, this is a most unprecedented event. It appears that President Daniel Gardner has been shot while giving his third State of the Union address."

Nita grabbed the beer bottle and rose, moving closer to the television for a better view. She tried to make out who was behind the podium but couldn't see well enough as the camera had pulled back. Capitol Police, and no doubt the Secret Service, had moved in and shortly the live feed cut off. The political anchors looked unhinged.

"What the hell just happened?" She watched the TV in disbelief with her mouth open.

Her cellphone beeped. She grabbed it off the coffee table and read a text message: "Did you see that?"

"Damn it." Why had she left Nick's contact on her phone and why hadn't she changed her phone number?

~~*

Perfect. The link to Jessie went dead as it should—the drone had exploded in the House Chamber. John signed out of the White House server, watched the Fox webcast for a few seconds and shut down his laptop. He stuffed it in the backpack and dropped the phone in his jacket pocket. Although he didn't know the death status of Daniel Gardner, he had comfort in the fact he'd accomplished what he'd set out to do. And somewhere, his wife Jessie would be proud of him for avenging her death.

He jumped off the back of his SUV and quietly shut the tailgate. Within minutes he was behind the wheel, exiting the Union Station garage and headed northeast on Massachusetts Avenue. He'd meander around for a while and then take the nearest bridge to get to the other side of the Potomac River, heading south to his hotel. He'd order room service and a couple of beers. His flight to Houston left early on Wednesday morning so he needed to get in some shut-eye.

Police car after police car rushed by him going the opposite direction. Guess the U.S. Capitol was all kinds of busy with the president being shot. He almost wished he were there, inside the House Chamber, to witness all the craziness. But that wouldn't work. If he'd been there, he would have been discovered for sure. This way was much better. *He'd done what needed to be done and now it was over.*

He checked his rearview mirror and nearly choked on his own spit. A police cruiser was directly behind his SUV. John checked the speedometer, not speeding, and took a deep breath. This cop on his tail was nothing. After a minute of following John's Murano, the cruiser's emergency lights flared and it blinked its headlights.

Pulling along the curb, his heart raced so fast he feared it would explode from his chest. Taking several deep breaths as the cop parked behind him, he rolled down the window, and watched in the side mirror as the police officer walked along the driver's side of the Murano.

"Good evening, sir. Is this your vehicle?" The officer looked to be about forty with tired eyes and a day's growth of beard.

"Yes, it's mine."

"May I see the registration and your driver's license?"

John dug the registration out of the glove box and reached in his back pocket for his wallet and pulled out his license. He handed both items to the cop.

The officer looked them over using a long flashlight then went to the back of the vehicle. After a moment, he returned and handed them back to John. "Mr. Smith, this vehicle has a failing taillight, it'll be burned out soon. Plus, you need to get it washed as your license plate has mud over it."

"Yes sir, I'll take care of it tomorrow."

"Good evening then." The officer returned to his patrol car.

With a sigh of relief, John rolled up the window, tapped on the left-hand turn signal, and eased onto the street once the traffic was clear. The cruiser performed a U-turn and drove the opposite direction.

Damn, that was almost scary. He continued with his plan to cross the river and his heart settled into its normal rhythm as he drove.

He turned on the radio, searching for news of the shooting, and then turned it off in frustration as he didn't know the local stations. The big question was whether Gardner was dead. He passed a hospital on his left. Would they take Gardner there? He shrugged, why did he care? All he needed to do was keep driving, nice and easy like. When he got to his hotel, he'd turn on the TV to the local news to learn what was going on in D.C. He chuckled to himself as he drove around Dupont Circle.

Damn right, something was going on.

Chapter Two

Wednesday, January 21

A LIGHT SNOW BEGAN falling around five a.m. Nita rose from her desk and walked to the kitchen for another cup of coffee. She added a fresh pod to the coffee maker, punched brew, and pulled a blueberry muffin from a bakery box. The coffee finished and she took the mug and her breakfast back to her "office" at one end of the dining room.

She remained standing, watching the snow from the wide window that bordered her desk, made from a cast off barn door. Illuminated by the streetlight on the corner, the snow looked so peaceful, so tranquil as it fell. Yet the world in Washington was not peaceful, nor was it tranquil this Wednesday morning.

God, she still couldn't believe that Gardner had been shot while giving the State of the Union. For the last two hours, she'd been on the phone with other bloggers, scouring Internet news sites, and watching the TV news for any information on his condition. The only White House disclosure was that he was still alive. The "most transparent White House in history" had closed up tighter than a hooker in a room full of rabbis.

Had Vice President Ross been sworn in as president? Why in the twenty-first century of 24/7 cable news feeds, did the American public not have any information about the health status of their president? Was this lack of communication one more example of a dysfunctional White House, clueless about protocol and lacking in the skills of basic crisis management?

Nita sipped her fifth cup of coffee, not that she was counting, and returned to her desk chair, rolling forward to get a better view of her computer monitors—one logged into CNN and the other to Fox News. Both websites hadn't changed their headline in eight hours— "President Gardner Shot – In Critical Condition." That didn't mean jack. The White House wasn't talking, that definitely wasn't normal. Usually, no matter the nature of the scandal over the past three years, someone had leaked a story, anonymously, of course. The fact that no one was talking must mean something, as this was a true crisis, not one of the usual embarrassments. In fact—

The front doorbell's chime startled her. What the hell? No one ever came to her house so early in the morning. Should she answer? Her curiosity got the best of Nita and she hurried to the front door, looked out the peephole. What? Damn it! Now he knocked, loudly. He'd wake up the whole neighborhood if she didn't open the door.

"Hold on," she yelled. She disarmed her security system then turned the deadbolt lock and a second lock installed for good measure. After taking a deep breath and slowly blowing it out, she calmly opened her front door.

"Hello, Nick. What the hell do you want?"

"Now, now, Nita, don't get that pretty blond hair of yours in a snit." Nick Romano flashed his sparkly brown eyes at her, followed by that sexy grin she knew so well.

"I'm not angry. Why are you at my door," she checked her watch with a dramatic flair, "at 5:15 a.m.?"

"Mind if I come in?" He had the nerve to walk past her into the living room. It had been a year since he'd been to her place. She wouldn't think about the night she'd broken their engagement—all that emotion was history, water over the bridge, done with. She followed close at his heels.

"Like I said, why are you here?" Rather than answering her, he went to the kitchen and she once again trailed behind him.

"May I make coffee?" He pulled a coffee pod from the snowman cookie jar and a mug from the shelf above the pot. Then he looked at her, a question in his eyes.

"Oh, all right. One cup and then you're gone." She went back to her desk for her own coffee. She sipped it as she again looked out the window—the snow seemed heavier now. Would that result in a D.C. shut down? She chuckled. The local authorities freaked at more than two or three inches of snow on the ground.

"What are you laughing at?"

Nita turned from the window toward Nick. Damn, he looked good, but that was irrelevant. "You have coffee now; tell me why you're here."

"Can we sit in the living room?"

She nodded and led him through the wide archway separating the two rooms. She lowered the volume on the TV and motioned for him to sit on the lime green, tweed sofa while she occupied her favorite reading chair by the fireplace. During their years of dating and engagement, they had spent many happy hours on that sofa, doing all sorts of things. She shook her head, nope, not going there.

"Okay, here we are. What's going on?" She figured this would relate to Gardner. No way would Nick be here to rehash their break up.

"I think we need to work together." His gaze was direct and impassive. He'd wrapped his hands around the coffee mug.

"Are you talking about Gardner?"

"Of course."

"Work together, how?"

He placed the mug on the rectangular table in front of the sofa. "Think about it. We're both writers looking for the big story that will make us famous. We have different D.C. sources. We've both given more than a casual thought to discovering the story behind Gardner's shooting. Right?"

Nita hated that Nick knew her well enough to zero in on what she'd been thinking the past few hours. Regardless, the story was the draw and he made a good point. By collaborating they'd have access to more Washington insiders via each other's contacts. In the four years they'd been together, they'd never joined forces professionally. Could they do this?

"What about the Chronicle? Will they allow their star reporter to work with a blogger?" Nick had worked at the *Washington Chronicle* ever since he graduated from Colombia University. His stories usually resulted in a front-page by-line. Of course, she hadn't looked at the newspaper for months and her friends and colleagues knew not to mention him.

"I don't work for the Chronicle anymore."

"What? You're kidding." Nita was truly surprised. She'd always figured Nick would one day be the Chronicle's editor-in-chief.

"Not kidding." He picked up the mug and drank. "I resigned six months ago. I got tired of the bullshit and decided to write stories *my way*. I'm a freelancer now, keeping busy. I finally started that book I talked about the last three years."

This definitely changed things. Could she work with Nick? Maybe this was the opportunity to put the past to bed and have a normal, non-romantic relationship with him.

"Okay, I'm interested. How would we do this?"

He threaded his hands through his hair then looked at her. "I haven't gotten that far. Maybe start with a list of who would want to knock off Gardner."

"Agreed. That'll take at least a week." Nita smiled and rose. "Let me get some paper."

"Are you hungry? Let's go to Denny's for breakfast. We can make the list there." He followed her.

"Hell no, it's snowing. I'll cook something and you start the list." She gathered paper and pen and set them on the long dining room table. "Sit here." Without waiting for Nick, she went to the kitchen and opened her refrigerator. "Bacon, eggs, and muffins okay?"

"Yeah, sounds great."

She watched Nick settle at the table, in the same chair he'd always used. Shaking off the image, she pulled out a carton of eggs and a package of bacon.

"Let's divide the list into categories," Nick said. "White House, Congress, lobbyists, military, national security, state governors, angry citizens . . . who else?"

"How about big corporations and small business owners?"

"Great ideas. Who haven't we included?"

Nita laughed as she whisked the eggs in a bowl. "Grade school kids."

"Gotcha. We'll start with this list and add to it as we go along. Next we list our contacts for each category."

Nita glanced at him, all hunky and adorable, and wondered if she was out of her mind agreeing to join forces with him. Then she pictured Gardner falling to the floor of the Capitol last night. Whatever brought that about would be one hell of a story, and she wanted a piece of that action.

Thirty minutes later they'd consumed the breakfast and Nita began to enter the category list into a document on her computer. Nick decided they needed a pick-me-up and stood at the bar in the corner of the living room making Bloody Mary's. She vowed to herself she'd keep this partnership strictly business, no emotion. She'd treat Nick like any other co-worker.

He handed her a tall glass and turned around a dining chair to face her desk. "Now, let's list everyone we know under each of the categories."

"You mean who we feel comfortable calling."

"Right you are." He raised his glass to her. "But that's never stopped either of us from going after a story."

"True. I'll make notations as to the status of each name." She continued entering the categories. "Would you turn up the volume on the TV? Maybe the White House has released an update on Gardner's condition. Nothing has shown up online."

He rose and grabbed the remote off the coffee table, then stood two feet from the television. After a couple of minutes, he returned to the dining room.

"A press conference is scheduled for nine. That gives us two hours to get our plan together." He sipped his drink and grinned at her. "Okay?"

Maybe it was the vodka in the Bloody Mary or maybe it was the circumstances surrounding this situation, but a slow burn of excitement rolled through Nita. This might be the story that would finally put her name on the big blogger map, on the writer-for-hire map.

She'd love to be the go-to ghostwriter for the Washington crowd—everyone wanted to write a tell-all book. As she sipped her drink, thoughts of Woodward and Bernstein, and the ultimate secret informant, Deep Throat, floated through her mind.

~~*

Nick watched Nita as she finished typing. She looked good, real good. She'd pulled her long hair behind her in a ponytail. He loved her hair; it felt like silk in his fingers. But she looked too thin, her cheekbones were more pronounced than ever. Her naturally slender frame had no extra meat on it. Was that because of their break up? It had nearly killed him but he figured enough time had passed and he could try a new approach with her.

He realized he'd taken a huge gamble by dropping by her row house without an invitation. Gardner's shooting had provided the perfect opportunity. The minute it happened he knew he wanted to investigate and figured Nita would as well. They'd spent many hours discussing Watergate and how Woodward and Bernstein had been so successful in uncovering the break-in story.

This was a once in a lifetime event and he was determined to be involved, with or without Nita. But she seemed equally determined to get to the bottom of Gardner's attempted assassination.

"I'm done." Nita gazed at him with a bright-eyed look as she sat perfectly still in her old desk chair. He could tell she was itching to get started.

"Print the list and we'll go through our contacts for each category."

She pulled the list from the printer and Nick opened the contacts app on his cell phone. "This could take some time."

"I know. Let's start with the White House. Who do you know

there?"

Almost two hours later, they were half way through the list and tired of the process. They took a break to watch television, hoping to catch the update on Gardner's condition. Nick followed Nita to the living room and joined her on the couch. A News Alert Bulletin splashed across the TV screen.

"Maybe we'll finally learn something," Nita observed.

"Don't count on it. Gardner's administration has the JV communications team. Hard to understand how they believe their own dribble. In fact—"

Nita raised a hand in front of his chest. "Shush, they're starting."

The press conference was at George Washington Memorial Hospital. The main speaker was Dr. Barry Appel, physician to the president. Nick didn't see anyone from the White House other than Emmett Garrett, Gardner's chief of staff, who stood off to the side.

"Ladies and gentlemen, I'm sorry for the reason we're together this morning." Dr. Appel paused and looked at the ceiling briefly, then he continued. "Due to patient confidentiality, I will provide only a high level summary of President Gardner's condition. He was shot twice—once in the upper right chest and the second bullet grazed the right side of his head. He suffered a severe blow to the side of his head when he fell backwards at the Capitol. The president is in a medically induced coma and is holding his own. That's all I have to report."

"Look at Emmett Garrett," Nita said, pointing to the television. "He's smirking. Why would he look like that? You'd think he'd be worried to the max about his boss."

"No kidding, but he's a weird duck."

Reporters yelled out questions to the doctor who initially seemed inclined to reply until Emmett whispered in his ear. Dr. Appel raised both hands in front of his chest. "That's it folks. We won't give another update for twenty-four hours. Thank you for coming." He turned away from the cameras and walked quickly to his left and through a door.

"That was short," Nita said. "At least Gardner's still alive."

"Right. Surely Vice President Ross has been sworn in. I wonder if she'll appoint a VP or wait to see what happens with Gardner."

"That's a good question." Nita tapped a finger against her lower lip. "Do you suppose it might relate to a motive for the shooting?"

"Maybe. Listen, this is the swearing in." Nick pointed at the TV and raised the volume.

"The White House has released a video of the Vice President

being sworn in as U.S. President at the Oval Office." The CNN anchor had a strange look on her face as the video started. VP Ross had her hand on a book held by Emmett Garrett. Chief Justice Shaw presided over the oath.

"I, Georgia Ruth Ross, do solemnly swear that I will faithfully execute the office of President of the United States, and will to the best of my ability, preserve, protect, and defend the Constitution of the United States." She smiled at the camera before the video ended and the anchor took over.

Nick lowered the volume. "Interesting that Garrett was there and not a member of her family, like maybe her husband."

"I bet he was out of town. Doesn't he go back to California a lot?"

"One more thing for our list."

"Let's finish with the categories and sources," Nita suggested. "Then we can do a preliminary action plan."

"That's sounds sexy."

Nita sent him an intense look and winked. "And you need a life."

~~*

John Smith slid the card key in the slot and the hotel door opened like magic. He loved technology. The room at the Las Vegas Grand was like a million other hotel rooms he'd slept in over his many years as an IT consultant, only nicer. He threw his carryon bag on the bed and flipped on the television before retrieving the room service menu from the desk.

He planned to order a meal and a bottle of Jack Daniels. He'd rest before moseying downstairs to the casino for a few hands of blackjack. Right then he had nothing better to do than gamble with a few dollars. On the flight to Vegas he'd come up with an idea to make even more money off Harry Roberts. One million wasn't nearly enough since old Harry was the one who benefited from Daniel Gardner being out of the way.

John flopped on the bed and flipped the channels until Fox News appeared. The anchor was doing an update on Gardner. It was a replay of a briefing earlier that day at the hospital. John listened and slapped his hand on the bedspread.

"Damn it. Two good shots into that son of a bitch and by a stroke of luck he falls and hits his stupid head. Dumb shit. He can't die quick enough for me." He performed a fist pump then opened the room service menu. A nice steak with a Caesar salad and a loaded baked potato, followed by a piece of chocolate cake sounded perfect. He decided to add a bottle of cabernet to the bourbon. Might as well enjoy the evening to the max.

He called in his room service order then pulled his laptop from the carryon. He had Harry's super-secret personal email address; the dumb shit shouldn't have given it to John. Now he could instigate his new and very clever "pay me more or Harry, you're going down" plan.

John laughed out loud. God, life was such a blessing, especially when he hadn't expected to make it alive out of Washington.

~~*

Emmett Garrett, Daniel Gardner's chief of staff, strolled into the Oval Office for his late afternoon, first official meeting with the new president, Georgia Ross. He'd had little interaction with her over the last three years. He considered her dumb as a rock so he'd done his best to steer clear of her.

Of course, under the present circumstances, that was impossible. He'd never understood why Danny accepted her as a running mate other than she was a very good-looking woman—tall, long dark hair, and good cheekbones—quite the package for the first female U.S. president.

"Madam President, I assume you've become familiar with your new office. Is there anything you need?"

"Emmett, how good of you to finally show up." Georgia did not look happy. "Where the hell have you been?"

"I've been doing my job—handling things. And, I've stayed out of your way while you get acclimated to your new role." He settled in a chair in front of the presidential desk. "What's on the agenda for the rest of the day?"

"I'm not happy with your attitude." Georgia leaned back in the rocker-style desk chair. "If you intend to stay on as my chief of staff, which I hope you do, I expect you to be available 24/7, just as I am. None of this playing games with me. Understand?"

Emmett smiled while seething inside. The stupid bitch thought he was her beck and call staffer? Well, two could play that game. "Madam President, forgive me if I offended you by not checking in earlier. Truly, I didn't want to rush you after the swearing in. With that behind you, what's next on your agenda?"

"Valerie Jones and the directors of the FBI and CIA will be here shortly." She turned toward the door as Betty Flowers, Daniel's secretary for decades, poked in her head.

"Madam President, your four o'clock guests have arrived."

Georgia nodded and Betty opened the door for the three to enter.

Georgia rose and motioned for the group to sit at the sofas arranged in the middle of the office. Emmett had no choice but to follow. Georgia sat in the chair at the head of the group. She showed no hesitation in occupying Danny's spot, which had Emmett wondering what she was up to.

"I know you've all been working on the attempted murder of President Gardner. At this point, I'm looking at it as a domestic issue. Do you concur?"

"I think it's much too early in our investigation to conclude that," Jim Brooks said. Tall and muscular, he'd headed the CIA for six years, carrying his twenty years in the military like a favorite suit. Both Emmett and Danny liked him immensely, even though he voted Republican.

"And why is that?" she asked coolly, looking straight at the director with her chin held high. Emmett felt a ripple of indigestion at her tone. Crap. Madam President might prove to be a problem.

"Ma'am, we have hot spots all over the world and most of those countries hate us. They'd love to see us destabilized. It's quite possible a foreign government or organization orchestrated this assassination attempt."

"All right then. Valerie and Adam, your thoughts?"

Valerie Jones was Gardner's senior advisor. She'd worked for him close to ten years. Emmett had no idea what she did other than attend luncheons and go to government conferences. He figured Danny kept her around because she was blond, had big tits, and was probably good in bed.

"I agree with you, Madam President." Valerie spoke with a confidence that Emmett knew was a Hollywood-level act. She was generally clueless about the goings on of the administration, but Georgia didn't know that. "There's nothing we've heard thus far that would indicate a foreign interest in Danny's, er, President Gardner's demise."

"Thanks, Valerie," Georgia said. "What's your opinion, Adam?"

"I concur with Jim. It's much too early in our investigation to eliminate any potential suspect or threat." Adam Martinez had started at the FBI right out of college and studiously worked his way up through the ranks. Although he was short in stature, he had the respect of everyone at the Bureau. Emmett wondered if Adam had a hidden life as a tyrant, since he seemed too good to be true.

Georgia nodded and turned her attention to Emmett. "What's your view?"

Emmett knew she'd do that to him—put him last to see which side he'd agreed with. Screw her. "At this point, not even twenty-four hours since the shooting, I believe we shouldn't rule anything out. Perhaps the most prudent course of action is to start broad and then narrow our focus as the investigation continues."

All eyes were on Georgia as she pressed her lips together. After a few seconds, she smiled and rose. "Let's look at all threats and see what shakes out. We'll do an update each day at four p.m. All right? Any news I need to know before then, direct to Emmett and he'll set up a meeting. That's all for now. Emmett, please stay for a moment." She walked around the desk and settled in the chair as Valerie, Adam, and Jim vacated the room.

Emmett again sat in front of the desk, wondering what she wanted from him. He now felt at a bit of a disadvantage since he'd ignored her for three years. Guess it was time to pay a visit to Speaker of the House, Harry Roberts. He could enlighten Emmett on how Georgia operated.

"Yes ma'am, how can I help you?"

"I have a question for you and I'd appreciate an honest answer."

"Of course," he replied, with as much politeness as he could summon from the depths of hell. "What is it?"

"Who has the most to gain from Daniel's departure, other than myself?"

"Madam President, that's not an easy question. I agree you are the most obvious person to gain from Danny being out of the picture. Have you had imaginary visions of being the president?"

"Ah, good avoidance, Emmett." She opened a file on her desk. "Let's leave it at that. I'll see you at 8 a.m. tomorrow morning. I told Betty to put you in the schedule for a daily briefing."

"That's fine." He rose, headed for the door, and turned back to her. "What about appointing a new vice president?"

"I'm waiting a few days. Let's see if Daniel's condition improves." Her gaze turned down.

"All right. Have a good evening, Madam President."

She waved a hand at him but didn't look up from the papers on the desk. Emmett let himself out of the Oval Office and headed to his own office in the West Wing. He needed quiet and a glass of vodka. Georgia Ross was not what he'd imagined the past three years. He did not need her questioning him and getting her nose into his little side business at the White House.

He had much to think about.

Chapter Three

Thursday, January 22

IT WAS AFTER NINE a.m. and Nita drank her first cup of coffee at her desk. She'd stayed up late the night before going over her list of sources and what she would say to each one. Plus, she had made copious notes to keep her strategy on track.

She wondered how things had gone at the White House yesterday. What she wouldn't have given to be a mouse in the Oval Office with the new president. The fact that Georgia Ross was the first female U.S. president was huge, historical, a big damn deal for young women across the country, including thirty-two year old Nita.

She hoped President Ross would have an easy time and change direction from the Gardner administration. Nita had never understood why Georgia had hooked up with Gardner's campaign in the first place. After her successful years in the Senate, she didn't seem the type to hook up with Gardner, a political lightweight. Maybe that was her plan all along.

And if going along with Gardner simply to be on the ticket was her real plan, then that made her the primo suspect for the assassination attempt. Nita rose and stared out the window. If Ross was behind the assassination, then that would make her plain stupid since she would benefit the most from Gardner's abrupt departure from office. Of course, one couldn't negate reverse psychology— who'd think she was dumb enough to do this, as she'd be the most logical suspect?

Sipping her coffee, Nita focused on the street below. The snow had just about melted, leaving a watery mess. If the sun came out, it would dry things up. Whatever, as long as it wasn't snowing, she was good. She picked up her cell phone and touched a contact name.

"Hey pretty lady, what's up?" Jimmy Crystal, her very good friend and head chef at Renoir, a popular high-end D.C. restaurant, was always in a good mood. The man simply saw the world through "God is good" glasses and never wavered from his faith in human nature. Despite their differences on the will of man, Nita and Jimmy had been good friends for many years.

"I'm still waiting on that recipe you promised me for stuffed mushrooms, and can you give me Jeff's work number?"

"You're a clever one, aren't you? I told you I'd trade it for your martini recipe." He chuckled and then continued. "All right. When are you coming in for dinner?"

"You know I can't afford your prices except for special occasions."

"Save up, girlfriend. Gotta go, my whipping cream is melting." He rattled off Jeff's personal cell phone number before disconnecting.

Nita entered the phone number in her tablet. Jeff Cannon and Jimmy had been living together for close to four years. They were a gay couple made in heaven. Nita loved to be around them as their relationship gave her hope for her own couple status—the right man had to be out there, somewhere.

Jeff had worked at the White House for nearly ten years as deputy chief of staff for policy. She figured she knew him well enough to ask a favor. The worst he could say was "no." She called the number and ended up leaving a message saying she hoped he'd meet her at the Renoir bar at six that evening to discuss the assassination attempt. Fingers crossed, he'd show.

Next she called her other best friend, Gina O'Brian, to set up a lunch date. They decided to meet at the cafeteria in the Supreme Court building. The food was typical but you never knew whom you might brush elbows with in the food line, plus it was over-the-top public—not reminiscent of a clandestine meeting.

She turned on the TV to see if there were any updates on Gardner's condition or who was responsible. Nothing new. The anchors kept repeating the same information with any expert that had punched out from under a rock. Nita concluded the White House had closed down tighter than a Democrat at a NRA rally. Why wouldn't they reveal any information? What were they afraid of? In her gut, she knew it had to do with secrets. That's the only thing that made sense.

Keeping secrets and a lack of transparency seemed to be the umbrella that shielded the Gardner presidency from criticism by the liberal media. Nita had a hunch this White House administration marched to a different drumbeat from previous ones. It had to do with something other than being a liberal. Gardner being so far left he might fall off the chart wasn't at the heart of the secrecy. Hmm, if she could learn the reason behind the White House shut down, she might learn why someone wanted Gardner dead.

She was eager to get her personal investigative show on the road and made another call, leaving a voice message, before heading to her bedroom and bath for a shower.

~~*

"Emmett, damn it. It's been almost thirty-six hours since Daniel was shot. Do you have any idea why we've not heard any concrete evidence as to who did this despicable act?" Georgia Ross sighed heavily, her frustration evident with the slump of her shoulders. "Sorry. I realize my lack of White House experience is getting the best of me. What *do you* think?"

Damn, she'd surprised him again. If he didn't watch himself, Emmett might just become a fan of Madam President. Right now, no matter how sincere she seemed, he didn't trust her. Subterfuge was the number one game in Washington and he had a feeling she was well versed in how to play the game. Thus, he'd keep his guard up and his head unfettered with praise for the new president.

"Ma'am, regardless of our frustration at being in the dark about who shot Danny, I do think our best course is to let the intelligence folks do their job." He crossed his legs and his gaze landed on a portrait of Abraham Lincoln. *That farmer was the best example of an American president.*

Emmett had dreams of writing a fiction book of a modern day Lincoln who rose from the city slums and gained national political prominence, restoring honesty and integrity to those who held public office. He sighed. Yeah, that was a pipe dream—not the writing but the reality of honest politicians in twenty-first century U.S.A.

"All right. I'll give it another twenty-four hours before I start to panic." Georgia opened a green file folder on her desk in the Oval Office. "I have another matter I need to discuss with you."

"Yes ma'am, what is it?"

"First, I need you to understand that what we say here is in complete confidence . . . one hundred percent confidence. Our words cannot leave this room." She gazed at Emmett like she had a bomb under her desk—direct and no bullshit. "Do you agree?"

Jesus, he hated these situations. He had no choice but agreeing with her didn't mean he *really* agreed. Everything in the White House had contingencies, strings, and alternatives—Emmett would go with the flow and adjust as needed.

Georgia studied him, her eyes narrowed for a moment or two, and then she slowly smiled. He had to be careful—very, very careful.

"Yes ma'am, I understand the need for confidence. How may I assist you?"

"We have an issue with Helen Capstone, our well-known secretary of DHS."

Emmett swallowed hard to hold back a chuckle. Helen was the epitome of the old establishment Democrat who hadn't gotten the message that the eighties were over. What the hell had she done now to screw up Homeland Security?

"I'm all ears," Emmett managed to say with a straight face.

"It appears that she's been conducting government business using personal email accounts from a server located at her personal residence in Florida."

His eyebrows stretched up and his chin edged down. "What? What the hell?"

"I know. It's hard to believe a cabinet member would be that stupid."

"Have you heard from the National Archives and Records Administration?" He wanted to squeeze his hands around Helen's skinny neck. How could she be so reckless?

"Actually, and this sucks, we received a heads up from the Associated Press. Apparently some watchdog group had filed a freedom of information request for Helen's emails related to those sniper shootings in Minnesota. That's how it was discovered she hadn't been using a dot gov email account."

He threaded a hand through his hair and stopped. Hmm, this might be an opportunity. Helen was a bitch and a pompous ass, trading off her father's many years as a U.S. Senator. Emmett figured Danny had named her secretary of DHS as a payoff to her father for bringing in big campaign donations. Those donations had enabled Danny to steal the Democratic nomination from Halley Hilton, the appointed front-runner, during the presidential election. Why else? Helen's four years as a junior house representative from Florida did not groom her for a cabinet position and certainly not one as important as DHS. He rubbed his jaw. Yes, this was an opportunity.

"That is unfortunate." He looked at the carpet, such a boring pattern of gold and green. "What are you doing about it?"

"What is the appropriate reaction?" Georgia leaned back in her chair and steepled her fingers in front of her chest. "My initial thought is to kick her to the curb. I don't like this sort of playing games. However, she is Daniel's appointee and I can't ignore that."

Emmett jumped in. "Ma'am . . . Georgia, I have an idea."

She nodded. "All right then, what is it?"

Emmett explained his idea to her then left the Oval Office. She needed time to think about it and he needed to get his butt in gear to meet with Harry Roberts. He called his car service as he walked through the West Wing. Within minutes, he'd settled in the town car, poured a Screwdriver and confirmed that Harry was on location, ready for pick up.

The car stopped on the Capitol Plaza in front of the House side. Harry Roberts slithered in the open door and settled in the bench seat opposite Emmett, who quickly pushed the button to close the window between them and the driver. Harry had a tendency to talk too much. The driver eased them into traffic for a leisurely route around the White House.

Harry accepted a drink and slugged a good dose. "Emmett, what the hell do you want from me now?"

Emmett loved these situations. They presented an opportunity to let the "big players" in Congress know they were on a level below the White House.

"Mr. Speaker, please, this a simple conversation. Relax." Emmett topped off Harry's glass. "You've worked with Georgia Ross for three years while she's been President of the Senate. What can you tell me about her?"

Harry narrowed his eyes briefly. Apparently that wasn't a question he'd expected. Good.

"I like her. She's easy to deal with, fair, does her homework."

"Have you had any disagreements on policy issues?"

"Not really, she tows the party line for the most part." Harry peered at Emmett over the rim of his glass then brought it to his lips and drained it. "Why are you so interested in my dealings with Georgia? Is she creating a problem for you?"

Emmett didn't respond immediately. He retrieved Harry's glass and took his time pouring a refill. Harry's face had reddened and the look—cold eyes, a flared nose, and lips flattened into a sneer—sent a chill down Emmett's back. This was not his old friend from Colorado and that realization hit him hard.

"No, of course not," Emmett replied as he handed Harry a full glass. "You know, if Danny doesn't make it, Georgia will be the logical choice to take the presidential nomination this summer."

Harry downed most of the fresh screwdriver. "I hadn't even thought about that."

"Yeah, things change quickly, huh?" Emmett tapped on the glass of the window, indicating to the driver to return to the Capitol. "Let me change the subject. Have you been interviewed by the FBI about the shooting?"

"I have a meeting late this afternoon."

"Good. Madam President is having a hissy fit that the shooter hasn't been identified."

"Welcome to the real world. Investigations take time."

"Unless the shooter is dumb enough to post on Twitter." Emmett stowed Harry's empty glass in a cup holder then he studied his friend of many years. Something had changed.

"Right. Wouldn't that give the NSA a boost?"

Emmett nodded and leaned back against the leather seat, giving him a good view of Harry. He'd known Harry for close to thirty years. He'd been Danny's roommate for four years at Princeton. Emmett didn't have the bucks or the grades and had attended Colorado State. At least he'd gotten a degree.

Harry had always been the guy with the family connections, the family money, and the family arrogance. Yet he'd never been an ass to Emmett or tried to belittle him. Because of that, Emmett had put up with him for the sake of his friendship with Danny. The three of them had spent a lot of time together in their twenties, chasing skirts and careers with equal gusto.

This version of Harry seemed off—tense and agitated. Was it because of Danny getting shot? Emmett needed to learn more. It was part of his job to keep tabs on all the major players and this worried him.

The car stopped along the curb where it had started.

"Harry, it's been too long. Let's get together for dinner."

"I could use a relaxing evening. Marjorie will be out tomorrow, how about then?"

They made plans and Harry exited the car, trudging back to the Capitol's employee entrance. Emmett watched him through the passenger window, unable to shake the uneasy feeling in the pit of his stomach. He added one more item to his list of worries.

~~*

"Who do you think would make a good Deep Throat?" Nita had explained to Gina about her plans to look into the Gardner shooting. She didn't mention she was working with Nick. That she'd keep to herself for now. She chomped on a tuna sandwich then spoke again. "And keep your voice low."

Rather than talking softly, Gina broke out in a raucous laugh that garnered the attention of other lunch-goers seated around them. Thank God, they were in a corner or the whole cafeteria would be staring.

"Keep it down. What's so damned funny?" Nita had no clue why Gina was laughing so hard that tears welled in her eyes.

Gina finally gained her composure and air-poked a fork at Nita. "You're what's so funny. Who would make a good Deep Throat? Seriously? Now this is a Watergate type investigation? Who are you? Woodward or Bernstein? Ooh, I know, it's Woodward. He's the good-looking one."

"Haha, you're such a comedian." Nita wasn't in a mood to joke. "I'm serious as a heart attack about this. Come on, help me out, I need an inside source."

"I know you're serious . . . but, an inside source, where? At the White House? The U.S. Senate? The FBI?"

That question stopped Nita. Yes, where?

"You're right." Nita popped a long French fry in her mouth and chewed while she thought over her question. "I got ahead of myself."

"Not to worry. I'll be a source in the Senate. I'll nose around some of the other staff members at the coffee bar and see if there's any gossip." She smiled and stole a French fry off Nita's plate. "I've always wanted to play spy."

Nita rolled her eyes. "Thanks. Have you heard Senator Booker mention the shooting?" Booker was the senior senator from New Jersey and Gina had been on his staff for three years.

"I've hardly seen him. He's been in non-stop meetings."

"I'd love to plant listening bugs in all those meeting rooms."

"Bugs?" Gina grinned. "The building security is so tight now that it takes forever to get in the door."

"I was only thinking out loud."

Like a diehard best friend, Gina chose to ignore Nita's admission of madness. "What exactly are you trying to do?"

"I'm trying to figure out the motivation for the shooting. Surely that will lead to who did it."

"I agree with that," Gina said with a definitive nod. "How do you narrow down the millions of Americans who detest their president into the one who's willing to take action?"

"Yeah, there is that." Nita leaned over the table and lowered her voice. "President Gardner has managed to piss off all the Republicans and a good portion of Democrats in only three years. Who doesn't want him out of the White House?"

~~*

For a late Thursday afternoon, the Las Vegas Grand was busy. A tour bus must have unloaded. John sat at a video roulette table, taking a break from blackjack. A waitress had just delivered him a fresh cocktail and he placed his bet, making sure the number "29" had a five-dollar marker. He'd decided to limit his betting to not draw attention from the dealer. Blending in was his new modus operandi.

He'd sent an email to Harry Roberts early that morning. It had been to the point: "Transfer four million dollars to my account or I'll go to the FBI." Four million was chump change for Harry. He came from a well-to-do family in Denver who had plenty in the bank.

Looking back on what he'd accomplished last Tuesday in Washington, John realized he had been much too eager to accept Harry's proposition. Yeah, he should have negotiated harder. This demand would correct that.

The roulette game was over and he won thirty-five dollars. He studied the winning numbers on the digital display, attempting to perceive a pattern. He shook his head, nope, just random numbers. He repeated the same bet with a touch of his finger to the screen. Too easy, just like getting Jessie into the House Chamber. Harry had done a good job of planting it in the balcony.

A dark-haired woman slipped into the empty chair next to him. Her arm bumped his as he raised his drink to his mouth.

"Sorry." She gave him a slow smile.

"No problem." He turned to look at the roulette wheel. The dealer released the white ball and it whipped around the spinning wheel before bouncing several times and finally landing on "black 14." He fist pumped and muttered "yay." He'd doubled his money from the last bet.

"You did good?" The woman next to him leaned in his direction with her shoulder touching his arm. She looked up at him and smiled. He noticed she had nice full lips and a nice pair of breasts. This might not be his smartest decision, but what the hell? He had time to burn.

"Yeah, I'm doing okay." He twisted around in the chair and stuck out his hand. "I'm John. How are you?"

She grabbed his hand and shook it with vigor. "Nice to meet you. I'm Candy from Hershey, Pennsylvania. Don't laugh, my mother loved chocolate."

"I love chocolate." He licked his lips. "You like to play roulette?"

"This is my first time. I'm here with my girlfriend and she took off with a guy she met last night so I'm hanging out by myself. This is a nice hotel."

He looked at her pretty face and decided a little companionship would help him pass the time. "You can hang with me if you want."

"Great." Her grin flashed pretty, white teeth. "Can you teach me how to play?"

"Sure can. Let me explain the roulette wheel first." One gaze from Candy's baby-doll-blue-eyes and he decided a break from thinking about Harry and everything else in Washington was in order. A cute brunette with a good rack—he could think of worse ways to pass the time.

Over six hours later, after a few drinks and a steak dinner, John and Candy ended up in his hotel room.

Carrying a bottle of Moet champagne, Candy collapsed on the bed. "Ooh, baby, this is nice." She pushed the bottle on the bedspread toward John, who stood at the side. "Open this, puleeeze." She giggled and rolled onto her back.

John shook his head to clear the fogginess and picked up the bottle. Sure he could open it. After tearing off the foil envelope, he untwisted the metal cap, and popped the cork. He managed to find two wine glasses at the bar and poured. With wobbly steps, he carried the glasses to the bed.

"Here, you awake?" He shoved a glass toward Candy who blinked and rose up, before scooting backwards toward the pillows. "Your champagne, Madam."

"Thank you, kind sir." She accepted the glass and patted the bed next to her. "Come on, take a load off."

He kicked off his cowboy boots and settled on the bed with the multiple pillows supporting his back. "Hmm, this feels good."

Candy sucked down her champagne then leaned over John and set the glass on the bedside table. She snuggled into his side and rubbed her hand over his chest, playing with the buttons on his shirt. "Do you really need this?"

He slugged down champagne, further befuddling his brain, and saw no good reason to be clothed. He tossed the glass to the carpeted floor then unbuttoned his shirt. "You take it off."

And Candy did, along with all her clothing and the rest of his. She climbed on top of him and slid her breasts up and down his chest then snaked her hand to his groin and grabbed his dick. "How does that feel, big guy? And I do mean big guy."

"Uh-uh . . . mmm, keeping doing that." John's head was foggy while his body felt heavy and slow. Candy's stroking had the opposite effect on him from what she intended. He yawned. "Oh, Jessie . . ."

Candy stopped and looked at him. "Who the hell is Jessie?"

His eyes popped open for a moment then closed. He tried to turn on his side and whispered. "Washington . . . big boom."

Candy rolled off of him and shook his shoulder. "What? What did you say?"

~~*

After lunch with Gina, Nita headed back to her house via the metro. She was home in no time and went directly to her computer. It was time to do a thorough search on all the reasons why Daniel Gardner had pissed off so many Americans.

As she opened the Internet browser, her cell phone rang. She dug it out of her purse. Hmm, Nick.

"How's it going?" His voice still had the sexy base that had always unraveled her best intentions.

"Good. I had lunch with Gina and she'll let me know what's going on at the Senate. How about you?"

"I've made some headway. Thought we might have dinner tonight to discuss."

Even as her heart fluttered with excitement, she chastised herself inwardly, disgusted at her reaction. "That might work. I'll be at Renoir at six this evening."

"Ouch, that place is pricey."

"My plan is to meet a staff member from the White House." She prayed Jeff had heard her message and would show up.

"Okay then. Maybe we can get chips and dip."

"Very funny. I'll see you at six?"

"Yeah, count me in." He clicked off.

Nita stared at her phone. Damn, she hated when he did that—one of the things she'd didn't miss after breaking their engagement. She set the phone on the desk and got back to business. First she searched the usual news sites for an update on Gardner's condition. Nothing new so she guessed the report would be in the evening just like yesterday.

She started her research by entering "President Gardner scandals" in the Google box. A long list of URL's appeared. *Good grief, the list of articles and blogs was huge.* She'd go one by one and inaugurate her serious research by creating a list of individuals who might want Daniel Gardner dead.

It took over two hours to go through every link. The result was a list of scandals that seemed awfully long for only three years of a presidency. In addition to that, Gardner had accomplished nothing even remotely related to his campaign promises. He operated primarily from a political basis, while the potential impact on the American people or the U.S. Constitution seemed irrelevant to his decisions. Nita shook her head. How in the hell had this man been elected after the previous president did the same thing?

She remembered he campaigned as the "candidate of change" from the tired old policies and political tactics of the past. Right. What specifically had he promised the American people if elected? She Googled "Gardner campaign promises"—another long list of links. It didn't take more than thirty minutes to gather a short list of the top promises:

1. Reduction of regulations that slow business development and job creation – employment rate increased to ten percent as regulations continue to strangle businesses
2. Marijuana legal in every state – nothing done
3. Return K-12 education administration and decisions to the fifty states – never mentioned how that would work, Common Core still law of the land
4. Abolish massive powers of the IRS with a total reform of the taxation system – hasn't agreed with any proposals from Congress, Gardner supposedly has his own proposal
5. Secure the southern border with a twenty foot electric fence – now says too expensive, will work with Mexico diplomatically to stop the flow of illegals over the border

None of these campaign promises had been fulfilled. Gardner did mention something about a new IRS and a new tax system Tuesday night. She grabbed her tablet and touched the Notes icon. Her last entry read: "Feb bill, simple tax sys, bdgt IRS java computer sys w/ train IRS empl."

Interesting. Gardner finally talks about one of his campaign promises and he gets shot. Coincidence, or related to the assassination attempt? She bet it related. Her gut told her that Gardner's agenda or lack of one was the motivation for the shooting.

That created a quandary—which scandal or which promise? She jotted a reminder in her tablet as this was worth mentioning to Nick. After printing out the list of scandals, she reviewed it one more time. Damn, no wonder some person had it in for President Gardner. This list made him look like an absolute jerk as a U.S. president. Abraham Lincoln must be rolling in his grave.

She checked the online sites for news about Gardner's medical condition—nothing new—and went to her bedroom to class up her outfit. Jeans and running shoes would not get her in the front door of Renoir.

~~*

Nick jumped out of a cab in front of Renoir and hurried in the door. It was two minutes after six and he hoped Nita wouldn't crucify him for being late. He looked around the space and settled in a leather stool at the long dark bar. She wasn't there. That was weird as she was a stickler for promptness. He motioned to the bartender and ordered a bourbon.

He stared at the image reflected by the mirror behind the bar. With its dark walls and bright blue accents, the restaurant oozed understated elegance and old money. The dining room had secluded booths along with private rooms, the reason why it was a favorite of the Washington elite. You could meet privately, out of the sphere of the press. He'd bet the walls could tell many a salacious story.

A hand rubbed his back and Nita slipped onto the stool next to him. "Did you order already?"

He nodded and motioned to the bartender with his finger. "What would you like?"

"Mm, vodka. It's been one of those days."

Both drinks quickly arrived and Nick ordered a couple of appetizers. He didn't think they'd actually eat dinner there—too pricey and too slow. They had things to do. He raised his glass to Nita. "Cheers. When will Jeff get here?"

"I'm not sure. I left a message for him to meet me here."

"Let's hope it's soon. This place makes me feel like a bum."

"Whatever." Nita sipped her drink. "What have you been doing since yesterday?"

He leaned in close to her. No one needed to overhear their conversation. "I've spent most of the day roaming the halls of Rayburn, Cannon, and Longworth trying to make contact with a house representative or their staff. You know, that's what us ace reporters do best—scurrying around like rats trying to sniff out a story."

"I'll ignore the mental image of you scurrying like a rat. Did you learn anything worthwhile?"

"Not much that you haven't already thought of." He sipped his drink and wondered if anything he'd talked about was truly relevant to the shooting. "Behind the scenes, Democrats haven't been happy with Gardner for a while. He's following the same road as the former president. Nothing has changed. And—"

"And his chance of getting the nomination in August isn't a shoe-in. Right?"

"Exactly. Sara Ward, the senior senator from Maine, might have a shot to oust him at the DNC convention. People are pissed and not afraid to let their Congressmen know."

"That's a topic at the House? Incredible how things have changed."

"Yeah, not good for the party overall and all that BS. It would be a welcome change if a politician thought first about the American people rather than their political party and getting re-elected." Nick realized he sounded like he'd climbed up a ten-foot soapbox. He wasn't alone in his feelings. "In fact, there are a lot of theories as to who pulled the trigger and how. Speculation says it wasn't anyone in the House Chamber."

"Yet there were two shots fired." Nita sat back in the bar stool and crossed her arms over her chest. Her gaze locked onto something over Nick's left shoulder so he knew she was thinking. Her typical thinking mode consisted of glazed over eyes and arms hugging her body.

He knew to keep his mouth shut and be patient with her process. He sipped the bourbon and eyed the plates of appetizers that had just arrived. Why did he love junk food so much? He grabbed a chili-cheddar French fry and stuffed it in his mouth.

"I saw something interesting today," he said.

"What and where?" Nita also ate a French fry.

"Walking down Independence Avenue, going from Longworth to Rayburn, I noticed Harry Roberts getting into a town car near the Capitol building."

"Really?"

"Yeah. I decided to wait a while and it returned after twenty minutes. Guess who was in the car with Harry?"

"No clue."

"Emmett Garrett."

"Ooh, Gardner's chief of staff. How very interesting." Nita grabbed another fry. "Wait, hold on. Aren't the three of them—Gardner, Garrett, and Roberts—friends from Colorado?"

"Exactly. This seems like more than a coincidence to me."

"Possibly, who knows?"

They sat in silence, immersed in their own musings. Nita nudged Nick's shoulder. "There's a Gardner update on TV."

They concentrated on the television to the side of the bar. The sound was off, but closed captioning enabled them to understand the latest press release from the hospital. Bottom-line: Gardner's condition hadn't changed and the doctors were taking a "wait and see" approach. Damn, the political stakes kept getting upped.

"I wonder if that's good or bad, him being in a coma for two days." Nick decided he needed another drink and motioned to the bartender.

"No clue. Guess we should add a neurologist to our list for interviews."

"I'll do it. I know a doc, someone I interviewed a couple of ears ago."

"Why didn't you order me another drink?" Nita glared at him like she hadn't heard his last comment.

Jesus, could he not make this woman happy? "I'm sure the bartender knew I meant a drink for both of us."

She rolled her eyes and looked away from him.

And that is why they were no longer engaged. She always sought out the worst in him, not his best. He rolled his shoulders and shrugged off the blast from the past—water over the bridge and all that. He pulled out his cell phone and opened the notes link. He added a reminder to call Brian Willis, a neurologist he'd interviewed about Alzheimer's. The bartender returned placing two fresh drinks on the bar.

"I'll give the doc I know a call tomorrow." He ignored her comment about the drink and spread Brie cheese on a cracker from the healthy appetizer plate. He knew she loved it. "Here, try this cheese."

She looked back at him and accepted the cracker. "The cheese is awesome."

He nodded. "Back to Gardner, where do we go from here?" Nick had his own ideas but figured giving Nita the floor was wisest.

"I have an idea." She sipped her drink then leaned toward him. "I looked at all of Gardner's campaign promises and the scandals over the past three years. It's a long list." She moved her mouth to his ear. "I think this is where we start. I bet someone has been hurt by Gardner and wants him dead in retaliation."

He gazed at her and nodded before whispering. "Or, it might be someone who wants his job . . . real bad."

She moved away from him and once again wrapped her arms around her midriff.

She might be onto something—a logical approach for their

investigation. "I think we should divide and conquer."

"Okay, how?"

"You look at who wants revenge for something Gardner's done or hasn't done and I'll look at who wants his job or wants him gone in general."

"That's a great idea. It will help us keep from tripping over each other." She toyed with the napkin around her drink. "I wonder if anything has been uncovered. Do you suppose the NSA is in charge?"

Nick laughed at that. "You know how federal agencies act in a crisis. They trip over each other to get involved then deny involvement when things get screwed up."

"Let's see," she started to name disasters on her fingers. "Katrina, Benghazi, Fast and Furious—"

"Hold on," Nick interrupted her, placing a hand on her knee. "Sorry. Isn't that Jeff Cannon over by the reception desk?"

Nita turned around toward the front. She nodded. "Let's see if he comes over first."

"Do we have a plan with Jeff?" Nick turned his attention back to Nita.

"Nope, go with the flow. He's walking over now."

"Nita, it's been a long time." Jeff kissed Nita's cheek and hugged her shoulder. "You're looking as beautiful as ever."

Nick hadn't seen Jeff in over a year and his movie star quality looks hadn't diminished. He accepted Jeff's outstretched hand. "Hey, Jeff, how's it going?"

"Good, I heard you left the Chronicle. Writing a book?"

"Something like that. Can you join us?"

"Actually, I'm here for a work dinner." Jeff rubbed Nita's shoulder. "But I can answer a couple questions. Off the record."

Nita looked relieved. You never knew whether a good source would come through or throw you to the curb. She gazed at Nick, raising her eyebrows. He nodded.

"Anything new at the White House the last couple of days?" Nita's query was broad enough to not garner interest from anyone who might overhear their conversation.

"Believe it or not, it's been calm." Jeff leaned forward between the two of them and lowered his voice. "It's been a hell of a surprise. I expected Emmett to be in a huge snit but he's been business-as-usual. From what I hear, President Ross is the exact opposite of President Gardner. She actually *works* in the Oval Office."

Nick made a mental note to remember every word Jeff said.

"Everyone there likes her?"

"So far the gossip is good."

"Do you know who's taking the lead on the shooting investigation?" Nita asked.

"I've not heard that anything definitive has been found so it could be any of the agencies. They all want to be the big dog."

"Interesting," Nita said shaking her head.

"More like sad." Jeff looked toward the reception desk. "My group is here. Call if you need me or have a question. I'll do my best, off the record. Good seeing you guys." He walked to the front of the restaurant.

Nick turned around in the stool to face Nita, his arm resting on the bar. "So?"

"So?" Nita grinned at him then leaned in close enough to kiss him. The scent she always wore floated over him. He damn near hyperventilated. "I'm excited," she said. "We need to get our asses in gear. The feds haven't figured out anything."

He whispered back. "Seems that way to me." Unfortunately she moved back from him.

Nita nodded and pulled her coat off the back of the stool. "Gotta go. I need to write a blog."

"Wait."

She slid off the stool to a standing position. "Wait for what?"

"Don't we need to talk more about who does what so that we don't cross our sources?"

She gazed at him through narrowed skeptical eyes then shrugged on her coat with Nick helping as best he could. She swung her purse over her shoulder and stepped away from the bar. "Sure. I'll meet you out front."

Nick quickly pulled a credit card from his wallet and waved it at the bartender. "Gotta go. Work to do."

Chapter Four

Friday, January 23

GEORGIA ROSS ENTERED THE Oval Office at 6:23 a.m. Her security escort turned on the lights and brought her a small tray with an urn of fresh coffee and a bear claw pastry.

"Thanks, Frank." She smiled as she accepted the tray. "The coffee here isn't half bad."

"Yes ma'am. I'll be right outside so holler if you need anything." He quietly shut the door and Madam President was alone.

She placed the tray on the side of the desk and sank back into the chair, allowing her body to relax in the leather rocker that was too large for her. Yet she wouldn't change one thing in the office until . . . well, until things had solidified. She wasn't a real fan of Daniel Gardner or his politics as president but she did have immense respect for his office. Of course, no one knew that, not even her husband who she confided in about most things.

She'd learned during her early days in Washington, as the freshman senator from California, to keep her most controversial thoughts to herself. No need for the voters or her colleagues to know that she was at heart a die-hard Independent, not the Democrat she portrayed herself as in the Senate. She'd run as a Democrat because at the time, it had been an easier race to win.

Over the years she'd managed to be the moderate who had succeeded at working with Republicans as well as Democrats. She sipped the coffee and chuckled to herself. For nearly twenty-five years she'd operated as the "clean up girl" who could get a difficult piece of legislation through the procedural bullshit and egos of the members of Congress without anyone realizing what she'd accomplished. Why in the hell had she stayed in Washington for so many years?

Georgia rose with her coffee cup and walked along the exterior walls of the office making a circuit. She'd had a short conversation with Rosie Gardner and Daniel's mother last night before they'd returned to the White House Residence. How awful for them. All

Georgia could do was hug them and say a prayer. She did hope that President Gardner would recover. She'd had no designs on the presidency herself and had agreed to being on the ticket with Daniel to satisfy the large liberal contingency of the Democrats. How in the hell could she have said no?

She refilled her cup, sat down, and logged into her federal email account. Good heavens, 312 emails loaded to her inbox. Were any of them important to running the free world? She snickered at herself— talk about a drama queen. Slogging through the messages, she ate the bear claw and finished the coffee. Most of the messages she forwarded to Emmett or Betty to handle.

A couple of emails from Lois Lynch, Commissioner of Internal Revenue, caught her attention. They'd originally been sent to the Secretary of the Treasury Department and Lois Talbot had forwarded them to her. From Georgia's viewpoint, Lois was another spoiled federal bureaucrat who had worked on the public's dime for years and had done little to actually deserve her hefty paycheck. But whatever, that was an issue for another day.

Lois had wondered about the status of the Gardner bill creating a simplified taxation law and new IRS computer system. Would the bill go forward on schedule? She stated she was keenly concerned about the bill's impact on IRS employees. Georgia snorted. Lois should be worried, as Georgia would cut the current bloated headcount by more than half if she could.

Although it was unlike Gardner to care about the cost of anything or to consider the benefit to the American public, she figured he'd finally gotten around to a campaign promise since this was an election year. "Politics first" should have been his campaign motto three years ago.

"Madam President, I'm sorry I wasn't here when you arrived."

Georgia removed her reading glasses and gazed at Betty standing in the doorway to her office. "Don't you worry about that. You keep to your regular hours while I'm here."

"Yes ma'am. Would you like a cappuccino?"

"Oh, I'd love one. Thank you."

"I'll be back in a jiffy."

Georgia stared at the door Betty exited. My God, no wonder people fought so hard for this office. It included world-class room service 24/7. She shook her head and reread the emails from Lois. She needed to get her hands on this proposed tax bill. Daniel had not consulted her so she was in the dark on the details. Typical. She jotted notes on a yellow pad in her red leather portfolio.

She looked up as Betty, followed by Emmett, walked toward her.

"Good morning, Madam President," Emmett said as he sat before her.

"Good morning, Emmett." Georgia accepted the cup from Betty. "Thanks. I forwarded a few emails to you. Once you've reviewed them we can discuss."

"Yes ma'am, I'll look at them this morning." Betty nodded and left.

Georgia waited for Betty to shut the door before she spoke. "I've thought about your suggestion yesterday related to Helen's extra-curricular email activity."

"All right, then. We—"

"Let's hack her. Now, today." She tapped her pen on the desktop. "I've thought about the what. How about security plans for the Super Bowl in Dallas. That's in a few days. Make up some group and they can announce it and demand fifty million dollars or the stadium will be bombed. Then tomorrow, a second announcement promising to reveal the names of every undercover ICE agent and Secret Service agent with a demand for the release of prisoners from Gitmo."

"I like your style."

"Good. I don't want to know who does it, or how it's done. When I'm asked about it I don't want to lie. Agreed?"

"Yes ma'am."

"Good. I'll watch the six o'clock news." Georgia heard a knock on the corridor door followed by Frank poking in his head.

"Ma'am, we'll be ready to go in thirty minutes. Any questions?"

She shook her head. "Thanks, I'll be ready."

Emmett frowned. "Are you going somewhere?"

"To the hospital to check on Daniel."

"Morning traffic will be bad."

"Not if you go in an ambulance." She laughed at the shock on his face. "Don't worry, they won't hook me up to an IV. It's the quickest way for me to get to the hospital without creating a traffic mess or telling the world the president is on the move."

He gazed at her intently then smiled. "You know, that's one of the best ideas I've heard in a long time. Why didn't you let me arrange it for you?"

"Sorry about that. I'm used to taking care of details myself."

"No problem. You'll get used to the extra hands. There are several items I need to discuss with you."

"First, I have a question. Do you have a copy of Daniel's new tax bill?"

"I can email you a copy. Jeff Cannon and Valerie Jones were the leads on it."

"Thanks. Now, what's on your list?"

Forty-five minutes later Georgia arrived at the hospital. The ambulance ride had been a breeze and she'd easily slipped through the ER to a back elevator and then the private floor. She slowed as she reached Daniel's room. She'd requested five minutes with his primary doctor and now realized he legally couldn't tell her anything, as she wasn't a family member. No one in the Gardner family was around. She decided to wait a few minutes.

"Doctor Appel, if it's okay, I'll sit with him for a while." The doctor nodded and moved to the nurse's station.

Georgia waved at the agents standing on either side of the door of the private room and walked in. Daniel looked small and very pale in the bed surrounded by medical equipment, yet his face looked bloated. The right side of his head was covered in a puffy bandage. His right hand lay on top of the white blanket and she gave it a couple of pats. She didn't feel comfortable with any physical interaction beyond that, but she could sit next to his bed and talk to him. Surely, he'd want to know what had been going on in the Oval Office over the last couple of days.

She scooted a chair close to the bed and began to talk. She'd reached today's meeting with Emmett when she heard voices outside the room. She turned around as the door opened and the First Lady entered followed by Daniel's mother.

"Georgia, we had no idea you were here." Rosie Gardner walked to the other side of the bed while her mother-in-law positioned herself at its foot.

"I wanted to check on President Gardner's condition in person." She glanced briefly at Mrs. Gardner, who didn't look happy. "I've been giving him a briefing on the Oval Office while he's been away."

Tears welled in Rosie's eyes. "Oh . . . that's so nice of you."

"Just want him to be up-to-speed when he returns." She noticed the grimace that Mrs. Gardner threw at Rosie. What was that? "Dr. Appel couldn't provide an update on Daniel's condition, privacy laws. Can you do that?"

"Hell yes, we can," Mrs. Gardner spat out. "My son is close to death's door because some . . . some jerk shot him. Dr. Apell said he has less than a twenty percent chance of surviving." She glared at

Georgia, daggers spitting out of her eyes. "There! Are you happy? You can complete the rest of Danny's term." She raised a fist to her mouth and rushed out of the room.

"I'm so very sorry." Georgia spoke softly as she gazed at the First Lady. The woman seemed barely able to control her emotions, based on her quivering lips and tense body. "Is there anything you need? What can I do to help you and your family?"

Rosie took a deep breath and wiped at her eyes with a tissue she'd pulled from the pocket of her dark coat. "Give us time to sort through all of this with Danny. Like Elizabeth said, the doctors have been very frank with me about his condition. The blow to the side of his head when he fell has done major damage. But it's much too soon to give up hope."

Georgia rose and walked around the foot of the bed. "Please take all the time you need. Nothing has to change right now." Rosie nodded hesitantly. The poor woman must be going through hell. "If it's all right with you, I'd like to declare this Sunday as a national day of prayer for President Gardner. Do I have your permission?"

"Oh . . . my." Tears once again welled in Rosie's eyes and she reached a hand toward Georgia. "Yes, Madam President, you have my permission. Thank you."

Georgia stepped forward, wrapped her arms around the First Lady, and gently hugged her. She had to take a step back in order to manage her own emotions. She'd be a basket case if it were Peter, her husband of thirty years. "I'll leave you with Daniel. Please take care of yourself and don't worry about anything at the White House. It's still your home."

"Thank you."

Tears rolled down Rosie's face as Georgia turned and let herself out the door. She immediately saw Frank. "Let's go." She pulled her cell phone from her purse and clicked on Emmett's number. He answered immediately.

"In addition to that other assignment I gave you this morning, I need you to do something else."

"Yes, Madam President, is it legal?"

"This time, yes. Talk with the Press Office about getting this out. I'm officially declaring Sunday as a national day of prayer for President Daniel Gardner. I want every church, synagogue, and mosque in this country saying prayers for his speedy recovery. I expect to hear about it on the six o'clock news." She clicked off the phone and followed Frank into the elevator.

Her tenure as President of the United States might not be long but she did believe in the power of prayer, and by God, each day of her presidency was going to mean something positive for the country.

~~*

PING-PING-PING. The annoying bark of the alarm drilled into John's muddled brain. PING-PING-PING. He flung out an arm in the direction of the bedside clock and pounded his fingers on every button. The sound stopped.

He groaned loudly and rubbed his bearded jaw. Jesus, his head hurt and his mouth felt like straw. He rolled to his right side and carefully slid his legs off the side of the bed, fighting with the damned overstuffed comforter. Pushing it aside, he slowly raised to a sitting position while his head pounded. Damn, what did he drink last night?

He heard a sound behind him and turned around to look, which made him dizzy. Crap. He'd forgotten about the woman who lay flat on her back. What was her name? She didn't look too good. He reached out and pushed her shoulder. Her eyes sprang open.

"What? What?"

"Just checking to see if you're alive."

"I'm alive," she whispered and brushed hair off her face. "But I feel like shit."

"Yeah, me, too. Don't you have a room here?"

She nodded.

"I'll order room service and you can get cleaned up in your room and come back here for breakfast."

She gazed at him with a wide-eyed stare.

"How does that sound?"

She blinked and rose up a bit, pushing a pillow behind her. "This isn't a one-night stand?"

"What kind of question is that?"

"I thought . . . hell, I don't know."

The IRS scam had nearly done him in and then Jessie died from breast cancer. He'd stopped caring about so many things. He realized he was tired of doing everything solo.

"I like you. Let's spend some time together while we're both here." He could see her processing his suggestion by the slight narrowing of her eyes. Would she trust him? She finally smiled.

"All right, I'd like that."

John went to the bathroom to take his morning piss. When he returned the room was empty. He assumed Candy would return and opened the room service menu. His stomach issued a ravenous growl, and for some odd reason, his heart pounded a bit faster than normal. He ignored the rush of emotion and picked up the phone. For once, he wouldn't be eating alone.

An hour later, the server left and John poured a much-needed cup of coffee, although the aspirin he'd taken before his shower had dulled his aching head. Candy hadn't returned. Had she chickened out? He wasn't one to waste food and pulled off a dish cover. He heard a knock at the door—good, she had some guts.

He quickly ushered her into his room and noticed her scent as she walked past him—something flowery and very feminine. "I'm happy you returned."

She tilted her head, smiling at him. "Me, too."

John's heart beat in a rapid tempo as he pulled the two easy chairs to either side of the room service table. "Have a seat. Would you like coffee?"

"Yes, please." She sat in one of the chairs and eyed the array of dishes on the table. "My goodness, this is a lot of food."

"I know, didn't know what you liked." He poured her coffee then removed and stacked the silver dish covers on the bar. "Do you like eggs or waffles? Bacon or ham? Tomato or orange juice?"

She giggled. "I just decided I eat too much. I like everything."

"Me, too." He laughed as he returned to his chair. "What would you like first?"

They chatted and ate breakfast for the next hour. John realized that Candy was much more than an airhead who had allowed herself to be picked up by a strange man. She was smart, funny, and very aware of the world around her.

Candy refilled their coffee cups and pushed her chair back from the table. "I have a question for you and I hope you won't think I'm prying."

"No problem. What's your question?"

"Last night, you said something strange. Something about Jessie, and when I asked you who Jessie was, you said 'Washington' and 'big boom'. Who's Jessie and what the hell were you talking about?"

Shit, that's why a person shouldn't drink. The booze makes you say stupid stuff.

He sipped his coffee, praying for the wisdom to respond intelligently—make up a story or be honest? Damn, even thinking about being honest with her had him considering the state of his sanity. Of course, what sane man builds a drone to assassinate the President of the United States?

"Jessie was my wife. She died a year ago from stage-four breast cancer. She didn't have a fighting chance to beat it after we lost our medical insurance."

"Oh, John, I'm so sorry. That must have been an awful experience."

"It was. She lasted three months. We were married close to twenty years." He topped off his coffee cup to give him a chance to breathe.

"I'm sorry for your loss. I'm divorced, almost fifteen years now. Decided I'm a bad picker."

"I've heard of that."

"What did you mean by 'big boom' and 'Washington'?"

Jesus, why the hell had he ever taken his first drink? This was his penance. Avoidance was the word.

"I'm curious, Candy. What do you do in Hershey?"

Her eyes looked to the side and her face looked pinched. "Me? What do I do? I'm retired."

Now he was curious and cautious. "Retired from what?" He enjoyed more coffee.

"I retired as a police detective."

John coughed and spit out coffee. "What? You . . . police?" He dabbed a napkin on his mouth.

She laughed. "I get that reaction a lot. Don't look much like a cop, do I?"

"Aren't you too young to retire?"

She held up her right hand and wiggled the index finger. "See anything weird?"

He squinted for a couple of seconds and then he saw it. "Ah, what happened?"

"First time I seriously pull my gun, I get shot at." She rose and went to the mini-bar. "If we're talking about this shit, I need vodka for my orange juice."

He totally understood. "Hold on, I'll get it." Candy returned to her chair while John opened the mini-bar in search of good vodka. He wasn't disappointed. He retrieved two small bottles and poured each one into a glass from the bar, filled it with ice, and poured in orange juice.

"Here you go." He handed a glass to Candy. "Nectar of the Gods."

She sipped the drink and smiled. "A Screwdriver is just what I imagined Zeus to be drinking."

"Haha." He really liked this woman, good sense of humor. "Finish your story. I'm interested."

"All right." She drank from the glass and set it on the table. "I graduated college with a degree in Forensic Science. Got a job in the Boston police department and I lasted two years. I hated the work. It drove me nuts being cooped up all day."

He nodded. "I can understand that."

"It was so claustrophobic being stuck in a lab. " She sipped the drink and continued. "I decided to attend the police academy and went home to Hershey. Being a cop was awesome. I loved every minute."

"Was your ex-husband a cop?"

She scowled. "Unfortunately. You know how that goes . . . you each understand how cop life works, yada yada. Until one of you can't keep his pants zipped and humps the head cashier at Pronto's Market for a damned year."

"How did you find out?" John had never dealt with infidelity in his marriage but knew a couple of men who had regularly cheated on their wives. He'd had the joy of firing one of them for being a terrible employee.

"Someone talked. People can't bear keeping the titillating details quiet. He finally admitted it and I kicked him to the curb. I can deal with a lot of stuff, but sleeping around . . . no."

"I've not had personal experience with it but I admire you for sticking to your guns." He sipped his drink as he watched Candy beam at his words. Damn, she was pretty. "Speaking of guns and your shot-off finger. What happened?"

"Yeah, that." She rose and went to the window. It overlooked the golf course and wasn't a bad view. John wondered about her thoughts. Was this shooting experience so painful she couldn't talk about it? Had it scarred her for life? After a minute or two, she turned toward him, her face devoid of emotion.

"You okay?" he asked.

"Just getting my thoughts in order." She walked back to the table and plopped in the chair. "This is the short story—it was a typical interview for a robbery that went haywire. The interviewee pulled a gun while I had my hands up saying 'calm down" and the gun went off. I lost half a finger and a four year-old boy behind me lost his life. It was awful."

John wanted to pull her into his arms and comfort her. But something held him back. She had survived this terrible event and a divorce and she didn't need some man to tell her all would be okay.

Instead, he raised his hand for a high-five. "You are my hero."

"Thanks." She slapped his hand. "You know you never did tell me the rest of your story. Remember, Washington and big boom."

"Let's walk the Strip for a while and then I'll tell you."

~~*

Living in D.C. was such a trip; Nick loved it. The snow had already melted and the cabbies were bitching about the weather getting too warm in late January. Go figure. The taxi pulled along the curb outside a medical building on Pennsylvania Avenue, not too far from George Washington University Hospital, where President Gardner lay in a coma. Nick paid the driver and quickly entered the ten-story building.

He sprinted into an open elevator and soon exited on the seventh floor. Willis Neurology occupied the entire floor and a wide reception desk stood to one side of the large waiting area. Nick headed to it.

"I have a meeting with Dr. Brian Willis."

A young woman in baby blue scrubs smiled at him then looked at her computer monitor. "Yes sir. I see it right here. Dr. Willis is on time today so let me take you to his office. Please come in to your left."

Nick followed her directions and then trailed behind her along a hallway to an office at the end. The door was open and a man walked toward them.

"Thanks, Sally." He held out his hand and shook Nick's. "Mr. Romano, good to see you again. Come on in."

"Thanks for agreeing to see me. I know you're busy." Nick settled in a chair in front of the cluttered desk. He knew Dr. Willis was not a man to waste time.

"No problem. What do you have questions about?" Dr. Willis sat behind the desk.

"I'm sure you're aware of the shooting of President Gardner."

"It's been on the news."

"I know you can't comment on whether you've consulted with his primary doctors." Although Nick hoped that he would comment.

"That's right." But the doctor did narrow his eyes when responding. Nick would take that as a "yes."

"Because of the public's interest in the president's condition, I'm writing an article on head wounds. Since you're an expert on the subject, I hope you can give me some insight as to the after effects of a bullet that grazes the skull, as well as a blow to the side of the head."

"I can do that," Dr. Willis confirmed. "A bullet that lightly grazes the skull more than likely won't do much harm. There's a lot of bleeding, typical for head wounds."

"What about a blow to the head? For example, President Gardner fell backwards and it looked like the right side of his head hit the top edge of the half wall behind him." Nick had watched Gardner's fall half a dozen times using Nita's recorded version of the State of the Union address.

"The damage depends on the specific part of the skull impacted." Dr. Willis rose, walked to a bookcase and retrieved something. He came around the front of his desk and leaned against it, holding an object for Nick's view. "Obviously, this is a model of the brain."

Nick had taken an anatomy class in college when he was in pre-med and was familiar with the model. He listened as the doctor gave him a quick lesson on the parts of the brain. He was most interested in the temporal lobe based on how it looked like Gardner's head had hit the wall divider.

"Say a person did hit the right side, the temporal lobe." Nick pointed to his head as he spoke. "What could be the outcome?"

"The key is the severity of the blow. This part of the brain deals with sensory input related to the retention of visual memories, language comprehension, and emotion association. Therapy and rehabilitation will be necessary. In fact—"

"Sorry to interrupt but what would have to happen to cause a person to die from such a blow?" Nick wanted to know if President Gardner could die from hitting his head.

"Something else that impacts the brain as a result of the blow. A good example is Dr. Robert Atkins, remember him?"

"I've heard the name." Nick had no clue but he wouldn't admit that to Dr. Willis.

"Good. He slipped on ice and hit his head when he fell to a sidewalk. He was dead in less than two weeks. The blow caused bleeding of the brain. I believe the official cause of death was blunt impact injury of the head with an epidural hematoma."

"Could that be a possibility for President Gardner?"

"Anything is possible," Dr. Willis said with a blank face. "But we don't have any information on his condition. I'm sure his doctors are monitoring him closely."

Nick rose and stuck out his hand. "Thanks for seeing me today. I appreciate your help."

Dr. Willis shook Nick's hand and walked him to the office door. "Now, don't be making any assumptions about the president's condition. We'll have to wait and see."

"Not a problem."

Nick's elevator ride to the first floor accompanied a bad feeling that Gardner wasn't going to make it out of his coma. *The assassination of an American president would change everything in D.C.*

~~*

"Okay kids, what's the 4-1-1 on Danny's tax bill? Madam President has requested a copy." Valerie and Jeff sat at one end of the small conference table in Emmett's office. He expected a quick answer to his query.

Jeff stared at the ceiling for a moment then glanced at Valerie. She frowned and chewed on her lower lip. He looked from one to the other, baffled by their reactions.

"What? Why aren't you saying something? I asked a simple question."

Jeff rubbed his jaw and fidgeted in the chair. "To be honest, there isn't a new tax bill."

"What the hell are you talking about?" Emmett fisted his hands to stop himself from pounding the table.

"Actually . . . well, Danny, er, President Gardner asked us to do a simple executive summary for a new tax system. You know, a list of bullet points." Valerie blinked at him like she'd just selected a new color of nail polish.

"Are you telling me there's no draft bill written?" He spoke slowly in an effort to calm his nerves. Otherwise, he'd be tempted to find a freaking gun and blow both their fool heads off. Damn, he needed a drink. Prolonged interaction with these idiots would pickle his liver for damn sure.

"No, sorry boss. President Gardner had us work on a suggested list of points for a new tax system." Jeff didn't seem to have a problem with his statement.

"Does it bother either of you that the president mentioned in his State of the Union address, not three days ago, that a new tax bill had already been written? When in fact, he lied to the American people? Because, well . . . there is no damned bill." Emmett's voice rose to fevered pitch as he spoke.

"Come on, Emmett, it's not a total lie." Valerie sounded so indignant. What a twit. "We've talked about the bones of a bill and have our list of policy points prepared."

"Where the hell is the damned list?" Emmett yelled, nearly jumping out of the chair. God, if he only had that gun—boom and then, boom again.

Jeff gazed at Valerie, his eyes narrowed. "Val, don't I have the latest version? Seems like it was my turn to do a good review of it."

Her chin lowered. "Absolutely, Jeff. You have the last version of the tax bill summary."

Emmett did not like the interplay between the two of them. But, he'd let it go for now. The White House had too damned many people playing games—political, sexual, power—you name it.

"Great." He checked his watch, three o'clock. "You have two hours to get whatever the hell you have into a format that looks like the summary draft of a tax bill. Don't forget the plans to retrain IRS employees and the new computer system. President Ross will be looking for it before she leaves the White House today."

Jeff and Valerie opened their mouths then quickly shut them. Yep, they both looked shell-shocked. Tough. They rose and headed for the door. Valerie went out before Jeff who turned back to Emmett. "Yes sir." He scurried out and shut the door with a quiet thud.

Emmett went to his desk and opened a bottom drawer. He pulled out a small glass and a bottle and poured two fingers of vodka. Twirling the liquor in the glass, he considered what he had just learned from Valerie and Jeff. Damn it! Why the hell would Danny play games like this? It was one thing to mislead with promises during the campaign, every candidate did that, but quite another to outright lie in the State of the Union.

He rose from the desk and went to the bank of windows. The sheers blocked a view but he could tell the sun was out. Sipping his drink, he turned and surveyed his large, somewhat regal-looking office. It reminded him of Harry's grandmother's drawing room in Denver; he'd visited the Roberts family mansion once. In addition, his office location was a few doors away from the Oval Office. He liked that and would do what was needed to make certain the whereabouts of his workspace didn't change.

That included a temporary halt to his skimming activity related to White House expenditures. Georgia might decide to do a review of the actual activity and her sharp eyes would no doubt discover his electronic payments to a non-existent vendor, otherwise known as one of his bank accounts. Danny never looked at anything so it hadn't been an issue for three years. Whatever. He was several million dollars richer for his efforts, and no, he didn't feel guilty. Considering his pitiful salary, the long hours he worked, and the secrets he kept, he deserved even more.

He released a drawn out sigh and wiped the empty glass with a small towel before placing both back in his desk drawer. He popped a peppermint in his mouth and sat in his chair, propping his feet on the desk. Only ten minutes until the four o'clock status meeting on the investigation. He didn't have a good feeling about any progress being made.

Emmett's lips thinned. He'd been to the hospital early that morning and nothing had changed. Danny seemed swollen and even paler. The president's semi-permanent golfing tan had disappeared. His gut told him that Danny wouldn't be making any miraculous recovery. Thus, Emmett needed to play his cards straight with Georgia. In fact, playing with her might result in something actually getting done. Progress—wouldn't that be a pleasant change of pace for the nation?

~~*

Although Nick hadn't stayed at her townhouse more than a couple of hours last night, he did manage to give Nita a couple of good ideas for her blog while he stuffed pizza in his mouth and washed it all down with a Mexican beer. His stomach was a bottomless pit. She'd loved cooking for him when they were together. Hmm, maybe she'd make that pork tenderloin with balsamic sauce he liked.

Stop it! Had she learned nothing? No, hell no, she wouldn't cook for him. She shook her head in disgust at her thoughts and opened her online blog, The Watch Dog, to look at the comments—342 after three hours, not bad. She made a habit of reading all the comments to her blog posts, and over time, her readership had increased. The more readers, the more influence the blog created with the Washington press and the Washington newsmakers. She regularly responded to comments and enjoyed the give and take of a spirited debate. She scrolled through fifty or so and came to this one:

BigDem:
What the hell do you mean by this: President Gardner has had quite the lackluster presidency the past three years. One has to wonder about the motivation for actually planning and carrying out the attempted assassination of POTUS. Someone must have had a really good reason, from their perspective, of course. Doesn't seem to me it's just another day at the office......You piece of shit blogger—I've got a bullet with your name on it. Watch your back. I'll be watching you.

Nita's eyes widened. OMG. She'd had hundreds of negative

comments over the years, but not one like this. Commenters that disagreed with her political view usually said she was stupid or misinformed. They didn't threaten her. She read more comments and concluded BigDem was the worst, although others had agreed that she was out of line with her conclusion that someone must have had a good reason to take a shot at POTUS.

Idiots, shooting the president didn't happen every day. The assassin had to be motivated by something.

What should she do?

She rose from her desk and out of habit, looked out the window. The sky was blue with a few puffy clouds. Most of the snow from two days ago had melted. Of course, if the temperature plummeted, ice would cover the roads, throwing the city into chaos. She chuckled. The weather was the one thing Capitol Hill politicians couldn't control.

Back to the blog comment—should she reply or ignore it?

Tapping her foot on the oak floor, she watched a small car attempt to parallel-park on the street below and she made her decision. "Screw it. I'll not feed this guy's insanity." If he made another threatening comment, then she'd take action of some sort.

She returned to her desk and pulled out the list of Gardner scandals. Research time—she'd scour the Internet for related stories. Maybe she'd spot a pattern, something to isolate a motive for the shooting. She didn't have the fancy tools of the intelligence agencies but she did have smarts and a passion for digging through the details. She reviewed the list of scandals during the first three years of the Gardner presidency she'd typed the other night:

1. Prime Minister of West African nation assassinated, U.S. doesn't send top diplomat to funeral, Gardner doesn't make public statement about situation, only written statement read by WH press secretary
2. Live Ebola virus stolen from U.S. government lab in Atlanta, not recovered to date
3. IRS official openly endorsed Democratic governor candidate, no condemnation by WH
4. State Department spokespersons constantly downplay issues around the world and threats to U.S. security
5. U.S. air craft carrier stopped at port in Muscat, Oman bombed via fresh food containers, one sailor killed/eight injured, Gardner does nothing to retaliate, says situation will be handled via diplomacy
6. Deputy chief of staff employee caught with a prostitute in D.C.

and retains his WH job

7. Secret Service allowed person to sneak in the White House through the North Portico and spray paint the walls of the Blue Room while agents watch the Super Bowl on TV, never caught

8. NSA attempted blackmail of a senior correspondent of Fox News in exchange for her notes related to the spray painting of the White House Blue Room

9. IRS computer system is hacked and millions of taxpayer records are stolen with name, SSN, address, refund bank information, and birthdate, WH assumed goal was to file fraudulent tax returns for Earned Income Credit, $$ loss estimated by OBO to be $6 billion over three years

10. Large military-type weapons consistently brought over southern border in Arizona and Texas by non-citizens

11. Franklin Foundation study of mainstream media, both print and TV, found little reporting of Gardner scandals, similar to the previous eight year presidency

12. Western Power Grid explodes in middle of July during Gardner's second year, electricity out for over a week, dozens die in several states, FEMA not prepared, no preventative action taken by WH

Good Lord, these were only the big scandals. She'd mentioned most of these events in her blog over the past three years as opinion pieces, not as in depth factual exposés. Reporters were more attuned to digging for the facts. She had no problem changing gears for this situation.

After studying the list for twenty minutes and making a cup of coffee, she concluded it was smartest to start with three of the biggest problems that would have consequences for individual citizens. Her gut continued to tell her this assassination was personal—maybe because someone wanted Gardner's job or maybe because he was so lousy at doing his job.

She identified a scandal as a "big problem" based on the number of people who had been negatively impacted by it. She selected three to start her research—1) one sailor killed/eight injured in the Muscat, Oman bombing, 2) IRS computer system hacked, and 3) western power grid explosion and deaths.

Nita sat back in her chair and considered the direct impact from these events on the American people. They sucked. She'd do her best to discover if an American directly hurt by one of these three events had a role in Gardner's shooting. Once at the end of that road, if she found the shooter, she'd have the basis for a killer article . . . hmm, maybe even a book. After all, Woodward and Bernstein wrote *All the President's Men* about Watergate.

She'd worked for almost an hour when her cell pinged with a text message from Nick: "Need 2 talk, will bring food, c u at 5:30." Damn, another evening eating dinner with Nick. Food was still at the top of his needs list. That didn't thrill her but they were working together and needed to share information. She went back to her research; Nick wouldn't arrive for over two hours.

First on the list was the bombing of the USS Barak Obama, a Navy destroyer stopped at the port of Muscat, Oman, on the west side of the Gulf of Oman, and south of the Persian Gulf. Since the bombing of the USS Cole, ships had discontinued using Arden, Yemen for refueling. Gardner had decided that was silly as the bombing was old news and approved Navy ships to stop in Arden. But for some reason, the Barak Obama had decided to stop at Muscat for fuel and to stock its galley with fresh provisions.

Nita wondered if part of the reason to stop at Muscat rather than Arden was to shoot the middle finger at Iran. A couple of months earlier, in the Gulf of Oman, an Iranian navy jet had approached the USS Eisenhower, a Navy destroyer on duty supporting Afghanistan war efforts. Apparently the plane was flying low and got within 1,000 feet of the ship. Although the Iranian plane wasn't threatening, the U.S. military didn't like Iran playing footsy with a Navy destroyer. She couldn't argue with that.

She shook her head—men and their toys—and searched for news stories first on CNN, then on Fox News, for the name of the sailors killed or hurt in the explosion. Finally she clicked on a video of a Fox interview with Mary Legend, the mother of the sailor killed. She was a nice looking woman with short gray hair and a tired smile. The anchor explained the bombing event and finally asked Mary if the White House had contacted her.

The woman dabbed a handkerchief to her eyes and took a visible deep breath. "As I said before, my son was killed in service to his country. No, I haven't heard from anyone at the White House. Those clowns are too busy vacationing at Martha's Vineyard and going to Hollywood parties to care about a dead sailor."

The anchor was visibly surprised by the mother's response yet she recovered quickly. "Mrs. Legend, are you saying you feel the president is too busy to deal with a tragedy such as the loss of your son aboard a Navy ship?"

"Yes ma'am, he's too busy, but not busy being a true leader. He's too busy playing at the role of president and not actually being president."

"I'm truly sorry for your loss, Mrs. Legend," the anchor said, closing the interview. "Our thoughts are with you and your family."

That seemed an abrupt end. Ten-to-one a producer was telling the anchor to cut it short. No good would result from pissing off the White House on national television. Nita entered the names in the notes file on her tablet. In addition to being a grieving mother, Mary seemed angry as hell—no warm, squishy feelings for President Gardner. Was that enough motivation to kill him? Guess it all depended.

She read another article and discovered Mary Legend lived in Seven Corners, Virginia. She looked at the maps app on her computer—Seven Corners was less than ten miles from Washington—an easy drive for an interview.

After obtaining Mary's number from the online white pages, Nita called, fingers crossed for an answer. The phone Gods were in a good mood.

"Legend residence." The speaker sounded like a teenage girl.

"May I speak to Mary, please?"

"Sure. Hold on."

Nita heard the person yell, "Mom, some lady is on the phone for you."

After a beat, another voice spoke. "This is Mary."

"Mrs. Legend, my name is Nita Andrews. I'm a blogger in Washington writing an in-depth piece on military families. I—"

"What about military families?" Mary's voice was soft and apprehensive.

"Well . . ." Nita had to think fast. "The impact on families from having a loved one gone for extended periods of time and the worry."

"How did you get my name?"

"I saw an interview of you on Fox News after the death of your son." At least that was the truth. "I'd love to interview you for my article."

"I see." Mrs. Legend was silent for a few seconds. "When?"

"How about tomorrow? Any time that's convenient for you."

"The morning is better for me. Let's say ten."

"That's perfect," Nita replied. "Where should I meet you?"

"I need to go shopping tomorrow. We can meet in the lobby of The Palace Hotel at Tyson Corner in Falls Church. My son, Michael, works there so you can talk to him if you need to."

"I appreciate that." Nita pumped her fist. "I'll see you in the morning. By the way, the blog I write is on BetterPolitics dot com. You can read my bio there."

"I'll do that." Mary clicked off.

Nita ran a search for the Palace Hotel. It was further than Seven Corners but that didn't matter. It would be a quick trip over all. She noticed the time on her computer, almost six. Where was Nick? Like magic, the doorbell rang.

She went to the foyer, retrieving the TV remote as she walked, and opened the door.

"Hey, there. You're late."

Nick walked past her carrying two large shopping bags. "I know. Ling's was crazy. Guess everyone else in D.C. wants Chinese tonight."

"Set the bags in the kitchen. I want to check the news." Nita plopped on the sofa and clicked on the TV. Fox was already on.

"We have breaking news this evening," the female anchor stated. "We've just learned that Director of Homeland Security, Helen Capstone, has had her email account hacked with a specific threat mentioned. Let me clarify—this is her work email account."

"Nick, get in here," Nita yelled. "Big news."

He rushed in, a corkscrew in one hand, a wine bottle in the other. "What news?"

She motioned with her hand for him to sit next to her. "Listen."

The anchor continued. "Let's turn to our chief White House correspondent, John Henry. What is the administration saying about this development?"

"At this point, the White House isn't offering much in the way of explanation. They're looking into the validity of the threat, which they didn't identify. However, we've learned that in addition to Director Capstone's email being hacked, she has been using a personal email account for government business. This account has been maintained via a server at her residence in Cocoa Beach, Florida."

"Oh, my God," Nita exclaimed.

"That's quite a revelation," the anchor said. "We'll have further information on this story later in the hour. Thanks, John. In other news, President Ross has declared Sunday as a national day of prayer for the speedy recovery of President Gardner, who is still hospitalized after the assassination attempt this past Tuesday. He continues to remain in a coma according to medical personnel attending him."

Nita punched Nick in the arm. "How about that? What idiot

would use a personal email account for federal or even state government business?"

"Apparently one of Gardner's cabinet members." Nick held out the bottle of wine. "Come on, let's eat."

In the kitchen, Nita grabbed plates and set them on the dining table with the food containers. Nick brought the wine and filled their glasses. He shoveled Chinese take-out on his plate while Nita did the same.

Nita chuckled after she tasted the wine. "Gardner may not be in the White House now, but his presidency keeps making the news."

"Can you believe Capstone? I wonder what she's been smoking." Nick took a bite of broccoli beef. "Using a private email account on your personal server is plain stupid. It's ridiculous."

"I know. Why do high-ranking federal employees believe the rules don't apply to them? This isn't the first White House with these type of yo-yo's."

"Yo-yo's?" Nicks eyes crinkled.

"You know what I mean." Nita forked a bite of cashew chicken. "You up for a short road trip tomorrow?"

"Like what?"

"Drive over to Falls Church and talk with Mary Legend. She's the mother of the sailor killed in the Oman bombing. I set up a meeting at ten. She's one angry mama."

"Okay, that'll work." He tipped his wine glass toward her. "We can have lunch at a bistro I know."

"Do you always think about food?"

"Only when I'm not thinking about you-know." He wiggled his eyebrows.

Nita couldn't decide if she should laugh or slap him. Instead, she ignored his comment. "What have you been up to today?"

"I talked to the neurologist, Dr. Willis. He wouldn't say outright, but I got the impression that Gardner isn't going to pull out of his coma. The questions are how long will he last, and when will the American people be told?"

"Damn, that's hard to hear, whether you agree with his politics or not."

"I know." Nick shook his head. "But we can't forget that his political strategy might be the motivation for this."

"I'm almost convinced his policies, or lack of good policies, motivated someone to shoot him." She had studied Washington politics for ten years and had no doubt that Gardner had some responsibility for this situation. "Regardless, it's gotta be awful for his family."

Nick gazed at her, displaying a half grin. "Ah, you have a heart after all."

"Of course I do, except where you're concerned. Now back to the issue at hand. Georgia Ross is the number one beneficiary of Gardner's demise. Have you looked into her background?"

"Yep, I started after I saw Dr. Willis." Nick shoveled chicken and more fried rice onto his plate. "It seems like everyone in Washington has credibility issues and she's not immune to them, or at least her husband isn't immune."

"Really? Did you discover something about Mr. Ross?"

"I'm not sure. On the surface it seems innocent, but anything involving one of the Gardner's starts my 'these people are crooks' scenario building in my head. Remember that one time when—"

"Nick, do not go off on a tangent. What have you discovered about the president's husband?" Geez, he had the worst time staying on track. Maybe that's why he strayed. Nope. Nita tamped down that thought. No thinking about the past.

"Sorry." He grinned again. Damn him. "I actually started looking into Peter Ross first, figured that would be a slam-dunk before Georgia. Not so much. Apparently, Peter and Elizabeth Gardner, mother of POTUS, are quite chummy."

"Chummy? How chummy?" Nita's mind whirled toward the ick factor.

"Not *that* kind of chummy. It looks like they're in business together."

She shook her head in disbelief. "That doesn't sound logical. Why would the VP's husband be involved with the president's mother in a business deal? Is it a spa or a trendy clothing boutique?"

Nick raised his hands flat in front of his chest. "I know, I know. It seemed weird as hell to me so I dug deeper. I've got more to do but I did discover that the two of them formed a corporation in Colorado that holds title to several commercial properties in Denver and the surrounding area."

"Where do regular people get the money to buy commercial property?"

"Peter Ross isn't regular people. He's loaded."

"What? I didn't realize that." How many more surprises would they uncover before this was over?

"They've not tried to hide it but his background has never been a target for the media. Georgia and Peter aren't part of the 'cool' crowd in D.C., so they've managed to stay out of the headlines."

"Interesting, but back to Ross and Mrs. Gardner. How did you discover they formed a corporation in Colorado?"

Nick refilled their wine glasses and grinned. "I'd like to say it's due to expertise on my part, but honestly, I discovered this as a fluke. I came across a photo at some function several months ago with Peter and Elizabeth looking cozy. That surprised me and I dug a little deeper and found an article in the *Denver Post* mentioning their names and their first real estate deal."

"Is the deal legal?"

"On the outside, but I find it awfully strange for the two of them to be doing anything together."

Nita raised her eyebrows. "Elizabeth is a very nice looking woman. I bet Georgia's had a busy schedule for years, leaving poor Peter to fend for himself."

"Gross, she's gotta be fifteen years older than him. No way."

"All right. But tell me about Peter. What do you mean he's loaded?"

"His family has been a major player in California commercial real estate development for fifty years. The family business started with retail space in East L.A. and expanded exponentially over the next ten years. Then the business took off and the rest is history. The business is worth a few billion dollars and Peter is executive vice president. His father, Gerald, is still CEO. They're very well-connected in California and give a boatload to charity."

"Then why the hell would Peter do a deal in Colorado with President Gardner's mother?"

Nick shrugged his shoulders. "Don't know, but that's the question at hand and I have more work to do. This doesn't make sense to me. I'm missing something."

"I agree . . . keep looking." Nita sipped her wine and considered the enormity of their task. "Are we nuts for taking this on? I mean, the NSA is probably in charge of the government's investigation. How can we compete with them?"

Nick rubbed a hand over his jaw. "I think we do what we do best—think outside the prescribed lines of government procedures. You know, be creative . . . travel outside that stupid box."

Nita laughed. "Absolutely. The feds are way too regimented in how they think."

~~*

With a stroke of luck from the Washington gods, Emmett managed to provide Georgia with a ten-page executive summary of Gardner's theoretical tax bill. Valerie and Jeff had no doubt engaged in a two-hour round of creative government bullshit suitable for a Pulitzer. Georgia had accepted it without question shortly after the end of the four o'clock meeting. She'd surprised the hell out of him by stuffing it in her briefcase and not asking one question.

Of course, she was distracted and not a happy camper. After three days of investigation, the NSA, along with their agency partners had not uncovered a credible suspect for the shooting, nor a reasonable motivation. Georgia found that incredulous and yelled at everyone in the room, including Emmett. It didn't bother him, as he agreed with her. The intelligence agencies had gotten lazy. After the former president, and now Gardner, the current posse wasn't accustomed to actually going after the facts. He concluded that apathy bred inaction.

Emmett bid her goodnight and headed home to take a shower and change clothes. Within the hour he was at the same corner by the Capitol as yesterday, waiting for Harry to arrive. He didn't know exactly how he'd play the evening. Go with the flow he guessed. But he sure as hell had to discover what was going on with Harry, who walked across the sidewalk toward the car. He moved slowly, as if he carried the weight of the planet on his shoulders.

The driver exited and opened the door for him.

"Good evening, Harry," Emmett said smoothly. "I hope you've had a productive day."

Harry plopped on the seat and sighed heavily. "Let's say it was annoying. Those damned Republicans say 'no' to everything. They won't work with us."

"I see. Kinda like the former president not working with the Republican Congress?"

"Hell no. This is totally different. They're obstructionists. Damn assholes if you ask me. Each and every one a loser."

"Not asking." Emmett wasn't pleased at Harry's tone. Constantly criticizing and blaming the other party led to stalemate. The former president had proven that, time and time again. He'd done his best to counsel Danny to learn from his predecessor's mistakes but more often than not, Danny wouldn't listen. Unfortunately, Emmett wanted to keep his job more than he cared about the integrity of his boss, so he backed off and kept his mouth shut. After three days with Georgia Ross as president, he wondered if he'd made a mistake not being more vocal with Danny.

"Damn. I need a drink." Harry rubbed a hand over his short hair. "Sometimes I wonder what the hell I'm doing here."

"I wonder the same thing every damn day."

They rode in silence as the car travelled to the restaurant. The driver opened the door and Emmett followed Harry out of the car and into Renoir. He'd made a reservation so they were quickly ushered to a discreet table in the corner. The waitress arrived as soon as their butts hit their chairs, handing each of them a heavy two-sided menu.

"Good evening, gentlemen. May I start you off with a cocktail and an appetizer?"

"Absolutely," Harry replied. "Bring me a double Glenmorangie, three ice cubes."

"I'll have a vodka tonic with Grey Goose. Bring a plate of those little crab cakes and a basket of the bread with smashed garlic and asiago." Emmett had been to Renoir so many times he knew the menu and set it on the plate in front of him. Now, down to business before Harry had consumed too much scotch.

"How was your meeting with the FBI yesterday?"

"Had it today. Interesting, but they've made little progress. It appears a drone carried the gun that shot Danny. They're working on putting it back together but the explosion did a good job of destroying it."

Emmett knew that—they'd discussed it at the intelligence meeting. "How in the world was a drone with a gun left in the Capitol building? That's a huge security breach." Emmett had mentioned to Georgia about talking with the Capitol Police. This was not normal for them.

"No shit."

The waitress appeared with their drinks. "I'll have your crab bites and bread in just a few minutes." She smiled and left. Harry took a long pull on his scotch.

"Harry, we've known each other for almost thirty years. I have to say you're not looking good. Are you having a health issue?"

Harry looked as though he'd been slapped and shock masked his face. "Why the hell are you asking that? Health issue? Hell no."

Emmett didn't believe him. "I'm worried, you don't seem like yourself."

Harry roared with laughter and pointed a finger at his dinner companion. "You . . . worried about me? That's rich. Truth is I'm working my ass off. Things have sped up with Georgia Ross as temporary president."

"Really?" Emmett didn't believe Harry. His gut told him this wasn't a work thing. Harry was hiding something.

"Yeah, she's asked for a list of all outstanding legislation and its status." Harry finished his drink. "Funny, Danny never asked, not once."

"I guess they have different management styles."

Harry responded with a dark frown and kept his silence. The waitress arrived with the appetizers and set them in the middle of the table. He rattled the ice in his glass. She nodded and left.

"These crab cakes are good," Emmett said as he placed a couple on his plate and covered them with the remoulade sauce. He added a piece of bread.

"Yeah, sure." Harry filled a plate as well. The waitress returned quickly with a fresh drink and they placed their dinner orders.

Emmett decided he'd try another tactic to get the truth out of Harry. "I hear that Mike McCain is switching gears in the Senate now that Georgia is in the White House." McCain was the Republican Majority Leader elected after Mitch McGuire decided to retire. He was much younger than McGuire and a hell of a lot more energetic. God bless young senators. Emmett actually had *no clue* about McCain's intentions now that Danny was out of action but Harry didn't know that.

Harry's mouth scrunched first to one side then the other. He was obviously thinking about the impact on the House of McCain changing tactics, along with any impact on the buckets of stalled legislation. "I haven't heard a thing about the Senate changing their procedures. This isn't acceptable. I should have been informed."

"Who knows? Everything is out of whack since State of the Union."

Harry nodded. "Exactly."

They chewed their appetizers and sipped their drinks, each silent for a couple of minutes. Harry broke the quiet moment.

"How's it going with Georgia in the Oval Office?"

Emmett had expected the question, as it was an obvious one. "To be honest, I wasn't thrilled the first day, that was Wednesday. But now, two days later, she's okay."

"I don't remember her being a standout in the Senate. Of course, she was the lead on that environmental bill a few years ago. Not sure what she's done since then."

Interesting. Now Harry wasn't a fan of Georgia. "Wasn't she Chair of the Homeland Security and Government Affairs Senate

Committee for eleven years?"

"Right, forgot about that."

Sure, he forgot. Emmett found Harry's cavalier attitude toward Georgia very curious. Why wasn't he thrilled that Danny's selection for vice president, four-plus years ago, had ended up being a wise decision? Perhaps he expected her to shift gears on Danny's policies. Or, maybe he suspected that she had orchestrated the assassination attempt. Since she benefited from Danny being out of office that sure as hell made sense.

Or, maybe it was something entirely different. He couldn't ignore any possibility.

"What do you know about this new tax bill Danny mentioned on Tuesday?"

Harry's question surprised Emmett. Surely Danny had consulted with him about the proposed bill's initial points even though a legitimate bill hadn't been drafted.

"I wasn't included in its development. I'm surprised Danny didn't discuss it with you months ago. Changing the role of the IRS is a big deal." Emmett drained his glass, weighing how much he should reveal. "Actually, Valerie Jones was lead on the details."

"You weren't involved at all?" Harry queried, seeming a bit baffled.

"Not when Danny assigns something to Valerie. I know my place."

"I never understood why he hooked up with that bitch other than she's blond and has big ta-ta's." Harry leaned over the table. "I'm sure she's kept Danny in a good mood for years."

Emmett was saved from commenting by the waitress arriving with their dinner selections, along with fresh drinks they hadn't ordered. Just what Harry needed, more alcohol. They dug into their steaks and baked potatoes. Renoir truly had excellent food.

After a few minutes, Harry laid his fork against the plate's edge and stared at Emmett for several moments, his eyes a little red rimmed and a frown creased his forehead.

"Harry . . . what?"

"Ya know, I was just thinking." He picked up his drink, brought it to his lips, and then set the glass next to his plate. "Washington is a vicious town."

Emmett nodded, wondering what had prompted this particular comment. "It's not a town for sissies, that's for sure."

"Damn right."

"This is a good filet." Emmett's gut continued to ping. Harry never talked like this.

Harry nodded and forked a slice of steak. "The worst thing about Washington is all the secrets. No one plays fair or tells the truth unless forced to by a subpoena. Everyone has his or her own agenda. Jesus, who could be worse than the Hiltons? Poor Halley, Danny fixed her but good. I like Bob, though."

"You're right. This is a tough town. But we work for the people and as federal employees we should do our best." Emmett cringed at his words, considering his own side business via the White House. Why in the hell was he second-guessing himself?

"You may be a federal employee, but I'm an *elected* official of the U.S. government. We work to a higher standard than you regular staff employees."

Emmett had just taken a sip of water and barely kept from choking at Harry's ridiculous words. What a pompous ass. He wiped his mouth with his napkin then chugged his vodka tonic. "I was wondering, Harry, how close have you worked with Danny on new legislation the past couple of years? You know, as an elected official and all?"

Harry stabbed his fork in the air over his plate. "Don't you dare be a smart ass toward me, you little punk. I've put up with you all these years because of Danny. Now isn't the time to push your low rung on the totem pole."

Emmett chuckled to himself as he ignored the jab; poor Harry, he was delusional about who actually ran the country. He raised his hand, motioning for the waitress who quickly arrived at the table. "My friend here would like another scotch. I'd like a cappuccino."

He drained his drink and glared at Harry, his feelings about his old friend mixed and confused. "I think the goal of elected officials has changed over the past fifty years. Rather than being elected to serve the people's mandate, Congress and the White House now have a personal agenda with politics driving every decision."

"Tsk, tsk, what a nasty attitude you have. What the people don't know won't hurt 'em." Harry belched, not bothering to cover his mouth. "Surely you understand that the people are clueless about what is best for 'em. Jesus Christ, they need our help for jus' about everything."

"Come on, that's an unjustified simplification."

Harry ignored the comment and stuffed his mouth with potato, chewed for a second, then added the last of his T-bone steak. Emmett was tempted to snap a photo on his cell phone and publish it on Twitter: "The people's Speaker of the House at his finest—stuffing his face with a $60 steak!" But he didn't. It was time to get on point.

"I need your help with something," Emmett said. "I'm putting together a list for Georgia of who would want Danny dead, other than her. Who do you think should be on the list?"

Harry hiccupped. The booze was getting to him. "How 'bout every damned American? People don' like him."

"Granted his approval ratings have fallen slightly the past few months. But I suspect the new tax bill would've changed that."

"Yeah, whatever." Harry wiped his mouth with his napkin. "Gotta wonder if Danny had it coming."

~~*

Georgia Ross had lived in the same little house off Pennsylvania Avenue in downtown Washington during her twenty-five years in the Senate. She saw no reason to change when she was elected vice-president but the Secret Service had other ideas. She was forced to move to Number One Observatory Circle, the official VP residence. Although she wasn't happy, she understood the move was a security thing. She made the best of it.

After three long days as POTUS she didn't care where her tired feet landed as long as she could sit in the corner of her comfy sofa and enjoy a glass of merlot in peace. She walked in the door behind Frank to a very pleasant surprise. She heard her husband's voice.

"Peter," she yelled. "You're home."

He walked out of the family room. "Yes, I am."

Frank nodded at Georgia and retreated out the front door. His nighttime replacement should be on site. She rushed to Peter's open arms. "I've missed you so much."

He kissed her temple and hugged her tight. "No more than me, Madam President." He held her at arm's length. "I'm sorry I couldn't return immediately. This has been a big week for you."

She shrugged. "No worry. Let's relax for a bit. I need to put my feet up." Setting her heavy briefcase on the foyer table, she went to the family room off the large kitchen and settled on a pale yellow sofa. It was her favorite spot in the house. "Would you mind opening a bottle of merlot?"

"Great idea. We have much to discuss."

While Peter fussed in the kitchen, Georgia took off her heels before pulling over an ottoman and placing her tired feet on it. Ah, that felt good. She leaned against the back sofa cushion and closed her eyes. Damn, the last three days had been hell on wheels. No wonder presidents aged and greyed so quickly after taking office. At least she could color her hair. She opened her eyes and chuckled at that truly vain thought.

"What's so funny?" Peter walked in carrying a tray that he set on the dark oak coffee table. "I added cheese and crackers just in case you're hungry. Let's order from Luigi's in a bit."

"Perfect." She watched him pour the wine and accepted a glass, sighing heavily. "It's so good to be home and to be quiet. The Oval Office is a madhouse of activity."

Peter settled in the yellow-cream plaid club chair adjacent to the sofa with his own glass. "Are you up to telling me about the last three days?"

She nodded and sipped the wine while gathering her thoughts. Where to begin? "Let's get the big dog out of the way—I'm the most obvious candidate as the orchestrator of Daniel's shooting."

"Yep, you're the big dog in that pound, for now at least. Any idea who fired the shot?"

"I've hardly had time to think about it, so that's a big no." She shrugged out of her suit jacket and laid it over the back of the sofa. "This POTUS gig at the White House is not for the faint of heart— much worse than being VP. It's one hell of a lot of work, and I've only been at it for three days."

"Do you think President Gardner feels the same?"

"Hmm . . ." She closed her eyes for a few seconds, thinking about the proper response to Peter's question. "I think he has a different definition of hard work. He copied the work style of the former president."

"You mean work as little as possible?"

"Uh-huh." She accepted a wheat cracker layered with a sliver of Gouda cheese from her husband. "Thank you. You're too good to me."

"Nah, you're worth it." Peter rose and picked up the wine bottle. He topped off their glasses and leaned in close for a sweet kiss. "I love you."

"Love you, too."

He patted her shoulder then returned to the chair. "So, what can you tell me?"

"You're my husband. I can tell you anything, at least I think I can." She cocked her head to the side. "Now this you must keep to yourself. I played the bitch card this morning. I told the chief of staff to hack the emails of Helen Capstone and demand a ransom, or the hacker would reveal something confidential. She's been using a personal email account for government business. The revelation should have been on the six o'clock news. I figure that's when Helen will learn she's been hacked. I'll watch the recordings later." Years ago, she had started to record the network and cable evening news broadcasts. It helped her keep current.

Peter chuckled. "You are my hero. I'm surprised you haven't received a call from her."

"My phone is on vibrate. I know that's a terrible thing to do but I need the break and Helen can stew for a while. She needs to learn a lesson about protocol."

"Other than setting up the Director of DHS, what else has been going on?" Peter handed her another cracker layered with cheese.

"Honestly, you may not be interested. Much of the president's work is reading and commenting, giving an opinion. Daniel has been a fan of giving speeches and riding in Air Force One."

"Will you be doing that soon?"

"I've cancelled the scheduled events for next week. None of them are important anyway." She sighed heavily. "After that, we'll see how it goes."

"You look exhausted," Peter commented quietly.

"Gee, thanks." She shook her head and sipped the wine. "Not exhausted as I'm accustomed to the long hours. Being the new kid in the Oval Office takes a toll, along with all the uncertainty of Daniel's condition. I'll make it work."

"Do you know how he's doing?"

"I went to the hospital this morning. He's in a coma. Rosie told me the doctors don't have much hope of him recovering. The blow to his head when he fell seems to be the problem."

Peter pursed his lips. "That's a shame. I've not been a fan of the Gardner presidency, but I sure hate to see his career end like this." He grinned at his wife. "Anyone I need to beat up for outright accusing you of this?"

"Not now." Yet she knew that had to be the favorite topic of conversation in Washington. "I'm frustrated our intelligence community hasn't made more progress. But we do know a gun attached to a small drone is what shot Daniel."

Peter's eyes widened. "How the hell did a drone get in the House Chamber?"

"Exactly. It was activated remotely so where was the controller located? I wonder how far away it could have been." She gritted her teeth. This bastard would not get away with shooting the president. "Someone went to a lot of trouble to kill Daniel, or try to at this point. What's the motivation?"

"Could be anything. But once you figure that out, it will lead you to the shooter."

~~*

John had made his decision that afternoon while he and Candy played the penny slots at the Palazzo and the Venetian. He hadn't had so much fun in years—way before Jessie getting sick. Candy concocted a slots contest game and they'd hit Spin for almost two hours. In the end, their individual winnings were only ten dollars apart so she declared them both winners. She kissed his cheek and smiled.

He rose and grabbed her hand. "Come on. Let's get a bottle of wine and go back to the room. We can relax and figure out where we want to go for dinner."

They stopped at the Grand's gift shop and bought an overpriced bottle of chardonnay. Within minutes they were in John's room and sitting on either side of the small table by the window, the wine poured and tasted. Candy had opened the curtains and late afternoon sun streamed in, illuminating a slice of the carpet.

She smiled at him. "Here we are again. I get the feeling you have something on your mind."

He nodded. "I do."

They stared at each other for several seconds before Candy spoke. "All righty then. What is it?"

John was momentarily tongue-tied. He didn't know how to divulge what he'd done. Would telling Candy be the biggest mistake of his life? Well, he hadn't accepted Harry's proposal expecting to come out of Washington alive. So be it. He breathed deeply, gathering his thoughts.

"What I have to tell you is gonna be a surprise so just hang with me. Okay?"

Candy nodded.

"I'm from Colorado, same as President Daniel Gardner and Speaker of the House, Harry Roberts. Six months ago I received a letter from the Speaker, expressing his apology for the IRS hacking fiasco. He—"

"You were one of the people impacted by that?"

"Sure was . . . I lost almost everything because some asshole hacked the IRS computer system and stole my identity. Damn IRS incompetents. First they target conservative groups, then they can't secure the personal tax data of the American people. Damn bunch of inept bureaucrats. That's why we lost our medical insurance." John took a calming breath and a drink of wine. Candy waited. "Anyway, Harry came to visit me at home about a month after that letter. He'd done quite the background check on me and had a ridiculous proposition."

She frowned. "A proposition? Not sure I like the sound of that."

"It gets worse." He drained his glass. "Harry's proposal for me was to kill the President of the United States, POTUS for short. Last I heard though, he's not dead yet."

Candy's jaw dropped fast and her eyebrows nearly hit her hairline. She recovered quickly. "How much did he pay you?"

"One million dollars. I just asked him for another four million. Guess I should check my bank balance to confirm he came through."

"Jesus, that's not nearly enough money for that job. You must be a lousy negotiator."

"You're not disgusted by what I did?"

"Nope, I dislike Gardner, glad he's gone from the White House. He's been a lousy president, especially after the eight years of incompetence from the former president. I have sympathy for the Gardner family though."

John chuckled at the shock and then relief of her words. "You would have gotten more money for the job than me?"

"Damn straight. That Roberts character is loaded. I read an article about him in the airline magazine on the flight over here. He should have paid you more like ten or fifteen million."

Now it was John's turn to be surprised. Candy was a firecracker. "All righty then, Miss Know-It-All, I have just the opportunity for you. If you're—"

She interrupted him again. "Sorry to cut you off but I need to make sure I understand. You are the one who shot President Gardner while he was giving the State of the Union speech, right?"

He nodded. "Uh-huh."

"How in the hell did you get in that place where he was giving the speech while carrying a gun?"

"I wasn't there." Being an ex-cop, he knew she'd appreciate the details and explained everything.

"You're a freaking genius having that Roberts guy plant the drone." Candy drained her wine and refilled both their glasses. "What's this opportunity you mentioned?"

"I received an email from Harry earlier this afternoon. He asked if

I'm open to another project. I'm thinking maybe. What do you say?"

"I think it depends on the project."

Chapter Five

Saturday, January 24

NITA SET HER COFFEE mug in the kitchen sink and hurried to her desk to dig her ringing cell phone out of her purse. Jimmy's name showed on the screen.

"You're up early for a famous chef. Everything okay?"

"You will not believe it. Jeff forced me to run this morning. I actually survived two miles and didn't embarrass myself." Jimmy sounded excited.

"Yay, you. At least one of us is getting some exercise." She couldn't imagine why he'd be calling since she'd talked to him on Thursday. "What's up?"

"Well," his voice had lowered. "I have a bit of juicy gossip for you."

"Very cool, what is it?"

"Emmett Garrett and Harry Roberts had dinner at the restaurant last night. Per the waitress they seemed stressed throughout the meal and Harry loves his scotch."

"Can't blame them for being stressed. Anything else?"

"As they waited outside for their car, they seemed to have a tiff with Harry yelling at Emmett. The valet said Harry called him 'a flaming asshole.' Nice, huh?"

"Yeah, interesting." She needed to think about this. "Thanks for letting me know."

"No problem. You and Nick come by the restaurant and I'll buy you dinner. Okay?"

She clicked off and shrugged on her jacket, then slung her tote bag over her shoulder. The meeting with Mary legend was in less than an hour. Nick pulled in in front of her house as she skipped down the steps. He got out and opened the SUV's door for her—quite the gentleman.

"Right on time. Thanks for driving." She shot a smile at Nick and climbed in.

"No problem." He shut the door with a thud and slid behind the wheel.

"Take New Hampshire south, okay?" Nita had the maps app active on her cell phone.

Nick grinned at her. "I know where I'm going so you don't need to follow every turn with your GPS."

"I like to know where I'm at, that's all." She almost stuck her tongue out at him but caught herself in time. Why did Nick always bring out the worst in her? She couldn't answer her own question so she checked her Facebook page on the smartphone.

"Whatever floats your boat." He navigated a right turn and pulled into the traffic on New Hampshire Avenue, headed toward the Theodore Roosevelt Memorial Bridge.

They rode without talking, listening to a satellite cable news show. Nick increased the volume at the mention of President Gardner.

"We have news on the attempted assassination of President Daniel Gardner," the anchor stated. "Per the Associated Press, the NSA has confirmed that the president was shot, while giving his third State of the Union address, with a gun attached to a small drone. How the device was placed in the House Chamber is unknown at this point. No other details are available. We will have more information as it's released. In other news, Secretary of Homeland Security, Helen Capstone, has issued a statement about her hacked emails."

"A drone," Nita exclaimed. "Wow, that makes so much sense."

Nick eased onto Interstate 66 headed to Virginia. "It would have been impossible for someone to actually be in the House Chamber, shoot twice, and not get caught. Unless there are false floors he could have dropped in."

Nita looked at him. "You know, that's not a half-bad idea. Maybe that's where the drone was hidden."

Nick frowned. "I doubt it. But the drone was hidden somewhere and by someone. And—"

"And someone had to control it. I wonder if that someone was in the Capitol building at the time."

"Don't know anything about drones. Guess we should add them to our research list." Nick glanced at her, his mouth stretched in a huge grin. "Our list is going to be so long we'll never get it finished before the feds find the shooter."

"We need to work faster. Remember? We're traveling outside the box." Nita turned her head away from him to look out the side window. How in the hell could a blogger and a reporter best the U.S.

intelligence services? She blew out a heavy breath, frustrated at her constant questioning of why she had signed on for this particular task. Then she remembered Woodward and Bernstein, yep, that was why.

After a few minutes they entered the Roosevelt Bridge.

"Love this bridge," Nick muttered.

She turned toward him. "Me, too. I haven't been to the memorial island in a while. I used to go there all the time when I needed to get away. For some reason I thought that staring at that huge statute of Theodore Roosevelt would give me wisdom."

"Did it?"

She grinned at him. "What *do you* think?" He shook his head and she checked the comments on her latest blog via her smartphone. Yikes, there were now 621 comments. This blog had topped all others. She scrolled through the new comments and soon sucked in her breath. "What the hell."

"What's wrong?"

"You would not believe the comments that asshole left on my last blog. What a jerk."

"What did he say?" Nick sent a quick glance at Nita, who looked straight ahead. The road turned north, along the west side of Theodore Roosevelt Island. It looked so peaceful in the winter sunshine.

"Let me read the first one to you. It was posted yesterday." She finished reading and gazed at Nick. "How about that?"

"That BigDem person is an asshole and obviously a liberal."

"And self-centered. Listen to this second comment: 'You chicken shit blogger...no reply to me? Now I have two bullets ready for you.' This is one unhappy guy. Two bullets? *Right*."

"Do you normally get threatening comments on your blogs?"

"Not like this." Nita bit her lip. "I wonder if I should report this to the police."

"More like the FBI. Has anything weird happened since you posted the blog?"

"Nothing other than these comments."

"I'd wait and see. Too many weirdoes on the Internet."

"You're right. Talk radio gives—" The sing-song tone of Nita's cellphone interrupted her, she touched the Talk button and listened for a couple of minutes—happy that Vito had responded to her voice mail. "Perfect. Thanks so much. I can do that." She clicked off and grinned at Nick. "Guess what I'll have by tomorrow evening?"

He glanced at her. "No clue."

"I have a friend who will provide a file with every name and address for the people who were included in the hacking of the IRS a couple of years ago."

"Way to go. I figured you knew a good hacker."

"Sure do. This guy is golden."

Within fifteen minutes, Nick pulled into the parking lot in front of The Palace at Tysons Corner in Falls Church. They were ten minutes early.

Nick pushed open the driver side door. "Come on. Let's get a cup of coffee first."

Nita climbed out of the SUV and met Nick in front. "I bet there's a Starbuck's inside."

With a tall mocha latte in her hand, Nita scanned the sofas and chairs in the hotel lobby for Mary Legend. A woman with gray hair turned her head for a moment. Nita turned back to Nick. "Come on, she's over by the ficus tree." She smiled as Nick followed with a muttered, "What's a ficus?"

Nita stopped a few feet in front of the woman. "Mrs. Legend?" The woman nodded and Nita moved forward, extending her hand. "Hi, I'm Nita Andrews. Thanks so much for agreeing to speak with me." The two women shook hands then Nita sat in the square chair directly across from Mrs. Legend. Nick sat next to Nita.

"Not a problem," she said. "Who's your friend?"

"I'm Nick Romano. Nita and I are working on a story together."

"Are you a reporter?" Mrs. Legend didn't look happy.

"I used to be, for the *Washington Chronicle*." Nick displayed a charming smile. "I'm a freelance writer now. We all want to write a book."

"I've heard that about reporters. Call me Mary by the way." She seemed to relax and her attention transferred back to Nita "Tell me again how you found my name?"

"I saw you giving an interview on TV, about the death of your son." Nita pulled her tablet from her tote and opened it for taking notes.

"I remember. The only people I'd talk to were the ones at Fox News and Jeb Stone on The Today Show."

"I saw the Fox interview," Nita replied. She was curious why Mary would allow an interview with Jeb Stone, a die-hard liberal. But she wouldn't ask. "We're so very sorry for the loss of your son."

Mary nodded. "Thank you. I don't know if I'll ever get used to it, Oscar being gone, I mean."

"Mrs. Legend, how did you learn your son was killed on the USS

Barak Obama?" Nick's voice was soft and respectful. Nita had always admired his interview skills—he was a pro.

Mary closed her eyes for a beat and wiped away a tear. Nita reached across to her and almost touched her knee before pulling back her hand. No, not appropriate.

"Actually," Mary began. "I first heard about the bombing and sailors being killed and injured on the TV news. It wasn't until the next day that I was informed by the Navy that Oscar had been killed." She fiddled with the straps of the black purse sitting on her lap. "It took them several hours to determine who was killed because of damage to . . . to his body."

Nita's hand went to her mouth—how awful to know that about your son. "You're a courageous woman."

"Not really. I doubt anything has changed." She closed her eyes briefly then shrugged. "You wanted to talk about the impact on military families when a member is deployed for long periods. Right?"

Nita exchanged a quick glance with Nick, who narrowed his eyes. "Yes, that's right. I imagine it's not an easy task. What's the worst part of having a loved one deployed?"

Mary waved a hand and a young man approached them. "Have a seat. This is my other son, Michael."

Nick shook hands with him, followed by Nita. She scrunched her lips together for a moment. "You look so familiar to me. Have we met?"

Michael laughed. "You probably saw photos of my brother on television. We're twins."

"I had no idea," Nita replied. Damn, why hadn't she discovered that in her research? She entered a note on the tablet.

"You didn't join the military like your brother?" Nick asked.

Michael shook his head. "He tried to talk me into it but I wanted to go to college after high school. It's a big regret on my part. If I'd gone with him he'd—"

"Don't say another word." Mary interrupted him and placed a hand on his arm. "Oscar's death is not your fault."

Michael sighed heavily. "I know, Mom. It's just so damned hard when nothing has been done."

Now they were getting somewhere. Nita considered the right question to ask. "What did you expect to be done?"

"Oh, I don't know, maybe have President Gardner going after the people who planted the bomb." Michael's voice had increased in volume and Mary again patted his arm. He shook his head. "I'll be calm. Gardner didn't have the balls to even call my mother to express his sympathy for Oscar's death. How's that for being the leader of the free world?"

That confirmed what Mary had said in the TV interview. "You've not been contacted at all by the White House?" Nita added a note to her tablet.

"I received a letter from Gardner," Mary said. "It was one of those form letters that didn't even have an original signature."

"That is truly disgusting," Nick said.

"Yeah, whatever. That's our president," Michael said. "Or at least it was. I haven't heard whether he's dead yet."

"I gather his potential death doesn't bother you." Like a good reporter, Nick followed with the right question.

"Hell, no."

"Michael, these folks don't want to hear about your issues with the president." Mary glanced from Nita to Nick, her face the portrait of a still grieving mother. "I'm sure they've figured out we aren't fans of President Gardner or his leadership."

"Unfortunately, you aren't alone. May I ask what you think the president should have done after the bombing of the USS Barak Obama?" Nita hoped she could get a gauge on their anger toward Gardner—generally pissed or the bastard needs to die.

Mary raised a hand to Michael. "First, he should have met with me at Dover Air Force Base when Oscar came home. Second, he should have told me what the government was doing to find the people who planted the bomb. Neither of those things happened."

"I've called the White House, sent emails, sent letters . . . and nothing, not one reply." Michael fisted his hands in front of his chest. "Gardner hasn't done jack-shit to hunt down Oscar's killer."

"Do you think he doesn't care or he's simply a lousy president?" Nick asked.

"Both. He doesn't care because he's a lousy president." Michael hit one fist on the arm of the chair. "Good riddance to him."

"Goodness, we've gotten off target," Nita said. "Let's get back to talking about being a military family. I have just a few questions."

After another twenty minutes of questions and answers, Nita and Nick thanked the pair for their time and openness and headed to the parking lot. They didn't speak until the SUV's doors closed.

"Holy shit. I didn't expect that honesty." Nita leaned against the leather seat, her hands on her knees. "Wow, just wow."

Nick backed out of the parking spot and headed for the street. "It looks like we have a name to add to our list of possibilities."

"We're going to have one hell of a long list."

~~*

Georgia slept in Saturday morning and enjoyed a leisurely breakfast with Peter. By nine o'clock she'd kissed him good-bye and was on her way to the White House. The caravan of three black SUV's slid through the streets without snarling traffic. The lights were on in the West Wing and Frank greeted her at the corridor door to the Oval Office.

"Good morning, Madam President."

"Good morning, Frank." She smiled and walked past him to the presidential desk. She liked the one she used as vice president better but it was a tradition the last few years using the Hayes *Resolute* desk. The damned chair was simply too big for her. She sighed and hauled the briefcase on top of the desk. She chided herself for worrying about such inconsequential things. Not liking a desk or a chair was nothing compared to Daniel Gardner lying comatose in a hospital bed. She'd stop by the hospital at the end of the day. Hopefully, the Sunday prayers of a nation would help him.

After starting her small laptop computer, she checked her email. She didn't know if that was presidential or not but it had been her first–thing–in–the–morning habit for years. The inbox had sixty-plus messages. She worked on them until Emmett knocked and entered.

"Good morning, Madam President. Are you ready for our ten o'clock?"

"Come on in." Georgia rose and grabbed her red portfolio from the briefcase. She settled in the lead chair as the group of men, along with Valerie and Helen, entered and settled on the chairs and sofa.

Everyone murmured "good morning." Good, that was out of the way.

"Thank you for coming this morning. I realize we all met a few hours ago, so please bear with me. Thanks for joining us today, Helen."

"Not a problem." Helen wiggled her ample derriere into the far corner of the sofa to Georgia's right. Georgia mentally slapped her for being a first class twit.

"Good. We need to talk openly." Georgia moved her gaze from Emmett to her direct right, to Adam Martinez, to Helen, all on the sofa. Across from them sat Valerie, Jim Brooks, and Ed Burnett who had recently come on board as the director of the NSA. He was a Navy commander and as straight-laced as they come. She'd never understood why Daniel had wanted him to lead the NSA. They were polar opposites in their political thinking.

"I'm not happy . . . in fact, I'm pissed as hell that the best of the best, meaning you folks, haven't made more progress into Daniel's shooting. People, he's lying comatose in a damned hospital bed. Tell me you know who did this despicable act."

As she expected, no one responded immediately. God, she hated politics. It spread an oily glaze over every damn thing that was done or said in Washington. That, too, needed to change. Yes, she had a heavy agenda in front of her if she intended to change how things worked. Ed Burnett interrupted her musings.

"Madam President, we do have an update for you."

"Good, please proceed." She twirled her index finger for a couple of seconds before realizing her impatience was on display.

"Yes ma'am," Ed said stiffly. "As you know, President Gardner was shot by a gun attached to a small drone. And that drone was computer operated."

"Is that typical for the operation of a drone, Mr. Burnett?"

"No, ma'am, most are radio operated." Ed hesitated, rubbing two fingers over his lips before he spoke again. "We've learned that the drone was operated by a computer inside the White House."

"What?" Georgia's angry shout was followed by multiple groans from the other occupants in the room. "That's preposterous."

"Ma'am, we—"

Georgia cut off the FBI Director. "Adam, do not 'ma'am' me. Give me the damn facts."

Ed jumped in. "The IP address of the operating computer was overwritten by a code that we're working on to uncover. All we know for sure is that the computer controlling the drone resided in the White House."

"Could the computer have been remotely controlled?" Emmett drummed his fingers on the arm of the sofa. How curious. Georgia had never seen him nervous. Clever of him to draw attention away from someone actually being at the White House.

"Absolutely, it could have been controlled offsite," Ed replied. "That's one of the many things we're looking into."

"I'm confused." Valerie uncrossed her legs and set her fancy shoe clad feet flat on the floor. Georgia noticed every male in the room watched. "So, okay. We know a gun attached to a drone shot President Gardner. How could that happen? Why would the Capitol Police allow a drone to enter the building?"

"Another excellent question." Georgia glared at Ed and then Adam. "So far we know Daniel was shot via a drone, somehow planted in the House Chamber, and operated from a computer inside the White House." She spread her arms in front of her. "This all relates to how the shooting was accomplished. Do we know why? What was the motivation to kill Daniel Gardner? Is it personal?"

"I agree," Emmett added. "Seems to me, that's just as important as how it was done."

Georgia looked around the room again, gauging how far she could push. What the hell, they all worked for her now. Although she didn't want to claim Helen who kept her mouth shut for a change. "Emmett is correct. Who do we have on our list of possible suspects? Let's start there. I want to hear every piece of information you've learned thus far."

"Madam President." Jim Brooks opened a messenger style briefcase on his lap. "We have a comprehensive report for you with everything we know so far." He handed her a thick stack of bound paper. "I believe the most interesting point thus far is that we've heard no chatter whatsoever that this assassination attempt was planned by a foreign organization. Our informants haven't heard anything, nor have our planted operatives. Social media has been quiet as well."

"You're leaning toward this shooter being home grown then." In her gut, Georgia knew this was correct—call it women's intuition because she had no clue as to the truth. "Good. Had there been any direct threats on Daniel prior to the shooting?"

"Nothing other than the usual crazies every president has to deal with." Adam attempted a small smile and failed. "We're monitoring Facebook, Twitter, Google Plus and all the other standard social media sites for consistent negative postings about the president."

"Are you listening to talk radio and reading all the conservative blogs? They're not happy with President Gardner either." Georgia had a hunch they were holding back from her. Well, she was patient and their butts were on the line for not finding the shooter, not hers. Gardner had appointed most of them. Hmm, maybe it was taking orders from a woman.

"Ma'am, we're doing any number of things to search for the shooter. It's detailed in the report." Ed looked at her, tilted his head to the side.

"All right. I'll read the report. Just one last question: Is what you're doing legal?"

Ed blinked. "Yes ma'am, for the most part."

Georgia nodded and stood. "Thank you for coming in on a Saturday. Emmett, will you stay please. Valerie, please forward the report on the Missouri riots I asked for yesterday morning." After the office emptied, she walked back to the desk and turned to the door. Rosie stood there, looking sad and defeated.

"I'm sorry to bother you, Madam President. You too, Emmett."

"Rosie, you'll never be a bother to me. Come sit." Georgia led her to one of the sofas and sat next to her while Emmett sat across from them. She knew this visit of the First Lady wasn't a social call. "Has something happened? Tell me how I can help you."

Emmett's face had paled. "Has Danny's condition worsened since last night? I stopped by after dinner."

She shook her head. "I wanted to tell you in person that I've decided to go home—home to Colorado. We're leaving on Tuesday." Rosie dabbed a tissue to her red-rimmed eyes. "Danny is coming with us. He'll transfer to a long-term care facility in Denver. We'll all be happier."

"I'm so very sorry this has to happen." Georgia couldn't imagine the pain Rosie must be feeling. "The doctors think this move is for the best?"

"Yes, this is the right thing to do." She looked at Emmett. "Would you mind helping me pack up Danny's personal things from . . . from this office? I want to be careful."

"Of course. It would be my honor. When?"

"In the morning. Is that okay, Georgia?"

"That sounds fine." Georgia smiled gently. She'd walk on fire if that would help make things easier for Rosie and her family. This situation was awful. "I'll be at home tomorrow so I won't get in your way."

"Ginny, my staff secretary, has arranged for boxes and tape to be delivered later today. She and a couple of other staff members will help us pack tomorrow and get everything loaded on Monday. It won't take long with all of us working."

"Let me know if you need anything." Georgia hugged Rosie then stood. "I'll give you and Emmett a minute alone."

"Thank you."

Georgia walked into the corridor and down the hall to the Press Office. She'd had little time to speak with Julie Jordan, the White House press secretary Daniel had pinched from the Northgate Foundation, a political think tank in D.C. that leaned liberal. She poked her head in the open doorway of the reception area. No one sat at the desk but she heard a muffled voice in the inner office. She walked to the door, knocked on the doorframe, and took a couple of steps forward.

Julie leaned back in her chair, with her feet on her desk. Her pixie cut blond hair completed the picture of a cute young staffer. Georgia had heard she held a master's degree in public administration from the University of Southern California. She held a cell phone to her ear. She glanced at Georgia, blinked, threw the phone on her desk, and jumped out of the chair, all in one fluid movement.

"Madam President, oh, my g—uh, how may I help you?" Julie stood beside her desk, obviously uncomfortable wearing an orange sweater, tight jeans, and running shoes in front of the new president. "I've been hoping to get on your calendar next week."

"That shouldn't be a problem. Dealing with Emmett has worked the last few days?"

"Oh, yes ma'am, that's been the normal procedure. I've had little contact with President Gardner. Emmett gives me everything I need for the daily press briefing."

"Really?" Georgia held back a laugh. How the hell had Daniel Gardner spent his days in the Oval Office? During this last year of his term, she'd make sure the White House staff had the opportunity to actually work with her. "I don't work that way, so welcome to my team." Georgia walked to Julie and extended her hand.

"Oh, ma'am, that sounds wonderful. Thank you."

"First, please don't call me ma'am, Georgia will do." She walked to the window and looked out, not a bad view of the West Wing entrance. "I need you to get with Emmett and whoever else is involved in preparing a press release."

Julie stood straighter. "Of course, what's the subject of the release?"

"President Gardner and his family are moving back to Colorado. He'll be going to a long-term care facility. They'll be leaving Washington on Tuesday. I'd like a press release ready for your Monday briefing. Is that doable?"

Julie placed a fist to her mouth and visibly swallowed. Then she shrugged off the emotion. "Absolutely, that won't be a problem."

"Good. Emmett is here. I'll tell him to stop by when we're finished." Georgia left Julie and went back to the Oval Office. Emmett was just walking out the door.

"Rosie went to the residence." He rubbed a hand over his face. "This whole things sucks."

"I know. Come in for a minute. We need to talk."

Georgia walked to the front of the presidential desk and leaned her butt against the front edge. "It's time now."

"Time for what?" He stood in the middle of the seating area.

"It's time for me to appoint a VP. Daniel leaving Washington is a clear indication he's not returning to this office. I need to move forward. I can't let the country down."

"I know . . . it's time." He blew out a heavy breath, wiped his hand over his jaw. "How can I help you?"

"I trust you and your knowledge of Washington and politics. I'd like your help with three names as VP candidates. Will you do that for me?"

"It would be my pleasure."

"Good." Georgia sighed. Maybe she would get the hang of this job. "May I have the list on Monday?"

"Not a problem."

"I have one more request. Who do I talk to about getting my house packed up as well as the VP office? I need my own chair." She started for the door.

"Where are you going?"

"To the VP office to roll my chair in here."

"Not to worry, Madam President, I'll get it for you." He smiled with humor. "We'll have you and your husband moved into the residence by the end of the week at the latest."

"Great, the traffic in this town to and from the White House is tough. It'll be nice to have a break from it."

Emmett laughed and turned to leave. Georgia stopped him. "Wait. I talked to Julie Jordan about a press release concerning President Gardner and his family leaving Washington. Would you mind checking in with her? She's in her office now."

"I'm on my way after I get your chair."

"I forgot to ask earlier. Is Helen getting hacked again today?"

Emmett grinned and saluted her. "You betcha."

~~*

Mozart filtered through the well-appointed study of Harry Roberts via his music player attached to a boom box, both Christmas gifts from his oldest daughter. He reclined on the sofa reading a Nora Roberts romance novel. He loved her characters. But this afternoon he couldn't keep his attention focused on the story.

Instead, the face of Georgia Ross kept blurring the page. Damn that woman. Even Emmett, the little weasel, was singing her praises.

His anger switched immediately from POTUS to her chief of staff. Harry had put up with Emmett for thirty years because of Danny. He wasn't the same as them. He came from nothing, working class family, and went to a state college. *Boring.*

He'd never understood why Danny had been so loyal to Emmett. Sure, they'd gone to the same K-12 schools but Emmett's father was a janitor and Danny's a CEO of a manufacturing company in Denver— worlds apart in life style and social status. Emmett was a twit, always trying to keep up with Danny, always in the way, and always a pain in the ass. God, Harry just now realized how much he hated Emmett. Maybe he'd get rid of him.

Or maybe not. Emmett was a good little worker and might become useful at some point. Danny had used him for years.

Poor, poor Danny is in a coma. Damn it, why hadn't he died already? Only Danny would have the luck of not being taken out by two shots. John had asked for another four million dollars for the job or he'd go to the FBI. Harry laughed. John had no idea who he was dealing with. But for now, John was useful and controllable. Harry would send the money. He had loved to play with puppets as a kid and dealing with John reminded him of that, and he came cheap. The puppeteer never failed to win.

Harry struggled up from the sofa, swung his feet on the floor, and shut off the music. He needed a drink. Thinking about Danny always made him need a drink. His cell phone buzzed as he walked to the bar. Screw it. He was taking a fucking break. He'd told his wife to give him two hours of peace.

He grabbed a couple of cubes from the ice machine under the bar and tossed them in a crystal glass. His favorite scotch sat on the bar in its usual place. He poured a good dose and walked to the desk to gather his mini-tablet. Perhaps he had a response from John to yesterday's email.

After settling in his favorite recliner, he turned on the large screen television over the fireplace to check the news before looking at his email. He sipped the drink as the TV opened to CNN and a repeat of yesterday's update on Danny's condition. The anchor gave a reminder that President Ross had declared Sunday as a day of prayer for President Gardner.

His mouth fell open. What the hell? Why hadn't he heard about this? That damned bitch, acting so compassionate and concerned about Danny. She didn't give a shit about him. She got the Oval Office, didn't she?

He slugged down the scotch. The Oval Office should have been his rather than Danny's. He still kicked himself for agreeing to support Danny's wild ass idea to take the 2016 nomination from Halley Hilton when all her scandal problems started to bury her in a pile of crap.

Harry should have run himself. Danny had been nothing but a jackass to Harry the last three years. And even with his falling approval ratings, Danny would still get the nomination in July. Thoroughly disgusted with his friend, Harry had a brilliant idea and created a plan to eliminate Danny. He'd campaign for a few months and then grab the nomination.

Now Harry had a new problem—Georgia Ross morphing into a decent president.

He rose for another drink. John had to finish the job this time with no screw-ups.

With another glass of scotch, Harry returned to the recliner and opened the email inbox on his tablet. The email address was more secure than the Pentagon thanks to the computer skills of his son-in-law.

"Ah, good." He had an email from John.

Might be interested. Details? You still owe me money.

Harry chuckled. John was a clown. Money was the least of his worries. He didn't need to work so why did he continue in the U.S. Congress?

Power.

Harry loved power. He needed power. He craved power. Real power. The kind of power you could find only in Washington, D.C.

And he'd do what was necessary to eliminate Georgia Ross and gain that power. She'd no doubt appoint an idiot as her vice president replacement so he'd have an easy time stealing the Democratic nomination this coming July at the DNC convention. He was just that good.

Sipping the drink, he considered his proposal to John. After a few minutes, he carefully typed a new email. He sighed and chuckled; John would be a fool to refuse this offer.

~~*

John and Candy had been at The Grand's pool for almost five hours. The weather in Las Vegas was beautiful for late January. They decided to get outdoors and experience fresh air away from the casino. They'd rented a cabana for privacy and had enjoyed a bit of canoodling in the shade. With remnants of their late lunch already gone, the two of them rolled up the canvas side of the cabana and stretched out on chaise lounge chairs in the sunshine.

"Are you sure you're okay not going home with your friend?" John asked. Candy had checked out of their shared room that morning and kissed her friend goodbye for the flight back to Pennsylvania. She was staying with him now. He didn't know for how long and wouldn't ask. Being nosy usually got him in trouble. One day at a time was his new philosophy.

She reached over and patted his thigh. "Yes, I'm okay. Great actually." She then pointed to her chest. "Big girl here and I know what I'm doing. I like you. Let's see what happens." She reached out again and stroked her fingers along his shoulder. "Okay?"

"Yeah, okay. I like you, too." He damn near shivered in relief knowing she was willing to give things a chance.

After thirty minutes they headed back to the room to cool off. They took a shower together, and then sprawled on the bed with the A/C cranked up.

"I didn't realize how hot I was at the pool until right now." Candy waved a hand over her face. "I'm getting old."

John rolled off the bed and walked to the mini-bar. He came back with a bottle of water and handed it to her. "Rub this over your neck."

"Or I can drink it."

He grinned. "That, too. I'll check my email. Maybe Harry has replied."

John pulled his laptop from his messenger bag and settled on the bed next to Candy. He tossed her the TV remote. "Let's check the news. Maybe there's an update on what the feds are doing."

Candy began to channel surf while John fired up his computer and opened the email program.

After a few moments, she nudged his side. "Listen to this."

The Fox News anchor mentioned that President Gardner's condition hadn't changed, he was still in a coma. "President Ross has declared Sunday as a national day of prayer for the stricken president. Her hope is that the prayers of a nation will strengthen the president in fighting this battle with his injuries."

"Are you sorry for shooting him?"

John raised his gaze from his laptop. "Sorry? No. Like I said before, his incompetence damn near ruined my life and it sure as hell killed Jessie."

"Okay, sweetie, I understand." She rubbed his shoulder slowly then leaned over and kissed it. "Is there an email from Harry?"

He looked at the laptop again and scanned the inbox list of messages. Bingo. Old Harry had responded. He was one anxious son-of-a-bitch. John clicked on the email:

New proposal: $20 million—that's it, $10M today $10M when job completed. Kill President Georgia Ross one week from today. Dead this time!!! Deal?

"Harry is one weird guy." John shook his head in disbelief at the proposal.

"How so?"

"Now he wants me to kill the new president. What is wrong with this guy?"

"What? Let me see the email." Candy leaned over as John twisted the laptop toward her. After a couple of seconds she jerked back and stared at John. "Harry is definitely one weird dude. What is his position again?"

"Speaker of the House."

Candy raised both her hands to head level and shook them. "And you wonder why Congress has such a low approval rating. I think not." She looked at the screen again. "What man uses exclamation points in an email? That guy is definitely out there."

John chuckled and squeezed her hand. "I know, it's scary. Who's running our country?"

"That's the ten million dollar question. What's your take on Harry the Weirdo's proposition?"

"It's a way to make more money. But I have no issues with Georgia Ross." He put both hands on his head and rubbed it. "I won't do it."

Candy leaned back from him, her eyes narrowed. "But the money would be nice, huh?"

"It sure as hell would." His voice had risen and his face was pale. "But like I said, I've got no beef with President Ross. I'm not some damned presidential assassin."

"Well . . . holy shit, John. I'm really glad to hear that."

"Good."

She rolled off the other side of the bed and walked to the window. Several seconds passed in silence before she turned around to John, grinning. "I've never seen twenty million dollars nor had the opportunity to earn even one million. I gotta tell you, I'm kinda intrigued by making that kind of money."

"Yeah? What kind of intrigued?"

"The kind of intrigued that lands us a payday without doing the deed."

"You mean fake out Harry." John was relieved they thought the same way on this second "offer" from the Speaker.

"Exactly. We're trying to make a difference here, stand up for the little guy, the average citizen who has no voice. Maybe we could start a foundation or something."

"Plus he's plain crazy." He looked into space, considering why Harry was hell bent on killing Georgia Ross. "When he first approached me about killing Daniel Gardner, I got the impression that he wanted Gardner out of the way for a personal reason. I assumed it was jealousy. It was one hell of a political coup to steal the nomination from Halley Hilton. Poor Halley—first the former president, then Gardner . . . both won."

"Jealousy is a bitch, believe me."

"You have personal experience with jealousy?" He threw her a pointed look.

"Never mind. Seems to me that if Harry's reason to off Gardner was jealousy, then he'd be dancing on the ceiling now. Instead he's plotting to kill the new president. Why? I bet he wants to run for president and Georgia Ross is his new competition."

Damn, Candy made good sense. "You've got me curious about Harry. I'll Google him." John rose and brought his laptop to the table. He did an Internet search on Harry Roberts that brought up a ton of links. "He's a popular guy."

"Start with Wikipedia."

He clicked on the correct link and began to look at the article. "Harry James Roberts was born April 30, 1970 in Denver, Colorado. He comes from a very wealthy family. Looks like the family construction business started with his great-grandfather and kept growing. He went to private schools in Denver and then Princeton for college."

"How did he get into politics?"

"Let's see. After college, he went back to Denver to work in the family business. He got a degree in accounting. Two years later, he was elected to the state legislature." John gazed at Candy and grinned. "Harry is one lucky son-of-a-bitch. After one year in the state legislature, at the age of twenty-nine, he was selected by the Colorado governor to fill a vacant position in the U.S. House of Representatives created by the untimely death of some dude named Howard Adams."

"Poor Howard," she commented. "I wonder why the governor chose Harry to fill the vacancy. He's been in Congress twenty years and he became speaker the same year Gardner came into office. I saw a PBS documentary on Congress a couple years ago and it talked about how difficult it is to get the support in the House to become the Speaker."

"I guess that means one of two things—Harry is so charismatic that he's capable of gaining incredible support or he paid people for their support."

Candy chuckled. "Gee, John, don't hold back."

"Smart ass."

She pointed at her chest. "Yes sir, that's me. But I think you're right. And I think Harry is certifiably crazy. Like I said, his desire to kill Georgia Ross is because he wants her job. The news said she hadn't yet appointed a VP. That means if she's dead, he'll be next in line as Speaker of the House."

"You're right." Damn, Candy was one smart cookie. "Do I fake accept Harry's offer or not?"

"Let's see if we can get fifteen million up front."

~~*

After a quick lunch of soup and salad at a bistro in Falls Church, Nick drove back to Washington. They rode in silence for fifteen minutes. He noticed the sign for the Roosevelt Memorial and decided they should make a stop. He signaled right to get in the exit lane.

"Hey, what's up?" Nita said. "Why are we getting off the Interstate?"

He glanced at her. "The weather is sort of decent so I thought we could stop at the Roosevelt Memorial. You said you hadn't visited the park in a while." He hoped this would keep her in a good mood. He had a topic to discuss with her that she wouldn't like.

"Thanks." She threw him a quick smile. "Great idea."

He merged onto the George Washington Memorial Parkway going north. It was only a couple of minutes to the exit for the parking lot. The lot held a dozen or so cars. January wasn't a popular tourist month for D.C. After parking, Nick grabbed Nita's hand and led her to the footbridge across the Potomac that led to Theodore Roosevelt Island.

"Be careful, don't want you falling in the river," he said as they stepped on the bridge.

"Not to worry, I can swim."

"Ah, I should have known that." He was making a joke yet he wasn't sure Nita understood as she rolled her eyes and pulled her hand from his. He shrugged it off and they walked in silence.

They reached the island and took the walking path toward the memorial plaza. The huge statue of Theodore Roosevelt soon came into view.

"Good to know Teddy hasn't changed," Nita commented as she stopped ten feet from the statute.

"Let's sit on the bench over there." He pointed to a marble bench across from Teddy and near a brick wall. The wind was picking up and the location should give them a bit of shelter. "Nita, uh . . . I need to talk with you about something."

"What is it?" She sat next to him on the bench.

"Please don't get mad at me for bringing this up." Nick knew he was treading on an unstable zone here, but it was worth it to him. He needed to know the truth. "Why did you break our engagement?"

"What?" She gazed at him with her mouth open for a moment and then snapped it shut. "You want to know why we broke up?"

"Yes, the real reason."

She stiffened and jutted her chin toward him. "The reason is that you had a one-night stand, affair, fling, whatever you call it with that redhead you worked with." Her eyes slammed daggers at him. "I won't marry a man who is unfaithful."

What the hell was wrong with her? She really thought he'd been with another woman. "What the hell made you think I'd been unfaithful? Really, Nita, that's disgusting."

She jumped up from the bench and faced him. "Disgusting, huh? How do you think I felt when Gina told me she saw you making out with a redhead at that club . . . uh, Revolution, that's the name."

The redhead had to be Julie Morgan, a young reporter he'd previously worked with. They'd never been involved or particularly friendly. He couldn't remember ever kissing her. "When was it that I was supposed to be kissing Julie?"

Nita glared at him. He was surprised she maintained control and didn't slap him. Damn, he was clueless about this making out session with a co-worker. She leaned toward him. "It was over a year ago, mid-December, at a company happy hour. I was supposed to meet you and Gina at the club after I interviewed George Somebody. Remember? I was late. And by the time I arrived, you and the redhead had left, arm-in-arm."

That's why she'd broken up with him? Of all the stupid, idiotic reasons—damn it to hell. "Yes, we did leave arm-in-arm—on the way to the damned emergency room. Julie is a diabetic and had too much to drink. Her reaction to the alcohol caused her to lose control a little and she kissed me—just before she started stammering and her eyes rolled back into her head. I took her to the hospital. I couldn't leave her like that."

Nick gazed at Nita, wallowing in equal parts of sadness and disappointment. "You wouldn't talk to me about why you were breaking it off. I guess that says everything about the depth of our relationship."

Nita twirled away from him and walked toward the statute. Screw it. Let her sulk. He obviously knew nothing about women. Which was funny as hell since he had three older sisters.

He slipped his phone out of the pocket of his jacket and checked his email. Thank you for big favors—the data had arrived. After a minute or so, Nita walked back to him and stood a few feet away.

"Nick, first off, I owe you an apology." He started to speak and she raised her hand. "Hear me out."

"Go ahead."

"First, I feel . . . like a fool, like an ass, like a jealous shrew." Her long hair swirled around her head and she fought to tame it. "I listened to Gina, my best friend, and didn't listen to my fiancé. How could I be so stupid?"

"Maybe we weren't meant to happen." Nick sighed. Perhaps this conversation wasn't such a good idea.

"Why do you say that?"

"Isn't that obvious? You didn't trust me enough to not jump to the wrong conclusion about what Gina said she saw . . . which wasn't accurate. Trust is a tremendous deal in my world. You broke our engagement because you didn't trust me."

"I broke the engagement because you were kissing another woman, a hot looking woman by the way." Nita had the smallest hint of a smile on her lips. "Gina would never be a good witness for a murder."

Nick rose from the marble bench and stood steady. "I agree."

Nita took a couple steps forward. "I guess I screwed up."

"Maybe . . . just a little." He moved forward and circled her with his arms, hugging tight.

Dark clouds had landscaped the sky and drops of rain began to fall.

She pulled back from him. "Holy cow, where did the rain come from?"

"We'd better make a run for it." Nick grabbed her hand, kissed it, and pulled her across the plaza and over the bridge. He helped her into his vehicle and jumped in the driver's side. The clouds unloaded with a downpour of rain as he shut the door.

"We made it just in time." Nita leaned over and ruffled Nick's hair. He caught her hand and drew it against his chest. "Teddy Roosevelt will always have a special place in my heart."

"Me, too." He kissed her gently.

"Let's get back to my house. I have something to show you."

He backed out of the parking space and headed for the exit. "What's that?"

"I have a new bedspread."

"Now you're talking."

He settled her hand on his right thigh.

They rode in silence for several minutes. Then Nick had one of those dumbass moments and prayed this wouldn't screw up their new peace.

"I forgot to tell you I have a friend who's a hacker."

"Really?"

"I mentioned to him about wanting to know who had security access to the Capitol building. He sent me a list."

"That's fantastic." She leaned over and kissed his cheek. "I can't wait to get the list of the IRS names. By the way, I have a plan for now."

"Yeah?"

"You stay over tonight and we can both do research."

"Research only?"

Nita wiggled her eyebrows. "I forgot to mention the subject of the research."

Chapter Six

Monday, January 26

THE FIRST LADY HAD never truly become accustomed to living in the White House Residence—too stifling and too protocol oriented for her East L.A. upbringing. It had been three years since they'd arrived and she had no qualms or regrets about leaving, even though the reason for their move was not a happy one.

The Gardner family belonged in Colorado, at their home, not in this relic of a house. The White House wasn't her cup of tea. She situated a box on the floor at Danny's dresser and dumped each drawer of underwear, socks, and tee shirts in the box. There was no need to be tidy. They were all packing their own clothes as there would be no extra help once they arrived back home.

"Mom, why do we have to do this? I wanna stay with my friends here." Drake leaned against the end of the dresser, a pout covering his face. "Can't Dad get better here?"

"No, he can't." Rosie would not reverse her decision to return to Denver. She did not want her husband to die outside of Colorado. "*Please*, go to your room and make sure everything is packed. Tell your brother to do the same." She stepped to her son and gave him a stiff hug. Teenage boys weren't open to a show of affection from their mother. Regardless, she hugged him again and patted his back. "I love you."

He pulled back from her and nodded. "I'll make sure Jake is packing." He hurried out of the bedroom, leaving Rosie to her list of tasks. Once the box was full, she left it. One of the staff would tape it shut and label it.

She walked into Danny's closet and lost it. Tears flooded her eyes and ran down her face. Danny's closet was always so neat, his clothes perfectly organized. He loved his suits and kept them in pristine condition. She ran her fingers slowly across the arms and noticed a piece of paper sticking out of a jacket pocket. It was from a notepad with the name "Valerie Jones" at the top. Rosie read the words written in purple ink: "Lover – Will meet u @ regular spot, 2 pm sharp. Don't be late, have a surprise – V" A heart was drawn below the writing with VJ + DG = HOT in the middle.

Rosie read the note again, folded it in half, then in half again. She slipped it into the pocket of her slacks. She wiped her cheeks with her fingers then rubbed her wet fingers over the lush fabric of a charcoal gray jacket. A long streak of mascara stained the fabric. She chuckled. Tough. Those were the last tears she'd shed for her unfaithful husband, President Daniel Gardner. For too many years she'd kept quiet— enough was enough.

Ginny had left several large boxes in the bedroom and Rosie pulled one into the closet. She neatly folded half a dozen suits and placed them in the box. Then she remembered the note from Danny's senior advisor and began to dump the suits into the box.

Within thirty minutes she had all of Danny's belongings in boxes. She didn't care whether they made it to Denver or not. She'd store them in the basement when they arrived. One dark suit, a white shirt, and a red tie had been left in the closet. She placed the outfit in a hanging bag monogrammed with Danny's full name and zipped it shut. This was the perfect burial outfit and he'd look perfectly debonair wearing it inside his coffin. Of course, she hadn't chosen her husband's coffin yet. Maybe she'd leave that up to Elizabeth.

"Rosie, where are you?" Speak of the devil. She patted the hanging bag and walked into the bedroom. "I'm here. I just finished with Danny's things. Do you need help?"

"Of course I do. Where is the help?" Elizabeth was dressed in a black designer pantsuit and wore four-inch heels. "Honestly, are we invisible now that we're leaving this ugly monstrosity?"

Rosie bit her tongue before replying to her mother-in-law. "Everyone is busy. Ginny has everything organized. Let's have lunch in the dining room. I ordered a bottle of your favorite chardonnay."

Elizabeth sniffed and nodded her head. "All right."

"You go on ahead and I'll make sure Ginny has your room scheduled next."

"Tell her I've packed what I'll need for the next week in my luggage. Everything else they can pack."

Rosie shook a fist as Elizabeth dismissed her and turned away. "I'll find Ginny and let her know and meet you in the dining room."

Elizabeth didn't respond as she was already out the door. Rosie fisted her hands at her sides and grimaced. *Damn that woman.*

Once she'd found Ginny, explained Elizabeth's needs and

checked on the twins, Rosie strolled into the family dining room to find her mother-in-law with her smartphone in one hand and a wineglass in the other.

She seated herself. "Everything okay?" Elizabeth nodded and turned away while she spoke on the phone. Rosie placed a peach colored napkin on her lap and sipped from her water glass.

After a bit, Elizabeth put her phone on the table, scooted around, and smiled at her daughter-in-law. "You're all set for leaving tomorrow?"

Rosie's heart sank and her stomach rolled. She had to be strong. "Yes, we'll be leaving here at nine sharp. Everything will be loaded on the plane this evening."

"Sounds like a plan." Elizabeth watched her over the rim of the wineglass. "I won't be going with you and the twins."

"What?" What the hell was this old woman up to now? "Why won't you go with us?"

"I'm staying in D.C. for a couple of days."

"To do what?" Rosie was aghast at the suggestion that Elizabeth wouldn't accompany her family back home. How could she even suggest such a callous thing?

"I have a bit of business here."

"Business?" Rosie spat through a clenched jaw. She took a deep breath and slid her hand along the tablecloth toward her mother-in-law. "What business is more important than the well-being of your son?"

"*My* business." Elizabeth snapped her napkin open and placed it on her lap. She picked up the wine bottle and poured into Rosie's glass. "Dear, you need some wine. You're getting that tight-ass look you wear so well."

While Rosie seethed in her gut and her hand itched to slap Elizabeth for her inappropriate words, she shrugged off the emotion. The outgoing First Lady did not conduct herself like a hooligan. Eventually she'd uncover what particular business was so very important to her mother-in-law. Rosie picked up the wine glass and smiled. "I do believe we're having salmon and asparagus for lunch. Doesn't that sound yummy?"

~~*

Even though she didn't drive to an office or work in a twenty-story office building, Nita still didn't like Monday mornings. It had to be something ingrained in her soul from all the many years of attending school. Of course, back in those good old days, all she had to worry about was homework, keeping her bed made, and doing the nightly dishes.

After her mother died when Nita was five, her father did the cooking and she cleaned up the kitchen. When she was a teenager, their roles changed and she began to try new recipes and experiment with flavors. Her love of cooking developed over the summer after her junior year in high school. She'd developed a recipe for chocolate pie that made her father cry, as it had been her mother's favorite dessert.

She glanced at the one picture of her mother she kept close to her desk. Her memories were hazy of the day she died. Nita was at her grandparents' house in Sugar Land, Texas. They'd installed a pool in the backyard and everyone was celebrating Nita's last day of kindergarten. Her mother, Julia, had dropped her off then left for a bible study meeting at their church.

Nita remembered swimming until she could hardly move and then plopping on a chaise lounge under a blue umbrella. She'd soon dozed off and the sound of her grandmother's sobbing woke her. A man in a dark blue uniform stood nearby. Everything was a blur as her daddy and grandfather soon arrived and all hell broke loose.

It wasn't until she was a teenager that Nita learned the whole truth of what had happened that day. Someone shot her mother at close range in the church parking lot after the meeting. The police never found the killer. Nita's father was convinced the killer was Donald Westbrook, an old boyfriend, but he had a rock-solid alibi. Perhaps the time had arrived for Nita to do her own investigation into her mother's murder.

She shrugged off the thoughts and blew a kiss to her mother's picture. Time to get to work. She needed to post a blog in the morning. The specific topic hadn't yet gelled. The news usually gave her plenty of inspiration so she opened her Internet browser and clicked on Fox News. She opened another page and clicked on CNN. She enjoyed comparing the differences of their lead stories; conservative versus liberal, but today she had no time for playing around. Looking at one front page and then the other, the stars aligned and she had her topic— "Washington politicians don't have common sense." Helen Capstone and the hacking of her emails—email-gate—would be the perfect subject. She rubbed her hands together. "Oh, baby, this one will be fun. I hate stupid politicians."

She continued to search for online articles on Capstone's email woes and found several. Bottom-line, Helen was an idiot for using her own private server in Florida to send and receive emails and relying on outdated commercial software to operate and protect the server. How in the hell could she put the Department of Homeland Security in such jeopardy? Nita shook her head in disbelief.

After staring into space for a couple of minutes and allowing random thoughts to roll around her mind, Nita had the first line for the blog. She began to pound her keyboard:

This last weekend in Washington, D.C. was an interesting one. I'll mention two reasons why this is true and they are polar opposites. First, the good news: our new president, Georgia Ross, declared last Sunday as a national day of prayer in honor of President Daniel Gardner. A gracious and kind gesture that will hopefully reap blessings for President Gardner.

Next is the bad news and the subject of this blog—dumbass politicians—specifically Helen Capstone, Secretary of Homeland Security. This is interesting to me because Capstone's "government" email account was once again hacked on Saturday, after first being hacked on Friday.

Yes, of course, we've heard of government records being hacked before. Case in point, the thousands of taxpayer names hacked from the IRS computer system two years ago. Who knows the amount of hurt that's caused?

It's amazing to me that a member of the president's cabinet would determine it's safe for the country to use a private email account on a private server to conduct official business of the Department of Homeland Security. Really? It's safe?

Apparently not.

Perhaps a cabinet member should have given

She rose and paced in front of the window. How far should she go with this blog? She always considered the repercussions of every word she posted online. The last thing she needed was a libel lawsuit from not being careful. She glanced out the window and her heart quickened at the sight of Nick's SUV.

He parked in the only open space on the street. She hadn't expected him so early. Maybe he'd found something. She hurried toward the front door, stopped and ran back to the desk. She slapped on lip-gloss, fluffed her hair around her face, and made it back to the door as he knocked.

Nick walked in with a backpack on one shoulder, a duffel bag on the other, and carrying paper grocery bags in his hands. "Hey, babe, I brought food." He kissed her cheek and headed toward the kitchen.

"What?" She scurried after him, her slippers slapping on the hardwood floor. "What food?"

He set the bags on the counter then turned to Nita and hugged her. "I missed you," he murmured against her hair. He stepped away and dug into one of the grocery bags. "I've got the fixings for a spaghetti dinner and breakfast. We have a lot of work to do."

She liked that idea. It meant he would stay the night with her. He was right; they had much work left to do. "I'll put the groceries away. Put your stuff in my bedroom and then we can get started."

An hour later, Nita had finished her blog and Nick was hard at work on his computer at the end of the table near her desk.

"I'm done," Nita announced. "I'll check the blog again in the morning before I post it."

Nick raised his head, smiled at her. "Good. I need your help."

"Sure."

He twisted around in the chair until he faced her. "I've been looking at everyone who has security access to the Capitol building. Plus, I have a list of who entered or the left the building during a twenty-four hour period beginning six a.m. on the day of the State of the Union using an entry or exit code. This doesn't include tourists doing the tour. I crosschecked both lists, not one name isn't on both."

"Hmm . . . guess that means one of the folks on your list is the shooter or helped the shooter, or someone came in through the visitor center."

"Exactly. Are you available for a bit of reconnaissance work?"

Ooh, she liked the way he said that. "What do you have in mind?"

Nick rose. "Let's play tourists at the U.S. Capitol and—"

"And see if someone without security clearance can sneak into a restricted area."

~~*

"Emmett, I've made my VP selection and he should be here shortly." He'd sent Georgia a list of names yesterday and she'd considered the options overnight. She and Peter had visited President Gardner late in the afternoon and that had helped her think clearly about the candidates. Georgia looked at her chief of staff with high hopes that he wouldn't protest what she was about to suggest. "However, I have a matter to discuss with you first."

"Of course." Emmett leaned against the back of the chair that Danny had normally occupied during Oval Office meetings. The significance wasn't lost on Georgia.

"I'd like you to switch positions in my administration . . . from chief of staff to senior advisor." She looked at him directly and didn't blink.

"What about Valerie?"

"I have another position in mind for her." She could see the gears grind in his head via his eyes. He'd be wondering how this change would benefit him and his own ambitions. What were those ambitions? Could he have ambitions beyond being a staff member of the White House? She'd not considered that.

"Wow, okay . . . I wasn't expecting this."

"I know it's a surprise." Georgia knew *how* to get him to accept her proposal. "I think you'll be more effective as a senior advisor rather than dealing with the White House operational details."

"Okay."

Georgia rose from her desk and walked past Emmett across the office to the fireplace at the opposite end. She had a trio of miniature paintings of flowers that would look nice on the mantel. She turned to him. "I think your talents will be best used in advising me how the White House responds to policy matters. I want you to be the lead in negotiating with Congress and any outside groups that become issues. I guess that includes anything that comes our way."

"Okay, that's different."

"I'm changing the job description for both senior advisor and chief of staff." She walked back to her desk, sat in the chair, and looked directly at Emmett. "I want you to be the pivot person for implementing my agenda as president. Can you do that?"

It was easy to realize when he'd made his decision to go along with her—his eyes narrowed slightly and he smiled. Her pitch had worked. Hopefully, she could keep a closer eye on him now. She didn't trust him but his knowledge of White House and Congressional politics outweighed the negatives. She would toss him to the curb if he got out of control. The integrity of *her* White House meant more to her than Emmett's hurt feelings.

"I like your idea." He walked to the desk and leaned forward, his hand reached toward her. "Madam President, I'm honored to be your senior advisor."

She shook his hand and glanced at the calendar on the computer. Her two o'clock appointment should be arriving soon. Betty poked her head in the door. Excellent, right on time.

"Ma'am, Speaker Roberts is here."

"Show him in. Emmett, please stay." Georgia walked around the desk and met Harry, shaking his hand. She pointed to the sofa. "Good to see you, Speaker Roberts. Please have a seat." She sat in her usual chair with Harry to her left and Emmett to her right. She noticed the two men eyeing each other. Something was up between the two or the typical Washington testosterone danced in the Oval Office. God, she was so tired of that damned dance.

"Madam President, you're looking well." Harry smiled at Georgia, his eyes betraying his nerves.

"Thank you." She glanced at her watch for added drama. "I have a busy schedule today so I'll get right to the point of our meeting."

"Of course." Harry crossed his legs at the ankle, showing her his nonchalance.

"If you agree," Georgia said lightly. "I'm appointing you as Vice President of the United States." The shock on Harry's face was extraordinary and real. His right hand splayed across his chest. He hadn't expected this. Good.

"I'm . . . I'm damn near speechless, Madam President." He leaned toward her. "I'm honored to accept your appointment as vice president." He glanced at Emmett, a slight frown on his brow, and then he turned back to Georgia, smiling large. "It will be such a pleasure to work with you. We'll make a great team in the White House."

"Excellent, welcome aboard." She rose and walked back to the desk. With her back to both men she said a small prayer that she hadn't screwed up with both appointments. Time would tell. "Harry, we'll get together in a couple of days to discuss details. Emmett, would you talk with Julie about the press release?"

"Absolutely." Emmett placed his hand on Harry's shoulder. "I'll walk you out."

"Show Harry the VP office since he's here," she suggested.

Emmett winked at Georgia and followed Harry out of the Oval Office. She collapsed in her own chair and wondered if she'd made a huge mistake. Oh well, eventually she'd stop second-guessing her every decision. It took time to grow into presidential shoes. She chuckled; at least she was dedicated to the task, unlike her two most recent predecessors.

"Madam President, the First Lady is here and needs to speak with you." Betty held the door open and Rosie rushed in.

"I need two minutes of your time," Rosie declared.

"No problem." Georgia stood at the side of her desk. Her concern for the First Lady and her family wouldn't diminish until they were safely home in Colorado. Like Rosie, Georgia felt that being "home" might have the power to set things right. "Is everything okay?"

"Yes, we're almost done with the packing." Rosie's head lowered and she pulled something from the pocket of her slacks. "I have something to give you."

"What is it?"

Her hand rose toward Georgia. It held what looked like a slip of paper. Georgia frowned—*what?*

"I want you to have this," Rosie said. "Please, understand this gives me no pleasure, but you need to know."

Georgia opened the folded slip of paper, read the words . . . understood the meaning. Her heart wept for Rosie. She raised her head and their eyes locked.

"I'm so sorry . . . sorry this had to happen to you and sorry you had to discover it now."

A single tear escaped from Rosie's eyes. "I've always believed things happen for a reason and for a purpose. Perhaps this is my time for proving that true."

Georgia stepped forward and wrapped her arms around Rosie. She hugged her tight, praying that blessings from a nation would flow into her. After a moment, she stepped back, withdrew her arms. "Madam First Lady, you are truly an enduring representative of our nation. Please, please let me know how I can help you going forward."

Rosie nodded and stepped toward the door. "Thank you for being so kind. One more thing before we go home. Elizabeth is staying here for a couple of days. I don't know what she's up to but it can't be good." She smiled and tipped her hand to her head. "Good luck, Georgia. I know you'll be one hell of a president." She waved and slipped out the door.

Whew. She had so much empathy for Rosie and the lousy position Daniel had created for her. Well, firing Valerie was next. Why the hell were Monday's so tough? She went to the door.

"Betty, please ask Valerie Jones to come around. Also, tell Frank to be close by."

Betty picked up her phone. "Yes ma'am."

She returned to her desk and spread the note on the blotter, smoothing out the creases. Georgia was far from a prude but she had no joy in discussing Daniel Gardner's extra-marital activities with his partner in the affair. She pushed her lips together. She'd do what she had to do.

Valerie walked through the open door and shut it automatically. Hmm, she must have spent of lot of time in the office.

"Come on in, have a seat. I have something to show you."
Georgia rose as Valerie settled on the sofa.

"Yes ma'am. How can I help you today?"

"Actually, it's I who will be helping you." Smiling, Madam
President walked behind the sofa then turned and stood in front of her
guest. "I think this belongs to you." She dropped the note in Valerie's
lap and sat in her usual chair.

Valerie eyed the slip of paper and her face blanched. After a
moment, it turned to red and her gaze rose to address her employer.
"How in the hell did you get this?"

"That is of no concern to you," Georgia said pleasantly.
"However, what is a concern for you is my take on the morals of my
White House staff. Apparently, you have no morals. I, on the other
hand, do—"

"You can't say that to me."

Georgia leaned forward. "Valerie, in addition to no morals,
you're not that smart. I have no place for you in *my* White House.
Your job is over . . . you're fired."

She jumped from the sofa so fast she nearly lost her balance.
"You can't fire me . . . you bitch, I quit."

"Perfect." Georgia rose and opened the door, wiggled her fingers
at Frank. "We need a security escort for Miss Jones." She turned back
to Valerie who had come close to her. "Miss Jones will clean out her
office and surrender all her federal ID's and keys."

Valerie glared at Georgia and her lips curled. "You'll be sorry
you did this."

"Young lady, I'll never be sorry you're out of the White House.
We both know why." Georgia smiled as Frank strode to them. She
pulled the note out of Valerie's grasp and watched Frank guide her out
of the Oval Office.

Betty came to the office door after they had moved in the
direction of Valerie's office. "I really wish I was a writer. The goings
on here would make a great novel."

Georgia patted her arm and displayed a wide smile. "That's
career number two. What's next on today's agenda?"

~~*

Harry followed Emmett out the corridor door and to the VP office. He
had an uncontrollable urge to raise and shake his hands and shout
"halleluiah", but of course, he couldn't due to the fact that he was in
the West Wing of the freaking White House. Instead he dutifully
walked with Emmett, making small talk about working in the building.

"I think you'll like working here. It's cozier than the Capitol building." Emmett smiled as he opened the door. He figured Carol would be around. They walked around her desk into the main office. She stood on a stool grabbing books off the shelf of a tall bookcase. She turned after Emmett banged his knuckles against the doorframe.

"Hey, Emmett, how's it going?" Carol smiled initially then frowned when Harry came around him and walked to the center of the office. "Speaker Roberts, how may I help you?"

"This is my new office," Harry said softly.

"Oh . . . sir, I'm so sorry, I forgot." She climbed down from the stool and went to him with her hand outstretched. He took it and she smiled. "Congratulations on your appointment."

"Thank you."

Carol stepped away and moved back to the bookshelf. "I'll be finished packing the president's belongings here by the end of the day. She asked me to stay on as your assistant for the time being."

Hell yes, he wanted her as his assistant. She was a million times cuter than the old biddy he had now and she knew the ropes in the West Wing. "That sounds fine, Carol. I know you'll be of great help to me. Thank you for staying on."

"It's my pleasure, Mr. Vice President. Is there anything I can get for the office?"

Harry looked around, noticed Emmett eyeing him, and knew he had to play it cool. "You can help me get organized once I move in."

"Absolutely, sir."

"Thanks." Harry turned from her and motioned with his head to Emmett. "I'd better get back to the Capitol." He needed some privacy to deal with this . . . *Jesus, what an opportunity.* He retraced his steps through the offices to the hall. Emmett was right behind him, like a dog following a bone.

"Harry, leave some time for me on your schedule tomorrow. We need to talk about your replacement in the House."

"Sure, I'll text you with a meeting time. I know all hell will break out once this hits the news."

Emmett pulled back his shirt cuff to look at his watch. "And, I need to go talk with Julie about that press release. You know your way back to the entrance?"

That question angered Harry but he smiled. "Of course, I visited many times while Danny occupied the Oval Office." He tipped his hand to Emmett. "See you tomorrow."

With that, Harry turned left to get to the lobby and his ride. He was thrilled—the West Wing beat the Capitol any day, of any week, of any year. Within fifteen minutes he was back in his Capitol office with the door shut. He had his secretary cancel his appointments for the next hour. Now he could sit down and breathe.

But he couldn't stay in the desk chair. Excitement coursed through him and he paced around the office. He looked out the window; damn, it looked like it was going to snow again. Stupid weather. Well, screw it, he was the vice president of the United States. Hot damn. He stopped pacing and gritted his teeth while fisting his hands. Only one small step away from having it all. He could beat that boring Georgia for the Democratic nomination in a heartbeat. Oh man, life was good.

And then, the balloon of euphoria deflated with a loud pop.

He scrambled back to the desk and lost his balance, nearly falling over. He steadied himself for a moment with both hands on the edge of the desk. The same thing had happened a couple of times last month. He put it out of his mind and sat down. He couldn't delay in sending a message to John. If Georgia were killed, the finger would point directly to him. The contract on Georgia had to be cancelled. Lucky for her, he was one step closer to the presidency and he'd reach his goal the usual way—through a national election. He chuckled at that thought. Jesus, he'd never been a typical politician. He'd always been way above normal, more like spectacular.

Harry sent the email using his private mini-tablet and breathed a sigh of relief. Although the contract to eliminate Georgia was over, John could keep the money. Fifteen million should be enough to buy his silence.

He couldn't wait for a televised debate with Georgia. He rubbed his hands together. He'd out campaign her for the nomination this spring and summer. Stupid bitch didn't have a chance against him and his superiority at politics. Oh baby, he could almost taste the cheesecake dessert at an inauguration ball.

The tablet pinged, indicating she had a new email. Good, John was paying attention. He touched the email icon. Hmm, what was this from John? He touched the email link and read the message.

"The email address no longer exists."

~~*

Nick led Nita down the stairs to the underground Visitor Center at the U.S. Capitol. The sky was gray and the wind had picked up. Tendrils of hair blew against her face. He loved her hair, so silky and he used to—. He stopped the train his thoughts were riding on. It's best to concentrate on their present task.

Once through the security line, they headed to Emancipation Hall and the Public Walk-up window at the Information Desk for same-day tour passes.

"Guess January isn't a big tourist month," Nita said a couple of minutes later as they queued up close to the front of the line for the tour.

"Which means fewer people will be walking around so we have to be careful." Nick slung his arm over her shoulder. He moved his mouth to her ear. "We don't want to get arrested on our first Capitol tour together."

Nita giggled as they followed the tour guide who motioned at them to follow her. The first stop was the north orientation theater. They sat halfway up at the end of a row. The spot had a good view of the screen and the entrance door. Nick turned around to look at the back of the theater. A wide door was at the top of the stairs. He bet they'd exit from there.

"You know it's sad, but this is my first time touring the building," Nita said. "I'm a lousy tourist."

"Nah, most people don't play tourist in the city where they live. Unless they have visitors from out of town."

She nodded as the lights dimmed for the film, *Out of Many, One*. It covered the struggle of the U.S. to establish the world's first truly representative democracy. Nick felt it did an excellent job in getting the audience interested in the history of the U.S. Capitol building. Less than fifteen minutes later the credits rolled. They walked up the stairs to the upper level of the Visitor Center for the start of the actual tour.

While they waited for their group to organize, Nick and Nita walked in opposite directions along the hall. After a few steps, a security guard appeared on the north end of the corridor. Nick took a picture with his phone before strolling casually back to the assembly of tourists. He sided up to Nita and whispered in here ear. "Security here is good."

"I know, Capitol Police everywhere."

They queued into a line and a tour guide in a red coat handed out headsets. Nick and Nita were the last to line up. The cute young girl with shiny red hair was their guide and led the group to a down escalator. They landed at the middle of the first floor of the Capitol, also known as The Crypt.

Nick didn't pay all that much attention to what the tour guide said or where they went as the group followed her. He walked on the left side and Nita on the right, both scanning the nearby area for a good location to exit the tour and then hide. Unfortunately, the Capitol Police were patrolling and neither of them could wander off from the group. He wondered if the number of police officers was normal or if it was due to increased security since Garner's shooting.

They walked up two flights of marble stairs to the Rotunda and huddled along one of the walls. Nick watched as police escorted a group of men in fancy suits from one end of the hall to the other. He realized then that dressing in jeans and a sweatshirt, typical tourist attire on the tour, would make it difficult for someone to breakaway from a tour and not look out of place in a non-tourist area. Wearing business attire while participating in the tour would look just as strange. This idea was a bust.

Regardless, they followed the tour guide to the end and soon headed back to the Capitol South Metro Station.

"I think we conclude that whoever planted the drone is a Capitol employee." Nita slipped her hand into Nick's as they walked along Independence Avenue.

"I agree and it must have been planted after the last security check before the State of the Union."

"I wonder what time that was. Do you suppose there's a security video of the House Chamber?"

Nick nodded. "I'd think that would be the first thing the feds would look at. Whoever planted the drone would likely know about the cameras and the timing of the last security check. It doesn't make sense otherwise."

"You're right. This whole scenario is one huge risk." Nita glanced at him and smiled. "Do you suppose this Capitol employee is working with someone else, someone big, like a terrorist group who wants to take over the country?"

"That blows our theory. I think if the shooter does belong to a terrorist group, they'd have done it outside where a lot of damage could be done. Seems to me they like blowing up stuff. It's not impossible, I suppose, but I think it's a long shot."

Within forty-five minutes they entered Nita's front door.

"I'll make coffee." Nita headed to the kitchen after stowing her jacket in the coat closet. "I have an idea."

Nick settled at the dining room table and pulled out the thick stack of papers he'd received from his hacker friend. Way too many people had security access to the Capitol building in his opinion. Of course, he knew absolutely nothing about the building's security.

Nita returned with the coffee and picked up her own stack of paper off her desk. "Let's see if any of the people on this list from the IRS hacking have security clearance at the Capitol." She sat next to him at the table.

"Good idea. How is your list sorted?"

"By state then by name."

"Perfect. Let's first check Maryland, Delaware, and Virginia. Read off the names by state on your list and I'll check my list of Capitol security." He had a hunch they were on the right track but had no clue what track they were currently on.

After three hours they'd not found one name on both lists for the three states.

"Is this a coincidence or just a bad idea?" Nita asked brushing hair off her face.

He shrugged. "Hard to tell, since we're making this up as we go." He rubbed her shoulder with one hand. "What are you planning to do with this IRS list?"

"I haven't quite figured that out."

~~*

"You left a vehicle at the airport? Is that safe?" Candy followed John away from baggage claim to the attached parking garage. Now she was wondering if he was nuts. Leaving a vehicle with guns at a public airport. Surely the police could figure out it was John's car.

"Shush," he said quietly as he patted her butt. They each pulled a rolling suitcase. "No one knows. They don't do security scans on cars in the parking garage." They walked down a long corridor then boarded an elevator.

Once they entered the fifth floor of the garage, John nodded to the right. "Over here."

"What kind of vehicle, make and color?"

He glanced at her and grinned. "Always the cop, huh? Nissan Murano, black."

She shrugged. "Yeah, always. I see it."

"I figured it would blend in with all the government vehicles." John used his remote to unlock the tailgate and it silently opened. He boosted both their suitcases to the cargo area and the door closed with a satisfying click.

"Nice," Candy commented. Her little sedan at home would fit into this SUV. John opened the passenger door for her and she climbed in. Once in the driver's seat after buckling up, he backed out of the parking space and headed to the exit. "Where are we going?"

"I made a reservation at the Marriott Woodrow Park."

"Is that far from here?"

"As the crow flies, not too far. But we're taking the lazy route to get there." He glanced at her and extended his hand to rub her thigh. "Just to be safe. I promise I'll buy you a very nice dinner to make up for the long ride."

She squeezed his hand on her leg. God, she was goof-ball crazy for this man. How in the hell had she been so lucky to meet him? Las Vegas luck was the real deal. "Sounds fine to me. Room service perhaps?"

"Now you're talking, sweet thing."

Once John had paid the parking fee and exited out of Reagan National, Candy pulled her smartphone out of her purse and touched on the GPS app. She wanted to follow their route to the Marriott. They were on the Virginia side of the Potomac River, heading north. It was noon so going home traffic wouldn't be an issue. Although the weather sure looked crappy—an Irish coffee would warm her up once they got to their room.

"You know, this vehicle has navigation," John commented and pointed a finger to the large screen in the middle of the dashboard.

"I know." Candy blinked her eyes at him. "I can't see that far. I really need to get glasses."

John nodded. "Understand that."

After several minutes of silence, she thought about this Harry character John had been dealing with. "I have a question."

The wind had increased and John kept both hands on the steering wheel. "Sure."

"I know Harry is a big shot in Congress. But how do you know you can trust him? He's not anywhere close to being a normal person by wanting two presidents dead."

"True. He seemed weird to me when he came to my house in Colorado."

"I get that. But why did you hook up with him?"

John threw her a quick look. "Money, of course." She noticed his jaw tensing. "Plus, Daniel Gardner owed me for the death of Jessie—an eye for an eye. Her death was a direct result of his incompetence. Damned asshole, he owed me big time."

Twisted or not, his explanation made sense to her. She totally understood taking justice into one's own hands. Sometimes a person had to do what a person had to do when the situation involved family.

"I wonder how many other people are in the same spot as you . . . you know, being screwed by the government." She kept her eyes on the GPS map.

"All I know is what the news said, thousands of people just like me getting hacked via the effing IRS. Assholes." He banged his fist on the steering wheel. "I know I'm not the only one who got royally screwed by identity theft. I have a file of names I put together."

"Really? It seems to me that the feds are out of whack. What happened to elected officials working for the people?" She noticed a bridge coming up on her GPS app.

"That went out the door with the president before Gardner." Sure enough, John took the lane for the Frances Scott Key Bridge.

"All he cared about was giving handouts in exchange for Democratic votes." Candy sighed. "Things aren't the way they used to be."

"I know." John chuckled. "My grandmother used to say that all the time."

She stared at him for a moment then punched his bicep with her fist. "Are *you* comparing me to an old lady?"

"What? No, of course not, no way." He turned right onto the bridge. His face showed no emotion. Which was definitely wise. "What I meant is that things around us keep changing and we're all missing the old days."

"I'm not missing the old days like that. I like change. What I don't like is politicians being so damned political these days. And that political correctness crap? *Please*, don't get me started."

"Message received. I won't compare you to my grandmother." He glanced at her and grinned. "Unless you're a good cook that is. That old lady made the best pot roast."

She grinned at how easy he turned around her potential bitchiness. "Lucky for you, I'm one hell of a cook. When this is over I'll cook you an exceptional shrimp dish I love."

"Exceptional, huh?"

She again punched him in the arm, softly this time. "That's right, mister."

A drizzle began as they exited the bridge into Washington and took a curvy route to the Marriott. Candy scoped it out on her GPS and kept track of their progress. They rode in silence for several miles until John turned north onto Connecticut Avenue from Rock Creek Parkway. The drizzle had turned into a soft rain so the traffic kept plugging along.

"We're getting close, right?" Candy had done an Internet search for the Marriott's address and realized the street was just ahead. "Hey, we just passed a sign, the National Zoo is on this road. Let's go visit."

John glanced at her and smiled slowly. "Sure babe, we'll add that to our agenda. Fake assassinate another president, check. Visit the zoo, check. Get out of Washington, check."

She laughed loudly. "You are such a smart ass."

He saluted her. "Uh-huh." He turned left on Woodley and soon pulled into the circular driveway in front of the hotel. "Here we are."

"Finally. I'm ready to relax."

John squeezed her knee. "I can help you with that."

Two hours later they had checked in, arrived at their suite, and ordered room service. John worked on his laptop at the desk. Candy had taken off her shoes and lounged on the bed watching the Rachel Ray show on the wide-screen television. John stood and pressed his nose to the window.

"It's raining harder now."

"I can check the weather."

"Nah, we're not going anywhere for the rest of the day. We can check later tonight."

"I like that idea. No worries for today."

"Yeah." He returned to the desk chair. "So you know, I deleted the email account I've been using with Harry Roberts."

"Why?"

"It's a safety precaution. Plus, I don't like Harry. Let him have some stress once he realizes he can't contact me." He closed the lid of the laptop. "I verified the fifteen million arrived and transferred it to another bank. We can forget pretending with the contract if we want to."

"Would Harry come after us if we don't appear to be fulfilling the contract?"

"Honestly, I don't know."

"If we leave now, we lose five million." Never in her forty-five years, could Candy have predicted she'd be having such a conversation in Washington, D.C. with a man she'd met last Thursday. What the hell had she gotten herself into? Well, she trusted John. She'd take it one day at a time as her granny used to say when faced with a difficult situation.

"True. Guess we need to think about this some more." A clatter sounded on the hotel room door and John rose from the chair. "Let's relax for a while. We can talk about this later."

~~*

Peter handed his wife a glass of cabernet. She had her feet on the ottoman and her butt snuggled against the back of the sofa. God, he loved this woman. He sat in his usual chair to her side, wine glass in hand.

"How was your day? Anything interesting happen in the Oval Office?"

Georgia raised her glass toward him and smiled. "It's the damned Oval Office, of course something happened . . . about every other minute. Not saying everything is interesting though."

He loved her humor. It hadn't changed in almost thirty years. And he admired her willingness to take a risk. The woman had the balls of an elephant in dealing with her mostly male "colleagues" in the Senate over the years. As president for the next year, she'd show them how it's properly done in the White House. No bullshit and no sex tapes.

"I did watch the six o'clock news. You appointed Harry Roberts as the new VP. Why?"

She downed half the wine in her glass before gazing at him. "A bunch of reasons. Number one being that Harry can cause less damage as VP than as Speaker of the House. I've never trusted his politics."

"I'm not surprised. He's always seemed like a loose cannon. Hard to pin him down on any issue." Peter trusted her instincts explicitly. She rarely misjudged a political situation. "What does your gut tell you about candidates for the new Speaker?"

"To tell you the truth, I haven't thought about that yet. I guess I should. And then send an unsolicited suggestion to Harry."

"Bet he will campaign for the opposite of what you suggest."

"Exactly . . . part of the plan." She leaned toward him and rubbed her hand along his thigh. "Just so you know, I love you. Especially for putting up with me and all this . . . political games stuff."

He grabbed her hand and squeezed it. "Keep that up and we'll need to postpone dinner."

She slid her hand from his and grinned wickedly. "I'll make sure you keep that promise after dinner."

He blew her a kiss. "It's a date."

"Good," Georgia replied. "Oh, I nearly forgot. Packers will be here first thing in the morning. We're moving on up . . . to the White House."

Peter grimaced. He was not looking forward to living in the President's House—much too restricting for his taste. "Do we have to?"

"I know. I'd just as soon be back in our little house. But moving will definitely help with my commute."

"That's true." He laughed. "Even the president has to deal with traffic."

"Terrible isn't it?" She winked at him and finished her wine, held out the glass to Peter. "One more glass."

"Are you sure? My God, what if there's a national crisis and the president is tipsy." He rose and took her glass with his to the kitchen island.

"And for how many years have I had two glasses of red wine every evening?"

He walked back to her with a full glass. "I know. Just teasing."

"But that reminds me, we'll have less privacy in the White House. I'm guessing the only time we'll really be alone is in the presidential bedroom."

"Probably." He grinned at her, even though he really wasn't looking forward to the move. The vice president's residence was bad enough with all the extra people around. "How about skinny dipping in the White House pool?"

"Not a chance."

They chitchatted for close to half an hour discussing the details of their days. Peter loved this daily interaction with his wife. It kept them grounded as a couple, and their conversations kept them honest with each other—which he was not doing concerning Elizabeth Gardner. He ached to tell Georgia his arrangement with the FBI but he'd vowed to tell no one. That included POTUS.

"Is something on your mind?" she asked. "You're frowning."

"No, nothing, just hungry." Peter prayed she'd forgive him.

Chapter Seven

Tuesday, January 27

EMMETT WAS ONE HUNDRED percent sure that D.C. had the absolute worst weather on the planet.

He hated the cold and he hated the wet streets. Whatever, he'd do his duty as the "new" senior advisor to POTUS and get his ass over to the Capitol to meet with Harry, the new VP. Talk about a buzz kill. Within thirty minutes, Emmett stepped into the Speaker's office. Too bad the walls couldn't talk, maybe then he'd get the truth out of Harry.

"Thanks for coming over this morning, Emmett. Have a seat." Harry seemed to be in good spirits. He motioned for his guest to settle in a parson's chair in front of his desk. "There's coffee in the pot over there." He nodded to his right.

"No, thanks." Emmett pulled a blue file folder from his leather portfolio and opened it. "The topic of discussion this ugly morning is your replacement as Speaker. I think the likely candidates are the majority leader, the majority whip, the assistant—"

"Stop. Jesus, your thinking is too basic." Harry wagged a finger at him. "That's why you're a low-level staff member in the White House and I'm vice president."

"Have you been drinking the garbage can punch again?" Emmett now truly hated Harry Roberts. The man was an imbecile. Why were assholes like him always attracted to national office?

Harry stared at Emmett for several moments over the top of his reading glasses. "You're such a plebeian." Finally, he removed the glasses, threw them on the crowded desk and leaned back in his orange leather chair. "Rather than approaching anyone in particular, I'm inclined to let the cream rise to the top of the House bucket. Let the members fight it out."

Emmett had been there for five long minutes, enough of this crap. He stood. "All right then, we'll give it a few days. Ross will expect the first House vote in a couple of weeks." He walked to the office door and turned back to Harry. "Make sure that vote happens . . . on time,

Mr. Vice President. You can do that, right?" He laughed and muttered "loser" loud enough for Harry to hear as he walked out of the office.

~~*

No doubt about it, the variety of events that Georgia attended could potentially result in a major tug on her heart. Today was such a day with that tug—the Gardner family's exit from the White House.

Georgia pulled on her coat and left the West Wing with Frank. They walked briskly to the North Portico. She swallowed hard as they exited the White House doors to the circular driveway. A black SUV with a small White House decal on the driver's side door occupied the driveway.

Rosie and her two sons stood near the hood of the vehicle. Georgia could tell by the body language and facial expressions that the twins were not happy campers. Rosie turned, her face blossoming, and she stepped forward.

"Madam President, how kind of you to come." She reached out her hand and Georgia grasped it, squeezing firmly. "Thank you so much."

"I had to say good-bye. I'm so sorry your family is leaving Washington on such sad terms." After punching each other, the twins climbed into the SUV. Georgia had sympathy for Rosie dealing with teenagers without a stable father.

"I am, too. But . . ." Rosie shrugged. "It is what it is. I can't do anything other than deal with the reality of the situation. We'll all be happier back home. That reminds me, Elizabeth has moved to a hotel for a couple of days. Says she has business to take care of."

"Tell her to contact me if she needs anything." Georgia rubbed the arm of Rosie's black coat. "It's cold out here. Please call me if I can help you . . . call if you simply need to talk. Okay? Also, Valerie Jones is no longer employed by the White House."

Rosie blinked and smiled.

"Now, you need to get on your way."

"Thank you, Madam President." Rosie leaned forward and hugged her. "You show all these men how a great president operates."

Before Georgia had the good sense to reply, Rosie pulled back and hurried to the SUV, sliding into the backseat. It slipped away from the curb. She waved as the vehicle quickly moved to the driveway exit from the White House.

Georgia shook her head; life could change so quickly. She glanced at Frank. "Back to work."

Gracie Evans waited for Georgia to return and chatted with Betty.

She turned as Georgia approached.

"Come on in, Gracie. We have much to discuss." She addressed Daniel's secretary with a slow smile. "I hate to bother you, Betty, but could we have a couple of your cappuccino's? I really need one right now."

Betty beamed. "Yes, Madam President. Give me two minutes."

"Thank you." Georgia waved her hand for Gracie to follow her into the Oval Office. She settled in her usual chair and motioned to Gracie to sit on the adjacent sofa.

"Glad you're here, have you had much contact with Betty in the past?"

Gracie nodded, her dark hair swirling around her young heart-shaped face. "We've both been on the employee Christmas party committee the last two years and I had the chance to get to know her. Betty is awesome. She's a gourmet cook who has a recipe for just about any occasion. Plus, she's a sweet lady."

"Glad to hear your appraisal. I plan to ask her to stay on as my assistant. No clue as to how she'll react."

"I don't know either. She's always been very loyal to President Gardner."

"We'll see." Georgia smiled as Betty entered carrying a small tray.

"Here's your coffee and my special White House brownie." Betty first offered the tray to the president.

"Thank you." Georgia eyed the brownie with the critique of an experienced calorie-counter. *Oh, what the hell.* She selected one and placed it on the edge of the saucer. She wanted to laugh but held it in. A heart showed on the surface of the cappuccino's froth—only at the White House.

Once Gracie had her coffee and brownie, Betty retreated and quietly closed the door.

They munched in silence then Georgia tossed aside her sugar high and went to her desk. She had a list of tasks she'd developed for Gracie. After speaking with the administrative officer for human resources, she determined it was acceptable to tweak the job description of her chief of staff and hire an assistant chief.

"Look this over." She handed the list to Gracie.

After a few moments, Gracie gazed at the president. "This is what you expect from me? And, I'll have an assistant chief?"

"Absolutely. I see your role as my right hand person, protecting me personally and the interests of my presidency. I expect you to negotiate with Congress and at all times to advance my agenda." Georgia smiled, pleased with the look on Gracie's face. "How does that sound?"

"All the administrative staff functions will go to my new assistant?"

"Exactly. I'd prefer you concentrate on major issues rather than hiring staff." Georgia had a good feeling about this change. "I'll expect you and Emmett to work together on policy issues and advancing my agenda. I'd like you to work with him on all congressional negotiations as well. I expect the two of you to provide some interesting debate."

She grinned. "Yes, Madam President, I believe you are correct on that. I will have hire authority for the deputy position?"

Georgia nodded. "Also, so you know the latest, Valerie Jones is no longer associated with the White House. Emmett will be moving to her office and you to his."

Gracie's eyebrows rose. "No kidding, you canned her? Good for you. That makes me happy."

"And that surprises me. Why are you happy?"

"May I speak freely?"

"Of course," Georgia replied.

"Because she's a lying bitch whose very presence disgraced the White House."

Georgia's eyes widened. She'd never heard Gracie talk about another staff member in quite the same vein. "Those are strong words. You obviously know something I don't."

Gracie's head moved back with her face pointed to the ceiling. Her lips thinned and her gaze swung back to her boss. "Over the past three years a lot of talk about Valerie and President Gardner has floated around the White House."

Damn—others knew about their affair. How widespread was it? "What kind of talk?"

"Talk that suggested they were much closer than president and senior advisor."

"I see." Georgia typically considered sharing completely with her chief of staff the wisest course of action. But this issue didn't relate to Georgia's job as vice president or president. "What's done is done, it's in the past. Do you have any questions about how I see your role as my chief of staff?"

"No ma'am, not right now." Gracie shook her head and smiled. "I'm sure I'll have them along the way. I very much appreciate you giving me this opportunity."

"How can you doubt that? We've been a winning combination for almost eight years."

"To be honest, I thought you might keep Emmett."

"No." Georgia rose and walked to the fireplace. She would tell Gracie the truth. "What I'm about to tell you is highly confidential. You cannot repeat this information."

"Yes, Madam President."

"Daniel Gardner has no chance of recovering from his head trauma."

Gracie's hand flew to her throat. "Oh, no . . . that's terrible news."

"The Gardner family is taking the president home to Colorado, today in fact." She walked around the right side of the sofa to her desk. "This White House administration we have here is all mine. The agenda is mine. And I own the outcome, whether it succeeds or fails."

Gracie nodded with determination.

"You will be my number one advisor. I expect you to work with Emmett since he's been here for three years." Georgia made a split second decision about her future. "However, that doesn't mean he will automatically be included in my administration if I decide to run for the presidency."

"I am happy to hear you're at least thinking about running." Gracie rose and walked to her boss. "Madam President, I hope I'm not out of line by saying I'm proud of you and honored to work in your White House."

Georgia held out her hand and Gracie shook it. "Now go talk to Emmett and let him know you're in charge."

She walked Gracie to the door and waved her hand at Betty. "Please come in. I need to speak with you."

Betty grabbed a notebook and hurried through the door. "Yes ma'am. How may I assist you?"

Georgia stood next to the back of the wing chair she usually sat in and mentally crossed her fingers. "I know you're aware that President Gardner and his family are on their way back to Colorado."

"Yes ma'am, I said my goodbye's last night."

"Good. What are your plans? I know you've worked with Daniel for a number of years."

"Yes, that's true." Betty's face scrunched for a moment. "Ma'am, I had hoped I could continue on with you. The First Lady and I had a nice talk about it and we both think it will help to keep things running .

. . uh, to help with consistency."

Georgia sighed in relief. "That's wonderful. I had hoped you'd stay on with me. Thank you."

"No, Madam President, *thank you*. If it's okay for me to say . . . I like your style." Betty face acquired a becoming pink blush.

"Good. I have a couple things I need to think over so let's get together first thing tomorrow to discuss logistics."

"Yes ma'am. Your next appointment should arrive in five minutes."

Betty retreated to her office while Georgia returned to her desk. *Hmm, maybe this POTUS job wasn't so tough after all.*

~~*

"Holy crap." John shouted as he sat on the foot of the bed watching the local news at noon on TV. "Candy, get in here."

She rushed in from the bathroom holding a small mirror in one hand and a tube of mascara in the other. "What? What's wrong?"

"Jesus Christ." He rubbed his hands over his face and looked at her. "Please . . . sit in the chair over there." He spoke softly and pointed to the chairs and table by the window.

She did as instructed and set the mascara and mirror on the table. "John, what the hell is wrong? You're scaring me."

"Sorry. This is too wild—incredible, in fact . . . yesterday, President Ross appointed Harry Roberts as the new vice president . . . of the United States."

Her face blanched and her mouth opened, like a fish struggling for oxygen. Then she snapped it shut and rose. "Holy shit. What is wrong with that stupid Harry? He shouldn't have accepted. He's not fit to be VP, he's an idiot."

"And a traitor."

"But President Ross doesn't know that." Candy paced across the suite and turned back to John. "In fact, she has no clue she became president because of Harry, or that Harry wants her dead."

"I know. This changes everything in my book."

"I agree. But how?"

"I'm not sure. We need to think long and hard about this." He rose and went to the desk. "While you finish up I'm going to do some online stuff."

In a little over an hour, they were munching hotdogs at the Atrium Cafe within the Smithsonian Museum of Natural History. It was too cold to go to the National Zoo. John had concluded that doing a typical tourist thing would give them a chance to relax and think about what they should do next.

"This hits the spot," Candy said and popped a French fry in her mouth. "I'm glad we came here. I almost came my senior year in high school but I got mono and missed the trip."

"Mono? Isn't that the kissing disease?"

"I guess, but I wasn't kissing anyone. I got it and it sucked. I had to be home schooled for a while."

"Bummer."

John had no desire to talk right then. His mind twirled from one thought to another without getting a good handle on what he was thinking. Why in the hell had he gotten himself mixed up with Harry Roberts in the first place?

Justice for Jessie's death.

Yeah, there was that.

He glanced at Candy and was once again grateful to the good Lord who had the wisdom to bring this woman into his life. He had changed because of her. Rather than expecting to lose his life after the drone had fired a week ago, he now had a reason to keep going, to make a new life for himself—a life that included Candy.

"Are you ready?"

He smiled. "You bet I am. Come on, babe. Let's check out the museum." He threw their trash in the can then grabbed her hand. This woman was his personal savior and he'd damned sure see to it that the rest of her life would be a happy one.

They took the escalator to the first floor and wandered through the exhibits. Candy pointed out this and that with John making appropriate comments, yet his mind kept going back to Harry and their contract. He nodded as Candy commented on the size of the African Elephant in the rotunda. Could it really be called a contract? No, it was more like an agreement. It wasn't legally binding. He wouldn't knock off President Ross even though he'd been partially paid for it. What could Harry do? Every option would implicate him or open him up to public reveal.

Checkmate.

He walked through the Ocean Hall with Candy. She seemed to enjoy all the displays. A huge replica of a North Atlantic Right Whale, named Phoenix, hung in the middle of the space. Now, that was a whale. She tugged his hand.

"How about going to the American History Museum? One floor of dead animals is enough for me." She winked at him. "Okay?"

"Good idea, let's go."

They went back to the ground floor and exited onto Constitution Avenue. The weather was still cold but the rain had stopped. They ambled down the street to the next museum.

"I was thinking . . ." Candy seemed pensive as they waited to cross 12th Street. "Maybe we should try to contact President Ross."

"How?" They started across the street, not too many tourists out. "Is there a number for the White House that goes to the president, or maybe an email address?"

"I guess we could look online. I know the White House has a website."

"What the hell did people do before Google?" John laughed as he sidestepped a puddle of water on the street.

"Or, maybe we could try something less direct." Candy scrunched her mouth. A sure sign she was thinking off the wall. God, he really liked this woman. He once again said a silent prayer to the Good Lord for bringing them together.

"Like what?"

"Surveillance."

"Of who?"

Candy stopped walking and stared at him. "Duh. President Ross."

"How do we do that?"

"I'm a damned cop. I'll show you how."

They stopped in front of the American History Museum. John's heart buzzed and he wondered if he'd lost his mind. "Is it necessary?"

"It's better than sending an email saying I've been hired to kill you, Madam President, even though I won't." Candy squeezed his hand. "It'll give us a chance to get acclimated here and decide how to move forward. You know, how to falsify our actions for Harry's last contract."

John hesitated. "You really know how to do surveillance?"

"Damn straight." She again tugged his hand and stepped to the museum's door. "Come on, I want to see Julia Child's kitchen and Dorothy's ruby slippers. This museum will be awesome."

John nodded and followed her. Faking the assassination of POTUS was a whole lot more complicated than just doing it.

~~*

"I'm opening the wine," Nick said as he held open the front door of Nita's row house. After she'd posted her latest blog that morning, they'd left to scout locations around the Capitol building that might provide a good spot to remotely control a drone in the House Chamber. They came to no conclusion. And now they had more research to do, specifically the maximum remote control distance for a drone.

"I'll make a snack to go with it." They both went to the kitchen. While Nick opened the wine, Nita grabbed sharp Cheddar and Gouda cheese and a couple boxes of crackers. She put the cheese on her cutting board with a knife and dumped the crackers in a basket. Not fancy, but it would work to satisfy Nick's bottomless stomach. They both transferred to the dining room table.

Nita set the cheese and crackers on the table then went to her computer. "Let me check the comments on this morning's blog. I'm curious if that BigDem person posted again." She logged into the computer and opened the blog. "Wow, 542 comments. This will take me a few minutes to check."

"Go ahead, I have an idea." He handed her a glass of wine.

She didn't hear Nick as she'd turned her focus to the blog comments. Scanning the remarks as she scrolled through them, she searched for one from BigDem. The consensus agreed with her that dumbass politicians did seem to be the majority rather than the minority in Washington. But what could one do but listen to the candidates running for office and vote for the one who seemed to be the most honest.

Then the candidate is elected and the voter learns the truth—politicians lie to get elected—perfect example is the former president. Not only do they lie, they misrepresent and distort actual current and historical events. It's hard for the average American to know whom to trust. Nita shook her head. How had she become such a political philosopher and so damned cynical at only thirty-two?

She stopped. BigDem was comment number 287:

Young lady, don't you learn? Are you brain dead? You shouldn't be calling any politician a dumbass…don't you realize how hard they work for the common good, for the individual American citizen? Seems to me someone needs to teach you a little respect. Didn't your wonderful father do that for you? Guess he was too busy.

Nita's breath caught. OMG. Who was this person? "Nick, I have another comment from that crazy person, BigDem. Listen." She read the comment to him then slumped in her chair. "Who is this person and why is he doing this?"

Nick rose and looked over her shoulder at the computer monitor.

"I wonder if this guy knows you. This last comment sounds personal."

"I know. Why would he mention my father? He's been gone for eight years." She turned around to Nick. "Do you suppose this guy knew him?"

"It's possible. Do you remember your dad's friends?"

"I'd have to think about that. I'll put it on my to-do list."

"Okay." He massaged her shoulders for a few moments then returned to the table. "Can you look at your comments later? We need to talk about the drone."

"What have you discovered?"

"A lot, and some of it is down-right scary." He sipped the wine and rubbed his jaw. "I had no idea it's so easy to obtain a drone. You can buy a DIY kit to build one yourself or purchase a ready-made one. I watched a video of a drone shooting paint bullets from a handgun turned upside down. It was pretty damned accurate, too. The fact that a drone with a gun walked in the Capitol is terrifying, even for a macho guy like me."

"No kidding, Mr. Macho-Man. We agreed yesterday that it would be difficult for a tourist to slip away from a Capitol visitor tour. I think it's safe to assume that whomever smuggled in that drone is on your huge list of people with Capitol security."

"We need to figure out a way to narrow it down."

Nita chuckled. "This will be like looking for a four-leaf clover in an acre of grass."

"Back to who had the most to gain—Georgia Ross and then Harry Roberts."

"I still don't think Georgia Ross had anything to do with it, not her style. She orchestrated a day of prayer for Gardner." She sipped the wine and grinned. "Now Harry, he's a weird guy to me and President Gardner's best friend. I can't see him doing this. Only a monster would want to kill his best buddy."

Nick steepled his fingers in front of his chest. "I agree. That's two names off the list. Who else would want Gardner dead?"

"Mike McCain is next in line as Majority Leader of the Senate. Of course he'd have to kill both Ross and Roberts to get the job." Nita laughed. "I know I just published a blog on dumbass politicians but he'd have to be a psychopath to think he could get away with killing three people simply to become president for eleven months."

"Doesn't make sense." Nick nodded and stuffed a cheese-topped cracker in his mouth.

"Are we shifting our entire focus to someone hurt by Gardner's policies or lack of presidential action?"

Nick winked at her with his wine glass raised in salute. "Yeah, I think we are."

~~*

Georgia, Gracie, and Emmett were finishing up a long policy meeting in the Oval Office. Georgia had an idea she'd been thinking about for twenty-four hours. "I'd appreciate your opinion on something—I haven't discussed this with Julie yet. I want to give a primetime address to the nation. It's been a week since Daniel was shot. I think it's time to reassure everyone they're in good hands with a new president."

"Absolutely, Madam President," Emmett said quickly.

"I agree as well," Gracie added. "Would tomorrow evening work? I can set it up with Julie."

"That's what I was thinking." Georgia turned her head after Betty knocked on the open door.

"Ma'am, we have an issue. You need to transfer to the Situation Room." Betty stepped away from the doorway.

This wasn't the first time Georgia had heard those words, but it was the first time as president. She rose and motioned for Emmett and Gracie to follow her. She nodded to Betty. "Please make sure Julie joins us."

The group of three along with Frank and another agent hurried down the staircase to the first floor of the West Wing and down the hall to the Situation Room. Georgia had been there before as vice president. It was a whole different vibe walking into the room as president.

Several men and Helen Capstone stood as the trio entered. Georgia walked to the middle of the long conference table, with Emmett and Gracie moving to the left, and scanned from her left to her right. Julie rushed in.

"What's going on?" She motioned for everyone to sit down.

"Madam President," Adam Martinez began. "We have a situation with an international flight on Western Airlines headed from Newark to Rome."

"What is the situation, specifically?"

Not to be upstaged, Ed Burnett from NSA spoke. "Ma'am, the onboard server on Western flight 89 has been compromised via a computer onboard the plane."

"What does that mean, in plain speak?" Why couldn't these people simply tell her the problem?

Helen Capstone stood. "Madam President, it means that a U.S. airliner with 342 people onboard has potentially been taken over by a terrorist."

"Thank you for the summary." Georgia turned her head to the right and then the left, attempting to make eye contact with every person seated at the table. Those who looked down spoke to her without words. "To confirm, either a crew member or a passenger has a computer onboard the plane that has taken over a server."

"Yes." Helen sat down again.

"What does this server control on the plane?" Georgia wanted to scream. Getting information from these people was like pouring country molasses—too damned slow.

"Ma'am, this is what we know." Adam picked up a remote control and the wide screen television at the end of the room came on. He scrolled through a menu and a slideshow appeared on the screen. "The aircraft for Flight 89 is an Atlas 767. Maximum passenger count is 340 and this flight has thirteen empty seats, with fifteen crew members."

"Do we know if the person taking over the server is a crew member or a passenger?"

"Ma'am, we're looking into that," Adam said.

"I'll ask my question again," Georgia said. "What does this server control on the plane?"

"This server is the direct control for the entertainment system," Ed replied. "However, it's part of the onboard WiFi hub and via a router has a link to the flight control systems. Obviously there are firewalls to protect the avionics system and the other flight control systems."

"Are you saying that some lunatic on that plane has the power to take over control of the plane using a WiFi connection?"

Ed nodded.

Georgia looked at her watch, 6:13. "Don't flights to Europe usually leave later in the evening?"

"Yes. This one left at 4:30 due to increased traffic in Rome."

"So the flight time is primarily in the dark?"

"Yes, that's true." Ed pointed at Adam. "Let's continue with the slides."

Adam narrowed his eyes for a moment then picked up the remote control. "Ma'am, these are photos of the inside of the 767. It's luxurious in first class and less so in economy."

Georgia studied the slides as they moved across the television screen. The plane's interior looked like that of planes she'd flown in the past. Nothing unusual other than it held a lot of passengers and was almost full. "Have we analyzed the list of passengers?"

"We're doing that right now," Ed replied.

"Do we know which seat on the plane holds the computer controlling the server?"

"Ma'am, we're working on that as well," Adam said.

"How soon before we have that information? Can't you get the IP address or something?" Georgia drummed her fingers on the table then stopped. It was too early in this situation for her to reveal her impatience with this group. "Aren't firewalls supposed to stop this sort of thing from happening?"

"We're working on it," Ed said. "Firewalls are software and unfortunately, that means they can be hacked."

"How did this situation come to our attention?"

"Ma'am, the plane's computer sent a message to the Western control center in Atlanta and they notified TSA." Adam sipped from a glass of water and gazed directly at his new boss. "My guess is this isn't some random hacker playing around with his PC while on a flight to Italy."

Georgia matched the intensity of his look. "What *do you* believe we're dealing with?"

"Madam President . . . Georgia" Helen, seated at the end of the table, waved her arm like a beauty queen.

Georgia shifted to her left. "Yes, Helen, what is it?"

"Well . . . I just now received an email from my TSA head and—"

Georgia cut her off. "Why isn't he here? Along with Transportation and the FAA, and Defense." She spun around to Gracie. "Please contact all four offices and tell them to get their butts over here." She turned her attention back to the Secretary of Homeland Security. "Sorry Helen, what were you saying?"

"I, uh, I'll wait for the others to get here."

"Great idea. Let's take a 15 minute break." Georgia rose, intending to go back to her office. Helen rushed to her.

"May I speak with you in private?"

"Of course, come with me." With Frank and crew following them, they made a quick trip to the Oval Office. Georgia nodded at Betty as they passed her desk. "We'll be here only a few minutes." Betty nodded and Georgia closed the door with a wink at her.

"What's on your mind?" She sat in her usual chair while Helen sat on the edge of the sofa.

"Uh, ma'am, I . . . well, I need to apologize for the recent issues concerning my government email account."

"Did President Gardner know you used a personal account for government business?"

"We never discussed it but I'm sure he did as we've emailed back and forth."

"Did you never consider that using a personal email account via a private sever might allow your email to be hacked?"

"I did it for control of the emails."

"Oh, so that you can decide which ones will be archived?" Georgia realized she was losing her patience.

"Well, yes, of course."

Patience had evaporated. "Damn it, Helen. Don't tell me you're that stupid. If you plan to continue on as Secretary of Homeland Security in my administration, you will use a federal email account or you won't have the need for one." Madam President's voice softened. "Your choice, of course."

Helen's eyes rounded and her hands fisted in her lap. "I will not be talked—"

"This isn't negotiable."

Helen's eyes were now close to bulging out their sockets. She appeared on the verge of speaking and fell against the back of the sofa while rubbing her eyes. Georgia remained silent as she allowed Helen to compose herself.

"Madam President, I'm truly sorry for this breach in protocol. I will obtain a federal email account as soon as possible."

Check and checkmate—power rules every damned time. Georgia nodded and rose. "Please inform whomever is at your residence in Florida that the FBI will be there within the hour to pick up the server for safekeeping."

"Thank you."

"I'll see you in the Sit Room in a few minutes."

Helen got the message and left. Georgia made the necessary call, used the ladies' room, and walked with her escort back downstairs.

"Frank, what's your take on human nature? Do you think people in Washington ever learn their lesson?"

He smiled wryly. "No ma'am, I don't believe they do. Unless, of course, a judge is handing down a sentence."

She chuckled. "Good point."

"Yes ma'am."

They arrived shortly and the group, with its new members, waited for her. Everyone stood as she entered—*that* would take some getting accustomed to. She shrugged it off and returned to her designated chair.

"What have we learned in the last fifteen minutes about this potential terrorist on flight 89?"

~~*

Elizabeth Gardner unpacked her large cosmetics bag on a thick towel in the bathroom of her mini-suite at The Lincoln Rose, a luxury hotel on 16th Street facing Lafayette Square and the White House. She needed to look fresh and formidable for her in-suite dinner in thirty minutes with Peter Ross. She'd already ordered wine and appetizers followed by a scrumptious dinner from room service.

This dinner was business, pure and simple. Although she might kick it up a notch to have a little fun with Peter. Men were such easy creatures to manipulate—like her late husband. James had died ten years ago from a stupid heart attack when she was in her mid-fifties. She'd used his death for a good two years to gain attention as the grieving widow. That had petered out and she'd moved on to more personally beneficial pursuits.

Like a real estate deal with the vice president's hubby. Danny had no idea she'd taken advantage of her grandmother role in the White House. James had taught both of them well in the art of the deal. Her dear son's ultimate deal turned into his campaign for the presidency, and then it became her turn. She couldn't use the benefits of the White House forever and the pitiful retirement James had accumulated before his death wasn't near enough to maintain the life style she deserved.

Thus she'd devised a plan to increase her bank balance.

She stroked mascara across her lashes then applied a beautiful shade of peach lipstick to her still full lips. She smacked them in satisfaction and walked to the full-length mirror on the back of the closet door. Hell yeah, she looked good. The soft blue sweater and skinny black jeans made her look like she was forty, not sixty-five.

She heard a knock on the door, right on time at 6:30. Elizabeth gathered the towel on the bathroom counter and placed it in one of her suitcases in the closet. She shut the closet door, fluffed her hair, and headed to the suite's entrance.

Both room service and Peter greeted her after she opened the door.

"Isn't this the perfect timing?" She reached her hand toward Peter and nudged him into the room in front of the room service cart.

The server placed the cart by the window and she signed the receipt, eager to get the little service person out of the room. Finally the door closed and she turned to Peter, beaming.

"Hello, Elizabeth. I thought we were going out for dinner."

She reached for one of the wine bottles on the cart. "I know. This has been a difficult day for me with Danny flying home. I thought a more comfortable setting would help me relax." She extended the bottle to Peter. "Would you open this, please?"

He accepted the bottle and looked at the label. "You have good taste."

"I know."

Elizabeth busied herself with uncovering the appetizer plates and convincing herself she could appropriately con Peter Ross. The biggest hurdle was the financing. Would he probe where her half of the money came from? Had she done enough to hide the true source of her funds? She shook off the thought and prepared two small plates of boiled shrimp, cheese, and mini-beef kabobs. She doubted he'd figure out the truth as she'd covered her tracks with the skill of one well suited for such "covert" activity.

Swallowing a giggle, she set a plate on the table near Peter as he poured the wine. "Here you go, a nibble before dinner arrives."

"Thank you," Peter said as he handed her a glass of wine. "Let's sit here by the window."

They settled with their wine and appetizers at a square table placed strategically next to the wide window. The drapes were open and the White House glowed in the distance. The sky had darkened in the winter night and the glow looked like a child's globe—Shake it and the world would right itself again. Elizabeth sighed, if only that were true for adults.

"Was today difficult?" Peter asked. "I mean, saying goodbye to the White House and moving Daniel back to Colorado."

She dabbed a napkin to her eye. "Yes, it's been one of the worst days of my life. But I'm determined to make lemonade out of a bushel of lemons. That's why I agreed to meet with you this evening."

"And I thank you for that."

She raised her wine glass. "Here's to continued business success in Denver." Peter raised his glass as well and she tapped hers against his. "Much success," she added with a demure smile.

She eyed Peter as she sipped the wine. Would he agree to her next idea for purchasing apartment buildings in Lakewood, a suburb to the west of Denver? These complexes would serve as the ideal vehicle to launder Mexican drug money—as she had promised her contact with the Los Gulf Cartel. They had been so generous funding the first set of transactions with Peter. How could they turn on her now? Especially when it was to the cartel's benefit to become established in Colorado. Legal marijuana was at the front of their drug goals for making money off Colorado citizens getting high. Heroin was next.

"To continued success." Peter smiled and stuffed a shrimp in his mouth.

Yes indeed, she had Peter in her grasp. He'd jump at this new opportunity. Men were so easy to control.

~~*

"Babe, we still haven't figured out a plan to fake a presidential assassination."

Candy rolled her eyes and sighed, heavily. They were hanging out and taking it easy after returning from the museums. It was one of those falsely relaxing times—the calm before the storm.

"Let's cut to the chase. I want to be sure. You're not shooting another U.S. president, right?" She slid her glance to John.

"Huh?" He blinked. "No, we already talked about this. But I want the rest of the money."

Good, they were on the same page. "I agree and I have an idea."

"I'm listening as long as it includes screwing Harry Roberts." John rose from the table, placed a hand in each front pocket of his jeans and walked to the window. He leaned his butt against the glass. "I think I'm certifiably crazy for agreeing to do his dirty work in the first place."

"You were angry and blamed Gardner for Jessie's death. Harry took advantage of you and your heartache after losing your wife. He's the bad guy, not you."

John rubbed a hand over his face while his eyes were hangdog droopy. "I wish I'd been stronger and acted differently. Not that Gardner didn't deserve it but the stress is a lot worse than I thought it would be."

"Am I to blame for that?" Had she been too hard on him? No, damn it, he had to emotionally accept it and move on.

"No blame on my end. You've helped me understand why I did it." He walked over to her and kissed the top of her head. "Seriously, you've been a life saver for me."

"Good. It's time to go forward and decide what to do about that extra five million."

"You said you have an idea." John sat across from her again.

"Not an idea exactly, more of a concept. We need to turn the tables on Harry and preferably after he transfers the five million."

"He won't do the transfer until he has proof that Georgia Ross is dead."

"I know, and that's the difficult part of the plan."

"Maybe we could fake a picture or something."

Candy rolled her eyes while smiling. John was so freaking cute. "You know, we better start that surveillance tomorrow. Harry might have someone watching to see if something new is going on."

"You're right. I think we should get a rental car rather than using my SUV. Won't we look all touristy around D.C. with a rental?"

"Probably so. A dark four door sedan should work."

"That's what cops always drive on TV."

"Uh huh, because dark cars blend in with the traffic."

"Tomorrow we begin. We have four days to execute our non-existent plan. I emailed Harry that I'd kill President Ross on Saturday."

"Geez, there's always drama with you."

~~*

"Everyone, what's the bottom-line here?" Georgia settled back at the long table in the Sit Room.

"Ma'am," Adam began. "The worst-case scenario is that a terrorist with a laptop is sitting among the passengers and has taken control of the airplane using its passenger WiFi."

Georgia nodded and made an honest attempted to suppress her frustration. Hadn't they already discussed that? "Do we have the passenger list and do we have the terrorist's seat assignment narrowed down?" She glanced around the table, hoping her facial expression didn't reflect the enormous concern churning in her gut. Weren't these people the best of the best for U.S. intelligence? "Surely, someone has an update."

Ed looked up from his cell phone. "It appears that the laptop is in seat 3K. It's the third row in first class, right side aisle. We should have a seat map sent over. Adam, can you check?"

"What's the passenger name for that seat?" Georgia asked.

"That's here, too." Adam clicked on the keyboard then used the mouse and a seat map appeared on the television screens at both ends of the room. A monitor built into the table in front of Georgia also came to life. "Ma'am, you can see easier using the table monitor."

Georgia studied the schematic for the seat map, zeroing in on 3K. That seat couldn't have come cheap. It was close to the cockpit—what a surprise. She looked at the side-by-side passenger list. "The name for the passenger in 3K is Alexander Hamilton. Really? What's his nationality? Do we have a copy of his passport? How did he pay for his ticket? Is it one-way or round trip? Has he flown this same route in the past? What other flights has he taken in the last year? And how long before this flight is scheduled to land?" She stopped to take a drink of water. "Do we know why this has happened?"

"Madam President, we do." Janet Brammel, the new administrator of the Federal Aviation Administration gazed directly at Georgia. "We had a posting to the FAA's Facebook page two minutes ago: 'Western Air flight 89 is now in the control of a passenger. If fifty million dollars isn't paid within two hours, the plane will head to the Atlantic Ocean. Call 434-555-1215 for details.'"

"What was that number again?" Adam had his hands poised over the keyboard. Janet repeated it and Adam clicked on the keys. "This will take a few minutes."

"Has Facebook identified who posted the message and their email account? And what about this Alexander Hamilton character? That can't be his real name." Georgia started to drum her fingers on the table.

"We need to discuss this demand," Helen said.

"Absolutely, and what we're going to do about it," Ed added.

"What do you mean, what we're going to do about it?" Georgia asked.

Ed glared at her. "Madam President, if this is a legitimate terrorist threat, we can't ignore it."

"Thanks for the clarification, Ed." She turned her gaze to Adam. "Anything on the phone number? Also, what do we know about the other passengers on the plane? Does the pilot have a gun onboard?"

"Ma'am, if you'll give me five to ten minutes, I should have some answers." Adam gave her "the give-me-a-break look" and she nodded.

At least the FBI director had his act together. "Let's take a five minute break." Georgia rose and grabbed her cell phone from the table. She went to the hall and picked up a house phone, punching the button for Betty.

"If I meet you at the top of the stairs, could you make me a cappuccino? I need caffeine."

"Yes ma'am, give me a minute. And, don't worry about the stairs, I'll find you."

"Thank you, you're a life saver." Georgia moved to the side of the wide corridor, waving off Gracie and Emmett as she pointed to her cell indicating she was making a call. She clicked on Peter's cell number expecting to hear her husband's voice. Instead the call went to voicemail. She scrunched her nose then left a message: "Hey babe, I'm in a little crisis here, not sure when I'll be home. Text when you hear this message."

She stuffed the phone in the pocket of her slacks and waved Gracie over to her. "Sorry, trying to contact my husband. Do you need to speak with me?"

"I was just wondering how you're holding up?" Gracie rubbed her boss's upper arm. "You've been president for not quite a week and this is our first big crisis."

"I know." Georgia tried to smile. "We'll get through it."

"Have you decided on your bottom line?" Gracie threw her a quick smile. "You know, that *red line in the sand*."

"Smart ass. Pay attention young one and watch me roll." Georgia's lips pursed for a moment then she spotted Betty. "Go into the meeting. I'll be back in a minute."

Georgia met her at the bottom of the stairs. Betty carried a tall travel coffee cup. "I made you a double, just in case."

"You are an angel, thank you." Betty handed her the cup and Georgia tasted the coffee, her eyes widening. "Goodness, stronger than usual."

"I added an extra espresso, figured you need to be in tip-top form." Betty chuckled and smiled. "Call me if you need anything else." She headed to the stairs.

Georgia liked Betty. At least Daniel had made a good decision when it came to his personal assistant. She returned to the conference table.

"All right, what have we learned?"

"Ma'am, this is what we know at this point." Adam looked up briefly then touched the keyboard and the page from a passport appeared. "This is the U.S. passport of the Alexander Hamilton who boarded flight 89. Does he look like an Alexander to you?"

Georgia studied the photo of the young, somber looking dark-skinned man with a full beard and dark hooded eyes. He had a hooked nose and his thick black hair had a choppy short cut. "No, I wouldn't guess Alexander Hamilton was his name at birth."

Georgia gazed at Helen then turned her attention to the head of the TSA. "Albert, wouldn't this passenger's name and appearance create a question for the TSA agent at airport security?"

"We don't profile," Helen interjected.

"But the TSA does use common sense . . . correct, Albert?"

"Yes ma'am."

"Do you know if the TSA agent who checked this passport had a question or a concern?"

"Yes ma'am, I do."

"Wonderful." Georgia mentally counted to five, controlling her irritation at this pompous man. "Do I need to sign a release or an executive order for you to simply tell me?"

"No, ma'am." Albert gazed at her, a slight smile on his closed mouth.

"You do have the information?"

"I do."

She waited at least ten seconds for him to deliver the details. Nothing. "Albert, how long have you been the head administrator at the TSA?"

"Almost three years."

"That's long enough. You're fired."

"You can't do that," Albert shouted indignantly.

"I can and I did." Georgia turned around and motioned to Frank. "Please show Mr. Owens out of the room and have an agent escort him back to his office to clean it out." She turned her attention to Helen. "You can sort out his paperwork when we're done here."

Frank nodded and waited for Albert to rise and walk around the table. He didn't look happy but that was to be expected when fired by POTUS in front of his peers. Georgia would analyze her show of temper later. Once Albert was out of the room, she again gazed at Helen.

"I trust you can answer my query, Helen. Did the Newark TSA agent have a concern about the passport in question?"

"No, he did not. The passenger boarded without an alarm being raised."

"Thank you." God, there were so many problems with the federal government—one crisis at a time. "Adam, what else have you learned?"

"The flight crew has been informed of the situation but the cabin crew has not. And, yes, there is a gun in the cockpit." Adam paused to drink from a water bottle. "The phone number on the Facebook post is for a burner phone purchased last night at a big-box discount store in Charlottesville, Virginia. The phone is currently turned off."

"Do we know this guy's real identity?"

"We're working on it," Ed said. "These things take time."

"Which we are short of right now." Georgia again drummed her fingers on the table. Did Alexander have the phone or did someone else? "Can this phone be used from the Internet?"

"It's possible. What are you thinking?" Ed finally looked interested.

"I'm thinking that if the phone could be controlled by the Internet and our bad guy has WiFi on the plane, maybe he is also posting to Facebook and has the phone with him."

"Ma'am, I think you might be right," Adam added. "Facebook has provided details on the account and the name is the same. We have the email address."

"Let's send an email. Surely I have a fake email account." Georgia glanced at Gracie then at Emmett and spread her hands. "For these type of situations."

Emmett grinned. "Absolutely, we do indeed have such an account."

"Are you sure that's wise?" Ed said. "I mean, is it prudent that he knows the president is involved?"

"What's the down side?" Emmett said.

Ed's face went blank for a moment. Then he recovered and sneered at Emmett before turning to Georgia. "Madam President, I'm concerned about the long term repercussions from terrorists realizing that a U.S. president is involved in dealing with them."

Yes, the job of POTUS was difficult when dealing with longtime federal bureaucrats like Ed. He'd been around Washington so long he'd forgotten why he occupied space in a federal office building. "I guess you're referring to Benghazi and the lack of high level involvement in that situation, resulting in the loss of four American lives. Not to worry. This president has no concerns about her involvement in dealing with individuals threatening her fellow Americans." Georgia zeroed in on Ed. "Unlike the past two presidents, I understand the concept of cojones."

Ed's eyes widened and his mouth narrowed into a thin line.

Whatever. "Emmett, do you have that email account pulled up?"

"I do."

"Good." Georgia picked up one of the standard issue White House pens and clicked it on and off . . . this was her first real test. "Please enter this as the email: Mr. Alexander, Message received. Difficult to accommodate. Need four hours—new at this. Sincerely, Mrs. Ross." She gazed around the table, trying to judge the reaction.

All these people were good poker players. She checked the time, 6:48. "Please send it."

"It's gone," Emmett said.

"How much time until flight 89 is scheduled to land?"

Adam glanced up from his computer. "Six hours, seventeen minutes. I doubt Mr. Hamilton will agree to four hours."

"Let's see with how he replies. In fact—" Georgia snapped her mouth shut as Ed began to speak.

"We don't even know if he will reply," Ed said.

The CIA Director, Jim Brooks, rushed into the room. "Georgia . . . Madam President, I'm sorry I'm late. I came straight from the airport." He pulled out an empty chair across the table from Ed.

"Glad you're here," Georgia said. "I sent an email to our terrorist, Alexander Hamilton, and Ed believes that wasn't wise. Adam, do you have an analysis of the passenger list?"

"Not yet, ma'am." Adam was the epitome of the cool FBI agent. "We're still reviewing the entire list. It will take another hour at least."

"We don't have all day," Ed added.

Adam gave Ed a thumb's up. "Got it."

"Let's discuss our options for handling this," Georgia stated. She had no clue how other presidents had handled crisis events. She suspected the men from the intelligence community were questioning her ability, or, perhaps it was dealing with a female boss in general. They had no choice but to deal with a new president. The buck stopped with her—she'd be held responsible for the end result of a terrorist taking over a U.S. airliner departing from Newark.

"Ma'am, if I may?" Jim said.

Georgia nodded. "Of course."

"We have a small window of time so I suggest we first concentrate on Mr. Hamilton and who he is and second, the other passengers on the plane. Is he a lone wolf or is this a group effort? Plus, the longer we can keep him engaged via email the better. I understand the Facebook post had a phone number. Have we attempted to call it?"

"I was thinking the same thing," Ed said.

"What number do we call from?" Georgia ignored Ed and smiled at Jim. She knew there were special phone lines set up for this sort of thing.

"We can patch into a secure line that shows The White House in the caller ID." Jim nodded at Adam. "Correct?"

"Absolutely. Ma'am, we haven't yet had an email response.

Would you like to try the number?"

"Yes," she replied. "The Facebook posting did say to call the number for details. It sure as hell can't hurt anything."

"Adam, can you patch us in?" Jim was a calming influence. Georgia appreciated that the CIA and the FBI were on good working terms. Or, at least it seemed that they were.

"We're ready," Adam replied.

Ed raised a hand. "We shouldn't proceed without knowing precisely what Madam President will be saying."

Georgia did roll her eyes at that statement. "I will inquire as to the details for the fifty million dollar transfer. I will also ask if my email was received. That's it."

"Perfect," Adam said as he slid a piece of paper across the table. "This is the call back number just in case the phone doesn't have caller ID."

Georgia nodded and within seconds. the ringing tone buzzed over the speakers. After five or six rings, the greeting kicked in. A deep male voice said: "Please leave a message. I will answer your call shortly." The words were spoken in a typical American accent.

"This is Georgia Ross, Mr. Hamilton. Did you receive my email? We need to discuss the details of your request. Looking forward to your call or email." She gazed from one end of the conference table to the other, assessing the faces of her national security team. Again, good poker players. "Now we wait. What is next?"

"Ma'am, we have an identification on Mr. Hamilton." Adam looked at her briefly then turned his attention back to the laptop in front of him. "Give me a minute to get it loaded."

"All, let's take a quick break while Adam loads the ID." Georgia rose and waved a finger at Gracie, indicating for her to join her boss in the hall. They walked out the door together.

Gracie shook her head. "That room is full of too much testosterone."

"No kidding. I guess I hadn't paid much attention before."

"I don't remember being in the Sit Room with President Gardner."

"You're right," Georgia said. "He handled everything in the Oval Office."

Gracie leaned in close to her boss. "I always thought that was weird. There's not much technology in there."

"Exactly," Georgia chortled. "He hardly looked at email. Too much bother, I guess."

"Let's face it . . . some males in your office have taken the easy road."

"You're absolutely correct. But it is what it is." Georgia smiled at her chief of staff. "In this case, I have a hunch everything will turn out fine."

"Georgia, we're ready." Emmett motioned everyone back to the room.

They returned to their chairs at the table. An ID of some sort appeared on the television screen.

"Ma'am, this is the University of Virginia employee ID for Alexander Muhammad Harron, an associate professor in the English department for five years. He was born in New York City so he's a U.S. citizen." Adam zoomed to the photo on the ID. "This man is our terrorist."

She studied the photo. In this one the man was clean-shaven and somewhat attractive, if one liked the brooding male look. "Any clue why he's doing this? I wonder where it got the fake U.S. passport."

"We're still working on that. Agents are almost to his house in Charleston. He's married with one young child."

"This man isn't what I've pictured as a lone wolf terrorist." Georgia tapped a pen on the table. "Although university professors have a long history as liberals, that doesn't automatically translate to terrorism. I bet there's more to this story."

"We should know something shortly," Jim added. "Agents are also arriving at the university."

"Good," Georgia replied. "Emmett, any response to the email?"

He shook his head.

"What terrorist events, other than 9/11, have we had with commercial airplanes?" Georgia suffered a wave of doubt. She had no experience with these situations. Daniel hadn't dealt with one like this so she'd had no opportunity to observe how all the intelligence agencies operated together when in the same conference room.

Adam nodded at her.

"You have any update for us?"

"Ma'am, we may have caught a break."

"Oh, yeah?" Ed said.

"What kind of break?" Georgia had no idea what had set off Ed— ignoring him was the safest course of action right then. Maybe it was dealing with a female boss. That wouldn't be a huge stretch for anyone's imagination.

"We have law enforcement on board." Adam used the penlight

pointer to highlight the name on the passenger list, now displayed on the television screen. "We have a Texas county sheriff in seat 24D. He's flying with his wife and two children."

"This is good," Emmett whispered.

"Who is he?" Georgia asked, eager to learn about a possible positive twist for this event.

"All we know is that he's on vacation with his wife and kids, twin thirteen year old girls," Adam explained. "His name is Troy Nelson and he's been sheriff of Brazos County Texas for nine years."

"I need to talk with him," Georgia said. "Can't we get him to the back of the plane and patch into one of the phones the flight attendants use?"

Jim raised his eyebrows while gazing at Adam. "That's entirely possible, right?"

"Of course, it's possible," Ed exclaimed. "But one of us should talk to him—someone with experience in these actions."

"I will talk to the sheriff, Ed." Georgia made a mental note to schedule a talk with Ed down the road if his current attitude continued. "Please set it up with the pilot and the head flight attendant who can contact him and escort him to the back of the plane. Mr. Hamilton won't see anything since he's in first class."

"Yes ma'am," Adam replied. "Give me five minutes." He rose and stepped out of the room with his cell phone to his ear.

Ed glared into space while Emmett grinned and Gracie performed a discreet fist pump. Nothing was lost on Georgia before she trained her eyes on the monitor in front of her. Even in a potential national crisis, the personalities of the individuals involved played a big role in how the event rolled along—so many things to think about and so much to analyze. Surely, the federal government could do a better job when dealing with these types of security issues.

"Madam President, we have an email reply from Mr. Hamilton." Emmett punched on his keyboard and the email appeared on the TV screen.

The email read: "Mrs. Ross—You still have two hours. The countdown starts now--7:35 p.m. eastern time."

"This guy has some nerve," Ed said.

"Not sure I agree with you on that, Ed." Helen had said little while in the Sit Room. Georgia wondered why. She glanced at Gracie who was grinning and wiggling her eyebrows.

"Why is that, Helen?" Georgia said.

"Come on, does this guy make any kind of logical sense as a full blown terrorist?" She raised her hands in front of her chest. "I know, self-radicalizing and all that. The guy was born here, was educated here, has a good job, and a family. My hunch is that this is something other than straight terrorism. This guy needs money. And he's desperate."

Adam walked in before anyone responded. "Ma'am, we'll have Sheriff Nelson on the line in just a minute. Jim, would you queue up the call?"

Jim punched on the keyboard in front of him and a buzzing tone followed by a female voice blared over the Sit Room speakers.

"Madam President, er, Mrs. Ross, uh . . . this is Ginger Foster, I'm the head flight attendant on flight 89."

"Yes, Ginger, this is President Ross. Thanks for keeping your cool and helping with this event. Is Sheriff Nelson with you?"

"He's here. I'm handing the phone to him."

"Hello, this is Troy Nelson."

"Sheriff, it's a pleasure to meet you. This is President Ross."

"President of the United States Ross?"

"Yes sir, that's the one." Georgia smiled. She loved this man's southern accent. "Sheriff, we have a situation on board your flight that requires the talents of a law enforcement officer such as yourself." She recited the executive summary of the event, ending with the promise that the gun in the cockpit could be provided to him.

"Ma'am, I'm a Marine and a Texas sheriff. I don't need a gun in a situation like this. This terrorist guy teaches English at a college? Not to worry. Do you want him dead or alive?"

Chapter Eight

Wednesday, January 28

IT WAS SEVEN A.M. and not quite dawn. Candy and John waited in a monochrome four-door sedan parked on the side of a four-story office building along Massachusetts Avenue NW. She sipped black coffee and scanned the area around the vehicle. They were three blocks down the street from a gate to the U.S. Naval Observatory. The U.S. vice president's official residence was on the grounds at Number One Observatory Circle. Since Mrs. Gardner had left only yesterday for Colorado, there was no way that President Ross had already moved into the White House Residence. This was still her home until the moving truck arrived.

The lady had too much class to move so quickly into the White House. Thus they waited. Candy guessed this would be the street the Secret Service would take to drive the president to the West Wing.

"What do cops typically do when they're on surveillance?" John glanced at her while also drinking coffee.

"I guess that depends on how friendly they are."

"Huh?" John pushed his back against the car door to face her more directly. "What do you mean friendly?"

"Oh, you know," she said as she raised her arms with two fingers of each hand making quote marks. "Friendly."

"What?"

Candy placed a hand over her mouth to hide a giggle. John was one perplexed man. Not necessarily good but she did enjoy playing with him. "I'm teasing. Nothing ever happened with any of my partners. Surveillance is generally tedious and you eat crap food out of boredom."

"Sounds like all the business meetings I used to attend. Boring as hell and always turkey/cheddar sandwiches for lunch. "

"Yep, same thing. Sitting in a car is boring until we see some action. I guess that depends on when President Ross goes to work. Once she moves to the White House we'll see nothing."

"I figure we have today and tomorrow at the most to follow her."
John shrugged.

"While we're sitting here being bored, we might as well figure
out how we're going to fake a photo of a dead president so Harry will
transfer the last five million." Personally, Candy thought there was no
chance in hell of Harry transferring the money without absolute proof
of the demise of Georgia Ross. And since they weren't killing her, the
funds were as good as gone. But she didn't want to say that to John.
He had a strange sense of obligation to Harry since he'd agreed to
eliminate President Ross. She had to get him one hundred percent
focused on screwing Harry.

"I have a photo program on my laptop. We could download a
picture of her and add blood and a bullet hole to it." John had a
hopeful look as he finished his coffee and stowed the cup in the take-
out bag.

"Don't you suppose Harry might expect to hear about a Ross
assassination on the news?" Candy kept her focus on a black SUV
coming toward them and noticed it was followed by another identical
vehicle. "We can't fake the news."

"You're right. We'll figure this out."

A third vehicle came into view. Candy placed a hand on John's
thigh. "Bend over in the seat. Three SUV's are coming toward us."
Thankfully, he didn't question her and bent down. Yay, she'd guessed
the correct street. She counted to fifty then rose, patted his shoulder.
"We're good. We need to follow those vehicles that just passed—at a
safe distance."

John looked behind him for a moment and turned on the ignition.
"Cool. I've never followed a car before." He backed out and turned
right onto the empty street.

"Don't go all Starsky and Hutch on me . . . you're simply driving
behind another car. Okay? Keep several car lengths behind that last
SUV. We don't want to draw their attention."

"Got it." His eyes gleamed.

"Good." What had she unleashed? Candy pulled her smartphone
out of her purse and clicked on the GPS app. She figured they were
headed toward the White House, but she wanted to be sure.

The traffic was fairly light for a few minutes after seven. People
must start the workday later in D.C. Within a few minutes, the first
SUV drove around Dupont Circle and turned south on Connecticut
Avenue. John was speeding up. "Slow down."

"I might lose them."

"No, they're on a straight shot to the White House," she replied while patting his thigh. "Take it slow and easy and we'll casually drive by. At least we'll know what gate they go in."

"Got it. Slowing down, now," He wiggled his eyebrows. "Yes ma'am, that's me, Mr. Slow and Easy."

She chuckled. "More like Mr. Smarty Pants."

"And you love it."

Now she squeezed his thigh. "No . . . I love you."

"Thanks, babe, love you, too." John drove slowly around Dupont Circle.

"Turn right at the second street, that's Connecticut, it turns into 17th Street."

John followed directions and they soon had the SUV's in sight again. They followed at a safe distance as the sun rose over the horizon and the sky slowly turned blue, a good omen. Candy's grandmother always said that sunshine on a winter day was a clear sign of God giving his followers a break. Yeah, before things turned to shit.

She kept her eyes on the last SUV or on the map on her cell's screen. A gate to the White House grounds at Pennsylvania Street was coming up. "Slow down a bit. I bet they're gonna take this west gate inside. I want to see where the first car goes."

Sure enough, the first SUV turned left and then stopped. A uniformed guard led a dog around the vehicle while another stuck a wand underneath and followed the first guard.

"What's that last guy doing?" John said.

"Probably a mirror at the end of the wand. Checking for bombs attached to the undercarriage." The next two SUV's stopped behind the first one. The first guard waved and the gate opened. The SUV slid through and the guards worked on the next one. They drove by as the second vehicle went through the gate. "Slow down."

She tried to follow the progress of the SUV's but there were too many trees. "I can't see where they're going."

"How about a driveway to the front door of the West Wing."

"You're right," she said with a nod. "It doesn't matter. There's no way in hell we can get in there."

John sighed. "Looks that way. Where to now?"

"Let's find a gas station or a convenience store. I need a bottle of water."

"First, I need to get out of this area. The traffic is heavier here."

John executed a number of turns and headed back toward the

hotel. "There's a Power Save. I'll pull in there." He parked in front of the convenience store and they exited the car.

Candy walked directly to the cold drink case along the far wall. After grabbing a couple bottles of water, she noticed a rotating rack of books. A good mystery or legal thriller would help her relax. She grabbed one and turned the rack. Sitting in the wire rack, right before her eyes was a dog-eared copy of *All the President's Men*. Hmm . . . Watergate and Deep Throat—now she had the world's best idea.

She hurried to the front where John looked at street maps of D.C. "Come on, we need to go." She pulled the map out of his hand, slapped it on the counter with the water bottles and the two paperbacks. "How much?"

John paid and they hurried to the car without saying a word. Once inside, she opened a water bottle and took a long drink. The coldness of the water sliding down her throat helped control her excitement, although she couldn't hold back a wide grin.

"What *is* going on?" John asked.

"We need to get back to the hotel to use your computer."

"Why?"

"I've finally figured out how we're going to screw Harry Roberts and get that five million dollars."

~~*

Georgia, accompanied by a cup of coffee and a chocolate croissant, settled at her desk in the Oval Office. She checked the time—7:33 a.m. Things would be easier once she and Peter moved into the White House Residence. Hopefully that would happen tomorrow. She needed to start using the gym. All these breakfast sweets would soon add to the size of her butt.

She took a slow breath, thinking back to the prior evening—her first test as president. It had ended with a big thud. The big crisis diverted by the kick ass actions of a Texas sheriff who neutralized the terrorist with barely five words spoken. Taking a sip of her coffee, she realized how fortunate they were that this English professor wasn't a "real" terrorist, simply a son who wanted money for his mother's cancer treatment and had made a very stupid decision on his way to speak at an academic conference in Rome.

As Peter had said more than once, "you can't fix stupid." The professor had ruined his life and that of his family. Why hadn't he reached out for assistance?

It could have ended so much worse. Georgia wasn't naïve and had a hunch this was a simple test run. Could this professor have been a plant? A trial run? A test of the U.S. response to such a threat on an airplane?

The former president had ignored the country's need for increased security from domestic and foreign threats. In fact, he'd made it worse by his inaction in the Middle East. Daniel had followed along in the same vein. There hadn't been a 9/11-type attack as far as loss of lives, but every month for the last six years, something or multiple something's had happened.

One thing for sure—Gracie poked her head in the doorway, stopping Georgia's thought.

"Do you mind if I'm early for our eight o'clock?"

"Not a problem." Georgia waved her in. "Sit next to the desk while I finish my coffee." Gracie had a look that Georgia recognized—debating whether she should speak up. "Something bothering you?"

"Not bothering me exactly. But I did find the situation last evening strange."

"Strange, huh?" Georgia had thought the exact same thing. "Okay let's compare notes like we usually do. What was odd to you?"

"That was my first time at a meeting with the FBI, CIA, NSA, and DHS. Interesting how they all meshed together. I thought the agencies had gotten better at working jointly."

"I thought they had after the Office of National Intelligence was set up in . . . what year was that?" Georgia tapped her index finger against her lips. "Hmm, probably around 2004. I think there's too much crossover of responsibilities."

"Exactly, it's like they were tripping over each other."

"Let's look into this." Georgia opened her red portfolio and jotted a note on the page headed Current Projects. "I'd like you to work with Emmett on this. I'll draw up some points and send a summary to both of you."

"Okay." Gracie turned around at a knock on the door.

"Madam President, I'm a couple of minutes early," Julie said. She had the nicest smile.

"Come on in." Georgia rose, as did Gracie, and they moved to the conversation pit as she now thought of the grouping of sofas and chairs. "Have a seat. I think it's time for me to assume a normal presidential travel schedule. What do we have coming up?"

Gracie opened a file folder. "There's a huge fundraising event on Saturday in Las Vegas and then a speech on Monday in Baltimore at the Historical Society of American Patriots."

"No fundraising events for anyone." Georgia crossed her hands in front of her to emphasize "no."

"Are you sure?" Gracie asked, clearly surprised.

"Yes, speeches are fine."

"I'm very happy you're doing the address to the country this evening." Julie had an earnest way of speaking, indicating to Georgia she took her job seriously. Thus, Georgia would keep her on as press secretary. "Ma'am, I have you booked at 9 p.m., Eastern Time. I've let everyone know to allow at least 45 minutes for your address."

Georgia chuckled. "I don't think I'll need nearly that long. I'm not that long winded. Plus, the average American doesn't have that much time to devote to a presidential talk. The have dinner to eat, homework to supervise, and baths to take. What ideas do you have thus far?"

Julie handed each of them a single document. "This is a bullet summary of the major points of the speech with support for each."

Georgia scanned the list: well wishes for President Gardner, welcome to VP Roberts, government is fully-operational, nation's security is number one focus, the usual. "Looks good. I have one more thing to add."

"Of course, ma'am, what is it?"

"I plan to file as soon as possible to run for president in the upcoming election."

"Wonderful," Julie exclaimed.

"Thank you, Lord," Gracie said to the ceiling.

"There's one more thing you need to know. I'll be filing as a Republican."

~~*

"The controller for these drones can have an incredible range." Nick stuffed another piece of toast in his mouth. They were having a late breakfast. "I say we concentrate on locations less than two miles from the Capitol."

"I agree. Wouldn't you want a clear path for the signal from the controller to the drone?"

He nodded. "It has to go through the walls of the Capitol itself so I bet he'd want a clear shot from his position to the Capitol. Less interference."

"That means he'd probably have a better signal being higher up, right?"

Nick crunched on a piece of crispy bacon and considered her words. A slow burn of excitement ignited in his gut. "Open your laptop. We need to look at a good map of D.C. We were wasting our time driving around yesterday."

She hurried to her desk and worked at the computer. "I've got one." She brought the laptop to the dining table. "Look at this." She pointed to the Capitol complex.

He drew a circle around the area with his finger. "Lots of possibilities."

"Don't you think the shooter would first look at locations open to the public?"

He looked at the map again. A public building with stories . . . bingo. "Union Station has a clear shot to the Capitol."

"That's what I'm thinking."

Nick stood and pulled his jacket off the back of a dining chair. "Come on. Let's find the spot where the shooter controlled that drone."

Within ten minutes, they were approaching Dupont Circle in Nick's SUV. "I'll take Massachusetts Avenue since it goes by Union Station."

"Might as well."

They rode in silence and made good time as the traffic lights were sequenced and they sailed through most of them. Nita again kept track of their progress using her phone.

"You're addicted to that GPS app," he teased.

"No, I just like to know how close we're getting. Just a couple more lights."

"Right. Union Station should be on the left." He pulled into the parking garage, pulled a ticket, and entered. "Help me keep oriented as to which side faces the Capitol."

"I'll figure it out as we go."

Once on the top floor, Nita said she knew the correct side and he made one turn to the left then parked in a space in the middle of the outside row. "Let's take a look." They both exited and went to the front of the SUV. The cement wall came to his waist. And sure enough, the U.S. Capitol loomed in the distance.

"This would be a perfect spot to control the drone. Nothing obstructing the signal until it reaches the Capitol. I bet it's less than a mile."

Nita nodded. "If the shooter didn't use this spot then he should have."

"If he didn't then we have a bigger problem. Look at all those roofs around the Capitol. Those are all federal buildings."

"Right." She leaned her butt against the wall. "The shooter would have to know someone to make his way to a roof or could have snuck in. Would that be easy in a government building?"

"I hope not." He tunneled the fingers of one hand through his hair. "It will be a ton of work to check out all those buildings."

"I think we should stay on track. The shooter is someone hurt by Gardner . . . someone who doesn't live here, and would use a location with easy access."

"I agree," he said. "Since we're here, let's talk to security." He pointed a finger at a nearby column across from where they stood. "See that camera up there?"

She nodded. "Maybe they'll show us video from it"

"If I mention I'm a reporter working on a story, I might be able to convince them." He led her to the elevator.

The garage had its own security office on the first floor. Nick hoped that would simplify things. He opened the glass door and they walked in.

"How can I help you folks?" An older gentleman with a bushy mustache and round rimless glasses manned the office. His nametag read Paul. He smiled as they reached the counter.

"Paul, I'm a reporter working on a story . . . a story about—"

"Actually, it's about my sister. She disappeared over a week ago. The last time anyone saw her was on the evening of January 20th. She loved coming here to study. Usually she'd take the metro, but that night my mom told her to take her car as it was supposed to rain. Anyway she always parked on the top floor of the garage facing the Capitol building, uh, something about feng shui. I don't know." Nita giggled. "Sorry I'm talking so fast, I'm so worried about my little sister."

"We're hoping you have video cameras in the garage. We want to see if the car was parked on the top floor that night." Nick did his best to look sincere.

"We do have cameras."

Nita swayed against Nick. "Oh, thank God. May we see the video?"

Paul glanced from side to side. No one else was in the office that Nick could see. "We don't usually do that kind of thing here unless you have a warrant."

"Oh, please." She leaned over the counter. "Sir, please, my mother is going to die of a broken heart if we don't find my sister." Her voice broke at the last few words.

Nick had no idea Nita was such a good actress. Paul fidgeted, clearly torn as what to do. "We'll be super quick and won't tell anyone you helped us," she added.

Silence.

"Please," Nita wailed.

"All right," he said. "Come around the counter and follow me. What was the day again?"

"January 20th," Nick said.

They followed him through a door to a short hall and then he opened another door to a small room. Shelves lined two walls and a desk with a computer sat on another. The man pulled a metal chair next to the desk chair. "Ma'am, if you'll sit here, I'll pull up the video." He sat and Nick stood behind Nita.

"What time do you want to start?"

"How about 8:30?" she replied. "Maybe we can see her leaving."

"Okay, give me a minute."

While Paul searched for the right video, Nick hoped this would tell them something. He dug his cell phone out of his jacket—just in case.

"Here we go," Paul said. "I'll fast forward a bit to speed things up."

The video gave a decent view of the row of vehicles. Several spots were empty. A sports car parked and a young couple emerged and moved out of camera range.

"Can you tell if the car is parked here?"

"I'm not sure . . . it's hard to tell," Nita replied. "The light isn't very good."

A tall man walked into view and went to a dark SUV backed into the parking space. He went to the back of the vehicle and the tailgate opened. Nick squeezed Nita's shoulder.

"Could you zoom in on the vehicle that man just went to?" she said. "I think my mom's car may be on the other side of it."

He zoomed in and Nick could tell the make of the SUV. He clicked photos with his cell phone, hoping for a shot of the license plate number. The man in the back was hidden from view. Nick squeezed Nita's shoulder again. They had played this as far as they could.

"No, that's not Mom's car." Nita rose and stepped back. "Thank you so much. I guess my sister lied about where she was going that night. We need to keep looking."

"Glad I could help." Paul led them back to the entry of the

security office.

Ten minutes later they exited the garage and headed to Nita's place.

"I wish I could have gotten a picture of that guy. I wasn't fast enough."

"That's okay." Nita rubbed his shoulder. "Maybe we'll luck out with a license plate."

They made it back in record time. Once inside, Nick grabbed his laptop and phone power cord out of his duffel bag and fired up the computer on the dining room table.

"I'll download the photos so we can see them better." He glanced at Nita in the kitchen.

"I'm making coffee."

Nick imported the photos from his phone as Nita handed him a coffee mug. "I hope one of these shows the plate." He clicked on the first of four and enlarged it.

"Too high. Is that a Cadillac?"

"Looks like a Nissan Murano." The next picture appeared, blurry. "I did a lousy job of taking these."

She sat next to him. "You didn't have much time." The third photo was also blurry.

"This is the last one." He clicked on it and they both leaned toward the screen.

"That's definitely a license plate . . . with mud smeared over the number."

"I'll try to adjust it with my photo program." He clicked on an icon on the desktop then loaded the photo and began to click. The plate became a bit clearer on the bottom.

Nita pointed to the screen. "Look at that."

"I know. Damn, we're good. That's a Colorado plate."

"I'm starting to tingle," she said, shaking out her arms to the side. "You know I decided to start looking at victims from Colorado for the IRS hacking. Do you suppose this is a coincidence or a clue?"

Nick didn't want to bust her balloon, but yeah, it more than likely was a coincidence. "Hard to tell. But why on that particular night did someone from Colorado back into a parking space at a public garage with a clear view of the Capitol?"

"And why did that person open the tailgate of their vehicle and sit on it somewhere around 9 p.m.? No fireworks that evening."

Hmm, maybe this wasn't a coincidence. "That is weird."

"Weird, my ass. That guy is the shooter."

~~*

John and Candy were back in their room at the Marriott after taking a leisurely drive from the Power Save and then backtracking to visit the Lincoln Memorial and the World War II Memorial. They walked from one monument to the other and then back to the parking garage. The historical presence of both memorials put them in a somber mood. What the hell were they doing screwing around with Harry Roberts? The man was a monster.

"Right now, I'm thinking we should walk away." John once again regretted getting involved with Harry. "We should take the money we have and leave."

"Not so fast, Mister. You started this and you need to finish it," Candy said.

"Why and how?"

"Why? Because Harry should be locked up and we're going to make sure that happens. And it's worth a try to get that last five million before he's locked up."

Candy was one smart cookie. He considered her words. She was right. No more bellyaching from him. "I'm in. What's your idea?"

"First, if you were to kill President Ross, how would you do it?"

"Hmm . . . probably the easiest method would be similar to how President Reagan got shot. Walk up to her with a handgun and pull the trigger in her chest. I'd need to know her schedule and have physical access to get close to her. Plus, not go through a metal detector."

"Isn't the president's schedule on the White House website?"

"Let's look." John opened his laptop and then Googled white house dot gov. "There's a link for the schedule—nothing public today. I'll scroll forward—nothing until Saturday."

Candy jumped off the bed and stood behind him. "What's on Saturday?"

"It's a speech at a conference here in D.C.—Literacy Volunteers of the USA." He completed a search for the conference. "It's at the Dupont Circle Hilton. I've passed that hotel before. I know where it is."

Candy paced around the room for a couple of minutes. John knew enough to keep his mouth shut while she walked. She finally sat on the foot of the bed. "Okay, there are two parts to my plan. The first is telling Harry what you're planning to do—you need the five million in advance as you'll immediately leave the country after you off the president and won't have online access. You need to get your affairs sorted out before you leave."

"Do you think he'll buy that?"

"He'll be thrilled you've shared your plan with him and then salivate over the details."

"I'll need to set up a new email account."

"Not a problem. The second part of the plan is how we screw Harry."

"I say we off him."

"John, no. This is much better. Everyone will know what a terrible person he is." Candy leaned forward. "You've heard of Watergate, right?" John nodded. "I think we should act like Deep Throat did back in the seventies. We feed information to someone who's in a position to publically bring down Harry."

"I like that idea." He jumped up and hugged her then kissed the top of her head. "You have the best ideas for an ex-cop. How do we do this?"

"Things have changed since Watergate so I think we should contact either a local reporter or a political blogger. Both would have access to stuff."

John sat in the chair by the table and crossed his legs. Candy sure as hell knew how to think off that damned wall. "I like that. Why don't you do an online search this time? Start with a blogger. I figure they're more flexible than those damned liberal reporters."

She settled at the desk and started poking at the computer. John considered the future. What would happen after Saturday? Where should they go? Would Candy really go with him? He thought she would since she'd come this far, but when push came to shove, would she actually start a new life with him? And if she did, where would they live? He hadn't expected to have a life after shooting Gardner so he'd made no plans for the future. His short sightedness hadn't been a concern at the time. He closed his eyes, chastising himself for not having more faith in his future.

"John, wake up. I found a blogger."

"I'm awake," he said with a quick laugh. "What did you find?"

"The website is BetterPolitics.com and the blog I like is called The Watch Dog. It has a really cute picture of a Doberman wearing a red bowtie."

"Who's the blogger?"

"Her name is Nita Andrews. Her last blog . . . um, posted last Tuesday, talks about dumbass politicians. I like this girl."

John rose and leaned over Candy's shoulder. "Where's that blog? I want to read it." She pointed to the screen and he read every word. "I like this blogger."

"There's a 'contact me' tab so we can email her. What should we say?" Candy turned around to look at him.

He sat on the edge of the bed. "Yeah, what do we say?" He rubbed his jaw as an idea came to him. "Maybe start with a question: Would you be interested in exposing the person responsible for shooting President Daniel Garner? If so, reply to this message."

"That sounds okay. Who's it from? How about Candy Girl?"

"No, we shouldn't use our real names."

"What's the twenty-first century version of Deep Throat?" John had no clue but he knew Candy would.

"Hmm . . . Dark Horse?" she suggested.

"That's fine with me. I'll set up the email addresses first." They exchanged places at the desk. Five minutes later, he rose and gave Candy a hug as she stood by the window. "This is a good idea. Thanks for hanging with me. I wonder what this Nita person will say."

"I'm sure she'll be interested. What blogger wouldn't want the publicity and the story of the decade?"

"Send the message," John said as he backed away from Candy. "Then I'll send a message to Harry. I bet he'll be surprised." Finally they were at the beginning of the end, only three more days. "This is almost over. I think we need to talk about the future."

"The future?"

Oh, crap. He froze at the look of panic flooding Candy's face. Not exactly the reaction he'd expected from her. So, if she didn't want a future with him . . . what was she after?

~~*

Emmett checked his watch for the third time. Damn it. He hated being stood up. He sipped his drink and figured this meeting was a bust. He hadn't been at a TGIF Friday's in ages and decided to get an order of potato skins—one of his favorite snacks during football season. He could eat them before heading back to the White House for Georgia's address to the nation. She'd expect him there to oversee any last minute changes to the speech.

He ordered the skins and another vodka tonic. Might as well enjoy a couple of free hours. He told Gracie he had an appointment on the Hill and she hadn't questioned him. He checked the television above the bar as it was on closed caption. The anchor reported that the hacking of Helen Capstone's personal email account had apparently been a hoax. He chuckled. Yeah, it was a hoax all right and Georgia had managed to get Helen's server as a result. The new commander in chief had played Helen like a drum.

He felt a hand on his shoulder and slid around on the barstool. "Hello, Valerie. You're looking . . . rested."

"You as well, Emmett." She slithered onto the stool next to him, giving him a good view of the cleavage under her white coat. "What are you drinking?"

"Vodka. What would you like?" He signaled to the bartender who sauntered right over. "The lady needs a drink."

"Yes ma'am, what can I get you?" The bartender winked at her.

"Double Jack Daniels on ice, please."

"You bet." As he moved off, Valerie removed her coat, revealing a thin red sweater with a deep vee in front.

What the hell was she up to? She'd been fired from the White House two days ago and now she was sniffing around him. He didn't trust her one bit but he was curious as to why she'd called him for this "meeting." No doubt she had an agenda.

"You look happy. I guess getting fired hasn't slowed you down."

"I don't remember you ever being so straightforward." She smiled at him like a beauty queen hoping to impress the judges. Her so-called charm wouldn't work on him.

"We never did work on quite the same level with Danny, now did we?" He flashed a sarcastic smile at her. "Why did you call me?"

The bartender interrupted them with her drink and the potato skins. He put a couple on his plate and loaded them with sour cream. He popped a bite in his mouth and watched her. She sipped the drink with her pinky finger pointing north.

"I have a question for you." Valerie set the drink on a napkin. "Actually, I'm a little embarrassed to even ask you this."

Hmm, this could get interesting. "You can ask me anything. After all, we had the same employer for several years."

"We sure did." She lowered her head. "I need a job recommendation."

He wasn't sure he heard her correctly. "You need what?"

She raised her blue-eyed gaze to him and touched his knee with a light hand. "A recommendation for a new job. Being terminated by President Ross doesn't look good on my resume and Danny is in no condition to write a recommendation." She leaned forward the slightest bit and her sweater tightened over her chest, exposing a bit more of the prime double-D real estate. "Please, will you help me?"

He swallowed, hard. Jesus, it had been a long time since he'd gotten laid. His long work hours didn't allow for much funky time with the ladies. How many years had he devoted the majority of his waking hours to Danny and what Danny wanted? Too many, damn it. He deserved a break and right then Valerie might be what he needed as an entertaining distraction.

Emmett leaned forward and played with one long earring that had three red beads at the end. He then traced a finger along the vee of her sweater. "Looks like you have a fondness for the color red."

She licked her lips. "Uh-huh, red always makes me think of . . . all things hot." She picked up her drink glass. "This is a new day and I'm moving forward with my life." She drained half the glass. "Mm, I love bourbon. Those potato skins look yummy." She slathered sour cream on one and took a dainty bite.

"Let's get another appetizer. All of a sudden I'm hungry." Emmett picked up the menu, selected a couple of items, and decided he needed a glass of wine. He selected one of his favorites from the wine list and surprise, surprise, the bartender appeared. Boobs were like neon lights at a bar.

"May I get you something else, sir?"

Emmett placed the order then turned his attention back to Valerie. "What job do you need a recommendation for?"

"It's a communications position at the Northgate Foundation. They are quite the Democratic think tank these days."

"Danny talked with them a couple of times. You think you'll be happy there?"

"Come on, Emmett. Happy has nothing to do with it. I need a damned job to pay my bills." She stuck out her lower lip. "Will you help me?"

Why the hell not?

The wine arrived and the bartender made a big deal of opening the bottle. Emmett did the obligatory taste test and the wine was poured.

"Your appetizers will be right out."

Emmett raised his glass and tapped it against hers. "I'll write that recommendation letter. I ask for one thing in return."

"Of course, what is it?"

"That we never mention Danny Gardner again."

She nodded with a sly smile and that was that.

They drank their wine, ate chips with queso along with cheese sticks, and then polished off a second bottle of wine. Emmett tried but couldn't focus on why he'd ever had an issue with Valerie. She seemed like such a sweetheart as they'd shared stories and laughed about the silliness of working in the White House. Nothing meaningful was ever accomplished.

His phone rang and dinged a few times and he turned it to vibrate without looking at the calls or text messages. He was having too much fun with Valerie to care about anyone needing his attention.

She ran her hand up his thigh, ending close to his groin area. "You wanna go . . . my place? I have a full bar." Her hand moved further and brushed his dick.

Oh, God, yes.

The bartender had already given him the bill so he stood with as much dignity as he could muster and signed the tab. He helped Valerie off the barstool. She swayed then gained her drunken legs and after a couple of attempts managed to get her arms into the coat sleeves. They weaved their way to the door and quickly hailed a taxi.

It didn't take long to arrive at Valerie's townhouse. Emmett tossed cash over the front seat to the driver before pushing her out of the cab. They struggled up the front steps and managed to unlock the front door after Valerie found the key at the bottom of her purse. Once inside, she grabbed his hand and pulled him toward what looked like the kitchen.

He pulled back. "Wait, stop."

She swung around and bumped into him, her hands ending on his chest. "Stop . . . for what?"

He swallowed. *The hell with it.* Lowering his mouth to hers for a long kiss, he placed his hands under her coat and pushed it off her shoulders. She slid her arms free then allowed the coat to fall to the floor. Her arms wrapped around his neck.

"Are you sure about this?" she whispered against his lips.

"Damn straight." He ground his erection against her. "Mr. Rock says hello."

"Ooh, I need to meet Mr. Rock." She stepped back and wiggled her index finger at him. "Follow me."

His head was so cloudy right then that he'd probably trail her to the ends of the earth. With an unsteady gait, he followed her down a short hall to her bedroom. She had a very large bed. The only light in the room came from a wide screen television.

"I left my TV on. Bad Valerie, wasting energy." She tripped over something on the floor and landed on the bed. Just where he wanted her.

Emmett shrugged out of his coat and tossed it aside. He watched

Valerie as she scooted backwards so her head rested on a stack of pillows. She again wiggled her finger at him. He didn't need to be asked twice and stumbled onto the bed.

She leaned toward him and started to unbutton his shirt. "Too many clothes." She gazed past him and pointed at the TV. "Emmett, honey—look, Georgia the bitch is giving a speech."

His soggy memory *knew* Georgia being on television was important. Wasn't he supposed to be there? Damn it, he needed to get to the White House. Valerie kissed his chest and licked her way to his belt. *Fuck it, he was getting laid.*

~~*

Nita had spent all afternoon and early evening calling numbers in Colorado from her IRS hacking list. She started with last names beginning with "A" and was down to "F." She said she was looking for the owner of a black Murano involved in an accident. It was slow going and she'd not had anyone bite. Nick had left several hours ago to interview a guy in Maryland who built custom drones. He wanted to verify the accuracy of their assumption about the maximum signal distance of a controller.

She'd keep calling until Nick returned. She punched in the next phone number and within two rings, it was answered.

"May I speak to Otis Foster, please?"

"This is Otis. Who are you?" Nita smiled at the raspy voice.

"Sir, my name is Nita Andrews and I'm looking for the owner of a black Murano SUV. It—"

"Why the hell would you be asking me that?"

"You're on a list I have of Murano owners."

"Are you trying to sell me somethin'?"

"No, sir. Do you own a black SUV?"

"Hell no, too damned big for me and Mama. But my neighbor across the street does. Well, he used to, I don't know now." Nita's grip tightened on the phone in her hand.

"Why don't you know now?"

"You're nosy." Otis cackled. "He lost his house after his wife died. All caused by the damned IRS. We both got hit but he was real bad off. He moved."

"I'm sorry to hear that. Do you have a phone number for him?"

"Yah, it's around here somewhere, hold on."

She heard a couple of bangs and then muffled voices. *Please Lord, let this be the guy.*

"Mama found his card on the frig. The mobile number is 303-

555-1211." She jotted it on the list of names.

"Thank you so much." Nita realized she didn't know the name. "Would you confirm your neighbor's name, please?"

"John Smith. Gotta go, *Jeopardy* is coming on."

The line clicked off and Nita jumped out of her chair. "Oh. My. God. This is incredible." She performed a happy dance all the way to the kitchen before returning to her desk and the list of names. She flipped the pages and looked for Smith, John. And there it was. The street name was the same as Otis yet the phone number listed was different from the one Otis gave her. She keyed the number from the sheet into her cell phone and discovered it wasn't in service. This story became better and better.

She tried the mobile number from Otis and the phone rang and rang. Hmm . . . the phone was either turned off or voice mail hadn't been set up. She'd try again. The doorbell buzzed and she smiled as Nick sauntered in carrying a pizza box, a six-pack of beer, and with a backpack slung over one shoulder. He kissed her on the mouth then hurried to the dining table and set the box on it.

"Seriously, more food?" she asked, thinking all they did was eat and drink.

"I told you, I love food. We gotta eat to live. Did you read my email?" he asked as he took off his jacket.

"No, I've been calling numbers from the IRS list." She walked to her desk. "I found a man on the list with a black Murano."

"No kidding? That's great." He opened the pizza box and pulled out a piece.

"Hold on, let me get plates." Nita hurried to the kitchen and brought back paper plates and napkins. She then opened two beers and stowed the others in the refrigerator. "Now we can eat like civilized people."

Nick laughed and sat next to her at the table. "I'm starved. That guy I talked with about the drones kept going on and on. I didn't think I'd ever get out of there."

"What did he say?"

"Basically, that our assumptions are good and a device at Union Station could have controlled the drone in the House Chamber. He even showed me how a gun could be added to a drone."

Nita shook her hands in front of her. "I'm getting that tingly feeling again. My gut tells me we're on the right track."

"I agree." He raised his right hand and they high-fived. "Damn, we make a great team for investigative work."

"Yeah." Nita bit into a hot and cheesy slice of pizza while her stomach flip-flopped. Right, great investigative team. What about a great team to build a life together? She washed away the bite and the thought with a slug of beer. Why the hell was she going where no woman should go when trying to discover who shot the president? She finished the slice and decided to check her email. Carrying her beer to her desk, she plopped into her chair.

After entering her password to open the laptop, she clicked on the email icon. She had twenty-seven new emails. She scrolled through the list for anything important. One was a contact from the BetterPolitics.com website. She opened that message first:

Miss Andrews....We read your blog yesterday about dumbass politicians. It was right on. Would you be interested in breaking the story on the crazy politician who orchestrated the shooting of President Gardner? Simply reply....Dark Horse

What the hell? "Holy shit. Nick, get your ass over here and read this email." He stared at her. "Now."

Nick rolled out of the chair and stood behind her concentrating on the laptop's screen. After a moment, he pulled back from her and walked in a tight circle between the kitchen and dining room, then stopped as he faced Nita.

"Shit, what the hell?"

"Sit down. We need to discuss this." Yes, discuss like intelligent adults. Nita went to the refrigerator for two more bottles of beer. She tossed one to Nick. "Yeah, this is a surprise . . . a very cool one indeed."

"How do we know this email is legitimate? Maybe it's someone playing a joke on you."

She considered that. It could be someone, like that BigDem jerk, trying to make a fool out of her. "What would be the motivation for that? I've not had cross words with anyone in quite a while."

"Maybe it's that guy who left the nasty comments on your blog."

"I thought about that, too. I know, I should report those comments to the police."

"Couldn't hurt."

"Okay, tomorrow or Friday." She read the email again. "I'm going to reply. Dumbass politicians, huh?"

"That confirms our belief that whoever planted the drone has security for the Capitol."

"You're right." She had to admit they did make a good investigative team.

"Ask for proof . . . something related to the shooting that hasn't been made public."

"Exactly." Nita typed this reply to the message:

Dark Horse---Of course, I'm interested. But first I need proof this isn't a joke. Tell me something about the Gardner shooting that hasn't been publicized and I can verify.---Nita

She read it out loud. "How does that sound?" He nodded and she clicked Send. "It's gone."

"Now we wait." He sat again and took a pull on his beer. "Now, tell me about this person who owns a black Murano."

"An old guy named Otis Brown lives across the street from where this guy used to live." She gathered her thoughts. "The guy's name is John Smith and he lost his house after his wife died, according to Otis. I verified his name and address on the IRS hacking list. We need to hack into the Colorado DMV so we can compare the picture on this guy's driver's license to that guy on the garage video."

"And neither of us are hackers." He grinned and held up his beer bottle. "Do you want to call your guy or should I call mine?"

"You call." She wrote the address for John Smith on a notepad and handed it to Nick. She also wanted to know about this guy's house. When had he lost it? And when had his wife died? While Nick moved into the living room to call his hacker friend, Nita started an online search for the name John Smith in Denver, Colorado. Naturally, it wasn't easy as that was a common name. She finally decided to try the appraisal district for property taxes. A few minutes later she had the correct website and entered the home address in the dialog box.

John Smith was still listed as the property owner and last year's taxes were in arrears. The house wasn't cheap either. The appraised value was close to six hundred thousand dollars. John and Jessie Smith had owned it for ten years. That meant John had a good job to afford an expensive home. Maybe he'd been forced to walk away from the house, especially after his wife died. Nita searched the Denver newspaper for Jessie Smith's obituary.

"We should have a picture by Saturday morning. My guy is on vacation and gets home Friday night." Nick returned to the dining table and grabbed a slice of pizza.

"Hackers take vacations? Perhaps I should call my guy. This is taking too long."

"They're regular people. Hacking is his job." He grinned. "It's better to be thorough, my guy is the best."

"Whom does he work for?"

"The feds mostly."

Nita shook her head. Okay, she'd accept the wait. They didn't yet have a plan to divulge what they'd been learning. "Give me a few minutes. I'm looking for an obituary for John's wife." It didn't take long since she had the name. And it didn't tell her anything other than the date of death, fourteen months ago, and the funeral home. She looked again. "Damn."

"What's wrong?"

"I can't find an obituary for Jessie Smith, just a notice of death from the First Oaks Funeral Home."

"Call them."

"Great idea." Nita reached for her phone as her email program dinged. "I have a reply from Dark Horse."

"That was fast. What does it say?"

Nita's heart pounded. She glanced at Nick and he nodded as she clicked on the message and read it out loud.

"This isn't a joke. The bullet used on Gardner was a .357 Magnum. Verify that and get back to us. We'll go from there."

"Can we verify that? Notice that Dark Horse uses 'we' and 'us.' Does that mean more than one person is involved?" She watched Nick. He pressed his lips together and shook his head from side to side.

"Not sure," he said. "Maybe the shooter is trying to throw us off or he's one of those 'we' people."

"What are 'we' people?"

"People who try to be inclusive saying 'we' rather than 'I'."

"Who knows?" Or cares. She didn't give two cents whether the shooter was a "we" person or not. Right then her focus centered on how they could verify the caliber of the bullet used to shoot President Gardner. "Do you have a contact who can confirm the bullet?"

"I do. I'll need a good story as to why I'm asking." He tipped his beer bottle at her.

Several times over the past ten years, Nita had considered writing a novel, a mystery more than likely. A fiction writer couldn't create a better plot than this situation. "Say you're writing a feature piece on the history of guns used to shoot U.S. presidents."

"I like that."

She liked it, too. Maybe she should start a book. How hard could it be? "I have a concern though. If Dark Horse ends up being or knowing the real shooter, shouldn't we go to the authorities at some point?"

"Yeah, that thought has crossed my mind. Let's see how things play out and then decide."

"We don't want to get on the wrong side of the feds with a silly story." Although in her bones, she knew Dark Horse was legitimate— woman's intuition or something.

"I'll call my guy first thing in the morning."

"Why not now?"

"Because he's not the kind of guy I can call right now."

Nita frowned then jumped from her desk chair and headed to the living room. "I just remembered, President Ross is giving her first address to the nation tonight."

"You're right." Nick followed her and plopped on the sofa while Nita clicked the remote. The speech was just starting.

The camera followed the president as she walked to the podium with Vice President Roberts next to her. Once she stood behind it, the vice president moved to the side and out of view.

Georgia smiled at the camera and took an obvious calming breath. "My fellow Americans, this is quite the historic occasion this evening. I believe this is the first time a U.S. president has given a national address on television in the Blue Room of the White House. Isn't this a lovely setting? Just so you know, that's a painting of Thomas Jefferson behind me."

"That's a different start," Nick commented dryly. Nita punched him on the arm.

"Shush, listen."

"And the elephant in the room is that this is the first address to the nation by a female president. Yes, it's true. I am the first female President of the United States. The circumstances that created this situation are difficult. President Daniel Gardner was shot in the House Chamber while giving his third State of the Union address one week ago. President Gardner, the First Lady, and their family have returned to their home state of Colorado where the president can receive the medical care he needs. We pray for his speedy recovery."

Nita nudged Nick in the side with her elbow. "Look at the way her eyes moved to the side at that last sentence."

"Huh?"

"She's lying. Gardner won't recover."

"That confirms what Dr. Willis said." Nick patted her thigh. "This whole situation sucks."

The president continued. "I want to assure you that the federal government is fully operational and . . ."

Nita tuned out the president's speech as it sounded like the usual political dribble—everything is fine and we're working hard for you and your family to stay safe and have a job. Whatever. Rather than listening to President Ross, she went over the progress in their investigation and made a mental list of what she needed to do tomorrow: call the Denver funeral home, more online research on John Smith, list of major players in Capitol who disagreed with Daniel Gardner, reply to Dark Horse after Nick confirms the bullet, and write another blog on—

She focused again on the president's speech.

". . . and I do have an announcement. I will be filing the necessary paperwork to run for President of the United States. I realize this is a late start but I hope to catch up quickly."

"No one will be surprised by that," Nick said.

"Also, I will be filing as a Republican candidate. Once I'm an official candidate, I'll discuss why I'm changing party. I realize this is most unusual so I do want to give everyone a clear explanation for my decision and my vision. Good night and God bless the United States of America."

"Holy moly, turning Republican is a huge surprise." Nita scrambled off the couch and went to get the last two beers and another slice of pizza.

"I guess that means Harry Roberts won't be her running mate." Nick had followed her.

"Do you suppose he'll run against her?"

~~*

Harry had finally returned home two hours after Georgia's speech. His wife was asleep so he went to his study for a nightcap. He poured scotch in his favorite crystal glass and sat in his easy chair. He had much to think about. First and foremost was filing to run for president, as a Democrat.

He was so damned excited he nearly giggled like a girl. Ah, life was good, good, and good. Georgia Ross had solved his problem like butter melting in a hot skillet by saying she'd run as a Republican. Neither party had any decent candidates. Danny had been the assumed Democratic candidate and a group of idiots were on the Republican side. Oh, yes, this would change everything. Roberts vs. Ross—bring it on!

His life was getting close to perfect for a change—close to everything he had imagined when he'd first entered politics. Then his heart thudded. Perfect except for that damned contract with John Smith. He rose and grabbed his personal tablet out of his briefcase. He had to try again to stop John, whatever the cost.

Lady luck was singing his tune—his inbox held an email from John.

VP Roberts....I assume your needs have changed since becoming VP. No problem. Contract is off. However, price is still the same. Transfer $5 million to same bank by noon tomorrow. Otherwise, feds will walk you to prison....John

Bastard! Who did he think he was?

Harry downed a swallow of scotch. Did he care about John? No. Hell no. He wanted to be done with him. John had served his purpose by eliminating Danny from the Oval Office. Although the notion of blackmail soured his stomach, he couldn't take a chance. John was a loser anyway. Who allowed their identity to be stolen due to hacking of the IRS website? Losers, that's who.

Harry transferred the money and replied to the email with "Done"—good riddance. Perhaps it would be wise to delete this email account as well. He didn't need to leave a trail or whatever. He snickered and reached for his glass, so much ahead.

Sweet Georgia Ross was going to get spanked like a nasty little girl in the national election. She had no idea what she was up against. Poor bitch.

Chapter Nine

Thursday, January 29

GEORGIA WALKED TO HER desk in the Oval Office and plopped in the chair. After last night's speech, she finally felt like she belonged here. Gracie had left for the ladies' room giving her a few minutes of solace after their intense meeting discussing Georgia's run for the presidency. Yes, she was far behind in getting a campaign organized but they could handle it. In fact, maybe all this being late to the party could work to her advantage. She had an idea she'd discuss later in the day with her new campaign director. Every once in a while, things did work quickly in Washington.

Emmett poked his head in the door. "Am I fired?"

She laughed. "No, but I may put you on probation." She motioned for him to join her. He sat in the chair in front of her desk.

"I'm sorry I missed your address last night." His head was down, no doubt studying the carpet.

"What happened?"

He lifted his gaze to his boss. "I got food poisoning. I ate Chinese for lunch and a few hours later it hit me and I went home. I'm sorry. I spent all evening in the bathroom."

She wasn't quite sure she believed him, something about the way his mouth curled. But she'd accept his excuse and move forward. They had much work ahead of them. "You're feeling okay now?"

He nodded. "Still a little queasy but I'll make it."

"Good. Take it easy today."

Gracie hurried back into the office. "Good morning, Emmett. We missed you last night."

"Yeah." He rose and headed to the conversation pit.

Georgia followed him and sat in her usual chair. Gracie settled across from Emmett. This meeting was a first for the three of them. "As you know, this is the fourth year in Daniel's presidency and it's now under my custody. I realize a year isn't a long time in terms of Washington politics. However, it's important to me to have at least two legislative initiatives for this last year of the term."

"Good idea," Emmett said. "I assume you already know the initiatives you want to support."

"Correct. Although I realized from the summary you gave me that a draft bill hadn't been written for tax reform, that is one of the issues." Georgia focused on Emmett. "Frankly, I'm surprised President Gardner would tell the nation that a tax reform bill had been written when the major policy points hadn't even been vetted."

"I'm sorry about that. I didn't know myself until you asked for the draft." Emmett shrugged. "That's how Danny rolled. I guess he was finally concerned that none of his campaign promises had been addressed."

"I'll need a copy of that summary." Gracie glanced at Emmett then she spoke to Georgia. "What's your second issue?"

"It's another tough one—beefing up the military. We need to increase our active enlistment by at least 150,000 men and women. The former president reduced the enlistment to a dangerous level and Daniel did nothing to change that. It's as important as tax reform." Georgia blew out a breath and gazed at her two most trusted advisors. "I'm officially requesting your help. We don't have much time to make *real* progress."

"Madam President, you have my one hundred and fifty percent cooperation. I agree with your two policy issues." Emmett's gaze focused on Gracie as he spoke. "I'd like to be in charge of the military enlistment. I assume this includes hardware as well."

Georgia nodded, a swirl of excitement pushed through her chest down to her abdomen. "You'll need to start from scratch as to the major points."

"Not a problem," Emmett said.

That was a relief. Maybe she could make this a meaningful year for the American people and create real progress for what mattered— easier personal taxes and a safer nation were good starting points.

"I'll work on the tax reform bill." Gracie's tone revealed a no-nonsense attitude. "Did Jeff do any serious work on this?"

"He worked with Valerie, whatever that means," Emmett said with a straight face. "He's a good guy so I'm sure he'll give you the details of what he has."

Gracie nodded. "Georgia, what's your bullet list for tax reform?"

She chuckled. "Let's start with what Emmett gave me. I'll have Betty send you my notes. That will fill in all the details. Basically, I'm in favor of a flat tax and a one-page tax return. I am willing to listen to arguments for a consumption tax. Maybe we can design a hybrid of the two. Also, make sure it includes an option for elimination of the payroll tax. We'll need a draft bill within a week. Get whomever you need to help with the language." Georgia rose and grabbed a glass of ice water from her desk. Gracie and Emmett seemed to be working together and that pleased her.

"What are you smiling at?" Gracie teased as Georgia settled back in the chair.

"Actually, I was being quite selfish." She wasn't about to share her real thoughts with them. "Peter and I will have our first night in the White House Residence this evening and that means I can sleep an extra thirty minutes in the morning."

"Awesome," Emmett said. "Living onsite will make your life a whole lot simpler."

"That's what I'm hoping." Georgia turned as Betty opened the door and stepped in the office.

"Madam President, I hate to interrupt but your next appointment is here."

"That's fine, we're done here." She smiled as Gracie and Emmett rose, wondering how she could be behind when it wasn't quite ten o'clock. At least the Oval Office ran on a tight schedule. "Let's get back together on Monday. Betty can put you on my calendar."

They hurried out and Adam Martinez walked in. Betty closed the door.

"Madam President, thank you for seeing me on such short notice." Adam sat on the sofa to Georgia's right. "Good speech last evening."

"Thanks. It's good to have the first one over." She knew he hadn't travelled to the White House to review her politics. "You have something to discuss?"

"We have a new development in our investigation of President Gardner's shooter."

"Wonderful. I've been frustrated we haven't yet had an arrest."

"Yes ma'am. As you know, we look at the event from multiple perspectives. We're concentrating on the drone as we believe it will lead to the shooter."

That made sense to Georgia. "Of course."

"We believe that whoever planted the drone in the House Chamber either works in the Capitol or used a valid ID from someone who does work there."

"That's what I've concluded as well. The drone didn't walk in by itself and the security is simply too strict."

"Yes ma'am. We're reviewing all the Capitol building video for eight hours before the start of President Gardner's address. It's possible the drone was planted in such a way that the normal security check by the Capitol Police didn't catch it. Or, it was planted after the last check."

"With either option, we have a problem."

"Yes ma'am, we believe a federal employee is involved in this assassination attempt." Adam shifted on the sofa. "We're concentrating on the flow of traffic around the House Chamber and tracking individuals throughout the rest of the building."

"At least we know everyone in the House Chamber that evening didn't pull the trigger."

"Anyone in that room could have hired the person who pulled the trigger." Adam stated the obvious.

"You're right." Georgia hadn't focused on that. "Could someone there have used a cell phone or small tablet to control the drone?"

"That's part of our current theory. We're checking all the cell traffic and WiFi usage in the building. Remember whoever did it, successfully hid their tracks by using Betty's computer to control the drone."

"I guess that means you're focusing on people who have technical knowledge."

"Which eliminates about every elected person in the chamber."

Georgia chuckled. "We have other talents. By the way, is there video of the chamber before the State of the Union?"

"Unfortunately, it was down for three hours in the middle of that afternoon for routine maintenance before the speech."

"Perfect time to plant a drone."

He nodded. "As you know, all this takes time. I'm sorry I don't have the name of the shooter yet."

"I'd rather you take all the time needed. There's no need to rush to an incorrect conclusion." She had personally questioned hasty and haphazard decisions made by Daniel and the former president that had left the country in a less than desirable state. The Democrats had agreed completely to those decisions—another reason why she had decided to switch parties.

"Thank you, this makes my job easier." Adam actually smiled. It looked good on him.

"Please keep me up to date with what you find."

"Yes ma'am. There is one more item."

"Oh?" And, now the hammer would fall—the real reason for this visit to the Oval Office by the Director of the FBI on a Thursday morning in late January.

"Ma'am," he said with a pained look on his face. "Damn, I hate this."

"What?" Georgia had no idea what was on his mind. But damned sure, he needed to spit it out.

"This wasn't a big deal while you were vice president, I didn't report to you then." Adam rubbed his jaw and his lips thinned for a moment. "But now . . . I feel obligated to tell you."

"Tell me what?"

"Ma'am, the FBI is conducting an undercover operation involving your husband."

"What?" Georgia had no idea what he was talking about. "Peter . . . in an undercover operation? That doesn't sound like my husband."

"It gets more complicated. Mr. Ross is helping us with a situation that focuses on the money laundering activities of Elizabeth Gardner."

Georgia's eyebrows went straight to the ceiling and her mouth dropped to the floor. "Elizabeth Gardner . . . Daniel's mother?"

"Yes ma'am." Adam blew a long breath. "We received a tip over a year ago about Mrs. Gardner meeting in San Diego with a member of the Los Gulf Cartel. That led to enlisting your husband's help with a—"

Georgia raised her hand. "Don't give me the details. I'm sure Peter will tell me in due time and I don't want to lie saying I didn't know."

He smiled slowly and rose. "I understand, ma'am. Thank you for your time today. I'll be in contact when I have something to report."

She rose as well and they shook hands. "Thank you, Adam, for everything."

He left and she walked around the desk and stared out of the windows behind it. A long, drawn-out sigh escaped as she slid her hands into the pockets of her tailored slacks. *What the hell was next?*

~~*

Nita started the day with a cup of coffee and zero enthusiasm for her usual Friday blog. This was unlike her and she wanted to scream. She couldn't even complain to Nick as he'd left thirty minutes ago to talk with his contact in the FBI. She crossed her fingers praying he could obtain verification of the bullet caliber without soliciting unwanted attention as to why he was asking. Now was the time for Nick-the-smooth-talker to shine.

She looked out the window behind her desk and noticed the sky. The bright sunshine of Tuesday was transforming into steel gray clouds and the wind swirled bits of trash along the middle of the street. The early morning news reported the approaching winter storm would dump a few more inches of snow on Saturday. At least the government wouldn't cancel the workday since the snow would fall on the weekend. Turning back to her desk, she thought about federal workers and remembered the research she'd done last year.

Maybe she could use the storm as a lead-in to all the benefits enjoyed by federal workers. She remembered the dust kicked up with the former president and the Affordable Care Act and the exclusion of federal employees from its mandates. Her personal insurance premiums under the ACA were horrendous, paying for services she didn't yet need, like maternity care and pediatric care. The medical insurance situation was a cesspool of corruptness she didn't have the stomach to think about right then.

Something that had bothered her was the federal employee union—the American Federation of Government Employees or AFGE. It had members from all areas of government and at every federal agency. Why the hell did federal employees need a union? In fact, labor unions were outdated and no longer needed to protect workers. The world had changed considerably in the last 150 years. From a long ago college course, she remembered the story of a 1911 fire at a clothing factory in New York that had killed over a hundred women. It had been an awful thing to happen. This was a good blog subject— Were Labor Unions Outdated in the Twenty-First Century?

Nita reviewed her online file of research and jotted a few thoughts on her notepad. For the next hour, she drafted the blog and was satisfied with the result. She'd review it Friday morning before publishing it.

She checked her email, no message from Dark Horse. Not that she had expected one. He or she or they were waiting on her, and she was waiting on Nick. He should be back in a couple of hours. In the meantime, she had calls to make.

The nice lady at the First Oaks Funeral Home in Denver couldn't provide much information, privacy laws and all. She did disclose to Nita, in a soft and sympathetic voice, that a service had not been held for Mrs. Jessie Smith and that the body had been cremated per the family's instruction. And, yes, the ashes were buried in a mausoleum on their premises. That was all.

Not one to stew over a dead end, Nita initiated a search for John

Smith using one of those paid services for instant background checks. Why hadn't she thought about this before?—because she wasn't a damned detective or a real investigator.

Entering the information she knew—name and address—she provided a credit card number for a full report. While she waited for it to be compiled, she decided to do additional online research of the IRS hacking scandal. Maybe John Smith had been mentioned in a news story. The scandal had received tons of press. On her notepad, she listed the big news channels. She'd check each website for stories and videos associated with John Smith.

Doing research like this was time consuming. After an hour she found a story on CNN with a video interview of John Smith from Denver, Colorado. The tall, bearded man appeared to be upset at the sight of a female reporter and a camera as he walked on a sidewalk in a residential area.

"Mr. Smith, you were one of the citizens hacked by the IRS, correct?"

Mr. Smith stopped walking and nodded. "Yes."

"How has that impacted you? Anything that's been negative?" The reporter shoved the microphone close to his face; he didn't back away.

"Negative?" His face knotted in anger. "You want to know if my most personal information being hacked from the IRS computers has been a negative experience for me?"

The reporter stood her ground. "Yes sir, I do."

"Hell, yes, it's been negative. I've lost everything." Then he lost it and jabbed a finger at the reporter. "Damned IRS and damned President Gardner. They're all incompetent." He turned around and walked in the opposite direction. The reporter ended the spot with a "back to you in the studio."

John Smith was one angry dude. Nita couldn't blame him. She played the video again and couldn't tell if he was the same man as in the Union Station garage video. That guy wore a ball cap and was clean-shaven.

She reviewed the background report on John Smith sent to her email address. What a joke. It didn't tell her anything she didn't already knew, except he had no criminal record. She'd wasted her money.

Damn. Her progress on identifying the shooter seemed to hit one brick wall after another. Maybe this Dark Horse would be the key. She rose and padded to the kitchen for more coffee. The house was quiet.

How long before Nick would return?

~~*

Nick's legs jiggled up and down as he waited for his "contact." He had no doubt Nita would be royally pissed if she ever learned the contact's identity.

Why did Nick keep lying to her?

Because he had to. He sipped a black coffee and pulled his coat around him. Damn, snow was forecast and it was getting colder, the wind licked at his ears. He waited.

A couple of minutes later his contact arrived and sat next to him on the bench near the Texas column on the World War II Memorial. The memorial and bench were one of Nick's favorite spot's in D.C.

"How are you, Nick?"

"Good. How's the FBI?"

"Busy. Why did you want to see me?"

"Adam, I have something to share with you." Nick squeezed his eyes tight before he began to tell the FBI Director what he and Nita had been doing the last week without providing the name Nita had uncovered. No way would he screw up some poor guy's life without absolute proof. He prayed she'd forgive him for not telling her the truth about his contact.

"You're telling me Nita received an email from this Dark Horse and used the caliber of the bullet shot at President Gardner as the proof that he-she-they knows the shooter's identity?"

"Actually, the email related to unveiling the dumbass politician who orchestrated the shooting."

"Not the actual shooter?" Adam scowled.

Nick shook his head, feeling like an idiot. "Sorry, I did a lousy job of explaining. But can you confirm for me the bullet used to shoot President Gardner was a .357 Magnum?"

Adam turned his head away from Nick and toward the pond. He was quiet for what seemed like hours but it was only a minute or two. Nick's legs began to jiggle again.

"I can confirm that's the caliber." Adam hadn't changed the direction of his gaze. "I think this is a silly hoax—someone is playing an elaborate joke on your friend. The caliber is a lucky guess. If nothing solidifies from your end in two days, I'll check into this Dark Horse just to be safe." He studied Nick. "Fair enough?"

"All right." Nick breathed easier. They had two more days to investigate. He rose with Adam. "By the way, how's Aunt Carolyn? Haven't seen her since Christmas dinner. I miss her cooking."

Adam smiled. "She's just fine. This has been a busy month for her at work. I'll mention we need to get back into the habit of Sunday dinners again."

"I'd like that." They shook hands and walked in opposite directions.

Nick smiled as he drove back to Nita's house. She had no idea that the Director of the FBI was dating his aunt, had been doing so for three years. They had both lost a spouse, had no children, and were dedicated to their jobs. Nick loved his aunt and had developed a soft spot for Adam as he made his aunt happy. Crap, he hoped he hadn't screwed up everything by asking an out of line question.

The traffic was light so he drove back to Nita's house in record time. His stomach growled as he exited his SUV. Maybe they should go to the grocery store. He let himself in using the house key she'd given him that morning.

"Honey, I'm home," he yelled as he closed the front door. He walked through the main floor and found Nita at her desk. "Hey, babe."

She pushed back in the chair. "How did it go?"

"Good. We have confirmation of the caliber." He stopped in front of her desk. "Dark Horse is the real deal."

Nita did a fist pump. "I knew it. That's awesome. Who confirmed it for you?"

He knew she'd ask. "You know I can't identify my source."

"Why not?"

"Nita!"

"All right, never mind." She grinned at him and moved back to the desk. "I'll email Dark Horse with the caliber and ask for the next step."

"That sounds like a plan." He rubbed his stomach. "You up to going to the grocery store? I feel like grilling a couple of steaks."

"Sure, I need to stock up since it's gonna snow over the weekend."

~~*

John massaged Candy's shoulders as she sat next to him on the foot of the bed. She'd been stressed since they'd sent the last email to that blogger last night. And when he'd again mentioned their future earlier, she'd gone all bug-eyed and had taken a long nap. He'd actually gone on a walk on the streets around the hotel to clear his head. She didn't even know he'd left. But the time was well spent; he now knew what he had to do.

Candy sagged against him. "That feels so good."

He kissed the side of her neck. "Babe, we need to talk."

She pulled away from him and butt scooted backwards to rest her back against the pile of pillows. "I know."

"We need to decide what we do next."

"What do you want to happen?" Candy stared directly at him giving no hint of her own thoughts.

John opened his mouth and no words formed on his tongue. He rubbed his jaw. Did he have the wherewithal deep in his soul to tell this woman the truth? His feelings had developed over a matter of days. Maybe it was his age—he was at the half-century mark—or maybe it was that he wanted to . . . no, needed to make an emotional connection with another. He hadn't imagined he'd have a future after shooting Gardner and now, a week later, he couldn't think about anything else.

He tried again and blurted out his words. "I want forever. I want you, and me, together . . . forever."

Tears began to trail down Candy's cheeks. "I was afraid you didn't want me anymore," she sobbed. He joined her on the bed and pulled her into his arms, holding her close. He brushed back her hair and kissed her temple. "Ah babe, I want you even more. Please don't cry."

She cried more. "I'm . . . I'm so sorry. La . . . last night when you said we needed to talk about the future you had such a look on your face." She buried her head against his shoulder. He rubbed her back for a while and pulled back from her, cupping her chin with his hand. "I'm sorry about my face. I guess that's what I look like when I have something serious to talk about." He kissed her mouth with the touch of a feather and rubbed her arms. "Better now?"

She rubbed her eyes, smearing mascara on her cheeks, and moved to the side of the bed. "I'm going to the bathroom."

While she was out of the room, John grabbed a bottle of white wine out of the mini-bar and poured two glasses. He'd always told Jessie that serious talking always went easier when one's hands were busy and smoking was out of the question. He expected the conversation they were about to have would define the rest of his life. No pressure.

The bathroom door opened and Candy emerged. Her face was clean of mascara and she was smiling with glossy lips. He figured that was a good sign. "Wine—very nice, Mr. Smith." She sat at the table and picked up a wine glass. "May I make a toast?"

He retrieved his glass and grinned. Things were starting to look okay. "Yes ma'am."

She gazed directly at him, their eyes meeting and acknowledging each other. She raised her glass. "May we have a long and healthy life together, wherever it may take us. We haven't been a couple very long but . . . our relationship is a keeper."

John sighed, happier than he'd been in years. They tapped glasses and drank. "Where would you like to go from here?"

"Have you considered how we'll get there?"

"Fly?"

"Do you think it's safe flying with your current driver's license? It's a Colorado one, right?"

He nodded, completely understanding where she was going. "You're right. We can't trust Harry. The jerk could have given my name to the police. What do we do?"

"I wasn't a cop for nothing. I know a guy who can get us new DL's and passports."

John slapped his forehead with his hand. "Thank God you're with me, I'd never think about that."

"You don't have a devious mind like me." She winked at him. "We can take photo's with my cell phone and then I can email them to my friend and transfer the funds to him. You can do a wire from that bank of yours, right?"

"Is that safe? Can it be traced?"

"Where's the bank?"

"The Cayman Islands."

She shrugged. "At this point, we have to take a chance. The guy I know is pretty sophisticated. He probably has an account in the Caymans as well."

"Okay . . . where are we going and when? Can you just leave your house and your family in Pennsylvania?" John had nothing to leave. Jessie was gone and they'd not had any children. No family or friends who cared two cents about him. His stomach churned, that fact was depressing as hell.

"I told my friend Sally when she left Las Vegas not to worry about me for a couple of weeks. Once we get to where we're going, I'll deal with Pennsylvania." She leaned forward and squeezed his hand on the table. "Let's take a couple of pictures of each of us then I'll email my friend. He'll be quick if we make it worth his while."

John rose. "Doesn't matter what it costs."

Candy followed him and they studied the walls of their hotel room. "I think we need two pictures with different backgrounds and us wearing different clothing." She pointed to the yellow-colored wall in the entry. "Let's use this wall for the passport photo."

With a change of sweaters and shirts, they took the photos and Candy sat at the desk to send the email. "I think we need the documents no later than ten on Saturday morning. Should they come here?"

"Yes, assuming we won't be leaving Washington until later in the day."

"That sounds good. What name do you want and what birthdate? Oh, I think we should be married and naturally have the same address." After ten minutes of haggling over names—Patrick and Elizabeth Warren—and their "home town" of Cody, Wyoming, Candy uploaded the photos from her phone to John's laptop and sent an email to her friend with the photos and a plea for immediate attention

John watched her send the message before returning to sit at the table. "Now, Mrs. Warren, where are we heading next?"

"Anywhere we can't go?" Candy raised her hand. "Hold on. We have an email from that blogger." After a moment, she swung her head toward John. "She's confirmed the caliber for the bullet and wants to know the next step."

"I wonder who gave her the confirmation."

"She must know somebody. What's our next step with her?" Candy tilted her head at him and grinned.

"I guess the question is how we feed her information about Harry—"

"And convince her that he's crazy and needs to be locked up."

"Yeah." John crossed his arms over his chest and let his mind roam for a bit. He pumped his fist. "I have a great idea."

"Good. What is it?"

"In addition to exposing Harry as the one who set up the shooting, we need to warn President Ross about him."

"How do we reach her?"

"Through this blogger gal." He warmed up to his idea. "We can't say anything to her that will identify me and no one knows about you. I think we feed her information that leads her to figure out that Harry is behind Gardner's shooting."

Candy rose, returned to her chair at the table, and picked up her wine glass. "And we convince her that Harry is so off his rocker that anything putting President Ross in a good light might set him off and do her harm."

John uncrossed his legs and leaned forward. "Exactly, we feed her just enough to get her to make the right conclusions. I think we need to leave Washington as soon as we can on Saturday. That will give us almost two days to feed her information."

"I agree. Where are we going again?"

John jumped from the chair and went to the laptop. "Hold on. I have an idea. What's the blogger's name again?"

"Nita Andrews."

"Give me a minute." John searched for the Washington, D.C. property tax records website then typed the name in a search box. "I have a home address for this blogger, on O Street NW. She has a house worth almost two million dollars."

"You're kidding." Candy rose. "Let's go take a look at it."

"That's what I'm thinking. Maybe we can communicate with her without using email." John jotted the address on a notepad on the desk and handed it to her. "You can use that GPS thing on your phone to find the address."

They shrugged on coats and were soon on their way in the rental sedan.

Candy concentrated on her phone for a minute. "Go south on Connecticut Avenue. This address isn't all that far from here."

John turned as directed and stayed in the right lane. Within a few minutes he drove around Dupont Circle and took the second right.

"O Street will be our first street," Candy said. She pointed to the street sign. "This is it, turn right."

The neighborhood seemed old but all the houses were tall and not very wide. "Are these townhouses?"

"Here they call them row houses. I bet this area is really old and they've been re-done." John drove slowly as Candy looked at the addresses. She pointed again. "It's on the left."

He braked in the middle of the street. "Blogging must pay good money. That's an expensive house."

"Yeah, that surprises me."

He shrugged. "That's one tall and skinny building. Who in the hell would want a house with four stories?" John had never seen a home like that. "It must be deep. Where's the garage?"

"Probably in the back," Candy answered. "Go around the corner and we can check the alley. I do like those wide steps to the entrance. Great place for pots of flowers in the spring."

John pulled forward to the stop sign and flipped the turn signal. "You like to garden?"

"Yep, I'm known for my geraniums back home. The alley should be open."

He followed her instructions and turned into a driveway with the red brick row houses on either side. Each one had a single garage door.

"Very nice," she exclaimed. "Usually these kinds of houses don't have a garage, just a parking space. No wonder it's valued so high."

They were close to the end of the alley, behind what had to be the blogger's house. "Not much going on here. This has been a waste of time."

Candy hit his shoulder with her fist. "Hold on. Someone's coming out the back door."

John noticed the tall blonde and hit the brakes. "I have an idea." He rolled down the driver's side window. "Miss, may I ask you a question? We're lost."

The blonde threw a bag of trash in a big blue can and walked to their car. "You guys need help?"

She was pretty and young—this had to be Nita Andrews. John nodded. "We're from out of town and trying to find an address." He turned his head toward Candy. "Hun, what was that address again?"

Candy leaned over and stuck her head toward the window. "It's on Newport Place, 2122, I think."

"You guys are a few streets off. Guess you're not from here. Tourists?"

"Yep, we're from Colorado," John said without thinking. Candy hit his thigh.

"Colorado, huh? I hear that's a pretty state." The woman's eyes narrowed and she looked directly at John, like she was studying his face. "You look familiar to me. Have we met?"

"No ma'am." They had to get out of there. He didn't like her scrutiny or her question. "Which way do I turn to get to uh, Newport Place?"

"Turn right at the end of the alley." The woman backed away from the car and waved. "Enjoy Washington."

"Thanks." John rolled up the window as he eased off the brakes. "Jesus, that was Nita."

"That was too freaky for me," Candy said as she pointed to the right. "Turn like she said. Do you still want to use something around here to leave notes for her?"

"You mean rather than email?" He turned and headed back to Connecticut Avenue. "If you're thinking she'll go to the authorities about me and use the email address, you're too late to worry about that. She could've already done it."

"Damn, you're right. We'll email her when we get back to the hotel." Candy ran a hand through her hair. "I'm officially losing my edge."

John reached over and rubbed her thigh. "But you're officially hot as hell."

She laughed. "And you're sweet as hell."

"Nah." John knew his cheeks flushed at her comment. "You know, we never did talk about where we're going on Saturday."

~~*

Per the gossip grapevine, Speaker Roberts and his staff had made considerable progress in moving him into the West Wing the last two days. It was remarkable at times how fast things could move in the nation's capital. As he strolled down a West Wing hall, Emmett shook his head and considered himself to be on the edge of insanity for what he was about to do. Regardless, he put one foot in front of the other and continued to the VP office.

"Hey, Emmett, how are you?" Carol greeted him as soon as he walked through the door. He wondered why he'd never asked her out. She was a nice looking woman with deep blue eyes. Of course, now his head was full of Valerie. He wanted her again and they had dinner plans for that evening.

"Doing good. Is Harry ready for me?"

"He just got off the phone." Carol went to the office door, knocked, and opened it. "Emmett Garrett is here for your appointment."

Emmett walked in front of her, giving Harry no time to refuse him. "Hello, Harry."

The new VP sat behind a large oak desk and stared at Emmett as he settled at the end of a green leather couch five feet away. "I forgot, why are you here?"

"Now Harry, don't be so prickly. I have an idea that will be beneficial to you."

He rolled his eyes. "You with an original idea . . . priceless."

"If you don't want to hear how I can help your new campaign." Emmett rose from the couch. "Fine."

"Don't be so damned sensitive. You're like a girl." Harry waved for him to sit again. "Now, tell me how you can help with a presidential campaign—if I decide to run."

"Come on, I know you'll be running. I bet you've already selected a campaign manager and the announcement speech is any day now."

"All right, tell me your proposal. I'm sure it's not without a quid pro quo."

Emmett took a deep breath; he'd so easily transitioned to the dark side without a look back. Scary. Could that be Valerie's influence? "First, this is a confidential conversation. If anything gets out, I will deny it and accuse you of being a sick old man with dementia."

"No one would believe that," Harry fired back.

"Try me." Emmett hated what he was doing but he had to look out for himself. Washington was a brutal town and he'd never survive for the long term if he didn't play hardball. "This is my idea. I'll be your eyes and ears as to what Georgia's campaign is doing. You'll have enough ammunition to stop her at every turn."

"Why would you do that for me?"

"Her changing political party doesn't work with my personal philosophy. I'm a Democrat, not some lame ass Republican."

Harry narrowed his eyes for a moment then smiled and leaned back in his chair. "I can buy that. What would you want in return for being my spy? Once I'm elected, that is."

Emmett figured Harry would balk at first but his desire to win the election at all costs would convince him to agree to the demand. "A position in your administration . . . as a cabinet secretary. I think interior, commerce, or labor would be a good fit."

"You're crazy," he shouted. "No, absolutely not."

"No problem, I understand." Emmett shrugged. "I'll keep Georgia's campaign strategy to myself."

"Now, hold on, don't be ridiculous."

Harry reacted according to plan. This was too easy.

"We should talk about this."

"My offer isn't open to negotiation. It's take it or leave it." Emmett did his best to manufacture an "I mean business" look on his face—when all he wanted was to laugh at Harry because he was such a dick.

"Give me a minute. I need to think about this."

"Sure." *I've got all day.*

Seconds later, Harry spoke. "I agree. I'll expect a report at least twice a week."

"Not a problem." Emmett crossed his legs. "Now, it's Thursday and Georgia expects an update on the progress in the House for electing the new Speaker. Where's the report, Mr. Vice President?"

~~*

Georgia hoped her stomach wouldn't turn on her. She'd been drinking too much coffee the last week and eating too many of Betty's sweets. She hadn't stepped on a scale for fear it would show a gain of five pounds. Thus, she'd refused afternoon sugar cookies and sipped from a water bottle. One small step for the size of her ass.

She'd just read an email from Rosie Gardner. The president's condition hadn't improved and he continued to gain weight from fluid retention. Georgia's heart ached for Rosie and all that she'd endured and would continue to deal with. Although, and she hated to be blunt, it would be better for everyone if he passed quickly. She closed her eyes. God, being honest made her feel like a horrible person.

"Madam President." Betty's voice curtailed her thoughts.

Georgia stood as Randy Booth entered the Oval Office. His arrival made everything too real. She was not living a melodramatic soap opera and had to deal with this next task.

They met by the seating area as Betty shut the door.

"Madam President, so good to see you." Randy offered his hand and she shook it, nice and firm.

"Thanks for meeting me on such short notice. Have a seat."

"I saw your address last night. Quite the bold move to switch to the Republican Party."

"That's why I asked you here. I need your help."

He nodded. "Help you with what?"

Georgia stopped herself from rolling her eyes. Wasn't it obvious what she had in mind? She sat and hoped she hadn't made an error with Randy. "I'd like to hire you as my campaign manager. Do you consider that a bold move?"

His eyes widened. Apparently, he hadn't considered she might require his services. "Oh . . . of course, I'd be honored to manage your campaign for the presidency. This is quite the challenge since it's so late in the normal election cycle."

"And that's why we need to be creative and think outside of the usual national politics. I want to be a different type of presidential candidate." Did her words make sense?

"Yes ma'am, I understand that. What differentiates you as a candidate, other than changing your party? Why are you what the voter will want as president?"

Hmm, good question, but . . . wasn't figuring out the answer his job?

"I'd like to be the candidate without a personal agenda," she replied. "One who does what's best for the American people without political concerns. People continue to be disgusted with Washington, both the White House and Congress, because every decision is made based on one's personal agenda and staying in office. What the hell happened to representation of the people?"

"Uh, big government?"

"Exactly, we need to remind the public that the United States is a republic and not a democracy." She considered her words and an idea formed. "How about if this is the 'back to basics' campaign? I can talk about the principles the founding fathers used in writing both the Declaration of Independence and the U.S. Constitution and make a comparison to the country today."

"Voters won't be interested in a history lesson."

"True. We have limited time so let's focus on three core principles and go from there. I do like 'Back to Basics' as the campaign slogan. Next we need to find some donors. " Georgia rose and stuck out her hand to Randy. "Thanks for coming on board. I know this is on the strange side but we can make it work."

"Yes ma'am, *we will* make it work."

Georgia walked with him across the office and he opened the door. "I'd like you to meet my husband, Peter. He should be here by now." They stepped into Betty's office and found Peter leaning on the edge of the desk and eating a cookie. "There you are. This is Randy Booth, he'll be managing my campaign."

Peter shook Randy's hand. "Nice to meet you. I'm glad you're in charge."

"Thanks. Georgia, we need to file the statement of candidacy form as soon as possible."

"The form is ready," Peter replied. "Just waiting for you to be official. Let's get together in the morning and I can update you on what's been organized so far."

"Sounds good. I'll work tonight on a schedule and a preliminary plan." The two men exchanged business cards. Randy said good-bye and then followed an escort to the visitor exit.

"Do you have time to check out our new digs?" Peter asked as he wiggled his eyebrows at her.

"Stop that." She punched him playfully on the arm. "Betty, wasn't Randy my last appointment?"

"Yes ma'am," Betty said. "I'll hold down the fort. President Gardner rarely worked past 4:00 so I think it's okay if you knock off early."

Georgia checked her watch—5:15. "Thanks, Betty. Make sure

you leave on time, okay?" She linked her arm in her husband's and they walked with Frank out of the West Wing and along the West Colonnade to the White House proper. Within minutes, they entered the residence on the second floor. They'd decided against moving in any furniture other than their bedroom set and their favorite living room pieces, so the transfer from one house to another was quick and easy.

They walked into the master bedroom.

"Looks just like home," Peter teased.

"*Sure.*" She opened a door on the right and walked into a small foyer with two open doors. "Here's the bathroom and the closet." She went into the closet, eyes focused on the clothes hanging in neat rows. "Our clothes are hung up and there's plenty of room for your over-abundance of suits and golf shirts."

Peter joined her and kissed her lips. "Who would believe that the husband is a clothes horse and not the wife?"

"Anyone who looked at our closet." She rubbed his arm and walked back into the bedroom.

He followed and grabbed her hand. "Come on, let's explore the other rooms. Maybe we can figure out how to order a cocktail or a glass of wine."

Georgia winked at him. "*Oh, Mr. Ross*, you are *so* the First Gentleman."

~~*

Peter made a lame ass excuse to Georgia about meeting a client who'd just arrived in D.C. and left the White House residence at eight o'clock that Thursday evening. The meeting couldn't take place anywhere close to his wife. He'd taken out his contacts and wore thick glasses, hoping to alter his appearance. God, he hated deceiving her but he had no choice. He'd given his word. His security detail drove him to a nearby Italian restaurant popular with tourists.

He found a spot at the bar, pulled down his ball cap, and ordered a light beer. While taking the first sip, he watched his FBI contact, Justin Jamison, in the mirror over the bar. Several women watched him as he walked from the back of the restaurant to the bar. There was something about these FBI guys. Peter didn't see the attraction but it oozed for women. Justin slid into the stool next to him.

"Mr. Ross, glad you could make it." The special agent shook his head at the approaching bartender.

"I don't have much time." *Georgia will have my head when she learns about this.*

"You've set up the meeting tomorrow with Mrs. Gardner at noon?"

"Yes, we're having lunch at the hotel's restaurant."

"Good. Go to room 1238 at 11:00. We'll put on the wire and go over the script." Justin stood and offered his hand. "Hey, nice running into you. Maybe I'll see you at the conference tomorrow."

"Yeah, I'll be there."

Peter waited five minutes, paid his tab with cash and walked to the door. His security detail materialized outside as well as his ride. No wonder people worked so hard, along with lying and cheating, to claw their way into the White House. The perks rocked.

Riding back, he thought about those "perks." Honestly, they weren't anything he hadn't provided for he and Georgia in the past. All it took was money, which they had. Why then, did Georgia declare herself a presidential candidate?

Peter knew his wife very well and had never dismissed or diminished her political career. Her ambition wasn't typical for a Washington politician. She was one of those rare politicians who truly believed in doing the right thing for the country. He realized she hoped to have a lasting legacy for her time in Congress and now, the White House.

Being POTUS made her a member of a very powerful club, one that by its nature was difficult to get into. Peter's heart welled with pride for Georgia. He knew her desire to shape the country for a positive future far outweighed any legacy for her time in office. Truly, her heart rested with bettering the lives of the American people and not her bio in a history book.

Damn, what a woman. What a patriot.

~~*

Nita's eyes ached. She'd spent so much time the last few days looking at a computer screen that she hoped she hadn't developed a cataract or something similar. Nick had administered eye drops that were supposed to be refreshing and placed a cold washcloth over her eyes as she reclined on the sofa listening to the late news.

"Nick, did you hear that?"

"What? I was in the kitchen."

"President Ross has hired Randy Booth as her campaign manager." She could hear him walk back to the living room.

"Wow, she's bringing in the big guns. That guy is ruthless."

She pulled the washcloth off her face, lifted her head off the decorative pillow, and gazed at him as he sat in a chair across from her. "Really? How many years has it been since a Republican won the White House?"

He raised both hands in front of his chest. "All right, I know. But still, he's a very talented guy. Maybe this crazy situation will be his time to finally make it to the winner's circle."

Nita shook her head and fell back to the pillow. Men were just weird when politics were involved. Maybe that came from them assuming they were the true big dogs for any elected office.

She closed her eyes and listened to the news, dozing off. Nick woke her by pushing her right foot back and forth.

"Nita, wake up. You got an email from Dark Horse."

She bolted upright, rubbing her eyes.

He stood next to the couch, holding her laptop. "Here, I didn't open it."

Scooting into a corner, she crossed her legs and set the computer on her lap. Nick sat in a chair by the fireplace. "This is both exciting and scary." She clicked on the email. "At some point, we'll need to go to the police."

"Will that be before or after you blog about it?"

"Good point." She looked at the email and read it out loud:

"Good. Now we can help each other. A VIP who works in the Capitol is responsible for the shooting. The big question is why get rid of President Gardner. Figure out the motivation."

"We've already done that." Nick crossed his arms over his chest. "This isn't helping, at all."

"I agree." She sighed with disappointment. "Maybe we should tell him what we think we know."

"I guess. Ask if we're on the right track."

"Or ask for the name of the VIP. Why make a game out of this?"

"That's what bothers me." He had that look of skepticism she knew so well. "So if this guy is the one who controlled the drone and he did it at the request of some VIP who works in the Capitol, then why not just give us the name of the VIP?"

"Maybe he's afraid we'll go to the cops and they can track him down through the Dark Horse email account." Nita was now convinced she'd watched too many cop shows on TV and had read too many mysteries.

"He could be emailing us from anywhere with an Internet connection. If I'd tried to assassinate a U.S. president, I wouldn't have stayed in Washington. Hell, I'd be in Rio or Hong Kong, even London or Paris. Somewhere far away from this country."

"You're right. If this guy is smart enough to build a drone with a gun and control it from outside the Capitol, then he's smart enough to have covered his tracks. He's not worried about us identifying him." *Why had he contacted her in the first place?*

"Okay, I'll buy that. Back to your question—why is he making a game out of this?"

"Yeah." Nita rose and carried the laptop back to her desk. She returned to her spot on the couch. "I have a silly idea. Maybe he's like me and thinking about Watergate and Deep Throat doling out information in a parking garage."

Nick snapped his fingers. "He is following the pattern of Deep Throat but the whole clandestine meeting thing is now outdated due to email." He paused and squeezed his eyes shut. "Even to me that sounds ridiculous."

"And we're back to square one." She considered their options. *What options?* "I think we should be honest with what we've concluded so far and ask Dark Horse to confirm if we're on the right track."

"Might as well. We've got nothing to lose."

"I'll send the email in the morning. I'm too tired to think straight and I don't want to screw up our response. We need to sleep on it." Nita rose and reached her hand to him. "Come on, let's go to bed."

Nick took her hand and kissed the palm. "I hope you're not too tired for . . . well, you know."

"No, I love . . . you know."

Chapter Ten

Friday, January 30

NITA WAS IN A freaking rut. She got up every morning around seven, lately a couple times with Nick, and trudged to the kitchen to make coffee. Then she started her computer, looked at her email inbox, and went back to the kitchen for the brewed coffee.

She wanted to jump up and down, her arms flailing, and scream "my-life-is-too-boring." Then she remembered Dark Horse. Who was she kidding? Her life this past week was a damned soap opera, Washington, D.C. style. She retrieved her coffee and padded to her bedroom. She could hear the shower running and muffled singing. Nick would be out soon.

Plunking down on the sofa, she clicked on the TV for the morning news. She had a few minutes to think about something that had been bothering her. First, were they correct in assuming Dark Horse wasn't concerned about being identified? And second, they'd assumed he built the drone with the gun. They had no evidence to prove either assumption.

Maybe Dark Horse was a random gamer who'd only been hired to control the drone and now wanted revenge on the VIP. The real culprit/assassin was the person who had concocted this scheme, had built the drone, and positioned it in the House Chamber. That person was a VIP who worked at the Capitol.

Hmm . . . VIP, Very-Important-Person. The definition of VIP wasn't universal. Ooh, she shook her head. This was making her crazy.

"You okay?" Nick spoke behind her.

"Yes, no . . . I'm not sure. I've been thinking about the VIP person Dark Horse mentioned."

"Let me get coffee and I'll be right back. I have an idea."

Of course he had an idea. She sipped her coffee and watched the news. She concentrated on a story about the latest poll numbers for the leading Republican presidential candidates. Georgia had just announced her intentions to run and she already led the field of four candidates. Interesting—did that mean the public considered the other three as unelectable against President Gardner? Hell, yes. But why had Republicans boarded the Georgia train so quickly?

"Why are you frowning?" Nick plopped next to her on the couch.

"I'm not frowning."

"O--kay. What are you thinking?"

"Do you suppose it's possible this VIP person built the drone and positioned it in the House Chamber and Dark Horse was only the controller?" She gazed at him and sent a silent wish that he had the answer, even though she realized he'd be guessing.

"Do you think a VIP, meaning an elected official in Congress has the technical ability to build a drone with a gun? Most can hardly make it to a session. Someone might be able to do one or the other but not both. I think Dark Horse is the hired gun."

His words made good sense. "Meaning VIP is the one who benefits from Gardner being eliminated and has the money to hire Dark Horse."

Nick nodded and drank coffee. "I don't see how anything else in this whole scenario makes sense."

Nita accepted that, it's the only thing that did seem logical. She finished her coffee and decided it didn't matter right then. They had bigger fish to fry. "We need to send a reply to Dark Horse."

He rose. "Let's get to it."

She followed him and settled at her desk. "Didn't you say something about an idea?"

He sat at the dining table. "Yeah, I know, but not really. I'm trying to get my head around uncovering this VIP person."

"The big VIP's in Congress are the House Speaker and the majority leader of the Senate."

"That includes Georgia Ross as she was vice president." He crossed his legs. "I think we should look at all three again. Maybe ask Dark Horse for guidance."

His response frustrated Nita. "He said to look for the motivation—"

"The motivation to eliminate President Gardner."

"Right." She rose and walked to the kitchen for more coffee. While the cup brewed, she realized that Dark Horse had confirmed what they had already surmised. The shooting of Gardner was personal and it went further than him hurting or angering someone due to one of his policies or lack of action. It had to be politically motivated if Dark Horse told the truth. She went back to the dining room.

"The motivation has to be political," Nick said as soon as she sat at her desk.

"I agree." *Why did he always say what she was thinking?* Damn. "But . . . maybe the political reason isn't to get Gardner's job, that's the obvious motivation. Maybe it's to be disruptive, to upset the dynamics of the November election, especially for the Democrats since their incumbent candidate is gone from the race."

"That would point to the Republicans." He rubbed his jaw then flattened his lips for a moment. "I don't know. Offing a president seems pretty far out there as a political strategy. Who are the crazy Republicans?"

Nita chuckled. "What true-blue politician isn't a little crazy?"

He nodded. "On the other hand, a Democrat could want the same thing, a serious opportunity to run."

"It's so late in the election cycle for someone to start a presidential campaign."

"Georgia Ross doesn't seem to have an issue with starting late *or* changing party."

"Right." She knew they'd earlier dismissed Harry Roberts as a possibility as he'd been Gardner's best friend for years. Could there be a motivation other than politics? "I think we still need to consider other motivations. Maybe the shooting was personal, like a pissed off girlfriend he broke up with."

Nick grinned. "Or a boyfriend."

"I don't think Daniel Gardner is gay."

"I didn't know an Olympic champion was a girl either. Maybe he has a secret admirer."

"Point made. So what's the next step? I don't think we should forget about John Smith."

"We should have that DMV photo in the morning. I guess now we do research on the VIP candidates. I'll take Ross since I've already looked at her husband. I'll also see what I can find about the wealth status of members of Congress. Dark Horse isn't involved in this for free."

"Good idea. I'll look into Harry Roberts." She rose. "But first I'll post my Friday blog."

"Let's reply to Dark Horse before you do that."

~~*

Harry stood in the middle of the Speaker's office at the Capitol. The room was devoid of any personal decoration and the paleness sucked the life out of the room. He didn't give a shit. His new office in the

West Wing trumped this piece of crap stuffed into a closet. However, this was a big day for him and he didn't relish nosey eyes from the White House gossip train witnessing this meeting. Thus, he'd trucked over to Capitol Hill first thing Friday morning.

A knock sounded at the door. He opened it and motioned for his visitor to enter quickly.

"Hustle up," he said. "I don't want anyone to know we're here."

Ben Howard scooted in and leaned his skinny ass against the edge of the desk. "You are such a douche-bag, Harry. Why the hell did you call me?"

"I see you haven't lost your incredible charm. Good to know." Harry hated sucking up to Ben who truly was an asshole, but a talented one so he'd do what had to be done. "I asked you here today as I need your help." His gut cringed at saying the words out loud, even though they were true.

"Help with what?"

"I'm running for president."

Ben burst out laughing, arms wrapped around his sides.

Harry's heart stopped beating, he fisted his hands, and it shrugged back into rhythm. "You're such a dick."

"Yeah, whatever." Ben walked around the office, looking at the pictures on the walls and out the window. "Nice view. You're really running?"

"Yep, filing this afternoon." Harry puffed out his all-important chest and pointed his index finger at Ben. "I want you to run my campaign."

Ben's eyes widened and his mouth formed a perfect "O." He was such a little drama queen that his ass twitched while he walked. His shock passed as quickly as smoke in a hurricane. "What's in it for me?"

"A very healthy salary and the opportunity for a position in my administration."

"What kind of position?"

"What kind do you want?" Harry knew the right buttons to push with Ben.

"All right. I'll need to get a staff organized real quick. We're way late getting started."

Harry sighed and nodded. "I know. Georgia Ross will have the same issues so I'm hoping the states will simply add my name to the ballot without a major hassle."

"We have a good argument as no one expected the presumed

candidate to be shot." Ben unbuttoned his coat and pulled a yellow scarf from around his neck. "Who is replacing you as Speaker?"

"Depends on the vote." Harry had figured out how this change could work to his benefit. "I'm pushing for Gary Nixon from Florida. He's a good man."

"And Florida has the highest number of electoral votes."

"That's what I've heard." *Haha.*

"Don't forget about New York as a back-up."

"Not a chance. Those people are all assholes."

Ben narrowed his eyes for a moment then blinked and hurried to the door. "I have an idea and I need to make some calls. I'll call you later today." He walked out the door and stuck his head back in. "Don't screw up getting that election form filed pronto."

Harry gritted his teeth. Could he handle dealing with Ben for the next nine months? Probably not but he'd make the best of it. Ben was ruthless in running a campaign and would turn the public's view of Georgia Ross to pond scum. Dirty and borderline illegal campaigning was his special talent. He'd never give Ben a job once Harry landed in the White House. The man was much too uncouth and wore clothes that were too tight. He'd take advantage of Ben's talents to win the election and then boot his ass to the curb.

That settled, Harry donned his special hat, opened the door a smidge and peeked through the opening, glancing right then left. The corridor was empty so he slipped out like a stealth warrior and headed for the nearest employee exit with his head down and his steps light and sure. He loved playing spy.

~~*

"I'm hungry," Candy said as she placed the book over her chest. She'd been reading *All the President's Men* and had developed a full-blown crush on Bob Woodward. She'd completed an Internet search on him and liked his looks, plus he was so damned smart. She had a thing for smart men.

John sat at the desk, playing a video game on the computer. He shifted around to face her. "What are you hungry for?"

She marked her page with a pen, closed the book, and stretched out on the bed facing him. "Pizza, something easy."

"We need to turn in the rental car so we can order one and pick it up."

"I like that idea. It'll be good to get out of here for a while. Let's stop at a liquor store for a cooler, water, and beer and wine."

John nodded. "Good idea. We'll leave as soon as that package arrives in the morning."

"I also want to—"

John held up his hand, stopping her in mid-sentence. "Hold on, we have an email from Nita Andrews."

"Oh goodie." Candy scurried off the bed and focused on the computer's screen hanging over John's shoulder. "Wow, this is something." She read the message out loud:

> *"Dark Horse---Thank you for narrowing down the shooter to a VIP who works in the Capitol building. My partner, Nick Romano who is a very successful investigative reporter, and I believe the VIP person is ultimately responsible for the assassination attempt on President Gardner, not the actual shooter. We believe two people are involved. We assume you are the shooter and not the VIP. Is this correct? Also, how much were you paid for your role in the shooting?---Nita"*

"She figured me out." John hit his fist on the desk. "Damn it to hell. We should never have started this Dark Horse thing."

Candy stepped back from the chair. Her calm in all situations training kicked in. "Come on, get your coat. Let's think about this and then we can talk once we've dropped off the rental car." She sighed, men were so transparent and temperamental, even the ones you love.

Nita had no freaking clue as to John's identity and didn't care. She wanted the identity of the VIP, not the shooter. Good, that made things easier.

They returned the rental car and ordered the pizza before stopping for gas and supplies. Next was the liquor store. Finally, John ran into Barry's Pizza for their lunch. Candy decided they made a good team in getting chores done. Neither of them brought up the email from the blogger.

A bellman with a cart helped them transfer everything to their room. The pizza smelled delicious and they opened the box once they were alone. Candy tore napkins off a roll of paper towels they'd bought for their trip. John opened a couple of beers and they sat across from each other at the table.

She wolfed down a slice without saying a word. It was good. Now she felt better and had the energy to examine Nita's email. She selected another piece of pizza and set it on a napkin in front of her. After a swig of beer, she was ready to talk.

"I'm ready to discuss our response to Nita's message. You?"

John saluted her with his beer bottle. "Sorry about before. Yeah . . . I'm ready to discuss this like an adult. Jessie used to fuss at me for jumping to conclusions."

Candy knew that without a doubt she and Jessie could have been friends. In another time and another place. "Not a problem. This is a weird situation for both of us. I say we stay focused on our goal . . . to safely get our butts out of here and to take down Harry."

"Agreed." John spoke with firm resolve. "We're running out of time, less than twenty-four hours before we head out."

"I know. I guess I should have thought about the timing before I suggested this whole Dark Horse thing." She felt responsible for ramping up the stress. Like shooting a first term U.S. president wasn't enough.

"All we have to do is tell this blogger the truth."

"The truth that doesn't include your real identity." She wouldn't agree to anything that compromised John. They had a plan for the future and she'd make damn sure nothing prevented them from going forward.

John swallowed his pizza with a slug of beer. "You know, I say we send this blogger a couple more bites of information. Then tomorrow, once we're on the road, we'll send her Harry's name and post all the messages I have with him."

"Erasing your email address, right?"

He chuckled. "You betcha. I can post them all to a document so it'll be easy to put them in the final email. Let's wait a while before we respond to her."

She nodded. "The weather is getting bad tomorrow so I say we go south."

"If we leave as soon as the document package arrives, we can beat the snow. Isn't it supposed to start in the afternoon?"

"That's what the weatherman said this morning." She smiled at him. "This is gonna be fun. I've never taken a long road trip before."

"Long hours of driving get tedious."

"Won't we stop to see some of the sights?"

"Yep, we're gonna be first-class tourists."

Candy finally saw an end to this whole Washington ordeal. "I'm excited. But shouldn't we trade cars at some point?"

"I've been thinking that, too. But once we change identities we'll need an insurance card to buy one or rent one with the new name."

"No problem. I'll contact my friend and he can create an insurance card and email it back. What kind of car on the card?"

John shrugged. "Nothing fancy, say a four door sedan, any make and model you want."

She rose and sat at the computer. "I'll ask him if he has the total we owe him." She clicked on the email inbox and noticed a new message. "Hey, we're in luck, he sent an email. It says the package has been sent via courier and we should get it this evening. Fantastic, he is one fast document forger. Of course, the fee is fifteen thousand dollars. Ouch."

"No problem with the fee. Tell him we'll add an extra thousand for the insurance card. Did he include his bank info?"

"Uh-huh, replying to him now."

John rose, wiped his hands with a towel, and joined Candy at the desk. "Let's send the money to get it over with."

"Why not wait until we have the package?"

"Nah, I want it done. If you trust the guy, I trust the guy."

She started to rise.

"Stay sitting. You can make the transfer."

"Are you sure?" She knew this was a huge step in their relationship. Realizing he truly trusted her, she damned near started bawling. Somehow, she managed to swallow the emotion.

"I trust you, too, babe."

"Same here. Tell me what to do." She followed his very precise instructions and finished the transfer in a couple of minutes.

"This reminds me of something." He walked to the closet and pulled out one of the rifle cases. After opening it on the bed, he pulled out a small envelope and handed it to Candy. "This is for you."

"What is it?"

"Open it."

She opened the envelope and pulled out a bank debit card with the name of Patrick Warren. She gazed at him. "What?"

"I told you I was already using that name. I got two debit cards just in case I lost one. Now, you can buy stuff without me and get cash."

Candy stared at him, tears once again threatening. God, she was such a mush ball. "Does this mean you like me?"

He grabbed her and hugged real tight. "Yeah, babe, I *do* like you. Come on, we need to talk about the details for tomorrow, or maybe we should leave once we get the package."

"I need another beer." Candy stepped back and went to the cooler. She grabbed two and handed one to John. She sat on the edge of the bed. "What route should we take to California?"

"I say we take I-95 south and then go west once we hit I-20. The storm is coming from the north."

"That makes sense to me," she said. "I'm still worried about your Murano being recognized. Did you drive it to or from your airport hotel the night you fired the drone?"

"Sure, I parked it at Union Station when I controlled Jessie."

Her heart nearly stopped. Crap. "Was that in a parking garage there?"

"Yeah, on the top floor. Is that a problem?"

She now wanted to scream. "John, the garage is more than likely full of security cameras." She rose from the bed. "Come on, we need to check it out."

"But . . . we shouldn't drive my SUV, right?"

"We'll take a taxi." She threw John's jacket at him. "Let's go."

"Damn, I screwed up. I wasn't thinking about having a future back then."

~~*

Playing detective or spy or macho man was not on the resume of Peter Ross. Why in the hell had he agreed to this getting wired scheme with the FBI? Plus, he'd lied to his wife by not telling her his role in the FBI's plan to arrest Elizabeth Gardner. His hand rose to knock on the hotel room door and he hesitated. He looked at his watch, right on time. Oh hell, might as well get this over with. The door opened before he knocked.

"Hello, Peter, you're right on time."

"Hello, Justin, we're you looking out the peep hole?"

Justin's eyes narrowed then he stepped back and swept his arm forward. "Come on in, we're ready for you."

Peter walked into the standard issue, king-bed room and noticed the half-dozen agents scattered around. From his viewpoint, they all looked the same but he knew each agent had been highly trained and would protect him in an instant.

"What do you want me to do?"

The agents took over. They outfitted him with a mini-microphone masking as a flag lapel pin and a small transmitter in the breast pocket of his jacket. They tested it in several positions with taped background noise from a restaurant. Satisfied that the recording would be loud and clear, Justin led Peter to a sofa to discuss the script for the meeting.

"You don't need to do this," Peter said. "I know how to lead Elizabeth so she admits to me who is providing her financing and why."

Justin sent him a pleading look. "I'd prefer that we go over it anyway."

"Sure," Peter shrugged off the comment. He'd do what he wanted when he met Elizabeth so he might as well play nice with the FBI. Georgia wouldn't be happy if she heard he'd gotten snippy with them. However, more than one set of statements could trap the mother of the stricken U.S. president. Whatever, he'd go with the flow. The results would make Justin and his superiors happy. Making his wife happy would bring on a whole different set of perks.

After reviewing the expected flow of conversation and the location of the FBI team during the meeting, Peter departed with an agent and his normal security escort, who led him out of the hotel through a side entrance. He dawdled walking to the hotel's entrance, timing his arrival to be five minutes late as he entered the restaurant.

The young hostess greeted him, indicating his lunch date had already been seated. He followed her to a corner of the dining room.

He noticed Elizabeth immediately. The sixty-plus year old woman somehow managed to create a vacuum around herself that screamed her superiority and importance. Incredible.

Peter almost felt bad, considering what he was about to do. Almost. He believed in playing by the rules to succeed and achieve financial security. Elizabeth did not. Based on her actions, she had no qualms about skirting legal issues—the end justified the means.

Reaching the table, he leaned down to kiss her cheek. "You're looking beautiful as always." He sat in the chair to her left. That would help with the audio per Justin.

"Thank you, Peter," she cooed. "You're looking quite handsome this cold Friday."

"Cold is right." He laid aside the napkin on the plate in front of him. "I hear a winter storm is on its way."

"Really? I'm flying to Denver in the morning."

A waiter arrived with a bottle of wine and displayed the label to Elizabeth. She nodded and then sampled the wine.

"Nice one. I thought we should celebrate our agreement today."

The waiter filled two glasses and set the bottle in a bucket. "Are you ready to order?"

"I won't have time for lunch," Peter said. "I'm sorry but I have an appointment at the White House in an hour."

Other than the slightest frown to reveal her displeasure, Elizabeth kept her emotions reined in—a true ice queen. She waved her hand at the waiter. "Give us a few minutes."

Peter reached inside the pocket of his jacket and withdrew a couple of typed pages. "This is our preliminary agreement for the purchase of Evergreen on the Mountain, giving me authority to act for both of us. The apartment complex is nearly completed so we need to get our offer in as soon as we can. Remember we're fifty-fifty partners for this deal."

"I remember. I wouldn't have it any other way." She reached for the contract. "I need to read these over, so chill for a couple of minutes." She finished her wine and refilled the glass.

He smirked inwardly at her use of the word "chill" and suddenly felt peevish and old. He blew a deep breath and sipped ice water. The wine would have to wait for another time.

He tapped his foot on the floor and counted to one hundred three times. He hoped his face looked pleasant as he waited for Elizabeth. She'd donned reading glasses and seemed to study the agreement like a shark-faced lawyer, all the while sipping wine.

Finally, she placed the papers over her plate, took off the glasses, and finished the wine. Not that he was counting, but that was two glasses within ten minutes. Maybe that would help. He poured the wine from his glass into hers.

"No need for this to go to waste."

"Thanks. Everything seems to be in order. Do you have a pen?"

He pulled one from his jacket pocket and handed it to her. "Do you mind if I ask you a question?" Hopefully, he could get their conversation moving along, and give the FBI something worth listening to. It didn't take Peter long to discover he wasn't comfortable in this type of situation. No doubt he'd have made a lousy spy.

"That depends on the question."

"Fair enough. I'm curious how you have the money for this purchase. I know your son isn't helping you." He raised his palms in front of his chest at her widened eyes. "Don't get me wrong. I'm not trying to be nosy."

"That's exactly what it sounds like to me."

"Sorry. I'm a businessman and I spend a lot of time looking at balance sheets. I can't write a check if I don't have cash under the assets column." He hoped this, along with the wine, would convince her to reveal her source. "I'd like to know where you're getting the funds for the purchase. We agreed together not to use financing. I—"

"Christ, Peter, don't you think you're getting a little too personal with me?"

Good, get her riled up. "Actually, no, I don't. Both our names are on this purchase agreement and we're equal partners. You know full well I have a corporate entity backing up my investment. I've not heard a similar assurance from you. Why is that?"

Elizabeth's mouth puckered, revealing age lines. She raised her wine glass and emptied it. She stared into space for a moment then fluffed her hair and smiled at him. "All right, but this is totally confidential."

Perfect. "I'm listening."

Her eyes narrowed before she grabbed the wine bottle and emptied it in her glass. "But you have to swear this is just between the two of us."

Being a gentleman, those last words caused him to take a breath. Why the hell had he gotten involved with her in the first place? He remembered, a favor to a new friend, the FBI Director. He'd push aside his usual distaste at revealing a confidential conversation.

"Not a problem. This is between you and me."

She nodded at him. "I have a friend who is providing my financing."

"Is this friend someone I know?"

She offered a cat-like smile. "I don't think so."

He imagined reaching down her throat to pull out the words. He did not like this woman and wanted this task over. In a small way, he felt sorry for her but she was an adult and had created this mess herself. Greed was a mighty enticement.

"Who is this person?"

She raised the wine glass to her mouth and leered at him over the rim. "My friend lives in Mexico." She sipped the wine. Setting the glass on the table, she almost knocked it over. "Oopsy. No more wine for me. Although chardonnay is my favorite, a good pinot noir is good, too. In fact—"

"Elizabeth, you were telling me the name of your friend who is financing your investment in Evergreen on the Mountain."

She wiggled her hand at him and leaned over the corner of the table. "Come closer and I'll tell you."

He moved closer to her. This was perfect for the recording. "I'm listening."

"Don't forget this is confidential." Her eyes darted from side to side. "My investment partner for this project is Carlos Montoya. He's the head of Los Gulf Corporation and he's filthy rich."

Relieved she made the statement, Peter nodded and moved away from her. He was feeling sorry for her again. She had no clue as to the true identity of Montoya and Los Gulf. Maybe plain old stupidity could be used as an excuse at her trial. Better yet, the FBI could use her to get the cartel leader.

"Did you sign the agreement?" he asked.

"Right now." She signed the second page with a flourish and handed the pen and the agreement to him. "I think I'll go back to my room now. Perhaps I can book a flight to Denver that leaves later this evening."

"Of course." He rose, glad this scenario was almost over, and moved back a step. "Let me help you." He offered her his arm.

She rose and surprised him by being steady on her feet. "Thank you, kind sir. I do like doing business with you."

He winced at those words and led her out of the restaurant. Two men were entering an elevator and Peter and Elizabeth followed them in.

Peter nodded at the tallest man and stepped out of the elevator. "I forgot to pay for your wine. Have a good flight home." The doors closed and he sighed heavily.

Justin appeared by his side along with his security guard. "It's done. You did well, Mr. Ross." He retrieved the microphone from Peter's jacket. "May I have the transmitter?"

Peter dug it out of his pocket and dropped it in Justin's waiting hand. "What happens next?"

"We'll read her Miranda rights, take her downtown, and then negotiate. If all goes well, you won't hear about this on the news. She'll cooperate and then you and she will be back as business partners."

"Do you think she'll go along with your plan?"

"If she doesn't want to go to prison she will." Justin pressed the elevator down button. "We'll let you know."

"I'm telling my wife about this."

"Of course." Justin winked at him. "You shouldn't keep a secret from your wife."

The threesome entered the elevator and soon departed company. As they drove back to the White House he thought about the FBI agent's last statement. Did Justin know something Peter didn't? No, he was being paranoid. This cloak and dagger stuff wasn't comfortable for him.

But still, what might Georgia be hiding from her husband?

~~*

"Are we still on for tonight?" Emmett said in what he considered his sexy voice. "Friday night is date night, you know."

"No, silly, Saturday is date night. Friday night you go out with your friends and hope to meet someone." Valerie giggled and her voice went straight to his groin. He shifted in his seat as he had a meeting in ten minutes with his boss.

"Then aren't we lucky we're past that."

"Ah, baby, you are so right," Valerie said in a breathless voice then she giggled again. "What time are you picking me up?"

"Seven. Let's go casual as this will be after a long meeting with Georgia."

"No problem. I know her meetings are draining."

"We'll do something fun." He didn't know what fun meant to her but he'd figure it out.

"Bring a bag. We can snuggle in front of the fire afterwards."

Just what he hoped she'd say. "Sounds good to me."

"Hey, did you hear that Harry Roberts is running for president against Ross?"

Bad news travels fast. "How did you hear?"

"I got a call from Ben Howard today, asking me to work on the campaign."

"That's fast. What did you tell him?" He held his breath, praying she'd said no.

"Hell no. I need a position with job security and Harry Roberts running for president is far from that."

"I understand," he echoed with a sigh of relief. "I'm done with campaign positions myself." He crossed his fingers at that false statement.

"It's amazing to me how many things we have in common. I better let you go."

"Have a good afternoon. I'll see you later."

Emmett clicked off his cell phone and slid it in his pants pocket. Not for the first time, he questioned his motives for dating Valerie. Was he out of his mind? What would Georgia say if she knew? She'd probably tell him to watch his back and leave it at that. He liked that about her.

After shrugging on his suit coat, he picked up a stack of file folders and headed to the Oval Office. At least he had something to look forward to once the meeting was over. Getting laid would be a bonus.

He walked down the hall and met Gracie and Harry in the corridor. "Is she ready for us?" He smiled as pleasantly as he could since Harry was within spitting distance. Had he sold his soul to the devil agreeing to help Harry win the presidency? All for a cabinet level position. *What did that say about him?*

"She's ready," Gracie said and opened the door. They filed in with Emmett last.

"Good afternoon," Georgia said with a smile. She sat in her usual chair waiting for the trio. "Are you looking forward to the weekend?"

"Should be quiet once the snow starts," Emmett said. He sat next to Gracie on the sofa while Harry sat across from them.

Harry pressed his lips together, looking disgusted for a brief moment. "A little bit of snow won't keep me from working, Madam President. I've much on my plate, considering the vote for the new Speaker won't be until next week and my VP schedule is full."

"Totally understand, Harry. We appreciate your dedication." Georgia opened her red portfolio.

"Before we get started, I have an announcement to make." Harry beamed and gazed briefly at each of them. "I filed paperwork today as a candidate for the Presidency of the United States, on the Democratic ticket. I've hired Ben Howard as my campaign manager."

"Congratulations." Georgia's face showed no reaction.

Emmett admired her for maintaining her composure at Harry's crazy news.

He gazed directly at her, a smirk thinning his lips. "You do realize this means you and I will be adversaries on the campaign trail."

What a sly fox, stating the obvious.

She nodded. "Yes, that's true. However, while we continue to operate in our current roles as president and vice president we will not be adversaries. We will work together for the American people. You do agree, don't you?"

"Madam President, of course I do. The American people come first, not our individual campaigns."

Emmett's stomach rolled at Harry's insincere words. He watched Georgia and noticed her eyes narrow for a second. She wasn't taken in by her VP's supposed concern for the American people. Good for her.

"Let's get to work. I want you all to know I just had a private meeting with the Directors of National Intelligence and the FBI. The subject of discussion was the investigation into Daniel Gardner's shooting. I'm sad to report they haven't made significant progress."

Harry wiggled on the sofa. "That's outrageous. How can they not know anything? Damn Republicans, they're responsible for this. Mark my words."

Emmett chuckled to himself. "You think this is another right wing conspiracy?"

"Absolutely." Harry's chest puffed up. "You betcha they orchestrated this. I bet Mike McCain is thrilled that Danny and his brilliant leadership are gone from the Oval Office. Has the FBI investigated him? Damn it, if they haven't, they sure as hell should."

"I'll mention that to Director Martinez," Georgia said, a tone in her voice indicating enough of partisan talking. "There are several items on the agenda today. The first is the speech tomorrow, my first event as president. I want everything to go without an issue. Are we ready?"

Gracie nodded. "Yes ma'am. Let me know if you want to tweak the speech."

"The literacy folks are a good place to start for this first talk," Emmett noted. "They're dedicated people so getting their support is good for you."

Harry coughed and Emmett smiled. The next nine months were going to be fun as hell.

"I'm happy with the speech so no need for tweaking. Now I want to discuss my travel schedule for next week."

Emmett tuned out for the next few minutes. He already knew the details of her travel schedule, and he would be going along to judge the reactions she received outside of Washington. He hated to admit it, but he thought they'd be good. Georgia Ross had blossomed as a politician in the little more than a week since she'd taken the oath of office. Working for her was almost fun—the direct opposite from his experience in Danny's administration. He rarely called meetings and preferred to talk with his staff and Cabinet one-on-one.

Whatever, Emmett should stop comparing the two. Danny was gone and Georgia was here and probably would be in the future. Perhaps he needed to re-think his deal with Harry.

Gracie suddenly rose with her cell phone in her hand. "Ma'am, I need to take this call." She hurried to the windows behind the desk.

"How rude," Harry muttered.

Georgia ignored him. "We'll wait for Gracie to return."

Less than a minute later, Gracie hurried back with a tense look on her face. "Madam President, I have bad news."

"What is it?"

"There's been a shooting at Camp Manning in Mississippi." Gracie visibly swallowed and her voice shook. "It appears that seventeen are dead and another eight are seriously injured."

"Do we know how this happened?" Georgia asked the question with a steady and controlled voice.

"Right now it appears rocket launchers were fired over a fence at a group of National Guardsman during a training session."

"I bet it was those damned extremists down there. They all love that Confederate flag." Harry crossed his arms over his chest. Emmett wanted to laugh in his face. What an ass.

Georgia once again ignored his outburst. "Do we know who's behind it?"

Gracie shook her head. "Not yet."

Georgia stood. "Meeting is over folks. I need to make some phone calls." She walked to her desk and turned back to them. "Gracie, I don't know who is responsible, but please make sure the flags at the White House are lowered to half-staff this evening. Harry, you make sure the same is done at the Capitol."

"Yes ma'am," Gracie said and headed for the door.

Harry stared at Georgia, nodded, and stomped out.

Emmett followed Gracie and took her to the side of the corridor once they were out of the Oval Office.

"Do you know what's wrong with Harry? He's acting like a grumpy old dwarf lately."

Gracie shrugged. "Honestly, I don't have a clue. He used to be very charming. Maybe President Gardner's shooting has been harder on him than he lets on."

"Yeah, maybe that's it." Emmett didn't think that was true, but he wouldn't share that opinion with Gracie. He touched her arm. "I'll see you later. I have some research to do for the boss."

Gracie smiled. "She keeps us busy doesn't she?"

Emmett walked back to his office while Gracie headed to Betty's.

Harry disgusted him. Damn, Emmett had some thinking to do. What did he want to do with the rest of his life? Funny, he'd never before asked himself that particular question. He seemed a little too old to be asking it now.

~~*

Harry damn near floated back to his VP office. What a meeting, one hell of a meeting, incredible meeting—his thoughts were twirling so fast he could hardly keep up with them. He nodded at Carol as he entered his office then he stopped and backed up.

"I don't want to be interrupted for an hour."

"Yes sir."

He shut his office door, itching to lock it. But he didn't as Carol might notice and become curious. The last thing he needed was to attract the attention of the White House gossip mill. Those staff people were lethal.

He rubbed the back of his head with his hand, another headache threatened. Damn, he was getting tired of them. He figured they came with the stress of public office. After that meeting with *Madam President* he needed a drink and opened a desk drawer and retrieved a short glass and a bottle of scotch. He poured a decent dose of liquor, stowed the bottle, and sat in his favorite orange chair. He'd brought it all the way from Denver for his first term in Congress.

Sipping the scotch, his mind calmed and he methodically replayed the meeting with Georgia in his head. He had to give it to her—she was damned organized. And that was the only nice thing he could say about her. The meeting had given him the perfect opportunity to study her in action. Oh, she played like she was a cool one, but that didn't fool him. He knew her type. She was another bitch who thought she could outsmart Harry Roberts.

Not a chance in hell.

He chuckled. Oh, this was all so perfect. He sipped the scotch and pictured himself giving his inaugural address on the steps of the Capitol. He'd order a new suit and a tailored topcoat, maybe a hat as well. Yes, a hat would add a debonair flair to his TV image. A politician always had to look good in front of The People.

Of course, there was one initial problem—getting ahead of whomever else might decide to get in the race now that Danny was out. He'd go to Des Moines on Sunday and Ben could set up meetings with the local caucus folks there and across the state. He'd make sure he gained their favor. All it took was a stack of cash to convince a lame farmer from Iowa to support his candidacy. Bullshit may walk but money always talks.

He shivered in anticipation. This election was going to be so much fun. He loved to travel and this would give him the chance to get out of Washington for a change. He'd get a speechwriter to write a stump speech and then all he had to do was give talks and shake hands. Easy.

Harry didn't give a shit about the people he'd meet on the campaign trail but they were a necessary evil during any election. Once he was elected U.S. president, he could ignore them just like Danny and the former president did. Easy.

Near bursting with joy, he rose and approached the window of his office. The sky was overcast and the stark trees were waving in the wind. A fire in his study would be just right that evening. Even with a speechwriter, he should think about his campaign promises. He'd go big for sure. Didn't have to worry about fulfilling them, no good politician ever worried about that. In less than a year he'd have a much better view from the West Wing. Just one election stood between him and the Oval Office. Easy.

He drained his glass, barely able to keep from laughing out loud. Georgia Ross was toast.

~~*

"Damn. Damn. Damn." John had stopped in the middle of the row of vehicles at the Union Station parking garage. The same space where he had stopped on January 20th. There was a camera just across from where the Murano had been parked.

"This isn't good," Candy said. "Hmm . . . maybe it's just for show. Not every camera in a public place actually works."

"How can you tell if a camera isn't working?"

"Can't tell by looking at it."

John was eager to leave. The garage now gave him the creeps. "Let's get out of here."

"I saw a security office on the first floor. I have an idea."

"What idea?"

"We'll stop by the office." She tugged at his hand. "Let me do the talking."

They re-entered the garage elevator and Candy pulled his ball cap out of his jacket pocket.

"Put this on and your sunglasses, just to be safe."

He did as told and they rode down in silence. He followed her into the office. An old guy wearing a security uniform sat at a desk with his feet on it. He rose quickly when they stopped by a high counter. He smiled and sauntered over to them. His nametag said Paul.

"How can I help you folks?"

"We were wondering if you have security videos for the evening of January 20th?" Candy sounded confident as she spoke. "Specifically the top floor of the garage."

Paul eyed both of them and pointed to John's glasses. "Are you hiding from something? How can you see?"

Dread shot though John but he didn't need to worry. Candy placed a hand on his forearm and said, "He had cataract surgery on Tuesday and needs to be careful about light."

"Oh, my wife had that done. You'll be back to normal in a couple of weeks." He nodded at John. "Funny you're asking about January

20th. I had another couple come in a couple of days ago asking about the same night."

"Really? Who were they?" Candy said. "What did they look like?" John had a sinking feeling this would not be good news.

"The guy was a reporter and they were looking for the car of the lady's sister. The guy was tall, good-looking. But the lady was a looker, long blonde hair and a beautiful face. Reminded me of my wife when she was younger. In fact—"

"Did they see the video?"

"Sure did. The guy even took pictures of it with one of those fancy phones."

"Do you know what he took a picture of?"

"Hmm . . . maybe the SUV. I think it was after some guy walked to the back of a big SUV backed into the space. Hard to say. I didn't actually see him take the picture, but I heard the click of the camera behind me."

"That sounds like my younger sister. Guess I need to call her. We've been arguing the last couple of weeks." Candy grabbed John's hand and pulled him to the door. "Thanks," she said over her shoulder.

They hurried to the front of Union Station and jumped in a taxi that had unloaded a huge family. John held his breath until they were headed back to the hotel.

"The elephant in the taxi is . . . was that you who they saw in the video?" Candy spoke in a low voice as she leaned toward John.

"It had to be. I parked as he said, backing in." Panic was creeping down John's throat and would soon explode in his gut.

"How about the license plates?"

"I rubbed black shoe polish over them. Kinda like dirt."

"Okay, we can talk once we've returned to the hotel."

They rode in silence back to the Marriott. After exiting the taxi, they headed for the parking garage. Once on their floor, Candy looked at both license plates on the Murano.

"The numbers are hard to see but I can make out Colorado on the front plate." She slid her arm through John's. "Come on big guy. We need to talk."

Once in the room, John made a beeline for their supplies and pulled out a bottle of wine. "Sorry, I need to calm my nerves."

"Doesn't everyone in Colorado use marijuana for that?"

"Not me. I'd rather drink my pain away." He opened the wine and poured two glasses. He handed one to Candy who had plumped up pillows on the bed and stretched out.

John sat at the table. He'd really screwed up in the garage. But like his granny had said so many times, "The good Lord gave you a good brain to use when you make a mistake." She was right; he'd make up for this screw-up.

He raised his glass to Candy. "Here's to our last night in Washington."

"I'm looking forward to moving on."

"Yeah," he chuckled. "This is the first day of the rest of our lives."

"Very true, you're quite the philosopher. I'm the practical one. We need to get rid of your SUV."

"You mean now?"

"I don't think it's safe to drive anymore." She sipped her wine and slapped her hand on the bedspread. "I bet that girl at the Union Station security office was Nita Andrews. The guard's description matched the girl we met in the alley yesterday."

"You're right. She was with a reporter. That must be the guy she said is her partner. I'm curious about something." John rose and went to his computer. "I'll do a search." Five minutes later he turned around in the chair. "I found an engagement announcement two years ago. Her fiancé is Nick Romano, he's a reporter for the *Washington Chronicle*."

"We don't have a choice now," Candy commented matter-of-factly. "We have to ditch the Murano."

John should have done it earlier. "I know. Don't you think it'll be safer to rent a car rather than buy one here? Plus we're running out of time." He checked the email inbox as he talked and found a message from Candy's friend with an attachment. "Good we have an insurance card. Would you get that dark gray duffle bag out of the closet?"

Candy retrieved it and plopped it next to him. "What's in there?"

"All kinds of stuff. Right now I need a printer and paper." He unzipped the bag and looked for the travel printer and paper he'd bought in Denver. He'd figured it was best to be prepared once he'd left on this journey. He located both near the bottom of the bag and tugged them out, placing both on the desk.

"You're like a boy scout, ready for everything."

He laughed, feeling better about the situation. Busy work kept stress from getting the best of him. "You never know when you might need to print a document." He turned on the printer and made sure the driver still worked on his laptop. He added paper and printed four copies of the insurance card. He handed one to Candy. "Keep this in your wallet. Never know if you might need it."

"Thanks. I think we should rent a car. Won't that be easier?"

"I agree. I'll—" John stopped talking as someone knocked at the outside door.

"I'll get it." Candy looked out the peephole and swung it open. "Oh, this is great . . . thanks." She closed the door and walked to John, handing him a large envelope. "We have our documents."

"They're early. This is awesome." He tore it open and pulled out the passports and driver's licenses. "Here you are Mrs. Warren." He handed over her documents.

She looked at them, smiled, and plopped on the bed. "All of a sudden this has become real for me. We're actually running away together."

Running away? John didn't like the sound of that. "Like I said before, I think of it more like the beginning of the rest of our lives. Exciting and scary at the same time but I'm sure we'll have fun."

Candy rose and leaned over him, wrapping her arms around his neck. "You always say just the right thing." She kissed and hugged him, then pulled back and picked up a small pad of paper off the desk with a pen. "I'll make a list of everything we need to do before we can get out of here."

"Good idea. The biggest thing is renting a car and then dumping the Murano."

"I was thinking about that. How about dumping it in the Potomac? That will keep it out of sight."

He nodded. "Good idea. We can do that after we get the rental in the morning. I think we should do it outside of Washington though."

"I agree with that. I don't think there are cliffs along the river. We'll need a spot that has a low bank so we can roll it in."

"A boat ramp would be nice." He snapped his fingers. "Maybe there's a park or a fishing area close to the interstate. I don't want to go too far out of our way. I'll look for a park." It took less than five minutes doing an Internet search to find the perfect location. "I found it. A park that has fishing and camping and two boat ramps, plus it's closed during the winter."

"How will we get in if it's closed?"

John grinned at her. "You leave that to me."

"Will do. Also on the list is packing, we still need to reply to Nita's last email, take the plates off the SUV before we dump it, rent the new car . . . and, get a good night's sleep."

"Good idea. We can dump the plates down the road. I'll rent a vehicle right now." He used the same agency where they'd rented the four-door sedan. "I'm going to get another SUV since we need the room. Any preference for Ford or Chevy?"

"Nope. I'll think about the email to Nita while you do that."

Within minutes, he'd finished and faced her. "A white Chevy Tahoe will be waiting for us at 8:00 a.m. tomorrow morning. What did you come up with for the email to Nita?"

"Since we'll reveal Harry's name once we're out of D.C. tomorrow, we need to keep her engaged. What nugget of information can we give her?"

John rose and topped off their wine glasses. He sat at the table, thinking about their options. Nita and her fiancé wouldn't have the ability to verify anything themselves. They'd need help. And if they were working with the feds, he'd probably already been found based on the video from the garage. It still pissed him off that he'd been so careless.

"I have an idea," he said. "We'll tell her that Dark Horse is the shooter. And we'll also tell her VIP planted the drone in the House Chamber. How about that?"

"Works for me. I'll type a message to Nita."

"Wait. Before you do that, I have a little surprise for Harry. It might take an hour or so."

"No problem." Candy leaned against the bed pillows. "I'll read while you work."

John nodded and returned to the laptop. First he had to hack into Harry's laptop, and then he'd copy the code he'd recorded while controlling Jessie through the White house computer. This was simply an insurance policy in case Harry decided to play hardball. Harry would never know his computer had been compromised. After forty-five minutes, he had it set and felt confident it would do its job. He rose and discovered Candy sleeping on the bed with the open book resting on her belly.

He removed the book and stretched out next to her. She snuggled against him and rested her head on his chest. Wrapped in his arms, her scent surrounded him, another reminder that he'd been one lucky son-of-a-bitch to have met her in Las Vegas. That day the good Lord was surely looking out for him.

Holding Candy felt right. This was home.

~~*

With her feet resting on an ottoman in the West Sitting Hall, Georgia accepted a glass of pinot noir from her husband. "Thank you. It's so good to relax. This has been a long day."

Peter sat in the matching overstuffed chair across from her. They'd had many, many evening conversations sitting in the pair of chairs.

"I suppose you heard about Elizabeth Gardner?" Peter said softly.

She'd figured he'd mention it as soon as they had some privacy.

"Yes, I did." She smiled. "Why didn't you tell me you were playing FBI agent? You could have gotten hurt."

He chuckled. "Not a chance with Elizabeth. I feel sorry for her."

"Sorry? I don't. She knew what she was doing."

"True, plus she's greedy. I wonder if she accepted the FBI's deal."

Georgia nodded. "Yes, earlier this evening. The two of you are still in business together. Adam thinks it'll be a several more months before they have enough evidence to arrest this cartel leader."

He sipped his wine and stretched out his hand to her. "Are you angry with me?" She accepted it and squeezed before letting it go.

"A little, but I understand." Well, she might as well fess up her part in this. "I need to confess I learned of your role in this case yesterday. Adam Martinez told me since I'm now his boss. Felt it wasn't right to keep the information from me."

"But I did."

"Yes, you did." She sipped her wine, enjoying the taste in her mouth. She wished good wine came without both alcohol and calories.

"And you didn't tell me you knew about my role."

She raised her glass to him. "Touché."

"I have a hunch our lives will get a lot crazier real quick. Can we agree to not keep things from each other, regardless of the subject?"

She appreciated that Peter was deadly serious with his request. Could she keep such a promise considering her current role?

"Honestly, I'm not sure. I have no idea what's ahead of me, what security secrets I'll be exposed to." Things had been so hectic the last week she hadn't given much thought to Peter's role in her presidency. "The less you know about the details of my job, the safer you are."

"Surely you're not worried about my safety." He motioned to the door. "Those burly escorts will keep me safe."

"Peter, the world isn't safe and we can't take any chances. You're the perfect target for a kidnapping." Damn it. She'd not considered that before. Was this job worth it? Had she made the right decision?

"Do not worry about me. I'm a big boy and know the risks." He grinned at her. "Come on, how many first ladies have been kidnapped in the past?"

"I know, but still, have I made the right decision to run? Maybe I've been in Washington long enough and should bow out when this year is over." Was she feeling sorry for herself? No, that wasn't it; whatever this was, she needed to deal with it.

"Are you having second thoughts?"

"I'm not sure." She sipped the wine, thinking she should have dealt with this before she declared her candidacy. Talk about getting lost in the moment. She shook her head; this behavior wasn't like her.

"Why are you shaking your head? What's wrong?"

"I'm mad at myself for not thinking through all the ramifications of being a candidate and then potentially winning the election. Should I even be running?" She might as well be totally honest with Peter. He'd been her favorite confidant for more than thirty years. He never failed to talk straight and give her the truth. "I hate to admit . . . I'm starting to second guess myself and whether I've made a huge mistake."

"Did something happen today?"

"The pertinent event is that Harry Roberts is also running and as a Democrat. Do I have it in me to fight with the vice president on the campaign trail for nine long months?"

"You're assuming you'll get the Republican nomination." He gave her one of his cute side-eye looks.

"Yes, I guess I am. Although, the other Republican candidates can't be happy I've entered the race."

"And will no doubt fight like hell for the nomination, especially since they've been at it for months. I don't think you're a slam-dunk."

She wanted to bury her head under a cloud of pillows. But she wouldn't. Running from the truth wasn't built into her DNA and escaping was beneath her. She would never intentionally avoid a difficult situation. Of course her running wasn't a slam-dunk, but damn it, did she want to do this? Why did she want to do this? She thought about those soldiers killed earlier that day. They didn't deserve to die and certainly, not without having a fighting chance to defend themselves. She sipped her wine. "You're right."

"The number one question is why do you want four more years in the Oval Office?" He raised his glass to her and smiled. "Answer that."

She remembered her vow a week ago to make her time in the White House mean something for the American people. A year wasn't enough time to succeed with a policy agenda. An agenda that included three goals she'd had for many years—first, substantially beef up the military; second, revise the system of taxation; and last, reduce the bloated federal budget by a minimum of forty percent. She'd not mentioned the last one to Emmett and Gracie. She definitely needed more than a year to accomplish any of them.

"I have things to accomplish for the American people. And no, I didn't think about how difficult a presidential campaign would be before I jumped in headfirst." Georgia sighed. "Oh well, I'm not afraid of hard work. How about you? Are you up to a campaign?"

"You bet I am. Let's make your presidency actually mean something for this country. I think we're all tired of politicians who *talk, talk, talk* and never accomplish a damned thing."

She rose and bent over her husband, kissing his mouth so he knew she appreciated his support. "I love you." She walked to the sideboard for the wine bottle then topped off their glasses.

Once she sat again, Peter spoke. "Now that we're running, what do you think of Harry Roberts as your eventual opponent?"

"I'm sure he'll be tough to beat. He's had good approval ratings while he's been Speaker."

"What do you think of him as a person?"

"Good question. He's an excellent politician and that's the side he's presented to his colleagues in Congress. I don't think it's the real person."

"What do you mean? Maybe he has a secret life . . . like as a cross-dresser or a circus clown." Peter chuckled to himself.

"You're being silly." She tucked her feet under her butt in the chair, feeling comfortable at last in the White House. "I think Harry's public persona is a façade. I'm not sure who he really is but . . . whatever, why are we talking about this? I'll maintain my usual work protocol when dealing with him and then fight like hell on the campaign trail."

"That sounds like a good plan to me. Why ask for trouble?"

"Exactly. By the way, I'll be flying to Iowa on Monday. I have my first speech Monday night to kick off my candidacy. Are you free to join me?"

"Will you introduce me publically?"

Uh-oh, she prayed he wouldn't balk at being in the spotlight. "I had hoped to. Is that okay?"

"I've never been to Iowa, so yes, count me in."

"Thank you. I'll be working on the speech all day Sunday so you can watch football or whatever without feeling guilty."

"The Super Bowl is Sunday night."

"Oh." Damn. Why didn't she keep up with these big sporting events? "I'll watch it with you then. Isn't it in the evening?"

He nodded. "Be done with writing your speech by six."

"Will do. You know how I love goals."

"That's my girl." He rose and offered his hand. "Come on kid, let's rustle up some dinner."

~~*

At Nita's request, Nick had started a fire and stood back from the hearth, enjoying the results of his skill at building a decent flame. Nita walked into the living room. "This looks great."

"It's cozy. Having a gas fireplace sure helps the logs to light." She handed him a glass of wine and sat on the couch. "Let's relax for a few minutes. The stew needs another thirty minutes to simmer."

A glass of wine is what he needed. His eyes burned from staring at a laptop screen and his back ached from being hunched over the dining table most of the afternoon. He plopped on the sofa next to Nita and put his feet on the ottoman. Ah, that felt good to stretch out.

"Thanks for this." He raised the glass a few inches. "I don't know why I'm so tired."

"Maybe it's hibernation mode when the weather gets cold. We want to snuggle in bed and sleep until spring."

"Maybe." He sipped the wine; it was smooth and slid down his throat. "Or maybe I'm tired of this whole investigation."

"That doesn't sound like you." She rubbed his thigh. "Come on, tell Aunt Nita what's bothering you."

What *was* bothering him? Well hell, it was everything, this whole deal. He'd never been a fan of Daniel Gardner but since the shooting, and he and Nita starting their own investigation, his opinion of Washington politics had hit an all-time low. Some asshole in this town had orchestrated the shooting of Gardner. And that sucked.

"You know . . . well, damn, I think this situation has gotten to me. If we believe Dark Horse, then it's the epitome of the crap that Washington dishes out. It disgusts me. The politicians here are bottom feeders. They don't give a shit about the voters who get them here. Look, some jerk decided to off President Gardner, why . . . we still don't know why. But the decision to do it was selfish and narrow-minded." He sipped the wine, pissed at the world.

Nita puffed her cheeks and blew out a breath. "You're right . . . of course, you're right."

Nick didn't give a shit about being right. He wanted Washington to change. And had no power to make that happen. "Okay, I'm right. Where do we go from here?"

"I haven't checked my email for an hour." Nita rose and went to her computer. She sat for a couple of minutes then shouted, "Damn it."

"What's wrong?"

"Come in here, please."

Nick hurried to her. "What's up? Is there an email from Dark Horse?"

"I haven't check yet. I looked at my blog comments first." She gazed at him with distress painted across her face. "There's a scary comment from that BigDem guy."

"What does it say?" He sat in his usual chair at the dining table.

"Basically he calls me an idiot for printing lies about labor unions and says I better watch my back as the labor bosses don't take kindly to being criticized for doing nothing substantive for their union members."

"Does it read like a definite threat?"

"I think so. I said I'd go to the police after last Tuesday but now I will for sure."

"Good. You have enough to show them now so they'll pay attention." Nick decided right then he'd ask Adam if he could discover the identity of BigDem. Sure he could, but would he do it?

"I know, but I don't want them thinking I'm a scaredy-cat." She again concentrated on her computer. "I do have an email from Dark Horse. He says that yes, he is the shooter and that the VIP planted the drone in the House Chamber." She gazed at Nick, her eyes wide and incredibly blue. "Is it time for us to talk to the feds?"

Her question made complete sense but he wanted to talk with Adam before they did anything official. "Can we wait one more day? I'm curious if we can get more information out of this guy. Since he's probably long gone from here, maybe he'll give us the VIP's name."

"Okay, one more day. I'll reply asking for more hints as to the VIP's identity. Hmm . . . the state he's from and whether he's male or female. I don't want to be too pushy."

"Good idea. That along with net worth should help us whittle down the names." While Nita typed the message, he considered that tomorrow would be the second day of grace he'd been given before Adam looked into Dark Horse. By the end of the day, he'd have to come clean with Nita. He didn't look forward to it. Honesty and trust were big deals to her and she'll probably say he'd violated both by not telling her his "source" for the bullet caliber was the Director of the

FBI. Yep, he'd be in big trouble.

"Okay, the message has been sent. The stew needs more time so let's sit down again."

Nick followed her back to the living room and settled on the sofa. "The fire puts out some heat."

She patted his arm. "Yes, I wonder how cold it is." She programmed the remote to The Weather Channel. "Look at that, 35°F right now."

"And the snow is coming late tomorrow afternoon." He threw his arm around her and pulled her close. "We can get snowed in together." He grinned wickedly. "You know, cuddle in front of the fire and keep warm."

"Uh-huh, big guy." She pulled back from him and picked up her wine glass. "Tell me about your research this afternoon that made you so tired."

"Right, that." He picked up his own glass and swirled the wine. "The data I found is from 2015. Honestly, what I found surprises the hell out of me. Voters have elected some very wealthy people into Congress."

"Oh? Were they wealthy when elected or became wealthy after a few years in Washington?"

"Good question but that's another story," Nick replied. "The top three in Congress are Mike McCain, Sara Ward, and Harry Roberts. Their net worth's range from 303 to 265 million."

"This gets better and better. Both McCain and Roberts have the means to carry out this scheme and they have the perfect motivation. Man, you can't write plots like this."

He punched her playfully on the arm. "What? Are you thinking of writing a book?"

"Maybe."

"Me, too."

"I thought you were already writing a book."

"I am but this one is a different subject."

Nita rose and stretched her hand to him. "Come on, you can tell me about the new book while I make a salad."

He allowed her to pull him up and they went to the kitchen. They both heard a pinging noise and Nita went to her computer.

"I have an email from Dark Horse. He says he's tired of all the questions and will give us the identity of the VIP some time tomorrow. That's all he says."

"Interesting," Nick said, not quite following the logic of this Dark

Horse. "Why, all of a sudden is he willing to divulge the name? Something must have caused this."

"Like what?"

"I don't know. It's like he wants to get it over with. You know, check this off the list and go forward with his life."

Nita shook her head. "Maybe he wants the bad guy stopped before he hurts someone else."

"Yeah, that, too."

Chapter Eleven

Saturday, January 31

"ARE YOU READY?"

"Yes sir, I'm ready to blow this pop stand." Candy grinned at John with one hand on her hip, surrounded by their luggage.

"Good. I have two carts so let's load up."

They'd already checked out of the hotel via the TV's online menu. The next task was to load up the Murano and drive to the car rental agency to pick up the Tahoe. They had the carts loaded in a few minutes and headed to the parking garage.

John held the elevator door open for Candy as they exited and pushed the carts to their vehicle. He punched the remote fob and the lift gate opened.

"I'll load the guns first," he said as he pushed off the cover over the spare tire well, which was empty. He placed the guns in the space and pulled the cover back in place. "Luggage back here and the cooler in the back seat."

In less than ten minutes, they had everything arranged and they were ready to depart.

"John, what's wrong with the front end? It looks low."

He trudged around the back of the SUV to the front.

"Damn it," he shouted. "We're screwed."

Candy followed him and viewed the problem. "Well, shit. This will put us behind schedule."

"Ya think? We need to take everything out from the back. The jack is in the spare tire well."

"Should we call someone, like Triple A?"

"Hell no. I'll get the tire off then we'll go to a tire store."

"Got it." She pulled out her cell phone to look for one nearby. *This was not good.*

After thirty minutes of huffing, puffing, and major swearing, John had the jack steady, had twirled the lugs off, and finally pulled the tire from the hub.

"Let's go." He rolled the tire to the garage elevator. "This sucks big time by the way."

She rolled her eyes as they entered the elevator and kept her mouth shut. Yes, a flat tire when escaping from D.C. was a major pain in the ass. Just one more crazy and weird thing to deal with since she'd met John.

Thankfully the first taxi on the scene had a big trunk for the tire. They were on their way to a store in below freezing weather. Could things get any worse this Saturday morning?

Why even ask the damn question.

The tire store did not have the correct size tire in stock. However, their local warehouse did have one. It would be about two hours for the tire to be delivered to the store where John and Candy now stood.

"Okay, we'll stay here and wait," John said to the clerk at the order desk "Extra money for you and the driver if you get it here faster."

Candy hoped John's cash incentive would hurry the tire along. They sat in pink plastic chairs in front of a television tuned to CNN. She ignored it and checked the weather app on her phone. The weather ahead of them should be arriving in two to three hours with snow flurries, wind, and the temperature dropping even lower. Great. For the first time in this whole situation with John, her stomach rolled and nausea threatened to crawl up her throat.

She jumped from the chair and hurried to the customer drink bar. She poured two cups of coffee. Returning to the chair, she handed one to John who stared at the television and barely registered her presence. That was okay. At least he wasn't yelling. She swallowed coffee then took several deep breaths, willing her nerves to calm. They didn't. She needed a distraction and pulled the mystery novel out of her purse. Reading would keep her mind occupied until they headed back to the hotel.

Almost an hour and a half passed before the order clerk waved John over to the desk. She watched John nod and take out his wallet. That was her cue. She stowed the book and walked over to him.

"Are we ready?" She touched his arm.

He smiled. "Yes, tire's on the rim and inflated." He handed the clerk two one hundred dollar bills. "This is for you and the driver for being so quick. Can you order a taxi for us?"

"Thanks for the cash, man. Where are you going?" The clerk was young and no doubt thrilled to get a tip.

"The Marriott at Woodrow Park," John replied.

"Hold on," the clerk said. He slipped out the door behind the counter with the money scrunched in his hand.

Candy checked her watch, 10:17. She puffed out her cheeks and blew. Damn, she wanted to get on the road and outrun the bad weather. She hated driving in snow or even being driven in snow. After a bad experience in high school when she slid off the road and ended in a deep ditch for hours, she vowed never to drive during a snowstorm.

It looked like that's exactly what was about to happen. She clinched her fists then wiggled her fingers, doing her best imitation of a woman not freaking out. John rubbed her back, sensing her anxiety.

The clerk returned wearing a huge smile. "The driver will take you back to your hotel. It's right on his way to the warehouse."

"Are you sure?" John looked at Candy and she nodded. Why not? It would be quicker than waiting for a taxi.

"Okay, we appreciate it."

"Follow me." The clerk motioned with his hand and they trailed behind him out the front doors of the store. She wrapped her sweater around her middle and stepped into the cold. A white van sat a few steps away. The clerk opened the passenger door. "This is Felix. He'll drop you off at the Marriott."

Candy stuck in her head and smiled. "Thanks for the ride." She climbed in. The seat was a bench and clean. John shook hands with the clerk then settled beside her.

"The tire is in the back," Felix said softly. "We'll be at your hotel in less than ten minutes."

True to his word, Felix dropped them off in the garage next to the Murano. John declined his offer to help after Felix pulled the tire from the back of the van. They waved good-bye and Candy checked the time again. Her stomach rolled.

John rolled the tire to the hub and lifted it on. "We're almost done. This is the easy part." He put the lugs back on, pumped the jack to lower the tire to the garage floor, and finally tightened the lugs. He rose slowly, rubbing his back. "I'm getting too old for this stuff."

"Ya think?" She kissed his mouth and picked up the jack and tools, throwing them on the floor of the back seat. "Can we go now?"

"Yes ma'am, next stop is picking up the rental."

Naturally the snow began as they drove into the empty parking lot in front of the rental agency.

"This place looks deserted." Candy squinted through the windshield as the building looked dark. "I hope they haven't closed."

John opened his door. "Stay here. I'll check."

Candy watched him walk to the glass door and pull on the handle. It didn't budge. Crap. Now what were they going to do? Her fingers started to stiffen, a sure sign of her heightened anxiety level.

John put his hands to the side of his eyes and pressed his face against the glass. Moments later his fist pounded on the door and she could hear muffled shouting of "open the door." A light inside came on and a man came to the door. He opened it slightly and spoke to John. She could tell by his body language that John was pleading with the guy.

It must have worked. The guy opened the door wider and John walked in. Oh, thank you Lord. She wiggled her fingers, easing out the nerves.

She moved over to the driver's seat and started the Murano. It was cold without the heater blowing. The snow seemed heavier. Once again, the weather forecast had been wrong. She watched the traffic in between watching John inside the rental agency. John and the man disappeared and the lights went out. She prayed that meant good news.

She released a squeal when a white SUV drove around the side of the building and backed into the parking spot next to the Murano. The driver's side window rolled down so she did the same.

John's grinning face greeted her. "Hey babe, like our new wheels?"

"I damn near had a heart attack."

"No worries. We're on our way. Follow me as closely as you can. We should be at the park in thirty minutes, depending on traffic. If you have a problem, call me."

"Yay, we're finally ditching this town."

He gave her a thumbs up and eased out of the parking spot. She backed out and trailed behind him. She checked the digital clock on the dashboard—almost three hours behind schedule and the snow continued to impair her visibility. She gripped the steering wheel. Thankfully, it wasn't far to the park and the boat ramp. Once the Murano was dumped in the river, she had a single task to complete, and then they'd be free. Forever.

And Harry Roberts would be screwed.

~~*

In the laundry room, Nita transferred a load of undies and pajama's from the washer to the dyer. She was behind on household chores. She walked up the stairs to the main floor and smelled bacon. Smiling at the thought of Nick cooking breakfast, she entered the kitchen.

The smile faded as she stopped and viewed the assortment of bowls, pans, and food items scattered across the granite counters. "Nick, what are you doing?"

He stood at the gas range and turned around. "Hey babe, I'm making breakfast. We gotta eat, ya know."

"I can see that. Why the mess?"

"Mess?" He glanced at the counters. "Right. I was thinking about the menu as I, uh . . . yeah, I made a mess."

She patted his arm. "That's okay, I have a dishwasher. What are we having?"

A few minutes later, he dished up bacon, scrambled eggs with cream cheese, and crispy hash browns. "This is good," Nita said and meant it. "Thanks for cooking."

"No problem and I'll do the dishes." He pulled his cell phone out of his shirt pocket. "I have an email." After a couple of seconds, he handed the phone to Nita. "Does this look like the guy in the Union Station garage video?"

She looked at John Smith's face on the Colorado driver's license. The guy was nice looking, dark hair, blue eyes, and fifty-one years old. The address on the license was the same as the one on the IRS hacked list. She studied his face but couldn't connect it to the brief look at the guy on the video.

"Damn, I wish we had a shot from that video." She stared at his face . . . nope, nothing. "I can't tell if it's the same person. But I have seen him before. I watched an interview of him after the IRS hacking. He had a beard then. Maybe I'm confusing myself but I swear I've seen him without a beard. I can't remember where though."

"Seriously? You think you've seen this guy in person? Here in Washington?"

She shook her head. "I don't know. Maybe it will come to me. Anyway, so we know for sure that John Smith owns or owned a black Murano and had his life turned upside down with his wife's death after the IRS hacking. Is that enough of a motive to go after President Gardner?"

Nick pushed back from the table and sipped coffee. "You know, maybe we should ask Dark Horse if he's John Smith from Denver, Colorado? We've got nothing to lose, right?"

"It might spook him. I think we wait until he gives us the VIP's name."

"That'll work. I'll do the dishes and you get dressed. The president's talk is at 11:00 so we should leave soon." They'd decided to check out the first public event for President Ross.

Thirty minutes later they searched for a parking spot at the Hilton. The outdoor lot was full so they drove into the garage and found a space on the third floor.

"Looks like the bad weather hasn't kept people from showing up for President Ross's first public speech." Nick grabbed Nita's hand and led her to the elevator. It opened in the hotel lobby. They followed the crowd to the ballroom and were stopped at the first entrance.

A young woman with long dark hair held out her hand to them. "Tickets, please."

Crap.

Nick fished his wallet out of his back pocket and showed her a card, then put it away. "We're with the *Washington Chronicle.* Where's the press section?" He winked at her.

The ticket taker grinned. "It's on the left in the back." She opened the door and they walked past her.

"Quick thinking," Nita whispered. She grabbed his arm. "Come on, let's get as close as we can."

They found center aisle seats on a row about halfway back from the stage. The chairs were close together and she rubbed butts with Nick. Nita studied the attendees, surprised at the wide-ranging crowd President Ross had attracted. She had expected it to be primarily middle-aged women. Instead it was a smorgasbord of ages, gender, and ethnicity. She liked that. It was nice to have a president who appealed to more than one type of voter. Yay, Georgia.

The program started with a speaker for Literacy Volunteers of the U.S.A. and Nita opened her phone for a quick email check—nothing from Dark Horse. She was itching to ask if he was John Smith but held back as it might backfire. Once she had the name of VIP though, she would ask for sure. And if he said he was John Smith, should they go to the feds? That would be the right step to take.

Could she get in trouble for not talking to them earlier? Crap. Nick would be in trouble, too. Maybe she should Google the laws related to withholding information. Nick elbowed her in the side and she looked up.

President Ross walked on the stage to thunderous applause and stopped behind a podium. Not one teleprompter was on the stage. Yay, Georgia. Nita decided she liked this president. The applause died down after a couple of minutes.

President Ross tugged the microphone out of the holder on the podium and walked to the front of the stage. She raised her hand and waved at the crowd.

"Hello everyone. I'm absolutely thrilled you've taken time on a wintery Saturday morning to venture out in the cold to hear me speak. Truly, I feel blessed to be here today. In fact—"

Applause interrupted her and she used her hands in a "quiet down" motion. "Thank you so much for your enthusiasm. I'm going to be honest and tell you I'm worried about the weather. It has started to snow and you know how the roads get around here. So, please hold your applause until the end to save time. Okay?"

The crowd shouted "okay."

She gave the thumbs up sign. "Excellent. Let's talk about literacy in our country. It hurts me to tell you that in the United States today, fifteen percent of adults can't read. Double that rate for adults who have a basic level of reading. And the percentages have not changed in the last ten years. Why? What in our society has created this and what can we do to correct this problem?"

"Running as a Republican," someone shouted from the right side. "You think changing parties makes you so smart."

Nick and Nita rose simultaneously. The female heckler was at the front and two policemen were closing in.

A male stood up next to her shaking his fist at the stage. "You're a loser, no one will vote for you."

The room was so quiet that his words were easy to hear. The police reached them. Nita swiveled her gaze back to Georgia who had walked to that side of the stage.

"Let them be, officers," Georgia said. "Please, tell me the real reason why you're interrupting my talk about literacy."

The man puffed out his chest. "Because you're a loser."

Georgia splayed a hand on her chest. "I'm a loser because I switched to the political party that aligns with my personal philosophy and political beliefs."

"Damn right lady," the woman shouted.

"All right then, "Georgia said. "You'd prefer I stay a Democrat and lie to the American people about my political views."

"Yes . . . well, no," the woman said.

"You're trying to trick us," the man shouted.

"How can I trick you if I'm telling the truth?" Georgia waved to the crowd. "Officers, you can escort these citizens to a happier place."

The two didn't fight as they were escorted out. Nick and Nita sat down as applause erupted.

Nick leaned into her and whispered, "Georgia has balls."

"No kidding," Nita replied quietly. "Finally a president who doesn't back down. She's gonna win in November."

~~*

"Why didn't I keep my mouth shut?" Georgia pounded her fist on the leather seat of her ride back to the White House.

"You were perfect," Emmett said, sitting in the front passenger seat of the SUV. "You didn't see the faces of the audience. They loved you engaging those two jerks."

"Emmett's right. The public is hungry for a president who stands up for herself and isn't afraid to defend her position." Gracie sat next to her boss and looked out the window as she spoke. "The snow is really coming down."

Georgia watched the snow build on the ground as they wound their way back. It was pretty if you were inside and warm. "It sure is. I'm not a fan of cold weather, period."

Frank and another agent sat behind the two women. "Don't worry, we know how to drive in snow and ice. We'll be at the White House in fifteen minutes."

The driver nodded. "Yes ma'am. A little bit of snow won't slow us down."

Thankful to be in such capable hands, Georgia again focused on the hecklers. "I'm sure I'll be asked over and over about switching parties. Not every audience will be as forgiving as the one today. I need to have a better response."

She watched Emmett open his tablet. "I agree. I'll make a list of our ideas. Today you said you switched to align your personal philosophy and political beliefs with the correct political party, i.e., Republican. That's a general statement. Let's have a few responses that hone in on the details of your beliefs."

"I totally agree with that," Gracie added. "The situation will dictate whether you go general or specific, you need to be ready to punt."

Georgia laughed. "Punt? Yeah, that's so me."

"Oh, you know what I mean, go either way." Gracie shook her head and smiled. "Come on, what statements will shut down a stupid heckler?"

"Gracie, please don't call them stupid. They have a right to express their opinion."

Emmett turned around to face Georgia. "You're far too generous. I've done a bit of checking on social media. Those two hecklers were plants."

"Plants? Seriously? I haven't even kicked off my campaign."

"So what? Harry Roberts doesn't care about that." He raised up his smartphone to the backseat. "Everything I've read online points to the Roberts campaign attempting to embarrass you today. We know that didn't work."

"It sure as hell didn't work," Gracie said. "And this is why I hate politics—all these stupid games. Why can't politicians be honest and talk plainly about the issues?"

Emmett pointed his index finger at Gracie. "That, my dear, is a question bigger than why elected officials leave Washington with more wealth than when they arrive."

Georgia raised a hand. "We're getting off track. Forget the hecklers, back to my campaign. I'm working on the kickoff speech for Monday night. Any ideas?"

"Since it's so late in the campaign season, I think you need to start right off with details." Emmett still faced them from the front seat. "No generalities and no political speak. I think you—"

"Talk from your heart, Georgia." Gracie interrupted Emmett and wiggled her fingers at him. "Tell the voters what you stand for and your proposed changes for how the federal government operates. Honestly, people are sick of the last two presidents who were all talk and no action that helped the American people."

"She's right," Emmett added. "Even though I'm a good friend of Danny Gardner, I'll admit he was a lousy president, just like the former president. They're guys you'd like to have a beer with at the local sports bar but neither of them had the talent to run a country. And yet, both of them got elected."

Georgia again raised her hand. "Okay, that's enough. My campaign is not about bashing former presidents. It's about looking to the future and making this country great again. Let's focus on that."

"Yes ma'am," Emmett grinned, saluted her, and turned around in the seat.

Gracie placed her hand on Georgia's arm. "Message received. This is why I love having you as a boss."

Georgia patted Gracie's hand then looked out the window of the SUV. The snow was heavier, she could hardly see across the street. She scooted around to the back seat. "Frank, how close are we to the White House?"

"It will take a bit longer than I originally thought. There are multiple accidents and we'll need to go around them." He pointed to his ear. "Don't worry, we have the best traffic report on the planet."

Georgia chuckled. There were definitely perks to living in the White House. "Let's continue our conversation and talk about the details. Modernizing the tax code and changing how the federal government collects income taxes is first. Emmett, you're taking notes, right?"

He raised a hand straight up. "Yes ma'am."

"Good. I've been thinking about this and my view has changed. Rather than a consumption tax or a flat tax for individuals, I propose we eliminate all exemptions and deductions other than mortgage interest and charitable gifts and stay with a progressive tax. The rates might be 1% up to $30,000 of net income, 5% up to $85,000, 10% up to $300,000, and 15% over $300,000. I do think those who make more should pay more. Taxable income would be calculated after the two deductions. We could do it on a one-page form."

"The IRS won't like this," Gracie commented.

"I know . . . tough. They're a bloated agency and the time has come to modernize how they operate. Plus this gets the tax code away from attempting to sway public or political policy or personal decisions about marriage, having kids, investments, whatever."

"What about investment income?" Emmett asked.

"Good question," Georgia replied. "I think realized gains and losses are part of your income. They're based on the receipt of or disbursement of cash just like W-2 cash is received from your employer."

"This sounds way too easy." Gracie grinned at her boss. "The Democrats will be certain you're trying to screw less fortunate Americans."

"And they aren't with unending handouts?" Georgia waved both hands in front of her. "Scratch that comment. Throw me some questions about this proposal."

"What about the earned income credit?" Emmett shouted from the front seat. "Will this proposal be revenue neutral or will it reduce revenue?"

"Yes," Georgia said. "We'll need to send various options to the OMB for a calculation."

"What about social security benefits, unemployment compensation, alimony, childcare support?"

Georgia nodded as Gracie spoke. "Yes, we need to talk about earned income versus passive income. I think in terms of cash. If you receive cash you didn't have before, then it's income. Naturally, this doesn't include gifts from your family or inherited funds. You know, the journey to change an institution like the U.S. tax code won't be simple or easy. Yet the end result of simplifying the code will be worth the work. Think about the positive impact this will have on the American people."

Gracie raised both hands over her head and pumped her palms toward the roof of the SUV. "Go, Madam President. Yay, Madam President. Go, Madam President."

"Very funny. What else? Corporate taxation is the next topic." Georgia loved these freewheeling discussions with Gracie and Emmett. They discussed various ideas for the next thirty minutes. By the time they arrived at the White House, the wind was blowing snow and drifting it across the lawns.

The group hurried into the main corridor of the West Wing.

"Whew. I'm glad to be back home." Georgia unbuttoned her winter coat. She nodded to Emmett and Gracie. "You two can stay here tonight if the storm continues. We have lots of bedrooms." She winked at them and headed to the Oval Office. "I'll talk to you later. I need to work on Monday's speech."

Frank accompanied her and made sure the office was clear before she entered. She threw her coat on a sofa and walked to the desk, placing her purse in the bottom drawer. "I need coffee. How about you, Frank?"

"Yes ma'am. I'll call the kitchen."

"Thank you." Georgia walked to the windows behind the desk and pushed back the drapes. She leaned over the credenza to get a good view out of the windows. What an eerie sight. It was mid-afternoon yet the streetlights cast shadows over the snow that continued to accumulate in drifts due to the blowing wind. She shivered and turned from the window, settling at the desk. This Washington weather had the power to shut down the city.

She took her cell phone from the pocket of her slacks and called Peter.

"Hey babe, how was the speech?" His voice never failed to soothe her soul.

"It was good overall. I'll give you all the details over dinner. What have you been up to?"

"Not much, reading, watching TV, taking it easy. When will you be done being POTUS for the day?"

"You've heard it's a 24/7 job, right?"

"Haha. That's only if the red phone rings."

"Yeah, yeah," Georgia chuckled. "I'll work another three hours or so and then I'll be up. Warm a spot for me. This will be a cold night."

"You got it, babe. I'll keep you nice and toasty all night."

She clicked off and opened her laptop to the email inbox. Emmett had already sent the notes from their earlier discussion. She leaned back in her chair and thought about her two closest advisors—Emmett and Gracie.

She was fortunate to have a good, loyal team.

~~*

John blew a slow breath, a feeble attempt to stay calm. Why in the hell was he so damned uptight? He'd orchestrated and shot Jessie without a blip on a stress line. But now, he was like an old woman with high blood pressure.

Shit, he knew why he was stressing out. Candy and her hang up about driving on snowy roads. And she was right behind him in the Murano. It had taken them nearly an hour to get out of D.C. People in that town could not drive in the snow. But now they were on I-95 south and close to the turn off for Paystone Park.

He pumped the brake a couple of times when he saw the freeway signage announcing the park. After taking the exit ramp, he came to a stop sign and checked to make sure Candy was behind him. She was there, good girl. With no oncoming traffic in either direction, he turned left and traveled under the freeway.

The road to the park was two lanes and covered in a dusting of snow that swirled as the wind blew across the pavement. They had fifteen miles to drive to reach the park and the boat ramp. He wasn't one bit sorry to dump the Murano. Jessie had selected the vehicle and he thought of her every time he pushed the start button. It was time to move on.

The drive became spooky and slow as large trees bordering the road blocked the daylight. The wind blew harder and the tops of the trees swayed from side to side. *How's Candy?* He touched her name on his phone's contact list. She answered after one ring.

"Hey babe, how ya doing? We're almost there."

"This road is giving me the creeps. It's like a Stephen King novel."

"Hah, think of it as the road to a fairy castle."

She laughed. "Where did you come up with that? A fairy castle with a big bad dragon."

"Doesn't every castle have a dragon?" He liked that she was laughing. That was a good sign. "Jessie and I used to watch all the *Shrek* movies."

"I'm okay but I'm hanging up now. I feel more comfortable driving with two hands."

After twenty minutes of steady driving, they reached the park entrance identified by a single sign to the right of a metal gate that crossed the road. John stopped and studied the gate and where it attached to a fence on either side. He put the Tahoe in park and stepped out to the road.

Damn, it was freezing. He zipped his bomber jacket. The wind hit him in the face as he walked to the middle of the gate and saw that it was two pieces held together by a chain and a large padlock—he had no choice. He walked to the Murano and Candy rolled down her window.

"The gate is locked?"

"I need to bust a padlock. Would you open the tailgate?" He walked to the back and waited a couple of seconds for it to lift. Then he rummaged around for a brown duffle, his tool bag. He first found his work gloves then a large bolt cutter. That should do the trick.

Walking back to the gate he knelt down and easily cut one side of the lock. He unwound the chain and wrapped it on the gate, hooking the open lock on a link. After he pulled the right side of the gate parallel with the road, he returned to the open tailgate, stowed the bolt cutter, and retrieved a screwdriver from the tool bag. He shut it and returned to the Tahoe.

The warm air from the heater warmed his face as he buckled up and started forward. He'd studied the map of the park so he had the route to the largest boat ramp in his head. They took a quick right turn to enter the main road that circled the various picnic activity areas. It took five minutes to arrive at the boat ramp. They parked side by side in a small parking area.

Candy met John at the open tailgates of the SUV's.

He raised the screwdriver. "I'll take off the license plates first. Why don't you get in the Tahoe since it's so cold?"

She wrapped a sweater around her middle. "I'll start to move stuff. The quicker we're done, the quicker we're on our way."

He nodded and went to the front of the Murano. It didn't take long to get the plate off. He walked to the back and finished transferring all the bags to the Tahoe while Candy worked on the stuff in the back seat.

"There's a trash bag in the right door pocket. We need to pull out stuff in the side pockets and the glove box. Start the Murano and get warm." John knelt down to remove the back license plate. The second bolt wouldn't budge.

"God damn it," he shouted. Snow plastered his hair and his ears were nearly frozen. He opened the back of the Tahoe and retrieved the tool bag, then searched for a can of liquid grease. He sprayed a heavy dose on the head of the bolt and tried it again. Thankfully it moved and he had the plate off in seconds.

Candy met him with a filled trash bag. "The Murano is clear."

He took the bag from her and stuffed it in the back of the Tahoe. "What about finger prints? I've never been printed," John said.

"I think we're okay as along as the Murano is submerged for a while."

"Good, let's do this." He placed everything else in the tool bag and closed the tailgate. "Get warm while I position the Murano at the top of the boat ramp. You'll need to help me push it down the ramp."

John wanted to do this alone. For some reason his heartbeat had picked up and his stomach felt queasy. He'd felt the same way the day Jessie had been cremated. All he had to do was to get through it. He jumped in the Murano, pulled down the sun visor, and found a picture of Jessie that he'd taped to it. Candy had missed it. Or maybe she'd left it for him.

He slipped his finger under the tape and pulled off the photo. Jessie stood beside the SUV in the angle of the open driver's door. This was right before she'd driven her new vehicle to her favorite grocery store on its maiden voyage. Fresh salmon, corn on the cob, and sourdough bread were on the list for their first barbeque of the summer. *God, he'd loved that woman, always would*. He tucked the ends of tape against the photo's back and placed it in the inside pocket of his jacket. It was time.

He backed out of the parking spot and crawled to the boat ramp, checking for any ice. He positioned the front of the vehicle about ten feet from the Potomac River, straightened the front tires, and rolled down all the windows. The angle should be enough for it to roll easily. He placed the gearshift in Park, turned off the ignition, and opened the door. Picking up the keys from the middle tray of the console, he stuffed them in the pocket of his jeans as his feet hit the ramp. Now he wanted this over with and quickly.

Candy had the sixth sense of a saint and was by his side as soon as he exited.

"How do we do this?" she asked. He knew she knew exactly how to submerge a vehicle. And that's why he loved her.

"It's in park now. I think it'll roll in on its own once we give it a strong nudge."

"I love a plan." Snow blew around Candy's face. "Let's go," she shouted as she moved to the back of the Murano.

John muttered a quick "Good-by Jessie, I love you," as he leaned in and moved the gearshift down. He moved back, slammed shut the door, and joined Candy at the rear.

They nodded to each other and placed their hands on the tailgate, pushing against the door below the open window. After one long groan, the SUV moved forward and picked up speed before it hit the water. It tipped forward in slow motion, water cascaded through all the windows, and within seconds, the Murano disappeared into the Potomac River.

Relieved the SUV had submerged so fast, John grabbed Candy's hand. "Come on, I'm hungry. Let's find a drive-through."

Candy grinned. "California, here we come."

They climbed in the Tahoe, adjusted the heater to high, and retraced their route to the entrance of the park. John parked and jumped out to close the gate. He replaced the chain and padlock in the same setup he'd found them. No one would know the lock was broken until next spring.

After ten minutes of driving toward the interstate, John noticed headlights behind them. "There's a car behind us."

"What?" Candy turned around. "Where did it come from? I'll check a map."

"It couldn't have been in the park. There has to be another road."

"Just a sec," Candy said, gazing at her phone. "There's a farm road crossing this road. We crossed it a couple of minutes ago." She turned around again. "John, that's a police car."

"Shit. Stay calm. He doesn't know that we didn't come from the farm road." John was sick to death of drama. He checked his speed, no problem. But still, he prayed a cop following them was random, a freak coincidence.

They drove in silence for a few minutes and the distant view of the freeway appeared. The cruiser was still behind them, following at a respectable distance.

It took only a couple of minutes to reach the intersection with I-95. Snow covered the road. The storm wasn't that bad away from the trees. John maneuvered to the left lane and flicked the turn signal. What would the cop car do?

As he waited at the intersection for the light to turn green, John watched the cruiser head to their right. "Halleluiah. The cop is going the other direction."

"Good. Do you mind stopping at Wal-Mart?" Candy still held her phone. "There's one a couple of miles down the road. I need new underwear."

"Sure. We can grab lunch as well."

"When do you want Dark Horse to send the final email?"

"Later." John glanced at her. "I just had a thought. Do we need to worry about the Murano's VIN number?"

~~*

Emmett clicked off his cell phone after a quick conversation with Valerie. His feet rested on the corner of his desk and he once again thanked the Dating Gods for his hook-up with her. He had no clue how long it would last but in the meantime, he had a smile on his face. She was making chili and expected him in less than an hour. Before he headed out, he had some business to take care of.

He checked his email—nothing much there. Then he remembered to send his notes from their discussion on the way back to the West Wing to Georgia. Funny, when he'd made his deal with Harry, he'd been convinced his political leanings sided with the Democratic manifesto. After listening to Georgia today and the nitty-gritty of her political thinking, he wasn't so sure he was a Democrat. Jesus, did he truly lean toward the Republican platform? This idea he should research and honestly consider. He figured that getting older had changed his views. He wasn't a silly kid any longer.

What would he say to Harry since he'd already agreed to spy for him? Talk about a deal with the devil. Emmett had been nuts to make a pact with dumb shit Harry. Or, maybe he could use it to screw him—that would be fun.

Just to be an ass, he checked the latest presidential polls that pitted Georgia against him. Yay, there were already a couple out there. Thank God for 24/7 political news sites. They were simple polls with two questions—whom would you vote for in November and whom do you find most likeable? Oh my God . . . Georgia won by over twenty points in each poll. This was awesome.

He couldn't let such good news go to waste and printed out the poll results. Maybe Harry was in his office.

This will be too much fun.

He grabbed the paper off the printer and headed down the hall. The door to the VP office was open as was the inner office. He tapped on the frame as he spied the VP seated behind the desk.

"Hey, fancy you being here on a winter's afternoon."

Harry looked up and scowled when his eyes slammed on Emmett. "What do you want?"

He walked into the office, sat on the sofa, and crossed an ankle over his knee, totally relaxed at being in the presence of the VP. "Guess what?"

Harry gave him a blank stare. "What, asshole?"

"A couple of presidential polls were conducted overnight. Fast, huh?"

"Yeah . . . so, whatever." Harry dismissed the concept of quick polls with a flick of his hand.

"They're from Fox News and NBC. Those folks are tigers."

"Tigers my ass." Harry closed the top of his computer. "I'm busy. Again, what do you want?"

"Like I said, I think you'll be interested in these polls. We don't want to ignore the people."

"Spit it out, Emmett. You're such a girl."

He clenched his teeth in disgust and then remembered who sat at the desk. "Well . . . Vice President Roberts the gist of both polls is this—you're more than twenty points behind President Ross as to both electability and likeability." Emmett stood. "Seriously dude, you should reconsider your candidacy. How in the hell can you make up those poll points in nine months? You can't and I quit. I don't work for losers."

Harry laughed. "You're the loser." He cocked his head to one side and tapped his cheek with an index finger. "Lame ass polls mean nothing to me. Now get the hell out of my office."

Emmett rose and quickly made his way back to his own office. He had no desire to deal with Harry again. He shrugged on his coat and stuffed his laptop and tablet into his briefcase. He exited the White House and walked to the employee parking lot. The snow was refreshing. He'd grown up driving on snowy roads and this was nothing compared to a Colorado snow storm. Washington residents typically panicked at more than an inch of snow and he considered it another day at the office.

~~*

Whatever. Harry congratulated himself for being so much smarter than Emmett, the weasel, who'd turned around and scurried out of the VP office. *He's the loser!* Who gave a shit about polls this early in the campaign? Emmett was another failure in the game of D.C. politics that misinterpreted the data. He opened the bottom drawer of his desk; his trusty bottle of scotch was almost full. He pulled it out with a glass and poured to the rim. He took a sip and grinned. This might be a long afternoon

Emmett might be an asshole but Harry couldn't take a chance with the polls and opened his laptop. Long ago he'd saved a list of news websites for his personal research and routinely checked them. A politician had to stay current with what his enemies were espousing. Losers all, but still, he couldn't be too careful. The last thing he needed was to get blindsided during an interview by some smartass reporter.

Journalism used to be a respected profession. Not any more. Every young asshole with a computer and a website sets up a blog. They all think they're political experts and the next . . . hmm, maybe David Brinkley or Walter Cronkite.

Fucking jerks, every one of them.

He sipped his drink. Damn, he loved scotch. It was better than just about anything else. He drank only the best.

His cell phone rang and he glanced at the screen of the phone next to his laptop. Crap, it was his wife. He'd better answer or she'd keep calling.

"Hello, Marjorie."

"Harry, where are you? Have you even considered the weather? We're having a terrible snowstorm."

"It started to snow? I've been working at the West Wing and haven't looked outside." He rose and walked to the window behind this desk, pushing back the sheer drapery thing. Well hell, it was snowing but not a whiteout. She always exaggerated. "Yeah, I see it."

"When will you be home? The roads will be awful . . . just awful." The usual whine entered her voice. Harry hated it. Damn, he'd get home once she was in bed so he wouldn't have to listen to her gripe in person.

"You know how it snows here. I'll wait for it to stop and then get a ride home. Don't wait on me for dinner."

"Are you sure?"

"Yes, I'm working on my campaign promises. You know how important this is to me."

"Of course I do." Her voice had hardened, so typical for his wife. She went from one extreme to the other in nano seconds. "All right then. Good luck with your imaginary promises. Love you."

"Love you, too." He clicked off and sighed. Why had he taken the plunge twenty years ago and married her? He'd not had one truly happy day since the day he'd said "I do." He downed the rest of the scotch and refilled the glass. No wonder he drank, being tied to a woman like Marjorie. He should've divorced her years ago and married some hot babe who knew how to keep a man happy. He snorted with laughter . . . a babe who could give a decent blowjob. A talent his wife had not yet acquired.

Seated at his desk, he focused on the computer and again reviewed the news stories on the presidential election. They all seemed to follow the same track—Georgia Ross was a much more favorable presidential candidate than Harry Roberts.

His fist hit the desktop in a loud thud. Damn it to fucking hell. Emmett had been telling the truth about the overnight polls. He lagged behind Georgia by over twenty points. That had to change.

What could he do? He sucked down scotch as he considered his limited options. His mind rolled from one idea to another. Like a fool, he'd cancelled the contract on her once he'd been appointed VP. He'd ended up paying John twenty million dollars to eliminate Danny, who was still alive, and to keep silent about Harry's desire to kill Madame President.

Now that he was VP, did he dare think again about truly eliminating Georgia? He could do it without John's help, one way or another.

He pushed his chair back from the desk.

Eliminating Madam President—for good. That was probably for the best.

Hmm . . .

He scooted back to the desk to top off his glass and then pushed back again.

Turning toward the window, he saw a sliver view of falling snow where the sheers separated. Falling snow had inspired many a poet—Shakespeare, Burns, Keats. Whatever, it created car accidents, too. Sipping the drink, he considered his options concerning Georgia, none of them good. He sure as hell didn't have time to recruit someone like John Smith to do the job. He'd have to eliminate her the old fashioned way—spending tons of money and pushing her candidacy into the ground.

He had work to do and pushed the chair back to his desk. Ignoring the websites and another headache, he opened a blank document to list what he'd talk about as his mandate for the country as the new president.

He sighed, always happy with the world while he sipped scotch. What words of wisdom did he have for the voters?

The West Wing phone rang, the button for the Oval Office lit. Crap, Georgia was in her office. He picked up the receiver.

"Hello Harry, I see you're working as well."

"Yes ma'am, how did your speech go this morning?" He didn't give a shit but figured it was polite to ask.

"It was good. We had a couple of hecklers."

"Really?" He didn't care about her hecklers.

"Yes, they were escorted out. But that's not why I called. Do you know how the House is leaning on the legislation for the Chinese trade bill? I'd like to know who is dragging their feet not supporting it."

Damn. She sounded so confidant, so sincere, and so earnest. Fuck, he'd used the word 'earnest' describing Georgia Ross. He shook his head, feeling a tad dizzy.

"I don't know the answer to that but I'll make a few calls and get back to you." He responded with just the right amount of "your wish is my command" bullshit logic.

"Thanks, Harry, I appreciate that," she gushed. "Don't work too long today. The roads are getting dicey."

Hadn't he already heard about the stupid roads from his bitchy wife? Damn. "Yes ma'am, I'll be leaving in an hour or so. Have a good Sunday."

"You as well."

He pounded his fist on the desk. God, Harry fucking hated Georgia Ross. He blew a breath and told himself to calm down. He had work to do and looked at another news website, forgetting that he'd intended to start writing his campaign promises. This site had Georgia twenty-four points in front of Harry.

That simply wouldn't do.

He refilled his glass and noticed the handgun in the same drawer where he stored his scotch. He'd had it in his Capitol Hill desk for years—insurance in case some terrorist broke in.

Hmm . . . his fingers gripped the barrel and he pulled the gun from the drawer and set it on his lap.

It was a very nice handgun, a Smith & Wesson .38 Special. He cleaned it every six months. He slid his hand softly over the barrel and then to the grip. The smooth surfaces felt like silk to his fingers. He loved this gun.

Maybe he could use it . . . use it to take care of his problem. He drank more scotch and the idea blossomed in his head. Why not? He could shoot Georgia and then go home. Hopefully, Marjorie would be in bed. Georgia would be caught off guard and wouldn't put up a fight.

He'd shoot her in the head, as he didn't want her to suffer. Get it over with. Yeah, that would work. Then he could go home.

No one would ever think the VP had killed the president. Perfect, he had a plan.

He drank more scotch, sniggered at his superior intelligence, and cradled the gun in his hands.

Very cool plan, Harry.

~~*

Candy loved Wal-Mart; she'd found everything she needed—girl stuff and road snacks. John hadn't been the typical male making lame comments as she shopped. He pushed the cart behind her and acted like a gentleman. They truly made a good team. After paying with cash, they headed to the exit with the cart full of their purchases. The door opened automatically as they reached it and frigid air rushed in.

"Holy crap," Candy said and they hurried to their vehicle. "The temperature must have dropped twenty degrees." She pulled her sweater around her middle and regretted not buying a coat. John had tried to talk her into it but she wouldn't spend the money since they were headed to California. He popped open the back and handed her the keys. Snowflakes peppered his head and shoulders.

"Hop in and get the heater started. You'll freeze out here."

She nodded and jumped in without hesitation. After starting the Tahoe and adjusting the heater, she scooted over the console to the passenger seat. No way would she offer to drive. Driving in heavy snow still made her nervous, plus it was downright scary.

John joined her and brushed his hair. "Man, it's really coming down."

"Do you think it's safe to drive?"

"Yeah, no problem. We'll get out of it in a couple of hours." He backed out and headed for the exit to the I-95 feeder road. "The weather report said the storm wasn't gonna move, but hang around Washington until tomorrow. We head south and we'll be fine."

"Okay," Candy said, relieved that John was so calm. She retrieved her phone from her purse. "I'll check the GPS app on my phone."

"Good. I had an idea while we were shopping. Let's stop in New Orleans for a couple of days. I've never been there."

"Me either. I like that idea. I'll check out the quickest route." She hoped the snow wouldn't impact the data on her phone. No problem, the maps app came right up. She found New Orleans and then went backwards to D.C. with a couple of different routes. After checking the mileage of each one, she had their route. "I've got it."

"You figured out our directions?"

She glanced up and noticed they were on the interstate. The traffic wasn't too heavy, which was good since they were traveling close to the posted speed limit. John was a safe driver and after living in Colorado, accustomed to driving on snowy roads. "Yes, I have a plan. We take I-95 to south of Richmond, Virginia and then get on I-85. We can stay the night in Charlotte, North Carolina. It's about seven hours from D.C. We'll get there after dark but it's interstate all the way."

"Sounds like a good plan. Can we make it to New Orleans by Sunday night?"

"Absolutely. I'll make a hotel reservation." She spent a long time looking at a map of the French Quarter and researching hotels. Then she discovered a Harrah's Casino and Hotel with a parking garage. Perfect. She grinned at John. "Would you like to do some gambling? New Orleans has a big casino."

"Hell, yeah. That'll be fun."

She called the hotel and reserved a mini-suite for two nights. She used her new debit card for the reservation. After she finished and thought about the name on the card, she remembered they had one uncompleted task.

"Dark Horse still has an email to send."

"I just thought of that myself. You have it ready as a draft?"

"Yes. Should I use your computer or your phone?"

"The phone." He took it out of his shirt pocket and handed it to her. "Finally we're at the end of this journey. Passcode is 1966."

Candy punched it in and touched on the Internet app. John provided the login information and nothing happened. "Damn, no signal. I can't send it."

"The snow's not any worse. It must be a cell tower on the blink."

"I'll wait and try again." *Hell no, it was God's way of getting back at her*. What? Why would God be upset with her? She sighed, why indeed.

It had to do with John. But from her point of view, John had done a good thing for the country. Yes, the shooting of Gardner was sad for his family but in this situation, the entire country was more important. Gardner was a lousy president, just like the eight years before him, and the U.S.A. was on track to changing for the worse. John had stopped that awful progression by enabling Georgia Ross to become president. She was smart and seemed to be dedicated to getting things back on track.

John had made the correct decision.

This weather was simply a winter storm and God had nothing to do with it. She understood the concept of collateral damage.

An hour later they, transitioned to I-85 and Candy noticed the snow was lighter. She looked at John's phone for a signal—three bars.

"I'll try to send the email again."

John sent her a smile. "Would you mind reading it to me . . . you know, just to be sure. This is the last one."

"You bet." She successfully entered the email login ID and password and touched on the Draft folder. "Okay, this is the body of the message:

Nita....You and your partner must understand the seriousness of this situation. Harry Roberts, VP of the U.S.A. is unhinged. He will do ANYTHING to become U.S. president. He paid twenty million dollars for the assassination of President Gardner. I would not carry out his plan to kill President Ross. She is in grave danger. Harry Roberts will try to kill her at some point. You must stop him. Emails with Harry are attached to prove he hired the shooter to kill Gardner and Ross....Dark Horse"

"I'm happy with the wording. How about you?" John said.

"I like the words 'grave danger', very cool. Ready to go?" She looked at John and he nodded. Good enough. She touched Send and the email winged its way through cyberspace.

John reached his arm toward Candy and squeezed her hand. "We're done, babe. Fun times ahead."

"Yippee, I hope Nita pays attention to what we said."

~~*

"Damn," Nick said as he maneuvered around the fourth traffic accident since they'd left the Hilton. "People in Washington cannot drive in bad weather. What's up with this town and fender-benders?"

"Oh, you know, no one is really paying attention . . . kind of like Congress."

He turned into the alley to park on the driveway behind her house. "Very funny. Just like you, I get frustrated with all the mumble-jumble from Congress. No one tells the truth." He turned off the ignition and opened the door. "Man, it's cold." He ran around to open the door for Nita and helped her out. "Hang on tight."

The entered the back of her row house and climbed the stairs to the kitchen.

"I'll start a fire." Nick tossed his jacket on a dining room chair.

"Good idea. I'll make coffee." She went to her computer first. "Nothing from Dark Horse."

"We wait then." He headed to the living room and first clicked on the television. Cable news sprang to life and the weather person pointed to a map. "Yes, we know it's snowing," Nick muttered. He opened the fireplace screen then reached into the wood box and dragged out three logs. He was glad he'd filled the box yesterday. It didn't take long for the flames to build along the logs.

"Nice fire," Nita said as he stood. She handed him a mug.

"Thanks." He plopped on the sofa and picked up the TV remote. "I guess now we wait."

"I'm too antsy to concentrate on anything."

"Ah, babe," he said as he threw his arm around her shoulder and pulled her closer to him. "Snuggle with me and we'll find a movie to watch." He began to click through the channels. They agreed on *Top Gun* starring Tom Cruise . . . good music and good action. The film had enough drama to keep both of them interested and immune to the email inbox on Nita's computer.

After a while, they both stretched their legs out, feet resting on the coffee table, and relaxed into the movie's drama. Nick tuned out the situation with Dark Horse and his personal dilemma of not disclosing the identity of his "source" to Nita. He prayed she'd understand his need for secrecy. If she didn't, their relationship would go downhill again and all because of him.

He was far from the point of thinking about marriage with Nita. Yet he did enjoy the time they'd been spending together. But the long-term—he wasn't sure they had the stuff to make it work. Maybe he wasn't ready to settle down with anyone.

Halfway through the film Nita shook his leg then rose from the sofa. "I need another cup of coffee. How about you?"

He clicked pause. "Thanks, sounds good." He handed off his mug and she walked away. He figured she wanted to check her email again. Thinking about Dark horse led him to an idea he'd been tossing around for a couple of days.

Writing a book—one about this whole experience, the investigation of the shooter. He couldn't decide whether to write it as fiction or non-fiction. Whatever, that decision would come. He could write it as a political tell-all, whichever way it went. Or, as a mystery or a thriller, both would be fun. He scratched the side of his face. Yes, the most basic decision about a book must be made before going forward. *Jesus, Romano, fiction or non-fiction?*

"Here you go; fresh coffee and brownies." Nita handed him the mug and sat next to him, placing the plate on the coffee table.

"Thanks." He picked up a brownie, leaned over and kissed her temple. "You always think of the right thing. Ready for the rest of the movie?"

She nodded. He settled back and touched the remote to resume *Top Gun*. Maverick was on the move.

They said little to each other until the movie ended an hour later.

"That was good." Nita stretched her arms over her head. "I'll check my email one more time." She walked around the sofa to the dining room.

Five seconds later she screamed, "Oh, my God." Nick jumped up and hurried to her.

"Is there an email?"

She fanned her face with her hand. "You will not believe this. Dark Horse says the bad guy is Harry Roberts . . . and, he attached emails. Oh. My. God. This is freaking incredible."

He'd never seen Nita so excited. Yeah, they had a big story here—if they weren't thrown in jail for withholding information, obstructing justice—yeah, something not good. He should call Adam. "I need to see the email."

"I'll read it to you." Nita read it aloud to him. The words that shocked him the most were that *President Ross was in grave danger*.

"Bring up the attachment." He leaned over her shoulder and read the emails she scrolled through. "Holy shit. We can't keep this hidden."

She turned around to face him. "Who would believe this?"

He swallowed hard. "My source would."

"Yeah? Who is this wonderful source?"

"Now, Nita, don't be mad. I can explain everything."

She rose slowly from her desk chair and stepped toward the window. It was still snowing. He had a hunch this wasn't going so good. She backed her butt against the breadth of windows and folded her arms over her chest. "All right, Nick, tell me what's really going on."

Nick held his palms out in front of his chest, a sure sign Nita wouldn't like what he was about to say. She twirled her index finger, encouraging him to start talking.

"Please don't be mad that I didn't tell you before."

"Spit it out, Romano."

He sat in his usual chair at the dining table. "My source . . . is Adam Martinez, Director of the FBI. He—"

Her heart slammed to the floor then bounced back as she gulped. "Why in the hell would you keep this from me? Why in the hell would you be so sneaky? Why in the hell are you such a jerk?" The last few words were yelled and she shook her fisted hands in the air.

"Babe—"

Nita wagged her index finger in front of her chest. "Don't you dare try to 'babe' me. Damn you, Nick. How could you be so . . . so, mean to me?"

"I wasn't being mean. I didn't know if I could tell you in the beginning. Finally, I asked Adam and he said okay if I absolutely had to. I am sorry."

"You've said that before." She pulled her length of hair over her right shoulder and raised a hand. "Stop. Now isn't the time to deal with you being a jerk. We need to get this information to . . . Adam, I guess."

He pulled his cell phone from his shirt pocket. "Send the Dark Horse email to me and I'll forward it to Adam."

"No, I'll send it directly to Adam."

Nick narrowed his eyes, which amped up her anger. He said, "No. I'm not giving you his email address. He hasn't given me the authority to do that."

She hated to admit his reasoning made perfect sense. "I'll send you the email." She sat at her desk and forwarded the Dark Horse email to Nick. "Dark Horse makes Harry Roberts sound crazy by saying President Ross is in grave danger. Should you call Mr. Martinez to let him know about this? We shouldn't take a chance. That email is starting to creep me out."

"I think you're right." He stood and worked with the phone in his hands then brought it to his ear as he walked to the living room.

Nita couldn't hear a damn thing he said. She printed out the last Dark Horse email and the attachment as he returned.

"He didn't answer his phone so I left a message."

"I don't have a good feeling about this," she said as she rose and stuffed her cell phone and the printed pages in her purse. "I think we should go to the White House."

"And do what? They'll throw us out and probably arrest us."

Nita threw Nick's jacket at him and shrugged on hers. "Details.

Remember, the end justifies the means." She held open the back door. "Let's go. You can call him again on our way."

They quickly loaded into Nick's SUV and headed to the White House via Dupont Circle and Connecticut Avenue. The snow slowed their progress but thankfully, the roads weren't filled with stop-and-go traffic. The streetlights illuminated the roadway with a fairy-like glow. While the snow falling seemed lighter than earlier that afternoon, the accumulation on the streets was an issue.

"This is a little bit scary," Nita said after the vehicle slid on a patch of ice.

"Don't worry, I'm being careful. What entrance of the White house should we go to?"

"I don't know. I've never been there before." Nita pulled out her cell phone. "I'll look at a map. Call Adam, he'll know."

"All right, I'll try again."

"Be careful driving and talking at the same time," she said quickly.

"Whatever."

Whatever indeed. She exhaled a long breath to relax her nerves before checking the maps app. Zeroing in on the White House compound, she saw a half-dozen entrances. Which one should they take? Where was President Ross?

"Presidents are always around Secret Service guys, right? I've got a really bad ache in my stomach that President Ross is in real danger."

"I wonder where Harry Roberts is? He hasn't been VP all that long, does he spend time in the Speaker's Office at the Capitol or at the West Wing." Nick had his phone to his ear. "Damn, he's still not answering."

"That doesn't make sense to me. How can he not be available by phone?"

"Maybe he has another phone."

"Hold on." Nick shouted. The back end of the SUV slid to the right. Nita watched Nick turn the steering wheel to the right, into the skid. It seemed like slow motion before the vehicle righted itself and stopped in front of a large tree branch blocking the street.

"Crap." Nita's hand flew to her chest. She coughed, not aware she'd been holding her breath. Damn, that was scary.

"Are you okay?" Nick turned to her and grinned. "Not bad driving for a kid from Texas, huh?"

She mentally bopped him on the head. They could've been killed in a car accident and he was bragging about his driving?

"I'm fine," she replied. "Now, get out there and move that tree from the road."

He looked out the windshield. "I'll need your help."

Of course he would. She opened the passenger door. "Let's do it." The air wasn't as cold as she expected. They reached the tree together and Nick kicked it with his foot.

"Is that how you propose to move it?" she said, grinning.

"No, just checking if it's heavy."

"I say we both lift on one side and pivot it around to the edge of the street."

Nick nodded as he took gloves out of his jacket pocket and put them on. Nita did the same. "Be careful, the road is slick, don't want any falls."

Nita ignored him and bent over; taking the end of the branch while Nick placed himself to her right at a thicker area.

"One-two-three," Nick yelled and they both raised the branch, moving carefully toward the side of the street. He must have hit a slick spot as his right foot slid sideways and he fell toward Nita and ended with his left knee banging against the branch they both dropped.

Nita bent over him, searching his face. "Are you okay?" His position looked awkward and painful. "Is anything broken?"

"I don't think so but the knee hurts. Help me up." She shoved her shoulder under his left arm and held on as he slowly moved his left leg and stood. He definitely favored that leg.

"You go back to the SUV. I can finish this." She turned away from him, bent over, and used both hands to push the branch the last couple of feet to the side of the street. Turning around, she found Nick still on the street. "We need to get going."

He hobbled to the vehicle and they both climbed in. The warm air was soothing to Nita's cold face. "How's your knee. Should I drive?"

"Banged up, I'll live," he replied as he pulled his cellphone from the middle console. "Damn. Adam called and didn't leave a message." He put the SUV in gear and drove slowly forward.

"No message? Doesn't he think President Ross possibly being in danger is an issue?" Nita fisted her hands. "I can't believe this."

"I didn't tell him she might be in danger."

Nita glared at him. "Why the hell not?"

"Because we aren't one hundred percent certain that Dark Horse is legitimate."

"Damn it, we tested him. He had the right caliber of the bullet that shot Gardner." Her voice rose as heat enveloped her face. "I

cannot believe you did that. Call him back." She retrieved her phone
and looked at the maps app. "And take the curve onto 17th Street. It's
a couple of blocks ahead." She thought about their earlier conversation
before they'd left her house. "You didn't forward the email did you?"

He didn't say anything for a good ten seconds. "No. I figured I
should talk to him first. Explain things."

"Explain things my ass. I should have come by myself." She
glared at him and he finally glanced at her. "You're worried about
upsetting or losing your precious source. *Damn it.*"

"That's not true."

"Whatever." She watched the blue ball crawl across the map on
her phone's screen. It was slow driving, as the streets needed plowing.
"The curve is just ahead."

"I know where I'm at."

"Really? You could've fooled me." Sarcasm frosted her words.
Why did he have to act like this? That was a question for another time.

"There's an accident ahead."

Her head snapped up from watching the map. "Great," she
snarled. "Would you please call Mr. Martinez again?"

He narrowed his eyes briefly and placed the phone against his left
ear. After a few seconds he spoke. "Adam, this is Nick again. I really
need to speak with you. This is very important and may involve the
safety of President Ross."

"Finally you mention her." Nita gazed out the side window, her
anger at Nick simmering below the surface. Now was not the time to
have it out with him.

They stopped at the rear of two vehicles behind the accident.
Police lights flashed in the falling snow and a wrecker driver worked
at getting a dark coupe loaded on the bed of his tow truck. The
streetlamps provided enough light to enable them to see the action.
Nita noticed the time on the dashboard clock, 5:09. They waited in
silence. Why couldn't the wrecker hurry it up? Jesus, now the driver
and the cop were talking next to the truck. Then the cop hauled
himself onto the truck bed and checked all of the chains in slow
motion.

"That guy is slow," Nick commented.

"Ya think?" She nearly gave him the finger but stopped herself,
as the action was childish. Instead she fisted her hands and crossed her
arms over her chest, tapping her right foot on the carpet in front of her
seat. *Come on people, let's move.*

At last, the driver climbed in the truck. He sat there forever before the wrecker moved and slowly headed down the street. The cruiser's lights turned off and it followed the tow truck.

Nita checked the time again, 5:28. "Let's go people." Why were the cars in front of them so slow to move?

"You don't have to yell," Nick said, as he drove forward.

She ignored his comment and looked at the map on her phone. "Go straight on 17th." Which gate to go to? Whichever route they took, two gates stood between them and the White House. Should they attempt to get to the West Wing first? She'd bet anything that President Ross would be working since she had a new campaign in front of her and the Iowa caucuses would commence on Monday. She studied the map, looked at the satellite image as well as a tour map, and shook her head.

"We have a problem," she said.

"What?"

"There's no way we can get in the White House grounds unless we're invited, we bop a guard on the head, or we jump over a fence and get arrested."

"You're right."

She had to do something. "I'm calling the White House. Surely the switchboard is open 24/7."

"Might as well since Adam hasn't returned my call." He stopped for a red light. Bordered by office buildings and restaurants, the street was almost empty. "I'll drive around the perimeter of the White House grounds until we reach someone."

Holding her cellphone, Nita entered the number she found on the White House website. After two rings, someone answered.

"The White House, good evening, how may I help you?" a crisp young female voice said.

She hadn't considered what she'd say, well, she'd wing it. "My name is Nita Andrews and I'm a political blogger here in Washington. I've recently received information that indicates President Ross may be in danger."

"Ma'am, you said danger, correct?"

"Yes." She had a brilliant idea. "I need to speak with the Secret Service at the White House. Honestly, this isn't a joke."

"Please hold."

While she remained on hold, Nick turned left on Constitution Avenue, the southern border of the grounds. The SUV plowed through the snow on the street like a bull charging a matador. With the streetlights and the glistening snow, the world outside their warm vehicle seemed off balance.

"She put me on hold." Nita glared at her phone in disbelief. "Why?"

"How many calls do you suppose the White House receives like that?"

"Right, I get it. They think I'm a flake. I bet she's checking to see if my number is on the 'crazy citizen list'. *Please* call Mr. Martinez again."

"I hate to keep bugging him." Nick was acting like an idiot.

"Damn it, Nick, the president could be in danger." She held up her hand as he started to respond.

"This is Special Agent Brown. How can I help you?" A deep male voice had Nita's heart racing.

"Are you with the Secret Service at the White House?" The tone of Nita's voice had gotten higher.

"Ma'am, how can I help you?"

She sucked in a breath. "Sir, first, I'm not a flake. My name is Nita Andrews. I have a website called BetterPolitics dot com, you can Google me. My friend and I decided to investigate the shooting of President Gardner and we've come across some information we think is important."

"Why haven't you gone to the authorities with this important information?"

"Special Agent Brown, that's why I'm talking to you." *Please, please take me seriously.*

"Who is your friend?" he asked in the same matter of fact voice.

"His name is Nick Romano. He worked at the *Washington Chronicle* as a reporter for ten years." She gazed at Nick. "Do you have a website now?"

He shook his head.

"He doesn't have a website. But he's been trying to reach Adam Martinez by phone. He works at the FBI."

"How does he know Director Martinez?" The special agent's voice had the smallest amount of interest in his question.

"Uh . . . I hope I don't get in trouble for telling you this." While they'd waited for the accident, Nick had explained how he knew the FBI Director. She glanced at him and he shook his head. She ignored him. "Nick's aunt is dating Mr. Martinez, for three years I think."

"One minute, Miss Andrews." She could tell she'd been put on hold via a desk phone.

"Damn it, Nita." Nick's closed fist hit the steering wheel, only once so he wasn't really mad at her. "Adam will not be happy you shared that piece of information. He keeps his personal life private."

"I'm sorry, but this is an extraordinary situation. I bet he'll laugh it off once this is over." She had no clue what he'd do and prayed it wouldn't be arresting her for withholding information or sharing personal details. Of course, he'd have to arrest Nick, too. Maybe Nick's aunt could intervene.

The SUV moved into a left turn lane and stopped at another red light. Nita kept the phone to her ear and said a small prayer for the safety of President Ross.

"Miss Andrews, I'd like to see this information you have. I'll send an agent to get it. Where are you?"

The SUV went through the light and turned onto 15th Street, on the east side of the White House grounds.

"We just turned from Constitution heading north on 15th Street. We—"

"You're outside the White House?" He seemed surprised.

"Yes. Once we got this last email, we rushed down here to warn President Ross that she's in danger. We hoped Mr. Martinez would meet us. Anyway, I realized we couldn't get in a gate and that's why I called. I'm very worried about the president." She heard a muffled sound on the phone.

"Continue north on 15th to Hamilton Place and pull into the gate area. I'll meet you there."

"We'll be there in a minute."

She repeated the conversation to Nick.

"You know this whole thing is nuts, right?" He winked at her. "No one just drives up to the White House and gets in."

"I know." Oh crap, they were going to get arrested. She rubbed her left wrist. She'd never been handcuffed before. Would it hurt? She opened the maps app again. "Hamilton is the next street."

After a hundred feet or so, she saw the gate. Someone was standing in front of it and pointing to his left once they reached him. Nick swung the SUV in and rolled down his window.

"Hi, I'm Nick Romano with Nita Andrews. The Secret Service told us to stop here."

"Yes, sir, I'll need both of your ID's please."

Nita pulled her driver's license from her wallet, handed it to Nick, and stretched over the SUV's console to get a look at the guard. It was a young female wearing a winter cap and a thick jacket over a uniform of some kind. She took the licenses from Nick.

"Turn off your vehicle and wait here." She bent over to look inside the open window. "Do not move." She walked through an open door into a small building while another guard stood outside, watching them.

Nick pushed the SUV's off button and grinned at Nita. "I'm not going anywhere. Look at the size of the gun that guard is holding."

"They don't mess around." She realized that by some stroke of luck they'd landed under a lucky star to get this close to the White House. It was taking time; valuable time if the nervous ball in her stomach was rolling around for a reason. A news alert flashed across her phone screen and she saw Ross and Roberts in it. She touched the news app and read the story. "Oh no, this is awful."

"What?" He touched her arm and smiled.

"One of those quick political polls was conducted last night and Ross is more than twenty points ahead of VP Roberts. This is bad . . . very bad."

A golf cart with a hard cover came out of nowhere and stopped at the guardhouse. A tall man in a long dark coat jumped out, hurried in the door, and came out carrying a sheet of paper he folded and put inside his coat. The original guard followed closely behind. The both stopped at the SUV.

"I'm Special Agent Brown. Both of you step slowly out of the vehicle." He stepped back for Nick to climb out while the guard went to Nita's side. Nick limped a bit as he exited.

Once Nita stood next to Nick with her purse slung over her shoulder, the agent spoke. "Mr. Romano, please hand your car keys to the officer." He pointed at the female guard and Nick handed them to her. "She'll look over your vehicle while we're gone."

"Where are we going?" Nita asked, praying it wasn't jail.

"The West Wing, but first . . ." He nodded at the other guard, a young man who walked in front of Nick.

"Raise your arms, sir." The guard patted down Nick, front and back. "He's clear." He looked at Nita. "Stephanie, this one is yours." He held out his hand to Nita. "Your handbag, ma'am."

Stephanie searched both Nita and her purse, and they walked in front of Special Agent Brown to the golf cart. A man, dressed in black and holding a long gun, emerged from the back and pointed to the back seat without saying a word.

"Please get in, it's a short ride." They climbed in and sat on the bench seat behind Special Agent Brown while the second man stood behind them.

The cart backed up before turning around and heading down the middle of a road. Nita pulled her cell phone out of the inner pocket of her jacket and then touched the maps app. They were traveling west on Hamilton Place with snow covered trees to their left and a huge building looming on their right—the Department of the Treasury— great, she'd probably get a tax audit as well as jail time. The cross street ahead was East Executive Avenue.

Suddenly, she realized the snow had stopped—that had to be a good omen but the air was still cold. The cart slowed and turned right and she had her first glimpse of the White House. Oh. My. God. This was surreal. All of her dreams as a little girl of working at the White House gelled into that first close up glimpse. Her stomach rolled and nausea threatened. She rummaged in her purse for an antacid.

"What are you doing?" Nick whispered, lowering his head.

"Looking for an upset tummy tablet." She found a roll, tore off the paper and popped two in her mouth. The cart stopped at another gate that opened magically and they sped through it. Trees on the left blocked the White House from view for close to a minute then the cart drove past the largest of the trees and The President's House was very close. It glowed in the winter sky and seemed to sparkle covered in fresh snow. She nudged Nick's side with her elbow and nodded toward it.

"It's beautiful," he whispered.

They went through another gate then traveled along the north drive to the West Wing. After rounding a corner of the building, the golf cart stopped and Special Agent Brown climbed out, as did the man behind Nick and Nita.

"Come on." The special agent motioned for them to follow him. He punched in a code on a keypad and they entered a wide door into the West Wing.

Nita barely felt the floor beneath her feet. Being in any part of the White House was bizarre and her head was swimming with the seriousness of what they would be sharing with the Secret Service. They walked down a flight of stairs then forward along a hall. Her skin crawled with anxiety. She had to get herself under control or she'd be arrested for out of control nerves. She stole a quick glance at Nick who looked straight ahead, his jaw tense.

Special Agent Brown opened a door at the end of the hall. "Come on in and we can talk about this situation involving President Ross." He waved at someone and led them to a small round table and four chairs tucked in a corner of the room. Moveable walls blocked the table from the rest of the office. Nick and Nita sat next to each other. "Would you like a coffee?"

She nodded. "Sure, black for both of us."

He stood in the opening between the walls. "I'll be right back. Stay here."

Nita itched to poke her head around the wall to see where he went, but she didn't. Instead, she turned to Nick. "Can you believe we're here? This is unreal."

"I'm curious how they'll react to our investigation. Not much has been reported in the press about the progress of the feds investigating the shooting. I'd feel better if I'd talked to Adam."

Nita stood, walked around the table, and sat in the chair on the other side of Nick. Good. She had a partial view of the Secret Service office. How many regular people had an opportunity like this? It wasn't much to look at. A couple of old looking brown sofas faced each other and behind them were ugly gray cubicles—actually, very sad and drab. Nick shook her arm.

"What are you doing?"

"Nothing, just looking." She swiveled around to face him as Special Agent Brown and a woman walked toward them.

He set two large paper cups on the table then pointed at the woman next to him. "This is Special Agent Pitt. We'll both listen to your story." The two agents pulled back chairs and joined them at the table.

Nita swallowed hard, the spit stuck in her throat. She sipped coffee and noticed her hand was shaking. Apparently, Special Agent Brown noticed as well.

"Miss Andrews, no need to be nervous. Just tell us your story. We're good listeners."

She set the cup on the table and wrapped her hands around it. "O--kay. It started the night that President Gardner was shot." She explained their activities for the past ten days and their logic for what they did. Nick added clarification of his role and whom he'd interviewed. She spoke without emotion as best she could—just the facts. The long tale ended with the last email from Dark Horse and the declaration that President Ross was in grave danger from Harry Roberts.

"That email was scary and creepy and something we couldn't ignore," she said. "I guess driving down here, hoping to get in was kinda dumb."

"Not so much," the female agent said with a slight smile. "You're in the West Wing, aren't you?"

Nita and Nick nodded at the same time, grinned at each other.

"I need you to load all the emails from Dark Horse on a thumb drive." Special Agent Brown placed a shiny black drive next to her cup. "I'd like to look at them as soon as possible."

"I brought a copy of the last one with all the emails with Harry Roberts." Nita picked up her purse from the floor and pulled out the folded pages. She handed them to Special Agent Brown. He looked at the first page then went through the others one after the other. He nodded at the other agent. He hadn't given any indication he thought they were nuts or crazy—calmly listened to them and asked a few questions. Surely, that had to be a good sign.

"We need to check on something. You two stay here and we'll be right back."

Once they were out of earshot, Nita spoke. "I'll bet you a hundred bucks they're checking on the location of Harry Roberts."

"That's what I'd be doing." Nick squeezed her hand.

"How's your knee?"

"Better."

Nita noticed a good-looking older man walking toward them. He stopped at the table and smiled.

"Adam, I've been trying to reach you," Nick said, a note of relief in his voice.

"So I hear. What have you and this young lady been up to?"

~~*

For once in his life, Harry decided he'd drunk enough scotch for one sitting. He did have to get home after his business was completed and didn't want to give anyone the wrong impression. After all, he was so close to being sworn in as POTUS that he wanted to be able to remember every little thing and word that would be uttered during the ceremony.

He stroked the handgun on his lap. It made a big boom when fired—he changed his mind and decided to shove the barrel against Georgia's chest—that would quiet the sound.

He reached over to his briefcase on the floor next to the desk. The tilting of his head brought on a wave of wooziness but it dissipated once he sat upright again. He laid the briefcase on his lap. He took a deep breath to settle his nerves. Another headache threatened but he'd ignore the pain like he always did.

Once Georgia was dead, he'd mess up the office like they always did on TV and open the door to the Rose Garden. No one would ever know he'd done the deed. He gave a drunken snort at his cleverness. They'd think the bad guy was some terrorist sneaking into the Oval Office after he left.

"I'm so fucking smart, I'm so fucking smart." He sang the words in a high childish voice. "Ding-dong the whore is dead. I'm so fucking smart."

Cackling at his very clever plan, he put the gun in his briefcase then placed the folder holding all the ideas for his first major campaign speech and his campaign promises on top. He had a meeting scheduled tomorrow afternoon to go over the speech with Ben Howard. He might even ask Ben to stay for the Super Bowl.

After popping a couple of breath mints in his mouth, he rose, a tad unsteady, put his topcoat over his arm, picked up the briefcase and opened the door to his office. Stanley, his new VP bodyguard, waited in the outer office and stood when Harry walked through the door.

He'd already given Stanley a large cash payment to occupy Georgia's security detail while he was in the Oval Office. These guys got paid so little that they were open to a bribe or two.

"I'm going to Madam President for the meeting we talked about earlier." Harry walked a step or two behind Stanley, intent on placing one foot in front of the other. They soon met Frank in the main corridor; the door to the Oval Office was open. He knocked on the doorframe.

"Cold day, huh? You have time for a quick talk? I've got some information for you." He smiled his best Sunday school smile. He was such a practiced drunk.

"Not a problem." Georgia waved him in.

This was so easy. Harry walked in and shut the door behind him. She started to rise.

"No need to move," Harry said. "I'll sit in front of the desk." That way she wouldn't see him take the gun out of his briefcase. He sat in front of her doing his best to look like a vice president and not an excited schoolboy.

"Thanks, it's been a long day." She smiled and shuffled some papers on the desk. "Did you hear anything about the Chinese trade deal opposition?"

"I made some calls but couldn't get anyone to give me a straight answer. I'll go over to the Hill on Monday and feel around. I also want to check on the vote for the new Speaker." Harry could play with her for hours. She wasn't that smart and so easy to lead.

"Have you scheduled that?"

"My plan is this Wednesday or the next. I'll verify with the Clerk of the House." He'd already tired of their conversation and opened his briefcase just enough to shove his hand in and grip the pistol.

"Good. The sooner we get back to full speed, the better."

"Sure, Georgia, but I don't think you'll be included."

"What the hell does that mean?"

Harry rose and turned his back to her, setting the briefcase on the chair. He rotated and faced her, the gun pointed at her chest. His head pounded like a stake was being driven into it. He ignored it and leaned toward her over the presidential desk.

"It means you won't be around to care who the next Speaker is."

Her eyes widened and she gasped.

"Yes, Georgia, now it's your turn."

~~*

Nita looked at her watch again. Special Agent Brown and Mr. Martinez had left them close to fifteen minutes ago. She figured they were doing a quick check of the email addresses on the messages. God, she'd love to have the resources the feds had to do research. She chuckled to herself; maybe she should have looked at the FBI for a job. Then she thought again, nah, she liked being her own boss.

The special agent returned. "It's going to take me longer than I thought. Here's more coffee. Please hang tight for a bit longer."

"Sure," Nick replied. "We want to help."

Nita nodded and grabbed a cup. Now, she was hungry. The Hunky Fed, as she now thought of him, walked off again. She pulled her cellphone from her purse as an idea percolated and she needed to verify her truly clever thought. Drinking the coffee, she did a search on whitehouse.gov and soon found what she needed.

She nudged Nick's side with her elbow. He'd closed his eyes, resting his head on his hand, braced on the table. "Hey, wake up. I have an idea."

He opened his eyes and sat up, rubbing his jaw with his hand. "Another idea? Come on, let's wait for these guys to do their thing."

"I need to use the restroom."

"Go ask someone where it is."

"I need to go to the restroom on the main floor here." She pointed her right index finger toward the ceiling. "It's on the floor above us."

"Whatever, go."

"The Oval Office is on the main floor."

His mouth rounded. "Oh."

She showed him her phone. "These are graphics of this floor and the main floor of the West Wing. There's a staircase just outside the main door to this office. If we go up the stairs we won't be all that far from a door that looks like the visitor door to the Oval Office."

He'd lowered his head and spoke in her ear. "Do you have any idea of how much trouble we'll be in if we go exploring?"

"While the feds are somewhere verifying the shooter and Harry's emails, President Ross may be in danger up there."

He rolled his eyes. "Jesus, Nita, don't you think you're being overly dramatic? She has a security detail."

"Whatever. I need to go to the restroom. Girls can't hold it like you guys." She rose and slung her purse across her chest, cellphone in hand. She took a few steps away from the table and looked back at Nick. "Coming?"

He shrugged but rose and limped to her. "If we get arrested, I'm turning you in myself."

She grinned and grabbed his hand. "Follow me."

They walked quietly around the cubicles and encountered not one person. This was much too easy. They slipped out the door they'd entered and turned right. Yes, there were stairs and no one was in the hallway.

They hurried to the stairs and started up. Nick winced.

"Are you okay? Here, lean on my shoulder." Nita pushed her right shoulder under his arm. "We'll go one step at a time."

They came to a landing and rested.

"I can't believe we haven't run into anyone," Nick said, hardly out of breath.

"Maybe it's because of the storm and the roads. You know how Washington is when we have snow accumulation more than an inch."

"Hope a terrorist doesn't know about that."

"Ready for the next flight of stairs?" She leaned over and kissed his cheek. "Thanks for coming with me."

"Always an adventure."

They made their way up the second set of stairs slower than the first. Nick's knee was obviously worse than he'd let on. Finally they stepped on the West Wing's main floor. Nita swore that tiny pellets of power descended over her. It felt almost sexual but she shook it off and checked her cellphone. She turned to her left and looked around the corner—all clear.

"The Oval Office is down the hallway and the Cabinet Room is on our left. You okay?"

He slung his arm over her shoulder. "I guess we should act

casual, like we belong here."

"Exactly. We're simply looking for the women's restroom."

They started down the hall, gawking at the décor. Nita pushed away a fan girl infatuation with their location—the freaking West Wing of the White House—now was not the time. She sighed and stopped, throwing her arm straight in front of Nick. She pushed him behind a tall statue on the left side of the hall. She peeked out to get a better look.

Two men stood in a wide hallway, talking and gesturing with each other. Hmm, guards, White House police? She looked at the graphic on her phone—they must be at the main floor corridor and the Oval Office was just ahead.

She pushed her butt against the wall. What the hell should they do now? So much for her smart idea of going to the restroom. They were stuck.

"Maybe we should go back," Nick whispered.

"Let's give it a few minutes," she murmured against his cheek and then put her finger over his lips, shaking her head. Being stuck was a relative concept.

He nodded, with a thumb's up gesture. They would wait like silent little mice.

I must be a crazy person. Nita could not believe she'd suggested they defy the direct order of a Secret Service agent and roam, without permission, the halls of the West Wing. Was plain old stupidity a valid legal defense? At least she and Nick had stopped yelling at each other.

After a few long minutes, the two men moved to the right and out of sight.

"Where are they going?" Nick said softly.

She put her mouth to his ear. "To the restroom."

His chest bounced as he clapped a hand over his mouth to stop the laughter from spilling out. She punched his arm.

"No laughing here. This is a serious place." She kissed his cheek and ignored the steady boom-boom-boom of her heart. "Let's see what those two are doing. Come on." She moved around the statue and turned to make sure Nick was behind her and walking okay. He smiled and she inched forward to the end of the wall on the left. She poked her head around and viewed an empty and elegant, wide hallway that angled to the right. This had to be the corridor in front of the Oval Office. And in the middle of a rounded wall on the other side was a door, slightly open.

She sensed Nick right behind her. "No guards in sight." She

turned her head back to him. "That door over there goes into the Oval Office. I wonder if President Ross is around?"

Nick stepped forward and poked his head left and right. "The coast is clear. Let's see if she's there. I mean, we've come this far."

"Okay, we're in this together." She grabbed his hand and they tiptoed and limped across the marble floor to the door. Nick stood at the opening side and Nita by the hinge side.

Nick frowned. "I hear voices, she must be in there with someone."

"How do we handle this? If we go in, she'll freak out when she sees us."

Nick's eyes grew large. "Something is wrong. She's yelling 'no, no.' I'm going in."

Before Nita could say a word, Nick opened the door and stepped into the Oval Office. She followed him.

Not in a million years will she forget the sight she viewed the first time she entered the Oval Office. President Ross stood on the front side of a huge desk with her hands out in front of her and a man stood about a foot from her holding a pistol.

Nick yelled, "Stop, stop" and took several steps into the office. The man with the gun turned from the president and pointed the gun toward them, all in one motion. President Ross moved forward, followed by a loud boom echoing in the room. The guards rushed into the office and stopped a couple steps past Nita. They both held guns directed at the man.

"Vice President Roberts, please, put down the gun."

What? This crazy man was Harry Roberts? The guards stepped forward and Nita finally had a view of Nick on his back spread eagle on the carpet with blood gushing out of his chest. *No. Oh, God, no.* She fell to the floor beside him and put her hand on his chest in a feeble attempt to stop the blood.

She looked up, as Nick needed help, and witnessed Harry Roberts place the gun under his chin. His eyes were wild and his face glowed a shiny red color. He said something Nita couldn't hear before pulling the trigger and parts of his head flew upwards. She closed her eyes briefly to block out the sight and bent over Nick scooting around to cradle his head in her lap. Tears streamed down her face and tripped onto his cheeks. The truth was evident as his beautiful eyes stared at her without seeing. *Please God, let him have peace.*

~~*

Georgia stepped into Peter's arms once she exited their bathroom after a quick shower and attired in fresh clothes. She needed the strength of his arms like no other time in their many years together. He stroked her hair and held her tight, not saying a word.

After a couple of moments, she'd stepped back and sucked in a shaky breath. "I need to talk to Miss Andrews. She's had quite the shock. You'll come with me?"

He kissed her cheek. "I want to shake the woman's hand and say thank you."

"Exactly."

They walked from the bedroom into the living room next door. Gracie held a glass of something and stood angled at the window holding back the shear drapery. She turned around and rushed to her boss. "Are you okay?"

"I'm fine, just a little rattled." My God, what had happened not quite two hours ago would haunt Georgia for the rest of her life. She had no intention of sharing that with her chief of staff. The aftereffects were too personal.

"How about a drink?" Peter said.

"Why don't you get a bottle of that cabernet I like? Maybe our guest would like a glass as well. She'll be here shortly." Georgia settled on a sofa with Gracie sitting in a chair next to her.

"Madam President, this whole event seems surreal to me." Gracie reached her hand toward Georgia. "Are you truly okay? Just tell me, I can handle it."

"Don't worry so much." She squeezed Gracie's hand. "I'm fine and I'll be as good as new after a good night's sleep." Movement at the door had Georgia shifting her attention.

Special Agent Brown and Adam walked in with Miss Andrews who had a haunted look—pale face and sorrowful eyes.

Georgia rose and went to Nita. "Miss Andrews, you found everything you needed?"

Nita gazed at her for a moment before speaking. "Yes ma'am, you have nice soap here." She nodded to the special agent. "Thanks for the clean jacket and shirt."

"Yes ma'am." He walked back to the door and stood on one side, always guarding.

Georgia extended her hand. "Miss Andrews, I'm Georgia Ross. I was very thankful to see you and Mr. Romano this evening in the Oval Office. And, I'm very sorry about what happened to Nick. I owe him my life."

Nita visibly swallowed and shook Georgia's hand. "Thank you.

This isn't . . . not how this was supposed to end."

"I know, let's relax for a few minutes. Please join me on the sofa." Georgia sat and patted the cushion next to her. Nita sat on the sofa exactly where she'd patted.

Peter returned carrying a tray and set it on the coffee table. He smiled and extended his hand. "You must be Nita Andrews. It is a pleasure to meet you. Would you like a glass of cabernet? This is one of Madam President's favorite vintages." His eyes twinkled as he talked.

"Yes, thank you, I like wine," Nita said.

Peter poured a glass for the three of them. Gracie was a bourbon girl and had left the room to get a refill. He first handed a glass to Nita.

"Thank you."

"My pleasure." He handed a glass to Georgia and sat in a side chair next to the sofa. "I owe you a huge thank you for saving my wife's life."

"Actually, sir, it was Nick. He's the one who determined something was wrong." Georgia noticed Nita's face was void of emotion while she talked about her friend—in shock no doubt. They'd have a conversation about this subject later as now wasn't the time.

"Nita, I understand you're a blogger," Georgia said, attempting to help her relax. "I don't have time to read blogs myself, are you a conservative blogger, liberal, or in between?"

Nita smiled and tasted the wine. "I like the wine. Hmm, well, as a blogger I'm conservative and sometimes in between, but I've never aligned with any liberal policies or ideas . . . thus far, that is."

"I see, good to know we're on the same side of the aisle then." Georgia smiled and pointed at Gracie who had walked in and sat in the chair on the other side of Peter. "This is Gracie Evans, my chief of staff."

Nita frowned for a moment. "Are you the Gracie Evans who attended Georgetown?"

Gracie smiled. "Are you the Nita Andrews who attended Georgetown?"

Nita rose as did Gracie and they gave each other a quick hug. "How long has it been? I lost track of you when you transferred to Harvard."

Georgia raised her hand. "Hold on. You two know each other?"

Nita and Gracie nodded at the same time then Gracie spoke. "We were in several study groups together and lived in the same dorm. What a coincidence meeting like this."

Adam Martinez marched into the room. "Good evening everyone. Madam President, I hope you'll have time for an interview in the morning—standard procedure for this type of event. Miss Andrews, I'm so sorry for the loss of your friend. I understand you were engaged at one time."

Nita nodded.

"I've spoken with Mr. Romano's aunt, Carolyn Helms. She'll contact Nick's family. May I give her your telephone number?"

Nita nodded again.

"Good. Special Agent Brown will take you home when you're ready." Adam's eyes narrowed for a mere second then he said. "We'll also need to set up a time for an interview. Monday will be fine. I'll call you tomorrow."

"Thank you. I need time to process all this."

Georgia understood her completely. "Nita, please don't worry and take your time. From what I've heard, you're a very brave young woman. I heard you were worried about being arrested."

"Yes ma'am, that was a concern."

"Don't worry about a thing."

"Thank you." Nita finished the wine and rose from the sofa. "I'd like to go home how. Is that okay?"

"Of course, follow me," Adam said and held his arm for her.

"Mrs. Ross, er, Madam President, thank you for your kindness. Mr. Ross, thank you for the wine." Nita tried to smile but didn't succeed. "Good to see you again, Gracie."

Adam escorted her to the door and the secret service agent led her out. Adam came back to the group.

"Ma'am, we need to agree on how we're going to handle the release of a blogger's part in discovering the shooter of President Gardner."

"I know, Julie Jordan should be here any minute in case you'd like to stay. We haven't released any details yet. Has Mrs. Roberts been notified? I need to call her."

"Let me check." Adam hurried out of the living room.

"I have a question about how this happened," Gracie said.

"What question?"

"Why was the door to the Oval Office left unguarded?"

"Good question," Peter commented. "I've wondered the same thing myself."

"I don't have an answer at this moment," Georgia replied. "But I sure as hell will have one soon."

~~*

The drive to Nita's house went by in a blur. She didn't want to talk to Special Agent Brown so she sat in the backseat of the Government Issue black sedan. He didn't ask anything other than her street address and shut the door. That suited her just fine. She hoped she'd never see him again. If he hadn't left them alone, she wouldn't have suggested to Nick they—

No! Don't think about what-ifs.

She fiddled with the long strap of her purse, thankful she'd had it slung over her chest as she had her house keys. She rubbed her now dry eyes, realizing she'd not shed a tear since watching the Medical Coroner's Office, she guessed that's who it was, gently place a drape over Nick's body. She'd promised herself to stay strong for him. He deserved that and so much more.

It wasn't long before the car stopped in the alley behind her house as Nita had instructed. The walk and steps were covered with pristine, beautiful snow. She hesitated exiting the car. Right then she couldn't enter her home via the back entrance—Nick's footprints were underneath the snow on the walk and the steps.

She leaned forward to the front seat. "Sorry, would you mind going around to the front?"

"Not a problem."

It wasn't long before Nita shut her front door after she'd begged off the agent's suggestion he make sure she'd be okay alone. She assured him she'd call her best friend for support. Well, that was partly true. First she wanted a shower and then a decent cup of coffee.

The shower was quick as she had an idea while washing her hair. She donned flannel men's pajamas and white socks and padded toward the kitchen. Passing the dining room table, she noticed Nick's laptop and his notebook. She quickly stuffed both into his backpack and set it on the floor of the front closet. These things belonged to his family, not to her.

She made her coffee, sat at her desk, and fired up her computer. Nick would agree to this. The idea from her shower had gelled in her head and she clicked on the email icon on the desktop. Ignoring the inbox, she selected New Message and typed a dispatch to Dark Horse:

Dear Dark Horse---I don't know if this information has been on the news or not. Earlier this evening, after your last email, Nick and I went to the White House to warn President Ross about VP Roberts. Long story short, we ended up going to the Oval Office and heard her shouting "no." We entered with Nick yelling, "stop." Harry Roberts had a gun directed at the president. Harry shot Nick, then turned the gun on himself and he is also dead. Don't know what will be on the news so please keep this version quiet, but I wanted you to know the truth. I have a question: Are you the John Smith who lived on Arlington Avenue in Denver, Colorado? Are you the John Smith who built the drone and fired at President Gardner?---Best, Nita

She re-read what she'd typed and satisfied with the text, clicked on Send. Hopefully, the Dark Horse email address would still be active. Sipping the coffee in her empty row house, she realized she did indeed need her best friend, and called Gina.

"Are you busy?"

"Not really, why?"

"Have you been watching the news?"

"No, I've been watching non-stop movies."

Nita sucked in a precarious breath as her wall of strength began to crumble. "Nick . . . Nick was shot this evening . . . in the Oval Office . . . by Vice President Roberts. He's . . . he's dead."

"Holy shit, I'm on my way over."

~~*

Emmett arrived at Valerie's apartment in the middle of the snowstorm. He had snow on his head and shoulders as she ushered him in the front door and helped him remove his coat.

"Oh, look at you with a red nose." She kissed his cheek, ruffled his hair to remove the snowflakes, and took his hand. "Come on, I have just the thing to warm you up."

He followed her to the kitchen. "Smells good in here."

"Chili is in the crockpot and I just took cornbread out of the oven." She smiled at him and poured coffee into mugs. "I thought an Irish coffee would warm you up." She then shook a can and topped the coffee with whipped cream. Handing him a mug, she grinned. "This should do the trick."

He tasted the coffee and his balls quivered. "This coffee definitely has some Irish in it."

"Yep." She winked. "The chili needs to cook longer. Come with me to the bedroom. I've missed you *all day long*."

As the man who'd endured a sexual drought the last couple of years, he followed her like a puppy dog, carrying his coffee.

"Climb into bed while I change." Valerie disappeared into the bathroom, leaving Emmett holding the mug. He downed its contents, shook his head and sucked in a deep breath. *Damn, that was strong.* But whatever, he followed her instructions and climbed into her bed, after folding his clothes over the usual chair in the corner. He chuckled at that; thrilled he had a chair he could claim in Valerie's bedroom. He slid under the covers and waited for her to join him. Valerie loved teasing him with the big reveal of her lingerie. The Irish whiskey and the warmth in the room leveled him out. After a minute, he dozed off.

Emmett opened his eyes with a bang; Mr. Rock was engaged and fully operational. Valerie had snuck into the bed while he slept and decided to wake Emmett in the best possible manner. He so enjoyed her efforts, and then decided it was time to play fair and reciprocate. He rolled Valerie on her back and slid down to the juncture of her legs.

"Hey, babe, what are you doing?"

"Relax. I'm here to thank you in advance for dinner." He so appreciated a home cooked meal.

"Hmm . . . baby, yes."

Some time later, Emmett stretched his arms above his head, sighed in complete satisfaction with his day. Well, almost. He hadn't enjoyed talking with Harry about the polls and now regretted bringing them to him. He rolled over in the bed and wrapped his arms around Valerie.

"Hey you," He kissed her neck and nibbled his way to her mouth. "Hmm . . . you smell so good."

Valerie kissed his mouth and tilted her head to the side. "I must tell you Mr. Garrett, you pretty much rock my world."

"Seriously? That's awesome, cause you do the same for me." This admission of hers knocked his socks off but he'd play it cool. "I'm hungry, is the chili done by now?"

She slid off the bed naked and presented her very shapely back to him. She grabbed a pink fuzzy robe in the closet and walked back to the bed. "Get dressed and we can eat. Meet you in the kitchen." She leaned over the bed, kissed his bare chest, and left the bedroom.

Emmett wasted no time dressing and hurried to the kitchen.

"The snow stopped," she said as she placed two bowls on a wide tray. "I thought we could sit in the living room and see what's on TV."

"Sounds good, maybe there's a movie." His stomach growled at the smell of the chili. "This looks good. I'll carry the tray."

"Go ahead while I get us a beer."

He set the tray on the coffee table in front of her dark leather couch. Never pictured her as a leather furniture type of person. He turned on the TV as he sat down. It was tuned to a cable news channel.

Valerie sat next to him and handed him a Mexican beer. "Turn up the volume. There's a news alert."

A sedate anchor spoke. "We have very sad news to report this evening. Vice President Harry Roberts died at the West Wing of the White House early this evening. Another man is dead as well. We don't have his name yet or the circumstances surrounding these two deaths. Repeat—"

"What the hell?" Emmett rose and went to the coat stand near the front door. He pulled his cell phone from an inside pocket of his winter jacket. He glanced at Valerie watching him from the sofa. "Give me a minute. I need to call President Ross."

"Of course."

He walked to the kitchen for privacy and touched Georgia's name on his contact list. She answered after the third ring.

"Hello Emmett, I guess you've seen the news."

"Just heard the news bulletin. What the hell happened?"

"Harry must have had a meltdown of some kind. He stopped by, we talked for a bit, and then he pulled out a gun. I started yelling and then this man burst in shouting 'stop.' Harry turned around and shot the poor guy. Then Frank and Stanley came in, ordered Harry to drop the gun, and he shot himself."

"This is terrible. Who was the man?" Emmett's gut rolled. Did his earlier conversation with Harry have anything to do with him going over the edge? Guilt poked at him.

"That is a long story. I'm tired now. Come by in the morning and I'll give you're the whole story."

"I was going in anyway. I have a couple ideas for your speech."

"Good." Georgia sounded tired. "Have a good evening."

He clicked off and went back to Valerie, stuffing the phone in his shirt pocket. He picked up the beer and slugged down half of it.

"I may need something stronger than beer."

"What happened?" Valerie asked and seemed genuinely interested. He figured she had no love lost for Georgia.

"Harry Roberts shot himself after killing another man who tried to stop him from shooting Georgia."

Her mouth fell open. She shook her head and spoke. "This is unbelievable." She picked up her beer bottle and stood. "You're right, we need something stronger then beer. I'll make you my special martini."

He followed her into the kitchen. "It's hard to believe this happened."

Valerie chuckled. "Doesn't surprise me one bit. Harry Roberts was a weirdo plus he drank too much."

Emmett agreed with her conclusion but how or why did she know Harry was weird? "Something happen with Harry that makes you say that?"

"Nothing specific." She retrieved vodka and two glasses from the freezer. "I've seen him at plenty of bars and events around town, plus I was in meetings with him and Danny. That guy didn't have all of his marbles."

"I guess something had to be off with him." Emmett hesitated and decided not to share what he knew about Harry and that they had talked earlier in the day. In fact he probably wouldn't share that with anyone unless he was asked. "Oh well, we'll learn eventually what set him off."

Emmett bit his lower lip as he watched Valerie make the martini. Guilt again prodded at him. Had he pushed Harry too far by showing him the overnight polls?

Perhaps he had.

~~*

John had been driving in the dark for almost three hours but at least they'd outrun the snow. He sighed in relief as they crossed the I-485 loop around Charlotte. As the miles from Washington, D.C. increased, his anxiety decreased.

"Hey babe, are you awake? You're quiet."

"Sorry," Candy replied. "I've been looking at motels along the interstate. We have quite the smorgasbord of inns, motels, and hotels to choose from. Any preference?"

"Nope, I need a good bed. That's all."

"I think that's covered. There's a Maywood Inn just outside the loop. It looks good."

"Okay."

The traffic through Charlotte wasn't bad for a Saturday night so they rolled into their stop for the night before 8:00. John circled the complex and stopped by a dumpster in the back.

"Time to ditch the Colorado license plates." He hopped out and grabbed the plates and the bag of trash from the back. After stuffing the plates in the bag, he tied it tight and threw it in the dumpster.

He climbed back in. "Happy to get rid of the plates. I'll dump the keys in New Orleans."

"Good idea. Remember there's nothing we can do about the VIN number now"

It didn't take long to get a room and unload the SUV. He went to the bathroom and Candy pounded on the door.

He opened it and she pushed him toward the middle of the small motel room. "Get in here. There's a news alert concerning Vice President Roberts."

He stopped in front of the TV and listened to the anchor report that Harry was dead along with another man at the West Wing. Additional details would be released the next day.

"My God, this is incredible." John's mind wrapped around the report and its impact on him. "You know what this means, right?"

"No, what?"

"It means I'm free. Harry is the only one who could identify me as the shooter. "

She grinned. "Yeah, there is that."

"I'm going to check online. Maybe they have better news." John opened his laptop on the table and plugged in the power cord to charge it. "I have an email from Nita." He read it and his heart dropped. "This is awful. Nita's partner, Nick, was the man shot at the White House . . . by Harry. And Harry tried to shoot President Ross and then killed himself."

"We were right to warn her then."

"Yeah, but her friend was killed." Once again John was sorry he'd gotten involved with Harry. Nothing good had come out it . . . well, other than Georgia Ross being a much better president than Gardner. "I guess this is one of those situations where you count the collateral damage and say it justifies the end. God, that sounds so . . . so unemotional."

Candy walked behind him and put her arms around his neck. "I know, but unfortunately in this case, I think it's true." She kissed his cheek and hugged him tight. "I love you."

"Love you, too." He patted her hands and she moved to the bed. "Nita also asked me a couple of questions." He read them aloud for Candy.

"She's a bright girl, not afraid to ask the hard stuff."

Right then he didn't know if, or even how he'd answer her. "I need to think about this. Let's sleep on it."

Candy patted the bed with her hand and began to unbutton her shirt. "Hmm, baby . . . sounds lovely."

~~*

Georgia climbed into bed and snuggled against Peter's chest as he wrapped his arms around her. She sighed. "This has been one hell of a Saturday."

"No kidding. I don't want to ever repeat it." He squeezed his arms around her. "I'm thankful you weren't hurt. I hope your security detail will be increased."

"Why Frank wasn't outside the door is a big question." She shook her head and thought of her constant companion. "Frank is dedicated so him walking away from the door doesn't make sense."

"How much of the truth are you going to release to the press tomorrow?"

"Everything we know for certain. I don't see how we can avoid it. But there will be no guesses as to Harry's role in the shooting of Daniel Gardner. That will wait until we have absolute proof."

He kissed the top of his wife's head. "Miss Andrews may become a media celebrity. I hope she's prepared for that."

"I doubt she's even thought of the impact of this situation on her personal life. I like Nita. Gracie had very nice things to say about her."

"Really? Sounds like you might have plans."

"I do have an idea. We'll see." Georgia would pass her idea to human resources first. She didn't want to get ahead of herself.

"Speaking of plans, what will the Democrats do now for the primaries? Without Daniel Gardner or Harry Roberts as their candidate, who do they have?"

"I'm sure the DNC will be scrambling. With an incumbent president, no one even considers running. This is a first."

He stroked his finger along her arm. "And you messed it up by turning Republican."

"Yeah, I guess I did."

Chapter Twelve

Monday, February 2

DAMN, HE WAS WARM. Emmett pushed the covers off his chest then realized Valerie would quickly become cold. He carefully tucked the sheet and comforter around her butt and bare back up to her neck. He leaned over and kissed her hair. He looked at his watch, only 6:00 a.m. She'd probably sleep for another two hours.

He bunched the pillows behind his head and crossed his arms over his chest. Time to plan his future. Right off the bat, he knew the first thing he'd do. Cover his tracks for his side purchasing business at the White House and halt it altogether. He knew Danny wouldn't have given a damn but Madam President was an entirely different political animal, with morals. Plus, after three years of operation, he had enough money tucked away for his retirement to live quite comfortably.

He had maybe ten years before he'd retire. He figured Georgia could win two terms and he'd be sixty at the end of the second term. He grinned. The timing worked perfectly. In retirement, he could travel and maybe do some consulting. And after working under two presidents who were polar opposites, he could write one hell of a political tell-all—or, a fiction novel about working in the White House, with . . . a string of murders of . . . hmm, maybe members of Congress. They still had a terrible approval rating with the American people. Why couldn't they just wise up and work for the people?

He stretched his arms over his head. *Um, that felt good*. He should make an effort to hit the gym more often. He'd already concluded he wasn't getting any younger thinking about his retirement. Like his mama always said, "one day at a time."

Valerie rolled over and her arm slammed against his head.

"Hey, watch it." The words came out louder than he intended.

"Seriously, Emmett, you're lecturing me on bedside manners." Valerie lay on her back with one arm over her forehead and her mouth quivered.

"What's so funny?"

"You and waking up so damned early on a Monday morning." She rolled toward him, scooting against his side, and threw her arm over his chest. "Come on, go back to sleep."

"We need to discuss something first."

She sighed without opening her eyes. "Okay, what?"

"Politics."

"Whatever."

"Going forward I'm leaning Republican and you just got hired for a Democratic think tank. Can we deal with this?"

She yawned. "You mean keep politics out of our relationship?"

"Yeah, that."

Valerie raised her head an inch, opened those beautiful eyes, and smiled. "Politics is just a job, not who I am as a person. You're more important to me than some stupid political philosophy. Okay?"

"Good enough."

~~*

Sipping her third cup of coffee for the morning and enjoying a moment by herself in the Residence living room, Georgia thought back to the previous evening. She'd had fun with a few single staff members accompanied by good food and good drink. Of course the Houston Texans winning their first Super Bowl was the icing on the cake, and in Dallas. In addition, it had been their first "social" event at the White House. Peter had given her a few ideas for parties and dinners. She intended to give others the opportunity to enjoy this beautiful building.

Her cell phone rang. "Madam President, I'm forwarding Rosie Gardner to you."

"Thank you, Betty." Georgia waited only a moment for the call to transfer.

"Georgia, he's gone . . . Danny's gone, a couple of hours ago. His kidneys finally gave out."

Her heart gave a heavy thud. "Oh, Rosie, I'm so very, very sorry. How can I help you?"

"I'll need to release a statement of some kind from the family and we'll need to arrange a funeral. I'd prefer a small one here in Denver but the Democrats will never let me get away with that. They'll want a big lavish state funeral in Washington. Can you have someone contact me and we'll get the details ironed out."

"Of course. But . . . how are *you* doing?"

"Honestly, I'm glad it's over . . . in so many ways. But now isn't the time to get into that. I'd like to talk with you when I'm in Washington. I have an idea."

"I'm available whenever the time is right. It will be good to see you again, even though the circumstances are so sad."

"Georgia, please don't be sad. Things have worked out for the best and Danny has finally learned you reap what you sow."

Georgia had no clue what Rosie meant by that statement. "I look forward to seeing you."

"The same here. Also, tell all the intelligence folks to stop looking for Danny's shooter. At this point, no one gives a damn. You're a much better president." The line went dead.

Georgia blew a heavy breath. That was a conversation she'd never expected to have. She quickly called Gracie and provided the pertinent details—bless her chief of staff for taking on the task of a presidential proclamation and a state funeral. The flags would be lowered to half-staff. Gracie knew whom to call.

Without a chance to catch her breath, Adam Martinez entered the living room. What now?

"Ma'am, everything okay?"

She nodded. "How can I help you today?"

"I know you're headed out soon, but I have a couple of items. May I come in?"

She checked her watch. "I have fifteen minutes at the most. What's up?"

Adam sat across from her. "First, we've done a quick analysis of the laptop of Harry Roberts. The preliminary analysis shows that his computer, via Betty's desktop, controlled the drone in the House Chamber. Frankly, I don't buy it."

"Was Harry a computer person?"

Adam chuckled. "I don't think so. My guess is that he had an accomplice, and the actual shooter knew his way around a piece of code. I think he's tried to set up Harry. We'll figure it out. Also, we have the results of Harry's autopsy."

"Anything unusual?" This was a topic she'd never before discussed.

"Actually, yes. Vice President Ross had a large brain tumor—an untreated one per his personal physician."

Georgia's hand flew to her mouth. "This is awful. Do you suppose that's why he . . . well, went so out of control?"

"Ma'am, it's certainly a good explanation for his behavior. Apparently this type of tumor can cause significant personality change."

"He must have been feeling horrible. I need to speak to Mrs. Roberts again. That reminds me. I just found out that President Gardner passed away. Mrs. Gardner sees no need to continue with the investigation of his death."

"I'm sorry to hear that. Not continue with the investigation—that seems strange to me. Why?"

"Maybe she wants it behind her. I'm not sure." Georgia would never reveal her personal belief that Rosie was relieved as she'd had enough of her husband, and the affair with Valerie Jones put the nail in the proverbial coffin.

"Regardless of her feelings, we will continue our investigation to discover the actual shooter," he stated firmly. This didn't surprise her. "The other thing is that Stanley White, the agent on call with Harry on Saturday, admitted to accepting a cash payment from Harry to divert Frank's attention from the corridor door to the Oval Office."

"Why would he do that?"

"Most likely so there wouldn't be a physical record of when Harry left your office."

"Aren't there cameras around here?"

"Yep."

"I guess Harry really wasn't thinking right."

"There you go. I know you're about to leave. Have a good trip, Madam President. My money is on you." He saluted and left.

Georgia raised her eyebrows—what was that? Did she just receive an endorsement from the Director of the FBI? This day was definitely picking up. She bent over for her briefcase and opened it— portfolio, electronic tablet, and a file of speeches. She was good to go.

Gracie and Emmett burst in, both laughing and high-fiving.

"What is so funny?"

"Nothing," Emmett replied.

"Are you ready for your first campaign trip as POTUS?" Gracie obviously wanted to get to the task at hand.

Georgia made a mental note of Gracie's avoidance of her question. "I'm ready to head to Iowa."

Emmett held out his arm. "Ma'am, may I have the honor of escorting you to Marine One?"

"Absolutely, at least to the door of the White House." She grinned and handed her briefcase to Gracie.

~~*

After hearing the heater kick on for the zillionth time, Nita raised her head and peered at her bedside clock, 10:58. Crap. She'd had an awful time getting to sleep last night and now she'd overslept. She clustered the pillows underneath her head and reached for the TV remote on the bedside table. The current news came first.

The TV screen roared to life with a live shot of President Ross walking to Marine One with her husband by her side. Gracie and Emmett What's-His-Name walked behind them. What a surprise to meet Gracie at the White House. It was a shame they hadn't stayed in contact with each other. They'd had some good times during their first two years of college. Maybe they could go to lunch at some point.

Marine One took off and Nita shut down the TV. She'd make a cup of coffee and decide what to do with the rest of her life. A few minutes later she stood at the window behind her desk. Someone had made a snow angel in the yard next door, probably her neighbor's grandkids. The snow glistened in the clear blue sky. What a difference a couple of days made in Washington weather. Even though the temperature hovered around freezing, the bright sun would warm things up a bit.

Of course, it didn't matter to her. She had no plans to leave her house—too many items on her to-do list. The first being her Tuesday blog. No, she'd make a flight reservation to Austin, Texas for Nick's funeral on Friday of this week. His aunt had called last night and given her the date but no other details. She said she'd send a text message with the time and funeral home address. Plus she expected to hear from the FBI for an interview.

Nita surveyed her desk. Where did she leave her cell phone? She thought for a minute and walked to the living room. There it was on the coffee table. She picked it up, touched the wake-up button and entered her passcode. She had a dozen missed calls with a few voicemails and two text messages. One text was from Gina asking her to lunch on Tuesday and the other was from Carolyn Helms with additional details on Nick's funeral service.

She went back to her desk and started her computer. She'd fly into Austin on Thursday and leave on Saturday morning. She'd not met anyone in Nick's family so she wouldn't think of this as a social trip. In fact, if she were completely honest with herself and there was no reason not to be at this point, she and Nick wouldn't have made it for the long term. They were too different. She fully believed that "opposites attract, but likes last" when it came to relationships. She and Nick were meant to be good friends, not lifelong mates. Now they were nothing.

She made online reservations for a flight, a hotel in Austin, and a rental car. Hopefully, she could slip in and out without a fuss. But the chances of that were small as she had a hunch that Adam Martinez would accompany his girlfriend to the funeral. Nita closed her eyes and sucked in a long breath. Somehow, she had to get her life back on track.

She had a shock when she opened her email inbox—a contact request sent via the BetterPoliticas.com website from BigDem. Why wouldn't this asshole go away? And why hadn't Dark Horse answered her questions. Anyway, this BigDem character said he wanted to meet with her and she had nothing to worry about, as he knew her father.

What the hell? If he knew her father, why had this jerk threatened her? No way. She deleted the email and remembered the voicemails on her phone.

The first number for the missed call was blocked, probably a solicitations call. She clicked on the voice mail anyway and had the surprise of her life:

"Miss Andrews, Nita, this is Georgia Ross, I'm sorry I've missed you. How are you? Are you doing okay? Oh, this is Monday morning by the way. I want to offer you a job, as the Director of Communications on my Executive Staff here at the West Wing. I know this is a surprise so I want you to have time to think about it and to do your research. I'll have Gracie text you with her phone number. You can talk with her as well as Kylee Abrams at the Office of Administration. They can give you all the particulars about the position. I'll be gone for a few days so take your time. Hope to talk with you early next week. Take good care of yourself."

Nita listened to the voice mail a second time to verify she had heard correctly. President Ross had offered her a job—and in the West Wing.

Wow . . . oh, wow. She performed a fist pump. But wait, what about her website? She needed to think about this and she definitely needed more information. What exactly did a director of communications do?

She'd talk to Gracie about the job but right then she needed to write Tuesday's blog and Friday's as well since she'd be out of town. She'd listen to the other voicemails later.

What were her blog topics? She sighed; she had no clue, her mind was blank.

~~*

"Boys, please come downstairs," Rosie Gardner shouted over the railing to the second floor of their Denver home. She had an idea that she hoped would make her sons happy. Before long, they stomped down the stairs.

"Come into the kitchen, we're having a family meeting." Thankfully, they didn't argue and followed her. She'd set their favorite shortbread/pecan cookies and mugs of hot cocoa on the table. A little bit of food always helped smooth over a tough conversation. The boys sat in their usual spots and reached for the cookies.

She waited a beat before speaking. She knew the drill with her twins and food.

"I need both of you to listen. This is important."

They both nodded. "Sure, Mom."

"On Thursday, we're returning to Washington for your father's laying in state at the Capitol Rotunda starting Friday morning and then the funeral on Saturday morning. The burial will be at Arlington Cemetery. It's a big deal and it'll be televised."

"So we need to be on our best behavior." Jake stuffed another cookie in his mouth.

"Yes. I'm not worried about that. You both will make your father proud." She sipped her cocoa wishing it were a glass of wine or bourbon. Later. "I know you haven't been happy returning to Denver after three years in Washington. I'd like to propose that we return to D.C., you can go back to the same school and we'll find a place to live. Plus, I intend to find a job of some kind."

Jake's eyes widened. "Are you serious?"

"Yeah, Mom, don't tease us about this," Drake added.

"I'm serious. I would never tease you about something so important." She smiled, pleased at their response. "Do we all agree to return to Washington?"

Jake raised his arms to the ceiling and Drake did a fist pump. "Yes, yes."

"Good. This means you both have work to do tomorrow and Wednesday. I need you to go through your bedrooms and decide what is going with us and what is getting donated. I'm putting this house on the market and nothing will go to storage." She gazed at her sons and was pleased with the eagerness she saw in their eyes. "You have two days to get all your stuff separated and packed. Okay?"

"Yeah," Drake said. "Can we order Diciccos's for dinner?"

"Great idea," Jake commented. "Lasagna, salad, and cheese bread?"

"You got it," Rosie said. "I'll make it a double order as your California cousins will be here in a couple of hours."

"We're glad they're coming with us," Jake said.

"Me too, we need our family around us," she replied. Her two sisters, plus their husbands and four children, were on their way to Denver and would accompany her and the twins to Washington. They were the only family Rosie had except for Elizabeth and she was questionable.

Once the twins went upstairs to scope out their belongings, Rosie found her cell phone next to the kitchen sink and touched the contact number for her mother-in-law.

"Rosie, is that you? Has something else happened?" Elizabeth's voice was soft and minus her usual accusatory tone.

"Yes, it's me and nothing else has happened. How are you, Elizabeth?"

"I'm fine considering I just lost my only son."

"I understand. It must be hell losing both the father and the son within a decade. I'm so sorry." Rosie surprised herself by not taking her mother-in-law's bait. Funny how the death of a cheating husband could change one's approach. "Actually, I was calling about your situation with the FBI. Has that been resolved?"

Based on her small cry, Elizabeth hadn't expected that question.

"How did you find out?"

"I have friends in Washington. Did you take the deal?"

"Yes, I had no other choice."

"Good. I'd hate for Jake and Drake to learn their only living grandparent is a crook."

"Rosie, that's uncalled for."

"No, canoodling with drug cartel people to make a buck is wrong. But now you have an opportunity to redeem yourself, with the FBI and with me."

Silence.

Rosie waited and finally Elizabeth spoke.

"What do you need from me?"

"Basic mother and grandmother stuff. You act like a grieving mother at Danny's funeral and you take care of the twins while I finalize things here in Denver. We're all moving back to D.C. and they're re-enrolling in their school. I'll need your help while everything gets settled."

Silence.

"I'll be honored to help my grandsons."

Yeah, right, Elizabeth would help the twins but not her daughter-in-law. Rosie clicked off and found a bottle of red wine in the pantry. Her mother-in-law had not one virtuous bone in her body.

Thank God Jake and Drake favored Rosie's side of the family.

~~*

The Mississippi River was an impressive body of water—mighty and majestic. John tingled just a smidge, thinking about the river's history with the people of New Orleans. He and Candy had taken a private car tour earlier that day and learned so much about this wonderful city. He gazed out the window of their room at Harrah's and watched a tugboat head north up the river. He wished he had a fancy camera to take a photo of the sight. He'd always enjoyed taking pictures on vacation when Jessie was alive. Hmm . . . maybe he could record his life with Candy.

She rubbed his back. "Hey, I'm itching to try the slots in the casino but first—"

"I know." John interrupted her and turned around, kissed her forehead. "We agreed to reply to Nita's last email before we hit the casino. Let's get it done—"

"And then we're officially done with D.C., right?"

"Why don't you do the honors?" He leaned over the desk and logged into his laptop and the Dark Horse email account. Waving his hand over the desk chair, he moved to the side. "Your laptop awaits you, fair lady."

Candy chuckled and sat down, poising her fingers over the keyboard. "Okay, hot dude, what do you want to say?"

"I'm not in favor of telling her the truth in answering her questions. What do you think?"

"I agree. But we do need to say something that will put a final nail in the coffin for Gardner's shooter. You know, convince her that it's over—he's gone. Stop looking."

They discussed several options then Candy raised a hand. "I think I've got it. Let's try this." She entered a reply to Nita's last email:

Nita....Your questions are understandable. No, I'm not the John Smith who lived on Arlington Avenue in Denver, Colorado. But my good friend John did live there. And, yes, he is the one who fired the drone at President Gardner, and was paid by Harry Roberts. His motivation was the loss of his wife Jessie, directly caused by Gardner's actions. John is gone now. He ended his life to be with Jessie. I am John's long-time friend and contacted you because he sent me his messages with Harry. Funny how things work out. I trust that John and Jessie are at peace now....John's Friend

"How does that sound?" She gazed at him, a frisky smile teasing her lips.

John leaned over her and grinned. "Babe, that is the perfect reply."

"Okay then, it's gone." She rose and walked to the window.

John sat in the desk chair. "Give me a minute to eliminate the Dark Horse email address." He did his thing and after several minutes rose from the desk. "Let's check out the casino. I've a hunch this is my lucky day."

Candy sidled up to him and gave John a one-armed hug. "Seriously? I thought it was the day we met in Las Vegas?"

He laughed, loving this woman, and they headed to the casino floor. Once they exited the elevator, John jingled keys in his pocket. Candy noticed and he knew she understood. She pointed to a large garbage can on the edge of the casino area.

"That will work," she said.

He tossed in the Murano keys and grabbed her hand. "John Smith is over and out. Patrick needs a drink. I bet Elizabeth does as well."

They soon found the perfect pair of side-by-side slots and each of them ordered a drink before slipping in a hundred dollar bill into the machine.

"I say we dual to the death. First one who loses a hundred bucks buys dinner." Patrick grinned, as he loved the competition.

"You got it, big guy." Elizabeth winked at him and rubbed her hands together. "Don't be surprised when you're buying me a steak dinner at a fancy restaurant."

"Yes ma'am. Also, I think we should get married when we get to Las Vegas." He held his breath, not sure how'd she'd reply.

She looked at him, her eyes narrowed. After a few seconds, which seemed like eons to him, she smiled and leaned toward him, wrapping her arms around his chest.

"Aw, babe, I'll be honored to officially become Mrs. Warren . . . uh, since I already have the ID."

Patrick hugged her back. "You're such a smartass."

"I know. But, can we live here, in New Orleans? I like this town."

Elizabeth batted her eyelashes at him.

"All right, all right . . . we can look at real estate tomorrow. But let's keep our options open. Have you been to California, or London, or Paris?"

"Good idea, Mr. Warren, my options are open."

Epilogue

Eight or so days later

THE PRESIDENTIAL STUDY IN the West Wing had a certain amount of ambiance well suited for Georgia's low-key style and her need to get a handle on her presidential schedule, as well as her campaign activities. Her too-full calendar was almost too much for one person to handle. How in the hell had the last two presidents had so much time for golf and basketball and fancy vacations?

She chuckled as she scanned the to-do list she'd hand-written on the front page of her portfolio. She had neither the time nor the inclination to take non-stop vacations while attempting to make this year a good one for the American people. The one fun item would be picking out a rug and new sofas and chairs for the Oval Office. The goal was to have it ready in three weeks time. That would work, as she'd spend most weekdays campaigning across the country. Thank heavens she'd received a special waiver to file and then be placed on the ballots in several states. The Democratic candidate from Vermont, Sara Ward, had received the same waiver. This was an extraordinary presidential election when it came to timing.

While thinking about the focus of her campaign, she'd had an "ah-hah" moment—people talked about the U.S.A. being a democracy while the founding fathers had envisioned the country as a republic, supported by the U.S. Constitution. Elected federal politicians were so far off track from their true roles as "representatives of the people" that their approval ratings were still in the gutter and after multiple years.

Georgia had an idea to fix those ratings. Granted, a Congress and a POTUS of the same party would help with her plan. Her head rose as she heard her name.

"Rosie, what a pleasure to see you again." Georgia rose and extended her hand to her new friend. They'd spoken several times related to Daniel's funeral, always surrounded by others. Now they could talk in private. "Please have a seat." They both sat on a small green sofa.

"Thanks for seeing me, Madam President." Rosie set her handbag on her lap.

"Please, we're friends and all my friends call me Georgia." Rosie smiled and Georgia spoke again. "I know you're relieved that everything is over. Daniel's service was beautiful. I'm so very sorry all of this had to happen."

"It's hard to believe Harry was responsible. I thought he was Danny's best friend." Rosie raised her hands then they fell to her purse. "I guess you never know what's behind closed doors."

"True. But how are you and your sons? You three are what's important."

Her eyes widened and she swiped away a tear from her cheek. "You are the nicest person. Thank you for thinking of us. I guess that's why I wanted to speak with you in private."

Now Georgia was curious. "What's on your mind?"

"The twins and I are moving back to Washington. They returned to their school this morning and I'll be buying a house or a condo of some kind."

Georgia squeezed her hand. "That's wonderful. I'm sure your boys will be happy to be back to their school."

"They're happy to be with their friends. Elizabeth will be living with us." Rosie picked at lint on the sleeve of her coat. "It helps with her cover story. You know what I mean, right?"

Georgia nodded. "I do. But what about you? Is this move truly what you want?"

Rosie smiled. "Yes. I need a change. Denver is in the past and I spent the last three years here. Granted, the experience was somewhat isolated but I like this town and I do have a certain perspective."

"As a former First Lady, you absolutely have a certain perspective."

"And that's why I'm asking for your assistance." Rosie rubbed her fingers over the leather surface of her handbag. "I need a job and I hope you'll be willing to provide a decent recommendation, if I even get to that point."

Now that was a surprise—and a good one. Georgia would do whatever was necessary to help Rosie secure a job. Absolutely— maybe something here at the White House.

"Of course I'll help you. Just tell me what's needed and I'll take care of it."

"Thank you. I won't take more of your time." Rosie stood and walked to the door. "I'm returning to Denver today to finalize our move. The twins are staying with Elizabeth at her hotel. Fingers crossed that no one is arrested."

"I'll make sure Elizabeth and the twins stay out of trouble while you're gone."

Rosie laughed. "Thank you. You're the best." She turned and vanished out the door.

Georgia returned to the small desk and looked at the electronic calendar on her laptop. What did she have scheduled for the rest of the day? In thirty minutes, she had a meeting with Mike McCain, her second appointment as vice president, to discuss his dissatisfaction with the legislative calendar. Welcome to my world Mr. VP. After Mike was Gary Nixon, the newly elected House Speaker. Mike should stay for that meeting. Yes, it would be fun to watch these two macho males duke it out over stalled legislation.

Then she'd share with both of them how things were going to work in the House and the Senate going forward. The bullshit of the last eleven years was over. This POTUS would always place the American people first. And damn it, the United States of America was a republic, not a democracy.

~~*

The snow had melted and another storm was predicted for that evening. Washington weather was just as crazy as Washington politics. Nita had watched the very sad funeral for President Gardner on TV and she'd closely followed all the news reports related to President Ross in the last week. She'd hoped to gain a view of the president that included both conservative and liberal views. And yes, the online articles and TV videos didn't disappoint. The surprise was the respect for President Ross.

After not quite three weeks in office, Georgia Ross had captured the heart of the country.

Nita stared out the window by her desk, holding her empty mug. After the emotion of Nick's funeral and meeting his family, she couldn't put it off any longer—she had a decision to make. Georgia Ross deserved an answer. She deposited the mug in the kitchen sink and then put on her jacket. A walk would help her sort out her options and the decision she needed to make.

Walking toward Constitution Avenue, she considered the issue at hand—the offer from Georgia Ross to work at the White House. *Was she an idiot to even examine her heart and head about this?* Gina had advised her to accept the offer and run to the West Wing.

But Nita didn't work like that—she pondered, she analyzed, and she evaluated the pros and cons of every major decision. That was her process.

She kicked at a piece of trash on the sidewalk.

Damn it. Screw her process. She'd accept the offer from Georgia Ross and work at the West Wing.

Also, maybe she'd summon the nerve to ask Adam Martinez to help her uncover the identity of BigDem. He'd sent her another message after Nick's funeral asking for a meeting to discuss her father and had mentioned her mother as well. This situation had taken an unnerving turn, and she couldn't ignore it any longer.

~~*

Candy-Elizabeth gazed at the Pacific Ocean—her first up close view of it—from the Santa Monica Pier. Her gaze caught the sparkle of the diamond on her left hand. They'd picked it out at a fancy jewelry store in Las Vegas, before their quickie wedding at The Bellagio Hotel. She'd thought one of those Elvis chapels would work just as well, but John-Patrick was determined the setting be more upscale.

"This is a nice view," he said, standing next to her with his forearms resting on the top of the railing that surrounded the pier. "What do you think about California?"

"Honestly . . . too many people and too many cars."

"I've been thinking the same thing. Nice place to visit though."

"Exactly." She watched a huge sailboat lazily cross the water in front of them. "New Orleans is still number one on my settle down list." She turned her body toward him. "Can't we buy one of those cute little houses we saw there? Please . . ."

"Funny you should mention that. I called the realtor yesterday and made an offer on the house with the kitchen you liked."

"No . . . you didn't."

"I did." He stepped forward and wrapped his arms around her. "The seller accepted. We'll soon be homeowner's."

She pulled back to look at his face. "You did? We will?" She performed a little jig then stood before him and kissed him smack on the lips. "Thank you. This is awesome." Then she thought about the practical side of this decision. "You do realize we have no furniture or household items, right."

"Got that all figured out. We'll stop in Houston on our way back. Buy a new car and then shop until we drop. We'll rent a moving truck and pick up the furniture and drive to New Orleans. Our neighbors will think we're moving from Texas."

"And what will we tell them why we moved to New Orleans?"

"Yeah, we need a good story." He rubbed his jaw. "Let's say I retired which is partly true and that we'd always loved New Orleans and decided to enjoy our retirement in our favorite city. How about that?"

"That will work." She walked a few steps further down the pier. The sailboat was still in sight.

She shivered, thinking about the rest of her life by the side of this wonderful man. A trip to Pennsylvania could be made after they settled in New Orleans. She could sell her little house there fully furnished. She looked back at Patrick. He was one good-looking hunk of a male specimen who had a heart of gold. *She was one lucky girl.*

Patrick walked to her and held out his hand. "Come on, babe, let's walk. We need the exercise."

Once they'd strolled to the end of the pier and then back to the street, Elizabeth was hungry.

"How about brunch? Isn't that popular here?"

"Sounds good to me. I wouldn't mind a mimosa."

Elizabeth laughed and walked beside Patrick back to their hotel. She had one last thought about their move to New Orleans.

"I was thinking about us doing something positive . . . related to politics, I think. Maybe a foundation, or a blog, like the one Nita has, but from the viewpoint of the common man, the average guy on the street."

Patrick didn't respond immediately. She waited.

"I like that idea. From the very first time that Harry Roberts contacted me, I've had a silent disgust for him and what he represented in Washington. I figure he's not the only one like that."

"That's what's so sad. We elect these people, expecting great things from them, and they go off the rails once they walk in the Capitol building."

Patrick smiled and squeezed her hand. "Think about it. How easy was it to eliminate one awful president? That sort of thing could happen again."

"Exactly what I was thinking."

THE END

Betty's White House Brownies

Ingredients
1 box devil's food cake mix
3/4 cup melted butter
1 large can evaporated milk
1 12-ounce bag caramel bits
1 12-ounce bag semi-sweet chocolate chips
1 cup chopped walnuts

Directions
* Preheat oven at 350 degrees
* Pour cake mix into a bowl and add melted butter and 1/3 cup evaporated milk.
* Mix and spread half of mixture into a 13x9 baking pan.
* Bake in oven for 18 minutes.
* While cake layer is baking, melt caramel bits in microwave with 1/2 cup evaporated milk.
* Remove cake from oven—sprinkle walnuts, followed by chocolate chips over it, and then spread melted caramel over all.
* Using a large tablespoon, place the remaining brownie mixture over the topped cake and press it down with the back of the spoon.
* Bake another 18-20 minutes. Cool and slice into squares.
* Enjoy!

Thank You!

If you enjoyed *Capitol Secrets*, please take the time to leave a review via the vendor where the book was purchased. Reader reviews are one of the best ways for writers to gain new readers and gain feedback about their work. Thank you if you do post a review. Also be sure to let me know via my website or on Facebook. I'd love to hear from you! Also, you can find a complete list of my books on my website.

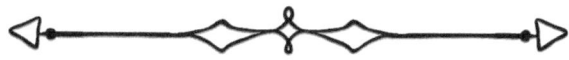

The Author

Karen Sue Burns has been a writer since 8th grade. Her former job as a CPA has provided interesting experiences: travel to Rio de Janeiro, London, and Oslo, auditing wine bottle glass molds in California, and taking a helicopter to a drillship off the Texas Gulf Coast. Now she spends her days living out her passion-- writing political thrillers, cozy mysteries, and Texas ghost novels sprinkled with romance. She enjoys cooking and creating recipes so her heroines do the same. All of her indie anthologies and novels include one of her favorite recipes. Readers may contact Karen via the Bio/Contact tab on her website. Check out the Recipe tab while you're there.

Contact:

Facebook: https://www.facebook.com/karensueburns
Twitter: https://twitter.com/karensueburns
Website: http://www.karensueburns.com

Notes